BIG HORN

A JENN HERRINGTON WYOMING MYSTERY

PAMELA FAGAN HUTCHINS

SKIPJACK PUBLISHING

FREE PFH EBOOKS

BEFORE YOU BEGIN READING, you can snag a free Pamela Fagan Hutchins ebook starter library by joining her mailing list at https://www.subscribepage.com/PFHSuperstars.

PROLOGUE

BIG HORN, Wyoming

THE CLOUDS DRIFTED in front of the sliver of a moon, blocking Jennifer Herrington's view of the snowscape behind the house. Deck boards creaked, and the cold against her bare feet shocked her fully awake. *What am I doing outside in the middle of the night, barefoot and without a robe, much less a coat?* She wasn't sleepwalking, per se. Something had woken her from a deep, warm slumber, and she'd responded on autopilot, like a reluctant protagonist from a Mary Higgins Clark novel.

She wrapped her arms around herself and shivered. In the distance, muffled by the wind, she heard sounds that didn't belong. Maybe that was what had lured her from bed. *Is it a voice?* The only people onsite at The Big Horn Lodge were Jennifer, her husband Aaron, and the proprietor and her client, George Nichols . . . and she'd left Aaron snoring in bed. Unless George was yelling at himself —not an impossibility, if he were drinking again—then either her ears were playing tricks on her, or the sound was coming from somewhere else.

Only there was no one else around.

Their location was remote and isolated, at the base of the Bighorn Mountains. Still, sound did carry like crazy out there. Sometimes, when the wind was just right, Jennifer could hear distinct conversations at the nearest neighbor's place, over a mile away. Or she assumed it was them and not the ghosts of Native Americans roaming the foothills, as the locals claimed.

The wind swept the voices to her again. Male, maybe more than one. Agitated. Angry.

"... your fault ..."

"... can't ... sorry ..."

Light shining from a window of George's cottage caught her eye. She grabbed the porch railing and peered more closely at the little house, wondering if that's where the sound was coming from. She heard it again. Definitely coming from another direction. But she paused. Something seemed off about the cottage, and she squinted. *What is it?* Then it clicked for her. His front door was ajar, a thin line of light crossing the porch. *In the middle of the night when it's thirty-degrees outside?* If he were passed out near the door, he might die of exposure before morning. She couldn't let that happen.

For a split second, she thought about waking Aaron. But as she turned back toward the lodge, she saw a pair of men's muck boots by the doormat. It would only take her a minute to check on George. She'd left her phone in the bedroom, but, if she needed Aaron's help, she could call him from George's phone. She slipped her feet into the too-big boots and clomped off the deck. Goose flesh pimpled her arms and legs. Her Texas fall sleepwear of silky pants and a baby doll tee wasn't cutting it in Wyoming, certainly not outdoors in this onslaught of early cold and snow. In her sleepy state—made worse by night-mares and insomnia that had plagued her since their arrival—the dry air had tricked her into thinking she didn't need a coat, but she wished she had one now. She broke into a trot, and her heels rode up in the boots. She caught a toe on a hidden rock and tripped, crashing onto her hands and knees.

"Ow!" The snow had an icy bite to it. She scrambled to her feet, brushed off her hands, and ran faster, lifting her knees as high as she could while still moving forward. Her quads and butt felt the weight of the boots almost immediately.

At George's front door, she poked her head inside. The light she'd seen was from the kitchen. "George?" she called. She knocked for good measure. Her eyes swept the floor. She was relieved not to see him crumpled around a bottle. "George?"

Best to do a quick bed check.

She walked in. A musty smell hit her. She'd only been in the ramshackle building once before. The sparse furniture was thrift-store and threadbare. The place was sorely in need of Lysol, multi-purpose cleaner, and elbow grease, not to mention an overall facelift. She made her way to the only bedroom and stopped at the open door. The drapes were drawn, and it was dark inside.

"George?"

The silence mocked her.

"George?"

This time, there was a noise, but not from his room. It was from somewhere outside again. The same man sounds, elevated. Her pulse quickened. Dread rooted her in place, but she forced herself to break its grip and enter the room.

The bed was empty.

Her eyes adjusted, and she hurried through. *No George, anywhere.*

Moonlight returned and shone through the window. For a moment, Jennifer imagined she saw something outside. She clutched the collar of her pajama tee. Should she call Aaron? But she didn't see a phone on the TV tray that was serving as a bedside table. She ran into the kitchen. No phone on the wall, the counter, or the table. In the living room—nothing, save an empty bottle of Wyoming Whiskey on the coffee table. She put her hand on the wooden surface and felt a few dribbles of liquid. *Darn it.* He'd found the liquor she'd hidden from him.

No phone anywhere.

The voices grew louder outside. One of them rose to a roar. Or was it really a voice? On the front range, it could be a mountain lion. Or a bear. She went out onto the porch and lifted her hair from her ear. The roar came from the barn, where a faint light glimmered. Only it wasn't a roar. It wasn't even a voice. She recognized the noise.

It was the log splitter.

Panic gripped her. George's pride and joy, a conical drill bit powered by a tractor engine, capable of rending thick sections of tree into split logs with the slightest pressure against its tip. Capable of doing the same and worse to a careless or drunk human operator. *George is out there after drinking so much whiskey that he left his door open in the middle of the night?* She'd told him earlier that day that the lodge was low on logs, and now she regretted it.

Jennifer would have preferred to have her big husband with her, but she didn't have time to go after him. She had to get George away from the splitter, without delay. She took off at a sprint for the barn, slipping and tripping but somehow managing to stay upright. It was only twenty yards away, but at nearly seven thousand feet in altitude, her chest heaved, and frigid air seared her lungs like she was sucking on a blow torch. A few feet from the hanging barn doors, she tried to slow down. She lost traction and caught herself on one side of the doors.

A person barreled out and past her, knocking her aside. Light from the barn revealed someone of medium-to-tall height, with a ball cap covering the hair and pulled low over the face, and layers of bulky clothing hiding body type. Except for the shoulder, where the clothing was ripped away, exposing skin. Not just skin. Skin and a dark patch. The brief glimpse slammed into her brain like a battering ram. A tattoo of a snake coiled in rocks with D-T-O-M below it.

She'd seen it before. It was a recurring image in her nightmares. For a fraction of a second, she was frozen in place, speechless. The tattoo was real. Did that mean the man in her nightmares was real, too—a memory instead of a phantom? That it was George, who she'd let into her inner circle? It was too horrible to contemplate. Because that man pulled out an AR-15 and opened fire on a schoolyard. On her and other children. But it was just a bad dream. Easily explainable based on events like Sandy Hook and Columbine and her own recent case in Houston. Wasn't it?

She pushed the thoughts away. The ripped clothing. The log splitter. Those weren't good things. She had to stay in the present.

"George?" she cried.

The person didn't stop. Didn't answer her. *George. It has to be.*

Inside the barn, the roar hadn't stopped either. *Why did George leave the log splitter on? Was the exposed shoulder a sign he'd been injured?* He'd moved like he was okay. Okay enough, anyway. She'd just go turn the machine off, then she'd follow him back to his cottage and make sure he was all right.

She stepped into the barn. A single caged bulb hung from the ceiling, illuminating the interior in meager light that was mostly shadows. Jennifer frowned, inhaling the scents of sawdust and motor oil. It was spooky, but warmer. She rubbed her prickly arms and strode past the big orange tractor that George used outside to get to the red tractor carcass that housed the engine powering his contraption. As she drew closer, hair rose on her neck like hackles. Something felt *wrong*. Instead of turning off the key, she kept going, intuition drawing her toward the splitter on the back of the tractor.

When she reached the rear corner, she looked around it toward the evil-looking cone. What she saw, she wouldn't be able to wash from her memory with a gallon of bleach and a stiff bristle brush.

Bloody boots. Red-splashed legs. A torso drenched in blood. A note on its chest. I AM A MURDERER. A photo by a hand of two men and a woman picnicking beside snowmobiles.

And an arm, ripped and thrown two feet away from the rest of the body.

She had to do something. Behind her, she heard a grating noise as the barn doors slid further open, then the distinctive action of a shell chambering into a shotgun.

ONE

HOUSTON, Texas

(ELEVEN DAYS EARLIER...)

AARON HERRINGTON RE-ARRANGED a vase of gerbera daisies for the third time. He smoothed the front of his fresh shirt, untucked from his Paige jeans, which he wore for the extra thigh room. He cocked his head and frowned, then repositioned one of the nodding blooms. Finally satisfied, he stood back from the dining room table and surveyed his preparations. A bottle of his wife's favorite pinot noir uncorked and poured, breathing in two glasses on the granite bar top. A low carb, gluten free veggie lasagna bubbling in the oven, emitting a tomato-and-herb aroma. The Houston skyline twinkling outside the high-rise condo with Sheryl Crow singing in surround. The framed picture of him in a football uniform with his wife in her cheerleading outfit on the sidelines of their last University of Tennessee home game, dusted and moved onto the table beside the daisies. He'd even picked his dirty clothes and wet towel up off the floor and thrown them in the hamper.

He was ready for Jennifer.

He took a sip of the wine, letting it linger on his tongue while the flavors revealed themselves. Cherry, followed by something leathery. He preferred a good craft beer, but the wine was nice after a grueling day. He'd packed in ten hours at River Oaks Pet Care, the veterinary clinic he co-owned with two partners. It had started with a before-hours emergency call from a crazy woman insisting her poodle was dangerously depressed. He'd dispensed a low dose antidepressant. It would help the dog more if the owner took it, honestly. He'd be plenty anxious and depressed, too, if he were in that dog's shoes. Or paws.

How did I end up in this life?

After his NFL career had ended before it had barely begun thanks to head injuries, he'd planned to be a country vet, à la James Herriot. It was the next best thing to inheriting the family farm he grew up on, which would never happen since he was the youngest of five brothers. Instead, here he was, living the high life, literally— prescribing poochie Prozac. He shook his head. *Well, it pays the bills.* There were times he wondered whether the injuries and his unful-filled dreams were punishment for the mistakes he'd made in his late teens. *That's not something I want to think about now or ever.* Yet somehow, the secrets of his past stuck with him, like the hot black tar on his bare young feet the time he'd run across a country road one sweltering August afternoon.

Not now. Not when Jennifer was due home any minute.

He forced his mind back to more pleasant thoughts. He'd finished up his workday coaching middle school club football. He loved coaching and ninety percent of the people involved, young and old, but he didn't love the parents who hovered, obsessed, demanded, and excuse-made, or the behavior of their offspring. *I'd be anxious and depressed if I were in the shoes of some of those kids, too.* He'd always imagined he and Jennifer would be parents by now, but not *those* kinds of parents. They'd be the kind that threw the ball around with their kids in the yard and cheered them on but kept it light—because youth sports was just fun and games. But Jennifer had begged off parenthood, so far, because of the demands of her job. Or so she said. They weren't getting any younger. If they didn't take the plunge soon, their kids could call him Grandpa instead of Dad.

But tonight, he was putting all that aside, because he'd gotten a text from Jennifer in the early afternoon. The message read: *Guilty!!!*

The trial that had delayed their Wyoming trip two days was finally over. It was a huge victory for Jennifer in a career that was already becoming legendary in the Harris County District Attorney's office. One less murderer out there victimizing children—in this case, school kids from the Third Ward, a neighborhood in strong contention for poorest and roughest in Houston. Only one of them had died, but that was one too many. The case had been challenging for his wife. The defendant was an identical twin, which meant standard DNA tests yielded identical results for him and his twin brother. In the end, she'd produced a witness who placed the other brother elsewhere at the time of the murder. That had been enough, luckily.

He was happy for her. Even more, he hoped the end of this trial and beginning of the trip would be like the push of a reset button for them.

A key rattled in the lock. He pulled a lighter from a drawer in the kitchen and lit a candle, then grabbed Jennifer's glass of wine. The door opened, and the grown-up version of his blonde-haired, blue-eyed dream girl walked through it. All five feet two inches of her, plus three-or-so more of fancy heels. She carried a briefcase on one arm, and a Neiman Marcus bag dangled from the other. As always, the sight of her put a little squeeze on his heart, to remind him what it was there for.

He smiled at her, holding out the wine glass. "Congratulations."

Jennifer kicked off her shoes. They fell over on the wide plank hardwood floors. *Is it my imagination or is she weaving?* "Thanks.

One for the good guys today." She didn't seem to notice the flowers on the table, but she took the wine.

"You're home late."

"Sorry. I went golfing and shopping with Alayah." She waggled the bag, then dropped it to the floor.

He should have expected that, he supposed. Jennifer and her best friend celebrated their wins and commiserated their losses with golf outings followed by retail splurges. His wife was a shockingly good golfer, with a handicap of five. The tiny woman could drive a ball farther than he could, and she wasn't even the best golfer in her family. That honor belonged to her twin brother Justin, who was a pro at a golf course in Tennessee. Jennifer had turned down golf scholarships at smaller schools to attend the University of Tennessee, where she'd walked on and made the team, but quit after she decided to cheer. Alayah? Well, she mostly caddied and refilled the drinks.

He said, "I made a special dinner for you. Veggie lasagna."

"Oh, you're so sweet. But I grabbed something to eat when we had drinks."

So that was why she was so late. Now he was sure the weaving wasn't his imagination. "You didn't text me."

"Time got away from me." She made a cute frowny face. "We can have it tomorrow, though, right?"

"We're leaving for Wyoming in the morning. For Hank's induction into the Hall of Fame. Remember?" *He* certainly did since he'd had to rebook their flights twice while they waited on her jury to come back. It was worth it, though. She'd always been close to her bull rider cousin, and the Cheyenne Frontier Days Rodeo Hall of Fame was a really big deal.

Her frown morphed into confusion and then recognition. "Crap. Right. Well, I'll wrap it up good, and we'll freeze it." She walked barefoot into the kitchen and retrieved a storage container from a large drawer. "I do love your veggie lasagna. Was it low carb and gluten free, too?"

He swallowed back the anger building inside him. Now wasn't

the time. He wanted to start their vacation without the lingering sour taste of a fight in their mouths. "Yes. But I'll put it up. I have to eat first."

"Oh. Of course." She floated past him toward their bedroom. "I need to shower and pack. Did you check us in?"

"Yes."

"Arrange for the doorman to come for our luggage in the morning?"

"Yes."

"And the concierge service to water our plants and bring in our mail and packages while we're gone?"

He ground his teeth. "Yes."

"Great." From the other room, she raised her voice. "How was your day?"

Before he could answer her, the shower came on. She wouldn't hear him unless he raised his voice, and he didn't feel like yelling. He felt like throwing the glass of wine across the room. Like stuffing the daisies in the trash compactor. Like putting his fist through the pantry door. But not like shouting for her attention.

Instead, he drank his wine like a shot and refilled it. Drank it. Refilled it again. Drank it, then drained the rest of the bottle into his glass. Swallowing the last of the pricey vino, he looked around their perfect condo, where everything was expensively in its place, except for the two of them, most of the time.

He couldn't wait to get out of there.

TWO

BIG HORN, Wyoming

JENNIFER SNAKED her hand under her husband's arm and jammed the horn on the rental car. The blast was long, loud, and discordant, but it didn't break up the traffic jam ahead of them—the traffic jam of massive bovines. She'd thought since they were booked in a lodge instead of crashing at her cousin's remote ranch, they'd be staying in civilization. Had been sure of it when they'd passed a golf course community, but now . . . this.

"Come *on*." She mashed the horn again.

There was zero reaction from the herd of beasts streaming down the mountain and blocking the dirt road. Tails swished at flies. Calves bawled. A cowboy whistled, then yelled "Yaw" and waved a coiled lasso at a cow that had taken a detour. Another animal slung its head and licked the inside of its nostrils with a long pink tongue.

Jennifer kept going. "It smells like a flippin' feed lot here. Are cattle drives still a thing? I feel like we've stumbled onto the pages of *Lonesome Dove* or something." It might have been her favorite book of all time, but that didn't mean Jennifer wanted it to come to life around her. She started to go for the horn a third time.

Her husband blocked her, but gently. Aaron had learned to be extra careful with people because of his size. At six foot five, he doubled her body weight and then some. His size came in handy with his two passions: veterinary medicine and football, although his playing days had ended long ago. Back then, she would have added herself to his list of passions, too.

"Honking won't do any good," he said.

"We're going to be late for Hank's dinner."

They'd already missed the hall of fame ceremony in Cheyenne. She hoped there'd been a good turnout of supporters, since her aunt and uncle—his parents—hadn't lived to see it. Her mother and Hank's father were siblings, and their two families had always been close, visiting each other when she was small. Her family had quit coming to Wyoming around when she entered elementary school, though, and everyone had started meeting up for destination vacations or family reunions in Tennessee instead. She wasn't sure why.

Anyway, Jennifer had really wanted to be there for Hank and to represent her side of the family.

Aaron lifted an eyebrow. Just one. She envied his ability to do that. It made him seem easy going. *Seem, schmeem.* He *was* easy going. A part of her believed that if she had his one-eyebrow trick in her repertoire, she would have seemed easy going, too. Which, truth be told, she wasn't.

"If we're late, it won't be because of these cows," he said.

The jibe hit its mark. They'd departed Houston a full thirty-six hours after their original flight. She flopped back into her seat. "The jury was still out. I couldn't just leave."

"The jury is always out. Or the judge has called an emergency hearing. Or you have to prepare for a closing argument." His voice was without rancor, until he added, "Like my patients don't have emergencies. The difference is I turn call over to my partners, but there's only one Jennifer Herrington, superstar Harris County assistant district attorney."

"It makes a difference, Aaron. If the jury had convened for questions with the judge, and I wasn't there, it could have signaled my lack of faith in the case. It was touch and go after he excluded my Eurofins test results. A child murderer could have walked." She'd gone way out on a fragile limb on the expensive Eurofins DNA test, which was the only test around that differentiated between identical twins' DNA. It had proved her defendant was the murderer. But the test hadn't yet been replicated by other labs or laid out in detail in any peer-reviewed journals, so the judge had ruled that she couldn't present the test and results to the jury. It had been a blow and left the entire case resting on the testimony of a witness little better than a jailhouse snitch. Given the nature of the crime and after all the money she'd spent on the excluded Eurofins test, there was no way she would have walked out on that trial before the jury was back. No stinking way. Not to mention how emotionally wrapped up in it she'd been. Sleepless nights and ten pounds she hadn't meant to lose told the tale. It had been her first school shooting. All of her homicide cases were heart wrenching, but this one had taken its toll.

Aaron didn't respond. She hadn't expected him to. The stalemate over her work wasn't a new one, and she knew he was mad she'd missed the dinner he'd made for her the night before, even though he was pretending he wasn't. The truth was, she hadn't expected him to go to all that trouble, or she wouldn't have gone for drinks with Alayah. And after she'd Ubered home, she'd been so buzzed that the magnitude of his efforts hadn't registered. She'd apologized that morning and still felt bad about it.

A cowboy galloped his horse down the hill beside the herd, breaking her reverie. Jennifer threw open the car door and jumped out, stepping in the hem of her red pantsuit. She recovered, but then wobbled in her Louboutin heels on the uneven ground. Rocks. Hummocks of grass. Divots and cracks. And, *ew*, cow patties. She hopped to the side, narrowly avoiding a steaming pile.

"Hey, there," she shouted to the cowboy. "Excuse me. Sir?"

The cowboy looked her way, then back at the cows. He shouted over their moos, which to her sounded a lot like moaning. *My God, these animals sound like a phone sex call center.* "Can I help you?"

She picked her way over the rough ground to get closer to him, struggling to maintain her dignity.

He threw a hand up. "Stay back, ma'am. These aren't pasture pets. If one of the bulls makes a run for it, I won't promise I can stop him before he gets to you, with you dressed like a matador and all."

Matador? What's he talking about? This is brand-new Michael Kors. Which she'd purchased after the jury came back the afternoon before. But she hadn't thought about the bulls. She stopped and smoothed her jacket. "We need to get up to our lodge. Do you mind letting us through?"

He tilted his head, then adjusted his hat. Down, up. "I wouldn't mind, but the herd might."

"How long will this take then?"

He scratched one shoulder. "Shouldn't be much longer now. Once we get a fair number in, the rest follow pretty nice."

She made a strangled sound deep in her throat and lifted her hair off her neck. "I don't understand why this is happening."

He frowned. "They have to come down some time now that summer's over or they'll starve up there, if they don't freeze to death first."

Another cowboy hollered, "Craig, coming your way."

Craig touched the brim of his hat, and, without seeming to give the horse any signal Jennifer could discern, he and the animal wheeled away from her as one to intercept three cows who'd broken ranks.

Aaron pulled the car up beside her. The slightly neon cobalt blue Ford Fusion that had seemed fine at the airport was looking out of place now. She settled back in it with a withering sigh. Suddenly, the sea of cows turned and flowed into the pasture. She watched through the window, her foot tapping on the floorboard. Craig the cowboy had been right. With the logjam cleared, the cows moved quickly, but it turned out there were a lot more of them than she'd counted on.

Finally, ten minutes later, Aaron accelerated up the steep hill. Not a hill, really. More like the side of the Bighorn Mountains, just outside the tiny town of Big Horn, Wyoming. The encounter with Craig and the cows seemed a bit more charming in retrospect. She sent herself an email with a few snippets of description and dialog. The subject line was "Someday novel."

They approached a crooked wooden sign on their right that read THE BIG HORN LODGE in faded green paint. Was everything around there named big horn-something? *A trend in naming conventions. Or maybe a rut?* She wasn't going to complain, though, since Aaron had made all the arrangements for their trip, letting her focus on her trial.

"This is it." Aaron bumped the car over the metal slats of a cattle guard.

"It's way out in the middle of nowhere, isn't it?"

The road crested a rise, then wound down to a cabin and outbuildings nestled at the edge of a forest. Above them, a row of flatirons in black and gray towered up, up, up toward a cloudless blue sky. Jennifer could almost imagine the faces of long dead presidents etched into the stone.

"Wow," Aaron said. "Just, wow." His square jaw hung open as he braked and leaned toward the windshield, admiring the mountains. She admired her husband. The man got better looking every year of his life, and he hadn't started from a deficit. His blond curls pushed against the back of his collar. He needed a haircut. He always needed a haircut. He turned to face her. "Isn't it amazing?"

She agreed. "Like something out of a movie." *Dances with Wolves.* Or *True Grit.*

He eased off the brake. The car coasted down the road—*driveway?*—toward a majestic lodge. They parked in front. The area could have doubled as a used car lot. There was an old Suburban up on blocks, an incongruous Porsche Cayenne, and a worn-in Dodge Ram two-ton, all lined-up in a row beside them. A stand of aspens shaded the front yard with shimmering golden leaves. Up close, though, the structure looked a little tired. Made of rough-hewn logs, it stood three stories tall, with a deep porch and tall, rectangular windows. The varnish on the logs had dulled, and graying wood was showing through it. The aged skull of a ram hung over the entrance, the curve of its horns forming a three-quarter circle on each side. Green paint peeled from the door.

Jennifer's phone buzzed and then chimed. She hadn't had a signal since their little regional jet had landed at the airport in Sheridan an hour before. Voice mail messages, texts, and emails all downloaded and announced themselves at once.

Aaron turned off the engine. "Ready?" He popped the trunk and got out.

The lure of technology tugged at her, but, after making sure none of the messages were from her twin brother Justin, her best friend Alayah, or her parents, she broke free of it. Her office knew to consider her unreachable through the weekend. She deserved a few hours away from the grind and could check her messages later. She slung her tiny purse and larger laptop bag over her shoulder. By the time she caught up with Aaron outside, he had hefted both of their suitcases onto the porch. She trotted up the creaky wooden steps, windmilling her arms to stay upright when she caught a heel between two boards. She jerked it out without breaking it. Aaron didn't seem to notice. A piece of lined notebook paper taped to the glass of the storm door wafted up and down in the wind. BE WITH YOU IN A MOMENT.

Jennifer rang the doorbell. After a minute with no answer, she heard voices outside. "Someone's over there." She pointed toward the side of the lodge.

She and Aaron left their bags and followed their ears. On the side of the house, they found two men in a heated conversation. They looked like the before-and-after photos for an anti-drugs and alcohol public service announcement. One wore pressed khakis, wing tips, and a button-down shirt. The other, soiled jeans, suspenders, and a buttoned blue chambray shirt that, as Jennifer got closer, she saw read THE BIG HORN LODGE over the breast pocket. Both men looked to be in their early sixties and had white blond hair, but the conservative cut on the business-type was nothing like the Rod-Stewart-on-a-bender look of the one associated with the lodge. Their ice blue eyes differed, too. Piercing versus dulled.

Rod Stewart crossed his arms. "Don't make me call the sheriff, Hadley."

Hadley, the Gordon Gekko wannabe, sneered at him. "I haven't done a thing."

"Right."

Gordon Gekko—Hadley?—pushed back his cuff, examining a shiny gold Rolex. "This isn't over, George. Not by a long shot."

"It never is," George-aka-Rod Stewart muttered. He looked up as if noticing Aaron and Jennifer for the first time. Louder, he said, "Sorry about that, folks." Then, staring at Jennifer, he added, "Oh, my."

"What?" Jennifer said.

"It's just, well, your outfit is—"

Hadley, "Loud," at the same time that George said, "Terrifying."

Jennifer's jaw dropped, and she gawked at them. Hadley nodded and walked away. Jennifer looked at her husband and mouthed *what the . . . ?*

"May I help you?" George took a few careful steps in their direction.

Aaron stuck out his big hand. "Aaron Herrington. My wife Jennifer and I," he gestured to include her, "have a reservation for tonight."

"Ah, yes. You paid for three nights, and then couldn't make the first two."

"That's right."

The men shook. Jennifer offered her hand, but she dropped it when George didn't turn her way.

"I'm George Nichols. Come on." He walked around them. Liquid sloshed in time with his steps. A glass pint protruded from the back pocket of his saggy, grease-stained jeans.

Aaron did the eyebrow lift again. Longing coursed through Jennifer. She wanted to be *in* love again, to *be* loved again. By Aaron. They had been so good together once. Had been for a long time, and she wasn't sure when they'd drifted apart, or why. The moment and the ache passed as quickly as they'd come, though, and she and Aaron traipsed behind George to the entrance. Aaron took one of their suitcases in each hand. She reclaimed her laptop bag, then glanced back into the parking area before going into the lodge. The Hadley fellow was watching them from beside the Cayenne. The scene between him and George had been off putting. Jennifer wondered who he was, why he was here, and when he was leaving. *Soon, I hope.*

George flipped on lights and motioned them ahead. "Let me check your room. I'll be right back." He disappeared down a dark hall, like a bowling ball searching for a gutter.

Jennifer paused to take measure of the place. The front room was spacious, with bulky furniture oriented around a cast iron stove. It had a throwback feel, circa 1970. Oranges, browns, golds. Stained wood finishes. Knubby fabrics. Gilt-framed pictures. A wide opening led into a kitchen with yellow Formica on every surface. Before Jennifer could get a closer look, though, the light overhead flickered and went out.

She said, "It's a little run down. I'm thinking *The Shining.*"

Aaron cocked his head, a pleased expression on his face. "More Wyoming meets *The Best Exotic Marigold Hotel.*"

"Maybe."

A shaggy, gray-muzzled St. Bernard struggled to its feet from a carpet with a jagged row of missing fringe around its edges. Jennifer thought the dog was coming to check them out. Instead, it lifted a shaky leg on the corner of the wall.

"No," she cried.

Aaron groaned, then he laughed. "Poor old guy. Here, boy. Let me take you out."

The dog wagged its tail and tottered across the floor like it had been trading nips with George. Before he and Aaron could reach the door, there was a screech, and a calico cat leapt from its perch on a rolltop desk, attaching itself by its claws to Aaron's chest. Aaron grunted—for him, a fairly dramatic expression of shock and pain— and grabbed the cat. In the brief and violent wrestling match that ensued, the cat scored a few major points, although ultimately Aaron wrenched it off and tossed it away from him. With a swish of its multi-colored tail, it jumped back onto the desk, where it licked its paws and studied the intruders as if imagining them stuck to a spec- imen board by long straight pins.

Aaron let loose a string of curse words. If his mother were here, she would have come after her son's mouth with a bar of soap.

"That dog is an incontinent pony, and the cat is a gremlin." Jennifer put a hand to her throat. "Your shirt. It's shredded."

He pulled the gray University of Tennessee golf-style shirt away from himself and peeked down the front. "So is my chest." He let go of the fabric and blood seeped through as the shirt settled against his skin.

"I'll find something to clean you up." Jennifer hurried into the kitchen, looking for paper towels and soap. When George returned, she'd ask him for hydrogen peroxide or rubbing alcohol, too. Aaron wasn't a stranger to wounds inflicted by animals in his line of work, and she'd doctored him many times. Once, when he was in vet school, he'd even spent a few days in the hospital with cat scratch fever— which had earned him the nickname Ted Nugent from his classmates —so both of them knew personally how serious cat's claws could be.

She stopped short in the center of the eating area adjacent to the kitchen. A sour smell undercut with something sickeningly sweet burned her nasal passages. Trash was stacked to overflowing, with a Wyoming Whiskey bottle balanced on top. Detritus from a meal of chips and sandwiches littered the countertops. Dishes were piled like the leaning tower of Pisa in the sink. By the faucet, a rusted coffee can was heaped with rotten food. A piece of medical tape on its side announced in black all caps letters that it was COMPOST.

But it wasn't the filthiness that gave her pause. It was the black and white animal scurrying through the food and dishes on the counter.

"Aaron . . ." Her voice quavered. She sucked in a whistling breath. And then she burst into tears. Sobs, really. Gasping, heaving sobs that bent her over on her knees.

Her husband ran into the kitchen. "What is it?" He straightened her by her shoulders, his eyes boring into hers.

She pointed at the counter. The little creature was standing on its back legs now, watching them. Through hiccups, she said, "Isn't it the most beautiful thing you've ever seen?"

Aaron's laughter scared the animal, and it squeaked at them and darted behind a standing mixer. "It's a skunk, Jenny."

"I never thought I'd get this close to one."

"You're almost close enough to get sprayed."

"I don't c-c-c-care." Watching *Bambi* as a little girl, Jennifer had fallen in love with Flower, and her heart had remained true. She inched into the kitchen. "Hey, there, little guy. Or are you a girl?" she cooed.

"You know you're probably the only person on the planet who's fanatical about skunks, right?"

Jennifer flapped her hand to shush him. "Come back, sweetie pie. Just let me get another look at you."

"It's so rare they probably don't even have a name for the disorder."

Jennifer sniffed. "They're so little and misunderstood. Their spray is just a way to protect themselves. They do lots of good things, like eat mice and rats and spread seeds."

She heard George's feet thumping on hardwood. At least, she hoped it was George, and not Hadley. But she didn't tear her eyes away from the skunk.

"That's Jeremiah Johnson," George said, sounding a little sloppier than a few minutes before. Glass clinked as he dropped something onto the trash mountain. "I found him as a baby in a live trap in my barn, dehydrated and starving. I bottle fed him until he recovered. After that, he didn't want to leave. We've been together ever since. Jeremiah, come meet the nice guests."

The skunk waddled to George and climbed into his arms. Jennifer trilled.

"Jeremiah's stink maker was removed, so it's safe to come close. He likes to get to know you before you handle him, though."

Don't we all. "If you're sure?" Jennifer was already halfway across the kitchen.

Aaron shook his head, grinning. "You're fulfilling a lifelong dream for her right now. A bucket list item."

George swayed like there was a stiff wind blowing through the kitchen. "See if he'll sniff your hand."

Jennifer held her hand out, palm down. Jeremiah sniffed it, then skittered up George's arm and perched on his shoulder like a parrot.

"He's *adorable*," she said.

"I don't know what I'd do without my little buddy." George set the skunk back on the counter.

Jennifer shuddered. Animals, even tame skunks, didn't belong on kitchen counters in her world. The lodge was a pigsty. Luckily, they weren't staying long and didn't have to eat here. She turned away from the mess.

"Do you have any rubbing alcohol? My husband had an encounter with your cat." Her voice was sticky sweet. As cute as Jeremiah was, the cat was a menace.

Aaron gave Jennifer a look. He knew what it meant when a southern woman used a voice like that.

George smiled. "Sorry about Katya. She thinks she's our guard dog, since Liam doesn't get around well anymore."

From the living room, the dog's tail thumped so hard at the mention of its name that it sounded like a tribal drum.

"Is Liam the incontinent dog?" she asked.

George beamed. "That's him. Isn't he a peach?" He walked out of the kitchen and into the hall.

Aaron and Jennifer followed him.

"Bless his heart," Jennifer said drily.

"There's rubbing alcohol and cotton balls in the hall bathroom closet." George motioned through a doorway. He took a few more steps and pointed to another opening. Jennifer couldn't see inside it. "This is your room. There was a famous mystery author staying in it last week. He rented the whole place so he could have peace and quiet to write in."

Aaron said, "Jennifer is something of a writer herself."

She frowned. "Am not." *An English major. A writer of trial briefs. An obsessive reader.* But she'd given up dreams of pursuing writing along with eating bad carbs in her thirties. Both had been painful.

Aaron's eyes clouded. "But you've always wanted to write murder mysteries."

And now I just watch them on the Hallmark Channel. She shook her head no at him.

Aaron seemed to cast off whatever negative feeling it was that had sprinted across his face. To George, he said, "Who stayed here, if you can tell us?"

"The one who writes stories about that detective in LA named after some famous wacky artist."

Jennifer knew exactly who he meant, and she couldn't help feeling a little excited.

George continued. "One of many authors that have stayed here, actually. I've had Craig Johnson—back before he bought his spread west of here—Rita Mae Brown, and, oh, others. I remember names better earlier in the day when my brain is working."

When he isn't pickled.

"There's a bathroom in here, but don't use it. Come on. Let me walk you through your water situation."

"Wait. What? Don't use the bathroom? Water situation?" Jennifer asked.

"The septic tank corroded and collapsed, so we aren't currently able to run any water. I've put some bottled waters in your room."

Jennifer couldn't be understanding him correctly. "What does that mean—not able to run water?"

He looked at her like maybe her question wasn't very smart. "We can't use the sinks, showers, or toilets until tomorrow."

Jennifer was too flabbergasted to respond. *No running water? As in zero, zip, nada?*

Jeremiah galloped down the hall. George scooped the skunk off the floor and tucked him in his arm like a football. He opened a door. It led outside, and the three of them exited onto a back deck. On it sat a hard-plastic camp potty, about twelve inches tall and hardly bigger than Jennifer's tush. *Aaron will crush the thing.* A roll of toilet paper sat on the deck beside it.

George cleared his throat. "These are the temporary facilities."

Jennifer's mouth dropped open. "It's so . . . exposed." No sheet or shower curtain or screen or anything.

"Nobody back here but animals and the mountain." George side stepped from the deck to a tree where a hose was attached to a pail hanging from a branch. "Here's the shower. You turn it on over there." He pointed to a faucet at the base of the house, about fifteen feet away. "The water comes through holes in the bottom of the bucket."

Jennifer was at a loss for words. With wide eyes, she turned to her husband and mouthed *no, no, no.*

"Is it, um, heated?" Aaron asked.

George was fiddling with the pail and didn't look over at them. "The water? No, but the weather's still nice out. If you're quick about it, it shouldn't be too bad."

Aaron avoided Jennifer's eyes. "When will it be fixed?"

"Black Bear Betty is working on it right now. Here she comes with the old septic tank." George lifted a hand in greeting as a tractor motored into view. He teetered but remained upright.

Black Bear Betty?

A woman with a silver pixie cut and a face like a bulldog sat high on the big orange tractor, waving a cigar. Hunks of metal with holes like lattice filled the tractor's bucket. Jennifer didn't know much about septic tanks, but she did know they were meant to hold things inside, not sieve them to the outside. The septic tank in the bucket was holier than the threadbare underwear her grandma used to mend for her grandfather.

Aaron's eyes wandered around the property. "We'd sure love a tour, if you've got the time." They might as well, since Jennifer didn't want to start over on her hair and make-up now, thanks to the outdoor "shower," which meant they'd no longer be running late.

George said, "I've got nothing but time. Let me put the critter in the house first, though."

Maybe he should put the incontinent *critter out.* "Does Jeremiah have to go in?" Jennifer leaned toward the animal. This time the skunk let himself be petted. She was touching a skunk for the first time in her life. The trip was worth it if for this moment alone.

"Only if we don't want him to be fox food."

"Oh, no, Jeremiah can't be fox food," Jennifer agreed, nearly purring. She peered up at Aaron. "But we should take care of your wounds first."

"Let's do the tour first," he said.

After putting Jeremiah away, George returned and led them across the property. The grass wasn't like Southern grass. It grew in the spikey clumps that Jennifer had already encountered by the cattle drive and made her wish she'd worn boots. When they reached a red wooden barn, George removed an unsecured lock and slid open the hanging doors. It was dark inside, but Jennifer's eyes adjusted quickly. The space was cram packed, except for a tractor-sized parking spot with wheel imprints in the dirt. Probably from the one Black Bear

Betty was using, Jennifer decided. She browsed the rest of the mess. Discarded paraphernalia from the lodge. Gardening pots. Winter shovels. Vehicle maintenance items. A couple of snowmobiles, one of which seemed pretty mangled. A set of stairs in the back leading to a trap door in the ceiling. The biggest portion of the interior was taken up by a red tractor with four flat tires parked in front of an assembly line of logs. Limbless trees, rather—a forest of them—laid cross ways between wooden guides. Beside them was a row of bins filled with split logs ready for a fireplace, and a chain saw hanging from a hook on a post. The whole barn smelled like sawdust and petroleum products.

Then Jennifer saw movement. A scrawny bearded man was sitting in a back corner, leaning against a giant backpack, whittling a stick with a black pocketknife.

George noticed him at the same time. "Dammit, Will. You can't stay here. I'm getting sick and tired of telling you."

Will's clothes were grimy and frayed, and his age was hard to estimate under all the dirt and facial hair. "It's a free country."

"Except for private property laws."

"And that's how you treat someone who used to work for you and is down on his luck. Nice."

"There are plenty of places to camp free on government land."

Will closed his knife, stood, and stuffed it and a water bottle into the backpack. He didn't zip it. Jennifer itched to pull it closed for him. "Not anywhere near here. Not with power and water."

"I'll give you a ride up to Big Goose myself."

"Do you think I have a death wish? I'm not going up the mountain with a drunk like you. I'll walk."

"Suit yourself."

Will hefted the backpack up and onto one shoulder. He worked his other arm through the strap, his back bowing under its weight. Without another word, he walked out of the barn, like a trekker in search of the Himalayas.

Aaron and Jennifer exchanged a long look, eyebrows up.

"This baby is my log splitter," George said, patting the broken-down tractor, and moving on as if he hadn't just evicted a squatter from his property.

"It runs?" Aaron walked around it and inspected it with the look of someone who'd grown up fixing the things he'd broken or wrecked.

"The engine does. She won't go anywhere, but she can still power this." George walked them around to the back of the tractor. A large piece of pointed metal protruded from its rear side.

George picked up a chain saw and mimed cutting with it. "I cut the big logs into useable lengths." He set the chain saw down and grabbed a pre-cut section of log. "Then I turn on the splitter." He held the wood against the stationary point of the metal. *A drill bit*, Jennifer decided. That's what it looked like. "It splits the log into pieces." He set the big piece down and lifted two others of the same length, only split. "Like these. Then I toss them in the carrier." He heaved them into the wheeled bin. "When I need firewood, I hook the other tractor to one of the bins, and I drive it over to the house."

"Wow, that's a nifty system." Aaron's eyes were gleaming embers.

George's chest expanded a couple of inches.

More like a great way to trigger a life insurance policy, especially for someone as obviously fond of Wyoming Whiskey as George. And how in the world can one person burn so much firewood, even in a lodge?

"Of course, I still have the manual splitter, too." He hefted a long-handled implement with an angled club at the end. It looked like it weighed as much as Jennifer.

Jennifer was more interested in the bag of ancient *golf* clubs she'd spotted. She touched the bag. "Are these yours?"

George barely glanced at them. "They belonged to the previous owner."

She pulled out a driver with a discolored metal shaft and scarred wooden head. Rolling her neck and shoulders, she settled into her stance, the old club as comfortable in her hands as if she'd held it a thousand times. Then she twisted into her backswing and unleashed like she was teeing off at Augusta.

Aaron whistled as the club cut through the air with a swish. "Fore."

George ducked with his hands over his head. "Shit! What was that?"

Aaron laughed. "A driver. Watch out for my wife. She's lethal with one of those things."

George was still shaking his head as Jennifer slid the club back in the bag.

After they finished with the barn, George led them to a stable that listed slightly downhill. A big, fenced vegetable garden ran along one side. A horned barn owl with a superior expression watched them from the open hay loft over the door. Jennifer stepped around a nasty pile of something below it that looked disturbingly like a regurgitated mouse.

George showed them stalls for horses and kennels for smaller animals. "Everything comes inside during the worst of the winter. But you'd be surprised how infrequently that is. The animals adapt. Especially the horses. I'd never been much of a horse person until I married. Shelly talked me into them, and before you knew it, we had four. I built this cedar tack room myself."

The workmanship was beautiful. The room was empty. Jennifer hadn't seen any horses outside, either.

"Where are the horses?"

"Sold 'em." His tone cut off the possibility of further discussion on the topic.

Next, he took them toward a cavernous metal building. They passed a section of fence on the way that looked like it had been built the day before.

It was quite a paradox to Jennifer how decrepit the stable was compared to the five tight strands of barbed wire strung between upright green metal posts. "New fence?"

"Nearly. I had a fellow running cattle here this summer. He put it in."

"It looks expensive," Aaron said.

George grinned crookedly. "Fences around here need to be horse high, pig tight, and bull strong."

Aaron nodded like George had just explained a revolutionary theory on quantum physics. "Exactly."

They entered the metal building. Inside were stacks of new lumber next to an assortment of woodworking tools.

"I've been meaning to finish out my shop, but I haven't got around to it. It has electric, heat, and water, though, and that's really all I need."

Aaron walked the concrete floors high on the balls of his feet, a bounce to his step. "Don't you love it, Jennifer?"

"It's peachy," she said. It was bittersweet to see her husband like this. *He's been unhappy,* she realized. She smiled at him, too late, and he didn't see it.

The last place George took them was a cottage. Rundown didn't begin to cover it. The wooden siding hadn't seen a paintbrush in far too long. A board on the little porch was broken. One of the front windows had been replaced with plywood.

But what drew Jennifer's full attention was a piece of plain printer paper plastered to the door with multiple layers of clear tape. The word KILLER marched across the page in precise capital letters.

George scowled and tried to loosen the tape with his fingernails. It didn't go well, and Jennifer pitched in.

Aaron's voice sounded concerned. "Do you know who left this here?"

George snorted. "Yes. My wife's ex-husband. The crazy SOB's been harassing me." He nodded. "You met him earlier. Hadley." *The Gordon Gekko guy.* He dropped his voice. "I'll show him harassment. You'd think he'd find a better way to spend his time than driving out here a couple of times a week." He peeled the last of the tape away. "He divorced her, you know, but he never loved my Shelly more than when she married me, especially after she died. He blames me for her death." He opened the door and muttered, "Not half as much as I blame myself, though."

Again, Aaron and Jennifer shared a significant look.

Aaron cleared his throat. "Do you live in the cottage?"

"It's where I sleep. I miss Shelly less out here," George said.

Jennifer peeked around his shoulder. Inside a dark, messy room, another Wyoming Whiskey bottle sat on a coffee table beside a tin cup.

He eyed it and licked his lips. "Sorry about the mess. I think I'm going to call it a night. If you have an emergency, call 911." He waved as if to shoo them away. "Have a nice evening."

Aaron and Jennifer backed out the door, which George shut firmly in their face.

"All right, then," Aaron said.

The two of them walked toward the lodge. Jennifer pressed the back of her hand to her forehead. Could this man, this place, and this day get any stranger? It didn't seem possible. They only had to spend one night here, though, and then they'd be back in their luxurious, beautiful, *normal* Houston condo—with functional plumbing.

Thank God.

THREE

SHERIDAN, Wyoming

"THANK you all for being here. As big an honor as it was to be recognized in Cheyenne, there's no place like home, and there are no people I'd rather celebrate with than you guys." Hank Sibley lifted a beer stein.

Not that Aaron checked guys out, but he always evaluated their physical potential, as if they were adversaries on the field. It was a habit he'd never broken after he left football. To him, Hank looked like a cornerback. Lean muscle and zero percent body fat, but not tall enough to be a wide receiver.

A swarthy guy nearly two heads shorter than Aaron lifted his glass toward Hank. "Any time you're buying, Sib."

Laughs erupted around the tables. Thirty, maybe forty people? The party was in the back room of a restaurant in Sheridan—Frackelton's, which was much better than he'd expected to find in Wyoming, based on the appetizers and drinks so far.

Hank grinned. "I'm just charging it to Double S, Gene. Thanks for picking up half the tab for everybody."

The laughs were even louder for that line. Gene was Hank's business partner in a bucking stock contracting business run on Hank's family ranch. Aaron had met Gene earlier in the evening. The woman sitting between Jennifer and Hank was iconically familiar to Aaron. Around Nashville, where he'd grown up on a farm, and Knoxville, where he'd gone to college and vet school, country music stars were gods. Maggie Killian had been scorching the air waves about the time he was graduating from vet school. She'd flamed out later, though. Drugs, if he remembered correctly. But she looked good now. Healthy. Straight.

"You probably all guessed I partnered up with Gene way back when because he made me look taller." This line got Hank the loudest laugh of all. "Last night, they told me I'm the tallest bull rider ever inducted into the hall of fame for Frontier Days. Which ain't saying much." Someone from across the room whistled and whooped. His face turned serious. "You folks know how much I miss my parents." Warm sounds of agreement and nods followed his words. "That's why I'm so happy to have family here tonight, especially since my sister Laura had to head back to New Mexico straight from Cheyenne. That's my cousin Jenny and her husband Aaron over there." He nodded at them. Aaron nodded back. "And, of course, my parents' longtime best friends, Patrick and Susanne Flint, who might as well officially adopt me. Patrick, thanks for patching me up, over and over, when the bulls got the best of me." A tanned and gray-haired man half stood, his hand on a woman's shoulder. She was fit and attractive, but Aaron assumed she was roughly the same age as her husband. "And of course, to my Maggie, the best thing to come out of Frontier Days for me, hands down." She blew him a kiss." So, here's to you all, drink up, eat up, and party 'til the sun's up. Cheers."

"Cheers," Aaron said, with the rest of the crowd.

Hank put the mug to his lips as he sat down beside Maggie. The two of them shared a searing gaze, then locked lips. It went on for so long that Aaron looked away.

Aaron took a sip of his Bomber Mountain Amber. He enjoyed trying out the local beers on tap—this one was from Blacktooth Brewery a few streets over—but tonight he was taking it easy, since Jennifer was on her third glass of pinot noir. One of them needed to stay sober for the drive back to the lodge, and she didn't have much weight to balance out the volume of wine she was consuming.

She flipped her phone over and dipped her head to check it. Again. She'd spent more time with her face in it than talking to any of the humans present. He frowned. Something was off kilter about her tonight. She looked great, flashing a little bit of side skin and shoulder in a slinky top. She always looked great. Her hair was twisted into a clip like she hadn't brushed it in a month, which he loved. She wore brighter colors than most women he knew and mismatched clothes on purpose. The way she dressed was bold and sometimes jarring, like her personality.

"You okay?" he said from the side of his mouth.

Annoyance crossed her pretty face. It caught at his chest. When had that become the norm? He tried to picture how she'd looked at him in the old days. She still had the big blue eyes, the perfect lips, a nose so cute he used to kiss it good morning, the blonde hair that was like silk against his skin, and a killer bod made even leaner by hot yoga and a stress diet than when she'd been into handsprings and herkie jumps. But he couldn't raise a mental image of the pheromone-charged gaze that had taken his breath away. It wasn't just the difference in her response to him, though. All of her expressions were harder. He felt another tug in his chest. His Jenny had lost her smile.

"I'm fine, other than I'm stuck beside her." She jerked her head toward Maggie. "Why do you ask?"

"Just checking on you. Did something happen between you two?"

Maggie leaned around Jennifer. "What are you two love birds whispering about?"

A fragile-looking waitress with red hair, flighty eyes, and a nametag that read MELINDA set plates down in front of Aaron and Jennifer. He'd ordered the Delmonico-cut ribeye. The scent wafting up from the plate made him salivate. They hadn't had time for lunch when they'd connected in Denver earlier.

Jennifer drained her wine glass and ignored her purple pasta. *What the hell makes it that color?*

Before Aaron could answer, Maggie drawled, "Must be important. Maybe it's about whatever Ms. Thing here has been reading on her phone all night."

The annoyed look on Jennifer's face deepened. She gave Aaron a *see what I mean* head tilt.

Aaron jumped in quickly. "Man, this food looks great."

"They do a nice job, although I've never ordered anything *vegetarian*." Maggie raised her eyebrows and nodded at Jennifer's plate.

"I happen to like beets." Jennifer swirled her empty glass. "And I need more wine."

Maggie shook her head. "Vegetarian plates and fancy wine aren't what you need in Wyoming." She raised a hand, and the waitress scuttled over. "Two Koltiska 90s, please. Rocks."

The waitress nodded and left without a peep.

"I like what I like," Jennifer said.

Maggie snorted. "Apparently that doesn't include the perfectly nice guest house at our ranch."

Ouch. Clearly it hadn't landed well with Maggie that Jennifer had insisted on staying elsewhere. A hand on Aaron's shoulder tore his attention away from the women. He turned to see a not-*un*familiar face under brown hair graying at the temples, but he couldn't place the guy. Thick but not fat, the man had a beard that was longer and darker than his hair, making him appear maybe ten years older than Aaron. He wasn't tall, yet there was an air about him that said "wolverine." Special teams. A small linebacker or fullback. If he'd been fast, a big running back.

"You're Aaron Herrington, am I right?" the man said.

Aaron stood, pushing back his chair. "I am."

"I'm Perry Flint. About twenty years ago, I was a scout for the University of Wyoming. I tried to convince you to play quarterback for us. You visited during a blizzard, and we never heard back from you again."

Aaron groaned. He remembered. It hadn't been a great time in his life. "I'm sorry. We don't get much cold weather where I come from."

The two men shook.

Perry smoothed his hand across the top of his short hair. "I was sorry to hear about your head injuries. The Lions lost out on a great tight end when you retired."

"Thank you, although I'm not sure you can call it retiring. I had to quit before I finished my first full season in the pros. If I'd come to Wyoming, maybe I could have played quarterback and avoided the nine concussions. But it forced my ass back to vet school, where it belonged."

"Yeah, bad luck signing at Tennessee at the same time as Peyton Manning."

Aaron sighed. "I wish I hated the guy, but he's just so dang nice."

Perry sang, "Nationwide is on your side."

Aaron laughed, recognizing the jingle from an insurance commercial. "And he got all the endorsements."

"Do you live around here?"

"No. Houston. Hank's my wife's first cousin. We came up for his party."

"How long are you going to be around? I coach at the high school in Big Horn. Maybe I can lure you out to talk to my players."

Aaron felt a twinge of regret. He ducked his chin as he gave his head one shake. "Rats. We're leaving tomorrow. I would have loved to. I coach youth club football in Houston."

"Next time. Are you staying with Sibley?"

"No. We're in Big Horn."

"Really? An Airbnb place?"

"The Big Horn Lodge."

Perry stretched his face into a surprised expression. "I didn't even know it was up and running."

Aaron considered the septic situation and the drunken proprietor. "By the skin of its teeth."

"It's a sad story. The owner, George, is a friend of my dad's. George used to run a successful electrical contracting company. Specialized in off-the-grid applications, like solar, wind, and generators. He sold out a few years ago to a big outfit, after he landed a statewide government contract for solar. He and his new wife Shelly bought the lodge and were going to fix it up. She wanted to be an innkeeper, and he was going to run snow machine tours."

"What happened?"

"Shelly died in an avalanche while they were back country snowmobiling. They say he dug for two days trying to get her out before someone found him."

Aaron had a new appreciation for the state of the lodge and George's liver. "Holy smokes."

On the other side of Aaron, a sharp female voice cut in. It was the fragile waitress, Melinda, holding a tray of drinks aloft. "Don't waste your time feeling sorry for George. The man killed my sister Sarah when he was driving drunk. He probably killed his wife, too."

Perry's eyes widened.

Aaron lowered his head a bit. "I'm sorry for your loss."

Her eyes snapped. "He might as well have killed the rest of my family while he was at it. My dad lost his shit, and my parents split up. I'm barely holding it together. I swear, I'd kill George for what he did to us, if I could get away with it."

She bit her thumbnail, dropped her hand, and stepped over to Maggie. She slammed two drinks down. Then she speed-walked away, ignoring Jennifer's request for more wine.

"What's her problem?" Jennifer's voice was loose and boozy at the edges. "Doesn't she know she works for tips?"

Aaron winced. *Something's definitely up.* It wasn't like Jennifer to be snippy about people in the service industry. She'd waited tables herself during college and law school. He leaned into her. "Her sister died in a car wreck. With George in the other car. We have to cut her some slack."

"Still."

Aaron let it go.

Perry made a face, showing his teeth. "I had no idea the waitress was Sarah Stiles' sister, or I would have been more discreet. That family has had a tough year. Sarah's death. An ugly, public divorce. Gerrianne, her mother, seems to have taken it especially hard. But I will say I read in the paper that Sarah ran a red light. Two sides to every story, I guess."

"True." Actually, Aaron couldn't have agreed more. It was like with his recruiting trip to the University of Wyoming. Sure, the weather had been severe, but what had really turned him off was the player who'd been assigned to show him around Laramie. The guy left a bar with a girl so drunk that Aaron didn't see how anything the guy later bragged about could have been consensual. *What a pig.* He wished his eighteen-year-old self had done something to stop it then, but he hadn't. He'd been far too wrapped up in his own problems, and he couldn't go back in time. If he could, he would have busted the guy's nose, and then some.

"I was actually there, right after the wreck," Perry said.

"Really?"

"George didn't look or smell drunk to me. But Sarah—it was clear the ambulance wasn't going to do her any good. She was in an old Volkswagen bug. It t-boned George's truck. No airbags. Her skull was completely caved in across her forehead."

"Sounds awful."

"It was." Perry clapped Aaron on the arm. "Well, enough of that. Too depressing. Great running into you."

"You, too, man. Thanks for saying hello. Take care." Aaron slid back into his seat and looked sadly at his cold steak. He tucked into it anyway. *Damn.* It was as good as any he'd had in the lone star state.

Still chewing, he glanced over and was surprised to see that the cocktail glass in front of Jennifer was empty.

"See?" Maggie was saying. "Isn't it just what you needed?"

Jennifer pursed her lips and nodded. Gone was the woman complaining about the waitress. She looked suddenly endearing. Again, he felt a tug in his chest.

Maggie drained her glass. "Makes you want to eat red meat, I'll bet."

And then his wife did the oddest thing. She laughed. His eyes met Maggie's, and he was sure he looked shocked. Maggie cracked a wide smile.

"She doesn't drink much back in Texas," he said, smiling, too.

"Well, she's not in Texas, is she?"

"I want another one." Jennifer stood, knocking her chair over backwards. Aaron caught it before it hit the floor. "I'm going to the bar." She was off so fast she made Jerry Rice look like a chump.

Maggie shook her head and raised her voice. "Trust me. That's not a good idea." Jennifer held up a hand and didn't break stride. To Aaron, Maggie said, "Men in Wyoming don't let the grass grow."

Aaron would have put his feisty wife up against a crowd of men, but if anyone tried anything, he still wanted to be there to rip them limb from limb for it. He nodded, finished his bite, and sawed off another huge one before he chased after her, one hand over his full mouth. He entered the bar and hung back a few feet from Jennifer, not wanting to crowd her unless she needed him. But ready. Very ready.

A pomaded man who looked ten years younger than her whistled between gapped teeth. "Damn, but you're one fine little filly."

Jennifer ignored him.

"Son, don't talk to a lady like that," a grizzled cowboy said from her other side.

The younger man's voice was taunting. "Who are you, old man—her daddy?"

The bartender handed Jennifer a glass of amber liquid. She

tossed it back like a shot. Aaron shook his head. *Who is this woman, and what has she done with my wine sipping wife?*

Beside Jennifer, the older guy put his beer in a buddy's hand. Then he stepped around her, reared back, and cold cocked the younger man in the side of the face.

Maggie wasn't kidding.

Aaron grabbed a wide-eyed Jennifer and pulled her across the floor and away from the flying fists. "Stay out of the way. Please."

Then he was back in the fray in a blink. He might be big, but he was quick. The older guy had his fists in front of his chin, ready. The younger one came up swinging.

Aaron stepped in front of him and caught his wrist, squinted, and in a low gravelly voice said, "Hey, buddy, disrespect my wife again, and I'll be the one who pops you next."

The guy's eyes bugged. "S-s-sorry, man."

Aaron shoved him away, and the guy landed on his butt again, skidding into the legs of a woman who spilled her drink on his head. "Sorry," Aaron said to the woman.

"He deserved it," she said. "No problem."

To the older man, Aaron said, "Thanks."

He nodded. "Younger generation needs to learn some manners."

Aaron returned to Jennifer. She stood on her tiptoes and looped her hands around his neck, pulling him down to her. "Hey, cowboy, thanks for defending my honor. Do you want to take this fine little filly home to bed with you?" Her voice was full-on slurred.

Aaron tried to focus on the fact that she'd made the offer, and not on how long it had been since the last time, or how drunk she was now. This could be the reset he was hoping for. The start of something good between them.

He'd take it.

He swept her off her feet and into his arms. "Yee ha," he said into her ear.

She giggled and put her head on his shoulder as he marched through the fracas, out of the bar, and into the dark Wyoming night.

FOUR

BIG HORN, Wyoming

WHEN SHE TRIED to open her eyes the next morning, Jennifer's lashes stuck together like they'd been superglued. She pried them apart with her fingers.

Everything looked blurry. Besides the alcohol, nightmares had kept her restless all night. She heard a sound next to her and rolled over toward Aaron's side of the bed, but he wasn't there. The motion sent a wave of nausea roiling through her. She jumped up, dislodging an angry Katya, the apparent noisemaker.

"Why can't you be the cute skunk?"

The cat yowled at her.

She looked around the room. The first thing she saw was the framed picture on the bedside table. Aaron in a Tennessee Vols football uniform, her in her cheerleading outfit. Aaron took it with them everywhere they went. The first time he'd done it, she'd asked him why.

"Wherever we're together, that's home to me," he'd told her.

"But we're children in that one," she'd said. "Use something current."

He'd refused, claiming that this one meant something to him.

It was endearing and totally Aaron. Her eyes traveled from the photo to the rest of the room. It seemed even shabbier than it had the day before. The sheets were thin with beads of sluffed off fabric. The comforter had coffee stains on it. The chintz curtains were faded and frayed. She sneezed. And she'd left out that it was dusty.

The nausea came back. She ran for the bathroom.

She was almost there when she remembered the toilet couldn't be flushed. Clapping her hand over her mouth, she sprinted for the back deck. She burst out the door and stopped short. The sight of the looming mountains draped in strands of low hanging clouds was breathtaking. They were so close that she reached her fingers out like she could touch them. An eagle screamed and winged in a wide circle over the property. Fresh air caressed her forehead like soft lips. Her nausea receded.

A woman's voice intruded on the moment. Was it her hangover or was she not alone? *Just the animals and the mountains? I don't think so, George.* She had a flash of memory from the night before. Propositioning her husband. Their laughing exit from the restaurant. Then . . . nothing until she'd woken up with the terrors. She patted herself down, relieved to find her jeans and silk blouse under her hands. Worse for sleeping in them, but better than being naked in front of God and who knows else. She'd even slept in her distressed Lucchese boots.

Relief gave way to a tinge of regret. So, she and Aaron hadn't finished what they'd started. When *was* the last time they'd been intimate? She couldn't remember. Or when Aaron had even initiated anything? Months. She touched the soft area above her cheekbone. Crow's feet. Little exclamation lines between her eyebrows. Loose skin under her chin. She wasn't a young girl anymore. Aaron was a gorgeous man. Maybe he didn't find her attractive. Her life was usually so busy that she could avoid thinking about it. But, here, on this still, beautiful morning, it stung.

She squared her shoulders. *Chin up.* Even though her stomach had settled, she decided to make the most of her time on the deck. Since the owner of the voice wasn't in sight, she squatted down on the camp potty.

"Glamorous," she muttered.

Right when she was at the point of no return, Black Bear Betty and Aaron walked into sight from the side of the house, the woman moving with a pronounced limp, like one of her legs was shorter than the other. They were headed for the deck, engrossed in conversation.

"Stop," Jennifer screamed.

They froze, but, of course, her scream drew their eyes to her. She clamped her knees together and lowered her hands to block their view of . . . things.

"Hey, honey," Aaron said. "Black Bear Betty and I are having a great conversation." His voice sounded buoyant.

"That's nice, Aaron. A little privacy here?" Aaron might be her husband, but Jennifer had never been into *that* kind of sharing.

He grinned and turned to face the opposite direction. Black Bear Betty didn't. Standing beside Aaron, she came to just past his waist. The woman couldn't have been four foot ten. *She makes me seem tall.* And her hair was flat on her head like a little cap, not adding a millimeter of height. Her pants were hitched high on her waist with a thick, men's style belt holding them up.

"Hello, there." Black Bear Betty's front shirt pocket bulged with a cellophane package. Wiping her forehead with the sleeve of her shirt, she took a drag on a fat cigar. "I'm Black Bear Betty, the only female septic system installer in the entire state of Wyoming, and backup caretaker for this place. Where are you from?"

"Right now, a little place called 'on the potty,'" Jennifer said.

With a grin and a gap-tooth smile, Black Bear Betty said, "Sorry to catch you in the act." She said catch like *ketch*, and act like *ect*. "I'll have that septic tank installed in a jiffy."

Jennifer nodded. "And I'm Jennifer. Thanks."

In the distance, a woman's voice clearly said, "Over my dead body."

A man replied, "Don't tempt me, woman."

Jennifer said, "Oh, my gosh, who *else* is out in that yard?"

Black Bear Betty cackled. "That's the neighbors. Wilma and Butch." *Thet's.*

"I didn't see a house next door."

"I guess they're near a mile away. Sound carries out here. Especially when they've had a couple."

This early in the morning? "I'll say."

"Some people hear Sioux out here, too."

"Sue? Who is she?"

"Not a 'she'. An Indian tribe. The Lakota Sioux. And a language."

"There's a reservation here?"

"Nope." Black Bear Betty waggled her fingers in the air. "Spirits. Just about everybody living up here has heard them a time or two. I've even heard them myself." *Mah-self.* "Wyoming is full of ghosts. Indians. Homesteaders. Trappers. Gold rushers. The land remembers."

Jennifer didn't believe it for a second. "Uh huh."

"Well, I gotta go." *Goh.* The word was short and clipped. Jennifer had never thought Wyomingites had much of a regional accent, but whatever George and her cousin Hank had was magnified times ten in Black Bear Betty's speech. "Get back to it, you know." Black Bear Betty walked into the yard to the parked tractor, which Jennifer hadn't noticed before. She climbed onto it, looking for all the world like a gray-haired Frodo the Hobbit, and motored away.

When she and the tractor had disappeared, Jennifer sighed. *Finally.*

Then a black and white figure waddled toward her at top speed. This one she didn't mind seeing in her current position.

"Jeremiah," she crooned. "Where did you come from?"

He cocked his head and watched her.

"Okay, skunk, that's a little pervy." She finished and struggled to pull up her tight jeans. Then she closed her eyes and drew in a deep breath before buttoning them. When she opened them, Jeremiah had gone to check out Aaron. *Show over.*

So far, she'd had a Katya and a Jeremiah experience, but she hadn't seen the shaggy old dog yet. He was probably somewhere in the sun and a puddle of his own making.

"Are you decent?" Aaron asked.

"I am now."

He swiveled around. "Wanna hear what I've been thinking?"

What she wanted was coffee and a toothbrush, in that order. "Sure."

She studied Aaron's light blue eyes and expressive face in profile. He didn't take her hand or touch her, or even look at her. He was excited, but not about her. Something had gone wrong last night. Really wrong. *So much for the romantic getaway I was hoping for.* They'd be leaving for home in a few hours. *Chin up*, she reminded herself.

The tractor noise stopped, then Black Bear Betty hollered. "Liam! Liam! Help! Somebody, help!"

Aaron sprinted off with the speed that never failed to take Jennifer's breath away. From man to lion in a blink. She finished buttoning her jeans and went after him, dodging Jeremiah as she left the deck. From ten yards away, she saw Aaron jump into a hole in the earth. Something big, blue, and plastic was tied to the tractor bucket poised over the hole.

Breathless, Jennifer stopped beside the tractor and Black Bear Betty. "What happened?"

Tears were running down Black Bear Betty's cheeks. "I was about to put the tank into the hole. I got down to check my position, and that's when I saw."

"Liam?"

"Liam. And ... and ..."

Aaron's head appeared, then his shoulders, a bloody Liam balanced against his chest. He lifted the dog. "Jennifer, help me." He slid Liam to the ground.

Jennifer crouched beside the old St. Bernard. Liam groaned. Blood was seeping through black fur on his shoulder. She slipped her arm under his head and cradled it. "It's okay, boy," she said, even though she could see it clearly wasn't.

Aaron ducked back into the hole.

Jennifer heard, "911, what's your emergency." It sounded like it came from Aaron's phone, but on speaker. She was surprised he was calling 911 for an injured dog.

Aaron's voice was crisp and business-like. "I'm calling to report a dead body."

Jennifer's eyes flew to Black Bear Betty. "A dead body?"

The older woman nodded and whispered, "Bout scared me to death. I thought it was George at first, it looked so much like him."

"But it's not him?"

"Nope."

"Have you seen George?"

"Not today. I got to talking to your husband then went straight on to work."

Jennifer smoothed Liam's fur and slipped her arm out from under the dog. "I have to find George. He needs to know what's going on." But first, she stood and leaned over the septic hole.

Aaron had taken his phone off speaker but was still talking to someone. Below him, a man with muddy white blond hair and wide-open ice blue eyes seemed to be staring straight at her. Unlike some ADAs, she always considered it part of her job in Homicide to hustle out to crime scenes as soon as her contacts in law enforcement called with a heads-up about a murder. Some of the deaths she'd seen had been gruesome. Mutilated corpses. Mangled bodies. Even headless torsos. But never had violent death hit so close to home.

She forced herself to take in the details, like she was trained to do, rather than looking away. The dead man wore a black t-shirt, jeans, and work boots. He appeared completely normal except for the knife handle sticking out of his temple, and a huge lump on his forehead, like he'd been hit with something there. The knife handle seemed ordinary, except for a first aid symbol on it. A dried river of blood tracked down the man's cheek and neck. A piece of paper was stuck in the blood. It read GUILTY in all caps. The lettering looked like the sign she'd seen on George's door earlier.

She put a hand to her throat. Black Bear Betty was right—the guy looked a lot like George. She knew exactly who he was, though. She'd seen him only the day before.

Hadley. George's dead wife's ex-husband. The one who had been harassing George.

Immediately her brain whirred through questions, trying to crack the case. Had the two men had a confrontation in the middle of the night? Was that George's knife in Hadley's temple? Oddly, the weapon seemed familiar to her. But, then again, how different did black pocketknives really look from each other?

And the most important question of all, had George killed Hadley? Suddenly, it was more critical than ever that she find George.

"I'll be right back." She took off at a run for George's cottage.

At his door, she knocked, then threw it open without waiting for him to answer. "George? Are you home?" She heard a grunt from the recesses of the house. "This is Jennifer. I'm coming in."

From behind her, Aaron said, "Jennifer. Wait. Don't go in there alone."

"Take care of Liam."

"Uh uh. You don't know what you'll find in there."

"Hurry, then. I'll be inside." She moved quickly through a dark, cluttered living room and turned down the only hallway. It was short and emptied into an even darker bedroom. She stopped at the door, slightly winded. "George, are you in there? We've got a problem."

A lump in the bed sat up. "Huh? What problem?"

"It's Hadley."

"What did that son of a buck do now?"

"He's, um, he's dead George. He was in your septic tank hole. Aaron called 911."

"What?"

"He was stabbed. So was Liam."

"Someone hurt Liam? Who would stab my dog? That's . . . that's . . ." The lump lurched to the side, and, at the bedside, a bulb without a shade flickered on.

It took a moment for Jennifer to comprehend what she was seeing. "Oh, my God," she shouted.

Aaron reacted like the 4.6 forty-yard dasher he used to be at the height of his playing days and was standing beside her in a split second. "What is it?"

Jennifer pointed.

George stood, fully dressed, and covered in dried blood.

FIVE

BIG HORN, Wyoming

WITH JENNIFER SHEPHERDING George to the lodge as fast as she could and the man in the septic tank hole clearly dead, Aaron devoted his attention and skills to helping the St. Bernard. He carried the dog to the wooden top of the breakfast room table. Liam was large but weighed less under all his bushy hair than seemed possible. *Poor old guy.* Aaron's blood simmered. How could people hurt animals like this? He understood grievances between humans, less so ones that led to deadly violence, unless it was self-defense. But when people took out their rage or depravity on animals, it made him feel close to deadly violence himself.

George lurched into the room with Jennifer hot on his heels. "Is he going to be all right?" In the bright light of the kitchen, he looked like a gallon of maroon paint had been dumped over his head and down his body.

Liam's tail thumped, fanning a short stack of napkins to the floor.

"I'm going to examine him now. What about you? Are you okay?" Aaron kept one hand on the dog and motioned George toward him.

George didn't approach. He gave one quick shake of his head. "I'm fine."

"What happened to you?"

"I don't know." He touched his scalp, and his face contorted. "I . . . I can't remember."

"Let me take a look. You need medical attention." Aaron wasn't a doctor, but a lot of his veterinary knowledge transferred well to humans, not to mention the expertise he'd developed in self-diagnosing his own football injuries. George appeared okay for now, although Aaron didn't like the glazed look in his eyes. It could be a symptom of a concussion.

George waved him off. "Take care of my dog."

Aaron nodded. Head injuries could generate a lot of blood. But an ambulance was on the way, and George didn't seem in any immediate danger. Liam needed Aaron now. And, if George *wasn't* injured, and that wasn't *his* blood all over him, it was best for Aaron to keep his distance anyway. He'd only known the guy for twenty-four hours. Less than that. No matter how nice he seemed, Aaron had no idea what he was capable of, not really. "At least have a seat while I work on him."

George pulled a chair away from the table, wincing. He sat gingerly, like the movement hurt.

"What do you need me to do, Aaron?" Jennifer asked. "Black Bear Betty is with the, I mean she's by the, uh . . . she's outside waiting on the cops."

"Get me some of that rubbing alcohol from yesterday, please. Scissors. A razor. And I'll need to stitch him up, too."

George raised a maroon-splotched finger. "I've got an emergency kit in my bathroom, under the sink. It's got needles and line to stitch with."

Jennifer nodded and disappeared.

Aaron started palpating Liam, searching for tender spots. "That's handy. Your kit."

"Been a snowmobiler all my life. There's nobody to take care of things for you in the back country. I've stitched myself and other folks up more than a couple of times."

Liam wasn't sensitive to Aaron's probing except at his wound site. Aaron was glad to see that it had stopped bleeding on its own, and that while the cut was long, it wasn't deep. He ran his hands along the dog's legs. No obvious breaks. He bent Liam's legs to check the joints. No reaction. He checked Liam's eyes, mouth, and nose. No bleeding, but his nose and gums were dry.

Jennifer returned carrying alcohol, scissors, and a razor in one hand, a bag of cotton balls between her elbow and side, and a shaving kit in her other hand, which she held aloft. "Is this your emergency kit?"

George gave the smallest of nods. "Yes."

She set the supplies on the table by Aaron and leaned against the breakfast bar. Her eyes flitted from Liam to George, like the metronome Aaron's piano teacher used while he fumbled his way unevenly through beginner lessons, until his parents released him from purgatory to concentrate on athletics.

Aaron said, "Could you get him some water, Jennifer?"

"Of course." She rummaged in the cabinets. Then Aaron heard water running from the faucet.

To George, Aaron said, "Good news. No breaks and no wounds besides the one cut, and even that's not too bad. I suspect what he needs most is rest and hydration. We need to watch him closely for trouble standing, walking, breathing, eating, or drinking. Or whining or getting too stiff. If any of those happen, he needs to get to a vet with real equipment. But if not, I think just cleaning him, stitching him up, and giving him something for his pain will do the trick for now."

George nodded with a little more energy. "I have some Tramadol in my bag, leftover from the last time I got hurt. The doctor prescribed more than I needed."

While Aaron didn't condone prescription sharing, he would make do with what was on hand. "All right. I may need your help holding him down for the stitching part."

Aaron rooted in the shaving kit. Jennifer brought a cake pan to the table. She set it in front of Liam's muzzle. A little water sloshed over the low sides. She wet her fingers and touched them to Liam's tongue. He licked, and she repeated the process a few times, then lifted Liam's head and let him lap at the water himself. When he seemed to be satisfied, she laid his head gently back on the table. Aaron found the Tramadol and guesstimated Liam's weight. The fifty-milligram pill would be just right. He scavenged a piece of raw bacon from the refrigerator and wrapped it around the pill.

"Here you go, boy." He offered the dog the bacon.

Liam sniffed it with interest. After a moment, he swallowed it whole.

The dog was calm, so Aaron began working on him without asking for George's help. He trimmed the hair around Liam's cut as short as he could get it, then shaved the skin, murmuring soothingly to the dog. "You're going to be fine, boy. Just fine." Then he rubbed in some topical Lidocaine to numb the area. "You still good, George?"

"As long as my dog's okay."

"He'll recover. Hadley, on the other hand . . ."

George sighed. "How did he die? Was it a fall?"

Aaron shot George a glance. Did he really not know? He really hoped George had nothing to do with Hadley's death. It wasn't impossible to imagine the bad blood between the men escalating into something serious. But even if George had hurt Hadley, he would never have hurt Liam. Certainly not on purpose. Not with a knife.

Aaron threaded a needle. "Hadley was stabbed, too."

"It wasn't Hadley that cut Liam?"

"No reason to think so."

"So, whoever killed Hadley stabbed Liam." George scratched his chin, flaking off dried blood. "We had a killer here last night. Hard to believe." His voice grew soft and thin. "I'm sorry. Not a great thing to happen while you're staying here."

Jennifer was standing near George. "We're fine."

Aaron closed the wound with one hand and stitched with the other. Liam didn't even flinch. "Good boy, Liam. Just keep holding still for me." The dog's tail thumped. Aaron wished all his patients were as chill as the St. Bernard. To George he said, "Who would come all the way up here and stab Hadley?"

George's voice was listless. "I don't know." His forehead dropped. "God, I'm so tired. So, so tired."

Again, Aaron worried about concussion.

Jennifer's phone rang. "Excuse me."

"Everything okay with you?" Aaron asked.

"Yeah. I just, um, need to pick this up." She headed down the hall toward the back of the lodge.

What's that about? For a moment, Aaron's mind returned to the night before. How hopeful he'd been when they left the restaurant. How badly things had gone back at the lodge. How much he dreaded returning to Houston. But right now, he needed to focus on the problems in front of him. Liam and George. George had said he was tired. "Did you not get any sleep, George?"

George waved a hand like he was shooing a fly. "What I mean is I'm so tired of *this*. Of all of it. I want to sell this place, simplify my life. Get back to doing what I love."

Aaron looked up. "You want to sell the lodge?"

"I talked to a real estate agent about listing it last week, then I got cold feet. I was worried it might not have been what Shelly wanted me to do. But this settles it for me. I'm done. It's all just . . . too much."

Images formed in Aaron's mind. The shop, converted into a veterinary clinic. The stables, with kennels and stalls ready for animal patients. The lodge, which, with a little TLC could be a wonderful home, with or without guests. Even the cottage. If he could talk Jennifer into a move, she could use it as an office. Maybe even as a writing retreat. The thought of getting out of the rat race was tantalizing. A longer dose of peace and serenity—a permanent one—might be the solution to their marital problems. Jennifer would probably say no. But it didn't hurt to talk to George about it.

"How much would you want for the place?" he asked.

"I'm not looking to get rich off it." George named a number.

Aaron tied off the stitching, thinking, calculating. He and Jennifer could afford that. "And that comes with how many acres?"

"Forty."

His heartbeat accelerated. "Water? Fencing?"

"It's all fenced. A nice five-strand. It's got a good producing well, seasonal drainage, and I've got rights on the ditch that runs alongside here. I'm pretty far down the line, but it's enough."

Suddenly, Aaron wanted this place like he'd wanted few things in his life before. To play quarterback for Tennessee. To win the SEC title. To be drafted into the NFL. To recover from his head injuries. To become a vet. To marry his wife.

Will Jennifer go for it if she realizes how important it is to me?

Yes, he decided. If they were to have a future together, yes, she would.

He stroked the dog, then picked up a pen from the counter and a paper napkin from the floor. He wrote, "I hereby make this offer for the Big Horn Lodge with forty acres and outbuildings." He scrawled the day's date, added a number ten thousand lower than the one George had given, then signed his name. "Would you take this much?"

George picked up the napkin and read it. His cheeks flushed. "Let me think on it."

A knock sounded at the front door. Liam stood, tilting the table, and Aaron helped him off of it.

Before either Aaron or George could get to the door, it opened and was filled by a tall man with a close-cropped beard and mustache. He was dressed in a tan law enforcement shirt and dark pants. "Anyone home?"

Liam woofed, a surprisingly robust and menacing sound given his age and ordeal.

George walked toward him. "Come in, deputy."

A second deputy—a dark haired woman half the man's height—followed, wearing the same uniform plus a cap that matched her shirt. She glanced at the dirty kitchen and wrinkled her nose. Then she gave George a onceover, and her eyes glinted. To her partner she muttered, "If I ever saw a cautionary tale about drinking, this is it."

The male deputy blew a horse's laugh, showing a discolored front tooth. George didn't react.

George doesn't smell like booze, Aaron realized. He imagined the blood away and looked past it, looked closely at George. His eyes were as blood shot as Jennifer's, but his pants weren't clanking with bottles today, and his speech had been distinct and their conversation clear, even with his head injury. But through the eyes of someone who didn't know him, someone in law enforcement, he looked like a good bet for a murderer.

The male deputy said, "Which one of you is George Nichols, and where's the body?"

George raised the hand that was holding the napkin Aaron had given him. "I'm George, but I haven't seen the body."

"I have," Aaron said. "It's out back. In a hole where a septic tank was being installed."

The deputy ignored Aaron. "Is that blood on your clothing, Mr. Nichols?"

George looked down. "Maybe." He touched his injured head. "I think so."

"You think or you know?"

"I'm fuzzy on the details."

The two deputies shared an intense look, eyebrows up.

The female deputy stepped forward, shoulders bunched. She looked like she could bench press twice her body weight. "Do you have any objections to special agents from the Division of Criminal Investigation coming onsite and working the crime scene?"

"No. Why would I?"

"Good. I'll let them know." She typed on her cell phone, then looked up sharply. "We need to talk to you sir. Alone."

"Where?"

"Here is fine."

Liam growled. Aaron frowned. The deputies hadn't seen the body or even given their names. He didn't like how things were going, and he wished Jennifer was with them.

"Without your dog either," she added.

Aaron reached down for Liam's collar. George gave him a wild look. Then he grabbed the pen from the table. He scribbled on the napkin, shoved it into Aaron's other hand, and walked over to the deputies.

Over his shoulder, he said, "Jeremiah Johnson and the rest of the animals are part of the deal."

Aaron stared at the napkin. Before his signature and the date, George had written one word in block capitals. ACCEPTED.

SIX

BIG HORN, Wyoming

A DUSTY WIND blasted Jennifer as she hurried onto the back deck-combo-bathroom. She lifted a hand in front of her face, thinking about all of the unread and unlistened-to messages from yesterday. Sure, she'd browsed social media at dinner when she was trying to get Maggie to leave her alone, but she hadn't checked in with work. She didn't usually unplug for this long. Now, according to her Caller ID, Quentin Jackson was calling. *The* Quentin Jackson, political party chairman for Harris County. She barely knew the guy. *Above my pay grade. Why's he calling me?* And his call request was for a Facetime. *Ugh.*

She wiped under her eyes with her shirt, smoothed and refluffed her hair, then pressed accept. "Quentin. This is a surprise."

The screen filled with a distinguished, craggy face dominated by a dapper white mustache. The man was a power broker, old enough to be her father, and he'd hit on her every time she'd come within ten feet of him. His voice was so vibrato that she felt it through the speaker. "Jennifer. You look lovely as always. How are you, dear?"

If he'd been her grandfather, she wouldn't have minded his lead-in, but as head of the Homicide Division of the Harris County DA's office, being called "dear" rankled her. "I'm fine. I'm on a jaunt to Wyoming, so I apologize for," she gestured around her, "the great outdoors."

"I'll make this quick since you're on vacation. Two words: district attorney. You in?"

Jennifer felt her forehead furrow and tried to smooth it. She wished she'd slept last night. And hadn't had so much to drink. Maybe then this call would make sense. "I'm sorry?"

"How would you like to be the youngest female district attorney in the history of Harris County? The party wants you on the ballot next year."

Her brain froze. Literally, blue screen and static. DA was a big leap from being lovely and a "dear."

"Jennifer? Are you alive?" He laughed. "Do you need a bucket of cold water? A defibrillator?"

"Yes. I'm sorry. I'm just . . . shocked. And flattered, of course."

He pulled the end of his mustache. "The party has had its eye on you. You've got the best win rate of any ADA in the office. You're the hardest worker. You have experience across all the major divisions. Your win this week was extremely high profile. And people like you, for the most part. We think you'd be a unifying candidate. All you need to do is say yes."

People liked her for the most part?!? She didn't pursue it, but she wondered which bastards had been bad mouthing her. Evan, proba-bly. He'd joined the office a few years before her and headed up the Sex Crimes Division. When she'd been put in charge of Homicide, he'd been her most vocal critic. *Take that, Evan,* she thought. It was her getting the call to run for DA, not him. Everything in her wanted to say yes, but she couldn't commit to something this big without thinking about it. And talking to Aaron, of course. Besides, if she just blurted out "YES!!!" she'd come off as desperate.

She smiled. "Um, maybe?"

His exaggerated frown was a little patronizing. "Probably is better than maybe."

"Probably. But it's a big ask, and I need to discuss it with my husband."

"Fair enough. We need you *both* all in. I don't have to have an answer today. Can you get back to me by the end of this week, darlin'?"

She couldn't wait to tell Aaron. He would be thrilled for her. "Yes."

"There's that word I was looking for."

She laughed. It was tinny and sounded slightly manic. Was this really happening? She'd dreamed of running for district attorney. Someday. Like, in ten years. She looked around her at the camp potty and shower pail. Remembered the dead body in the hole only yards away. *Yes, this is real. She couldn't have dreamed up anything this strange.* "Thank you, again. I appreciate the party's confidence in me."

"Have a nice break." His picture disappeared.

She did a happy jog in place, pumping her arms and punching the air as she lifted her knees. Her moves segued into a hip swiveling victory dance, one she'd been doing since her high school cheerleading days. "I'm gonna be the DA, I'm gonna be the DA."

"Jennifer?"

She wheeled, mid-dance, to find her husband and Liam. The dog flopped down on the mat outside the back door.

Aaron crossed his arms. "Do you have sun stroke?"

She threw her head back and laughed. "No. I have news. Big news."

"Me, too."

That surprised her. They'd only been apart for five minutes.

Aaron had been doctoring Liam and babysitting George. "You go first."

"Okay." Aaron wiped his hands on his hips. "Well, here goes nothing. George said if we want to take this place off his hands, he'd throw in Jeremiah."

Jennifer stared at him, waiting for the punchline. When none came, she said, "This place—the one where a murder happened last night? The one in *Wyoming?*"

Aaron sucked in a deep breath and started talking faster. His eyes were doing that gleaming thing again, like topaz on fire. "We could have the life we always dreamed of. I could be a country vet." He jerked his thumb over his shoulder. "The cottage would be a perfect office for you after we fixed it up. You could write murder mysteries. We'd have pets and—"

She held up her hand and interrupted him. "Talk about sun stroke. Are you out of your mind? We can't buy this place."

"Sure, we can. We have more money than we know what to do with."

"I'm not talking about money. I'm talking about our life. Your vet practice. Coaching kids. My job. Which, by the way, just got a lot more interesting. Brace yourself for my news." She savored saying the words aloud for the first time. "The party chairman just asked me to run for district attorney. Me—district attorney. I'll be the youngest female DA in Harris County history if I'm elected."

A strange expression came over Aaron's face, one she'd only seen a few times before. Once, before his senior year in college, when a doctor had told him he should give up football because of his head injuries. The other, when one of his partners had suggested they start doing plastic surgery on pets for their wealthy clients. "I'm not putting an animal through anesthesia, pain, and recovery, endangering their life in the process, for *cosmetic* surgery to please an owner," he'd said, outraged.

Both times, Aaron had held his ground. Like he would this time. She felt it in the pit of her stomach.

"Congratulations, Jennifer. Is that what you really want, though?"

"To be DA?"

"The political infighting. The stress. The long hours. The lack of privacy."

"Well, yes."

"Then I'm happy for you. But it's not what I want."

Her jaw dropped. This was not the reaction she'd been expecting. "What do you mean?"

"I moved to Houston for your career fifteen years ago. You wanted to put off kids? Fine. We put off having kids. You wanted to live in a high-rise, so we didn't have to take care of a house? Fine. That's what we did. You didn't want pets, because of the responsibility and your long work hours? I gave in. You've been the quarterback calling the plays this whole time, and, honestly, I'm tired of blocking for you. This time, I'm the one calling an audible."

What is he saying? He can't mean what it sounds like. Jennifer's throat constricted. She choked out a few words. "You'd compare our life decisions to changing a play on the line of scrimmage—us, really?"

He chuckled softly, but in a way that told her he didn't think anything about this was funny. "What us? I used to be in love with a girl named Jenny who left me notes every day about all the reasons she was grateful for me. I haven't seen her—or a note—in years."

Her eyes burned. "I am grateful for you. I always have been. I can write you a note right now if it makes you feel better."

He shook his head. "It wouldn't. Because it would feel forced and insincere. Like a frown wearing a big, stupid smiley face mask."

"Come on. We have a great life together in Houston, Aaron."

"Not really. I have a roommate in Houston named Jennifer. We don't spend much time together, but I hear she's really good at her job."

Her face flushed with so much heat, she wouldn't have been

surprised if her hair went up in flames. "Oh my gosh, how can you, what the, Aaron Herrington, I . . ." She tapered off, staring at him.

His voice turned icy. "You don't touch me. You don't look at me. *Jennifer* doesn't love me. If Jenny shows up, tell her I will always love her. But Jennifer? I don't really even know her."

"I *do* love you."

"Yeah. That's what you call last night. Love."

The heat and blood drained from Jennifer's face. She'd had too much to drink. *What did I do?* If she admitted she had no memory of what happened, would that make it better or worse?

Aaron started nodding and kept going as he talked. "You do you, Jennifer. Like always. This time, I'm going to start doing me." He walked off the deck and toward the barn without another word.

Fear, hurt, and humiliation raised her defenses. They triggered her long-held, secret fear that Aaron didn't love her anymore. They short circuited the rational Jennifer and rendered her a raw, reactionary nerve ending. After a few seconds staring after him, she whirled and ran back to the lodge. She had to get out of there. Away from Aaron and this feeling, to . . . somewhere else. Anywhere else.

To home.

For goodness sakes, there'd been a murder right outside their window last night. That would have been reason to leave in and of itself. She punched up her Uber app to order a ride. But after a few fruitless minutes, she realized Uber apparently didn't exist in Big Horn, Wyoming. Or Sheridan. Or most of the state. She stormed into the kitchen, startling George, who was talking to some deputies. He dropped a glass. Water splashed in all directions, but the glass must have been made of plastic, because it bounced. He grabbed a rag off the faucet and scrambled to clean the mess. Katya hightailed it to her perch on the desk. Jeremiah jumped on the table and started pacing nervously. The deputies stared at Jennifer.

Jennifer said, "I need a taxi or something. Is there anything like that around here?"

George stood, rag in one hand, glass in the other. "There's WYO Rides. I have their number taped to the refrigerator."

"WYO Rides. Thanks." She walked over to the refrigerator. There was a crude WYO Rides flyer on it. She entered the number in her phone.

"Whoa, miss. Who are you?" the female deputy asked.

"Jennifer Herrington. I'm a guest here."

"Are you the one who found the body?"

"No. That was Black Bear Betty."

"I'm going to need a statement."

Jennifer crossed her arms. *Of course she does.* "I have a plane to catch, deputy, so if you're going to get a statement from me, I'd appreciate you doing it soon. And since I didn't see or hear anything, it should go pretty fast." She didn't know exactly when her flight would be, but she'd figure that out when she got to the airport. Whichever one was next would do.

"Can you wait for me here, Mr. Nichols?" the female deputy said.

"Yes," George said.

She walked Jennifer into the living room. The male deputy followed. Their questioning didn't last five minutes, including the time it took for Jennifer to write down her account of the events on a piece of notebook paper.

"If that will be all?" Jennifer said.

"Did you include your phone number?" the male deputy said.

"I did."

"You can go, then. George, we're not done with you."

As Jennifer stomped to her room, an image of the deputies and George stayed in her mind. They seemed to be treating him like a suspect. And why not? She'd wondered herself if he'd done it when she'd found him covered in blood. He'd certainly hated Hadley. But Aaron was right. No man tender enough to bottle feed an orphaned baby skunk could ram a knife into another man's temple. Or into his own dog. Not in her world. The deputies would redirect their investigation quickly. If they had a good county attorney to work with, anyway, they would. She pushed her worry about George to the background and pressed Call.

A gruff voice answered. "WYO Rides, Rory speaking. Why-oh-why-oh-why would you ride with anyone else?"

The odd greeting left her speechless, but only for a second. "I need to get to the airport from The Big Horn Lodge."

"That place up off Red Grade Road? On the mountain?"

"Yes."

"Okey dokey. I'll be there in fifteen minutes."

"Thank you."

The line went dead. Fifteen minutes. She hurried, brushing her teeth, washing her face, changing clothes, then throwing all her stuff in her suitcase. By the time she made it to the front porch, a truck was parked with its back end toward the lodge, right between the Sheridan County Sheriff's Department truck and the blue rental Fusion. A brown and gold magnet on the rear gate said WYO Rides. A sticker in the rearview mirror warned the world, "Don't tread on me," complete with a coiled snake. For some reason, that one gave her a weird feeling, but she brushed it off. She eyed the unpaved ground, then her footwear. Heels. She'd forgotten about the terrain. *Fine.* She pulled her suitcase down the steps. It bumped and wobbled over the rough ground, as did she.

The driver saw her and jumped out. He was a slim, older man in pressed indigo jeans, a loose-fitting paisley buttoned shirt, a cowboy hat, and a big silver belt buckle. "Good day, ma'am." How strange to be called ma'am by a man old enough to be her father. He took her suitcase and tossed it in the truck bed. "I'm Rory."

She tried not to stress about the probable scratches to her expensive luggage. "Jennifer. Nice to meet you." *I think.*

He opened the door to the passenger side, brushing dog hair off the seat and stashing a stack of newspapers in the center console. There was no second row of seats.

Unreal. She climbed in and shut the door, careful not to step on the extension cord coiled up in the floorboard. A pinecone scented, pine tree shaped air freshener hung from the mirror, doing its job, and then some. She breathed through her mouth. There was no bottled water, mints, or hand sanitizer in the truck either, which was de minimis with Houston Uber drivers. Wyoming was truly another planet.

Rory got behind the wheel. "Lawmen out here for something?"

"Yes." She didn't elaborate, but once again she thought of George and hoped the deputies weren't blinded to other possible suspects.

"Where to?"

She'd told him on the phone. "Airport."

He nodded and set his hat on the console, crown down. He wasted a few minutes trying to get his navigation system to work, muttering to himself as he fiddled with it. She couldn't help noticing the bright red low gas light was on. The nearest gas station was over ten miles away, and the airport was twenty, if she recalled correctly. *I hope I don't end up walking. Or pushing.*

"I'm just going to the airport," she repeated, in case he'd gotten her destination confused in the last few minutes.

"Huh. You in a hurry, ma'am?"

"Kind of."

"Okey dokey." Rory tore away from the lodge and up the driveway, turning on the left blinker at the road. After he made the turn, it stayed on. He didn't seem to notice.

As he picked up speed, he started to talk. And talk. And talk and talk and talk. He'd worked the oil fields, which is where he met his partner, and they'd moved to Sheridan because it was more gay-friendly. He liked it here. He liked driving people around. He liked to *talk*. And, oh, by the way, where was he taking her again?

Jennifer was lost in her own thoughts and emotions and, besides reminding him she was heading to the airport, only interjected a lack-luster *you don't say* and *oh my* occasionally when he took a breath. But he didn't seem to need much encouragement. She kept her eye on the red gas light and mouthed a prayer that he wouldn't run out of gas before he dropped her off. On the outskirts of Sheridan, the gas warning tone started dinging in chorus with the ticking of the turn signal. Jennifer's fingernails bit into her palms.

They reached the airport in only half an hour, but it felt like a decade. She jumped out at the curb with her little purse and laptop bag. She took two steps toward the tail gate and nearly collapsed. She caught herself on the side of the bed. It felt like she was dissolving into the sidewalk. *What's wrong with me?* Rory set her suitcase at her feet and waited. It took her a moment, but then she realized he wanted to be paid. How long had it been since she'd paid for a ride with cash? She fished three twenties out of her purse and handed them to him, still hanging on to the side of his pickup.

"Thanks for the ride, Rory. Keep the change."

"Thank you, ma'am."

She didn't respond. She couldn't. Her lips were numb and no longer working.

"Are you okay, ma'am?"

She nodded. But she wasn't.

He saluted her. "Take care." Then he settled into his truck but stayed parked at the curb, messing with something on his dash again.

She stared at the road leading into the airport, searching for Aaron in the obnoxious blue Fusion. Her mouth tasted bitter, like disappointment. A puff of air escaped her lips. How very Scarlett O'Hara of her, pushing Aaron away and then wanting him to come after her. What would she even do if he did show up?

Why, let him change her mind, of course.

She waited for almost a minute, giving him time to catch up with her, but to no avail and no Aaron. She almost asked Rory for a ride back to the lodge since he was still at the curb.

But she didn't. Instead, she hauled herself, her suitcase, and her battered, confused heart into the tiny airport, and changed her reservation to an earlier one back to Houston.

SEVEN

BIG HORN, Wyoming

AFTER AARON GAVE HIS STATEMENT, the deputies were still questioning George. Aaron didn't like it. But there was nothing else he could do for the inn keeper, and there was something he could do about Jennifer. He ran to the Fusion, crammed himself into the tight front seat, and drove pell-mell down the dirt lane and onto Red Grade Road. *Thank God the cows are all behind the fence today.* He pounded the steering wheel and groaned. He had to catch Jennifer before she left. The things he'd said had come out too strong, which is what happens when stuff is left all bottled up under pressure for too long. That was on him for not speaking up earlier. Yes, they were true. He'd even meant most of them. But he hadn't wanted her to leave. He'd thought he could shock her into talking to him, working things out with him, loving him again.

Well, he'd shocked her all right. Shocked her right out the door and out of Wyoming.

Red Grade Road made a sharp turn into Big Horn. The tires

squealed a little. He barely hit the brakes as the descent grew steeper. The football field flashed by on his right. Briefly, he caught a glimpse of young men on the field. Then he saw red and blue lights oscillating in his rearview mirror.

"No. Dammit. No!"

He pulled to a stop across from one of the three bars he'd counted in the little town the day before, an impressive ratio of booze to people for only a few hundred residents. In his rearview mirror, he saw a white Ram pickup like the one parked at the lodge behind him, its lights still wigwagging. He got out his wallet and had his license and proof of insurance in his hand and window down by the time a deputy sauntered up.

"Where you headed, sir?" the dark-haired deputy asked.

With a quick glance, Aaron took in a generous belly and big, rounded shoulders. Tall, although not as tall as Aaron. Definitely offensive lineman.

He handed the deputy his license and insurance. "Airport."

The deputy read them. "Late for a flight? I ask because you were driving thirty miles over the speed limit. In a school zone. Lucky for you it's a Sunday."

Shit. "I'm trying to catch my wife before she leaves."

"Leaves Wyoming?"

"And me."

The deputy leaned over and slid his sunglasses down his nose. Aaron saw a nametag that read TRAVIS. "Leaving *you?*"

"Yes. I'm sorry I was speeding. I'm not from here. The last speed limit sign I saw said fifty-five."

"You were probably going too fast to see the thirty-mile-per hour sign."

"Now I know, and I'll respect it. I understand you need to give me a ticket, but I'm in a huge hurry." Aaron clenched and unclenched his fists. Clenched and unclenched. Clenched and unclenched.

"Have you been drinking?"

"It's not even noon."

"Question remains the same."

"No, sir. The only sins I've committed this morning had to do with running off my fool mouth."

"Hence the runaway wife."

"Yes."

"Where you coming from?"

"The Big Horn Lodge."

Travis's eyebrows shot up. "We just had a call about the Big Horn. I was on my way up."

"A body was found out there in a hole in the yard this morning. A septic tank hole."

"And you're tearing through town, away from the lodge?"

Aaron realized it looked bad. "I've already given my statement and had permission to leave from the deputies."

Travis pushed the sunglasses back up his face. "I'll be back in a minute."

He returned to his truck. In the rearview mirror, Aaron watched him use his radio. *Come on, come on, come on.*

Travis returned in less than two minutes. "Your story checked out, Mr. Herrington. My wife has forgiven me a time or two. Slow down. And I recommend flowers."

That's it? God, I love this town. "Thank you, Deputy Travis."

"Welcome to Wyoming." The deputy walked back to his truck.

Aaron couldn't believe he'd gotten out of a ticket, but the wasted time gnawed at him. He kept an eye on the speed limit signs and used his cruise control the rest of the way. Although Jennifer would have loved daisies, he didn't stop for them, since he was afraid he would be too late already. Thinking about the flowers only increased the pain in his heart. He used to bring them to her when they were first married. When had he stopped? And why? He should have kept it up, no matter what, and then maybe he wouldn't be chasing across Wyoming now after the woman he loved.

At the airport, he parked at the curb. Buccee's Gas Stations in

Texas were larger than the entire airport, and his was the only vehicle pulled up outside the main terminal. He dashed inside—his heart hammering worse than it had at the start of the SEC championship game against Auburn his senior year—and went straight to the ticket counter.

A curly-haired woman with rose-colored John Lennon glasses greeted him. "How can I help you today, sir?"

"My wife. I'm trying to catch her before she leaves."

"Where was she headed?"

"Houston. Well, Denver first, I guess."

"I'm sorry, sir, but that flight just boarded. Was she that sad little blonde?"

The words made him feel like the kind of person who clubbed baby seals. *I made her sad.* Was this what a heart attack felt like? "Jennifer Herrington, yes."

"I'm sorry about her mother's hospitalization. She was in such a hurry. We held the plane to get her on. What a good daughter."

Aaron was confused, until he realized Jennifer had spun a story for the agent to explain her mood and her rush. "Is there any way I can catch her?"

The sound of a plane overhead answered his question before she could. "Oh, I wish there was. But it sounds like they're airborne. If it's an emergency, we can have a message waiting for her in Denver."

"No. That's all right. I can text her." He started to walk away, then turned. "But thank you."

"You bet. Have a nice day, Mr. Herrington."

"You, too." He trudged back to the rental. From behind the wheel, he texted Jennifer. *Don't do this. Call me as soon as you land.*

Half an hour later, he was back at the lodge, with no memory of the drive.

The deputies' truck was gone, but another truck was parked in its place. Aaron saw George through the front window. There was a man with him. Aaron wasn't up to talking to George yet, so he paced the side of the house, back and forth, back and forth, kicking rocks.

He picked one up and threw it as far as he could. He still had arm strength and great throwing mechanics. He shook his head. He should have gone to Wyoming and played quarterback. He imagined for a moment an alternate life. His body was tailor made to be an NFL quarterback, especially after he'd lost the pounds of bulk he'd gained to play tight end. He might only now have been hanging up his jersey, after a successful career. But if that had happened, he would have been in Laramie, Wyoming on that September day during his freshman year, instead of leaving practice in Tennessee, hangdog because he wasn't staying for the quarterback meeting, the disappointment piled on top of his recent personal loss crushing. He wouldn't have stopped at the ice cream shop in Knoxville, which had been empty, except for him and the cute little blonde who made him a hot fudge sundae.

Jennifer.

The two of them had been together ever since.

Even if he'd played quarterback at Tennessee instead of tight end, he would have been in that QB meeting and missed the encounter with his future wife. His smart, beautiful, ass-kicking wife.

Damn. He hadn't even told her how proud he was she'd been tapped to run for Harris County DA. He couldn't imagine a job he'd less want her to have, but that didn't change what a validation it was. She deserved it, if that was what she wanted—even if she wanted it more than she wanted him.

He grimaced and threw another rock. If she'd have even hesitated before she stormed out, he could have explained himself. But she hadn't. She'd lit out for her bigger and better things and left him in her dust here.

Left him. His wife had left him.

He exhaled slowly and gazed up at the mountains. Here wasn't so bad, though. It would have been better with her, but, in fact, here was amazing, and he really was done living like they had been. The rat race. The sterility. The grind. Playing second fiddle.

He was going to make the best of it. He was going to do this.

Maybe he could change Jennifer's mind. Or maybe she would agree to split time between Houston and Wyoming. He would keep trying.

He marched to the lodge past the crime scene and through the back door, checking the bedroom they had stayed in. It was eerily empty. He swallowed. Raised voices drew his attention away from his own situation. *George.* Following the sound, he hurried to the living room and stopped in the doorway.

"I heard in town that Hadley was dead. Had to see it with my own two eyes." A man no bigger than a thoroughbred jockey was jabbing his finger into George's chest. "That's another person you're responsible for putting in an early grave. I suppose I'll be next."

George's glare was withering.

The small man didn't stop for a breath. "I can't put bread on the table, and you're living here like a king. It's not right, George."

"I'm a dry well, Tim."

"You say that now, but last month you said you'd cover me in your will. If you can do that, why can't you make it right between us now?"

"I put you in the will not because I owe you anything, but because you used to be like family to me. I don't like seeing you on hard times." George sighed. "I'll see what I can do when this place sells."

"You're selling it?"

"Looks like it."

"And then you'll pay me."

"It won't be much, Tim, but I'll see if I can help you some."

The man nodded. He spun on his booted heel, rattling the windows with each step, and slammed the door.

Katya ran after him, as if to make sure Tim wasn't coming back. Liam whined from where he was resting his injured body on the rug. George took a flask from his shirt pocket, popped a stopper, and swigged several gulps. Then, still holding the bottle, he swept up the little skunk, who was pawing his leg. "It's okay, Jeremiah. He's gone."

Aaron cleared his throat. "Are you okay?"

George nestled Jeremiah to his chest and stroked him. Aaron

could smell the animal across the room. For a skunk without a stink maker, he still tended to smell a little skunky.

"That was my former business partner, and he's in bad financial straits. He's been after me for money ever since Shelly died. Thinks I got a big life insurance payout and wants to believe I owe him." George shook his head. "No insurance, and I owe him nothing."

From the looks of the lodge, Aaron thought it was probably George who needed money. How could Tim accuse George of living like a king?

Aaron took another step into the room. He pulled their hastily entered agreement from his pocket. "Were you serious earlier about selling to me? I don't want to hold you to something you regret."

George shook his head. "It's time. Running a lodge was Shelly's dream, not mine."

"What's yours?"

He smiled wistfully. "When Shelly and I first had this place, we used to host progressive dinners. We'd get a group together, hop on the snowmobiles, and go from cabin to cabin for cocktails, appetizers, dinner, dessert, after dinner drinks, the works. Sometimes we'd go sixty miles or more in a night. Great times." *Drunken snowmobiling in the dark—sounds dangerous.* "I'd love to put together something like that for one of the shops at the big mountain lodges. I could guide for them, too."

It surprised Aaron that George still had a passion for guiding after how he'd lost his wife.

As if reading Aaron's mind, George set Jeremiah on the counter and continued. "My wife died in a freak accident. I can't let that take the only other thing I've ever really loved besides her away from me." He picked up a bottle of whiskey and swished the liquid. "Of course, I'd have to dry out to do that, if I ever really sold this place."

"I think you're going to need to give up the sauce then, man."

"Yeah?"

"I'm buying this place from you."

"I don't want you to regret this either. Didn't Jennifer go rushing off to the airport? What was that about?" George flushed. "I'm sorry. I shouldn't have—"

"No, that's okay. We're in a rough patch. She went back to Houston without me."

"I'm sorry to hear that."

"I'm sorry, too." Aaron pulled out his wallet and walked into the kitchen. "Now, how about I write you a check for a down payment?"

"I don't know how much to ask for."

Aaron filled out a check and twirled it around to face George, who squinted at it. "Will this work?"

Jeremiah scurried across the counter to sniff his pen, which Jennifer would have loved. Thinking of her hurt. *She really left me.*

George pulled at his chin, breathing through his mouth. His lips moved like he was figuring numbers in his head. "I think so."

"Yes?"

"Yes."

If Aaron gave the check to George, he was crossing a point of no return, with his wife and his life. *Something has to change. It might as well be this.*

He signed his name.

Ripped the check from the book.

Drew in a deep breath and handed it over to George, as red and blue lights starting flashing through the front window of the lodge.

EIGHT

HOUSTON, Texas

JENNIFER SHOVELED cold bread pudding straight from a Styrofoam container into her mouth, damn the carbs. Monday night, she'd had a four-star dinner with Quentin Jackson and his cronies, as they tried to sweet talk her into committing to run for DA. Today, she was in a ratty velour robe with bed head and an aching heart, skipping hot yoga, sitting on a bar stool in her immaculate gourmet kitchen with a *Murder, She Baked* mystery blaring from the living room. A stack of boxes was waiting for pick-up by the front door. She'd just finished packing the things Aaron had texted her to ship to him, and she was entitled to a pity party.

Aaron. She'd expected him to be back in Houston on her heels. Hoped he would. He'd been blowing up her phone by the time she connected flights in Denver, and he hadn't stopped since. *Don't do this* and *I can't believe you left* and *Sheriff served search warrant on George for the entire place* and *Please come back* and *Liam is healing well* and *We can work this out—I love you.* She gazed out over Buffalo

Bayou, the skyline, and a gridlock of traffic on Interstate 45, so different from the gridlock of cows a few days before in Wyoming. Aaron had left her, and she couldn't even talk about it. Not to him, her mom, Justin, her co-workers, or her friends. Not to anyone.

Of course, he insisted she was the one who left him. But how could that be? Before the weekend trip, they'd lived in this condo together. After it, she lived here alone. She'd asked him to come home, and he'd shot her down. Ipso facto, he'd left her. *Or maybe it wasn't that simple.* He *had* asked her to join him in Wyoming, over and over.

Another of their famous stalemates.

The buzzer sounded. Her heart skipped a beat. *Aaron.* But no. He wouldn't need to buzz her. He had keys. She wasn't expecting anyone. A guest? A delivery?

She pressed the intercom. "Yes?"

Her best friend Alayah's irrepressible voice reverberated through the condo. It served her well as an ADA, where she worked in the Sex Crimes Division with Jennifer's nemesis, Evan. It was jarring to Jennifer today. "It's me, bitch. Buzz me up."

Jennifer and Alayah had been friends since law school at Baylor. They'd joined the Harris County DA's office at the same time and suffered through Alayah's bad relationship choices together. But Jennifer hadn't said a word to Alayah about Aaron or about the possibility of running for DA.

Groaning, she buzzed her friend in the building. The elevator would give Jennifer two minutes. She used the time to brush her teeth and splash water on her face and was back at the door to open it before Alayah rang the bell.

One hundred and twenty-five pounds of Filipino dynamite in a flared leg black jumpsuit rolled in on stilettos. Alayah smoothed the slick sides of her hair toward her low, tight bun, then scowled at Jennifer's attire. The slitted eye, the glowering brow, the jutting lips— no one could scowl like Alayah. "What's up with *you?*"

"I called in sick."

Alayah turned off the TV. In its absence, her voice was overpowering. "Two days in a row? You never miss work, so I had to assume you were dead."

"Close enough."

"Evan was telling people he saw you at the Pink Poodle getting your nails done."

"He did not!"

"Sit." Alayah pointed to the stool Jennifer had been perched on earlier. "Speak."

Jennifer sat. *I'm a good doggie.* She picked at another bite of bread pudding. "Aaron left me."

"Impossible. He adores you."

"Adored."

Alayah swept across the kitchen and retrieved air freshener from under the sink. She sprayed, turning the condo into a citrus grove. "Is there another woman?" She depressed the nozzle at Jennifer.

Jennifer coughed and waved her hand in front of her face. "No. There's another house. Another state."

"You're not making sense." Alayah set the can on the countertop with more force than was necessary.

"He wanted to change things up. So, he bought a lodge in Wyoming and plans to turn it into a country vet clinic. He thought I'd want to quit work and move there with him to write murder mysteries."

"You are kind of obsessed with them."

Jennifer glared at her. "Not relevant."

Alayah put her hands on her hips and shook her head. "He had to have more reason than that."

Jennifer swiped at a tear. "He said we're miserable together and that he doesn't know me anymore. That our entire relationship has been about him doing what I want, and that he's ready to do what he wants for a change."

Alayah took Jennifer's hand. Jennifer's nails were bare and bitten to the quick. Alayah's manicure was on point. "Well, he's kind of right about that last part."

"Whose side are you on?"

"Yours. Always yours. But you do see his point, don't you?"

Jennifer exhaled a shuddering breath. "Maybe." Then, "Yes." It came out as a wail.

"Do you love him?"

"I . . ."

"Yes or no?"

"I . . . yes."

Alayah released Jennifer's hand. "Is the practice of law illegal in Wyoming?"

Jennifer couldn't help but laugh. "No."

"So why not try it?

"Because . . ." Jennifer thought about the possible DA campaign. Her current ADA job. Her beloved high rise. "Because I have a life here. But there's something else."

"What?"

"It's a secret."

"Since when have your secrets not included me?"

Since I don't want to hurt your feelings that you're not the one the party asked to run. "I'm being considered to run for DA."

Alayah's penciled eyebrows shot up. "Aren't you the big shot?"

"Yeah, so big." Jennifer rolled her fork in the bread pudding. *And getting bigger all the time.*

"So, if you're elected, will your job grow old with you and keep you warm at night?"

Jennifer's jaw dropped. "I thought you didn't believe in marriage."

"I've never been married to an Aaron, have I?"

In actual fact, Alayah had almost married first an unsuccessful rap artist then an unsuccessful television producer, both of whom were players with a capital P. If nothing else, she had a type. "What are you saying?"

"I'm saying your tight end with the tight end is your constant. Go be the DA in Montana."

"Wyoming."

"Whatever. A place with cowboys and mountains. Go there. Here is always here if you need to come back, although not for you just to wallow, binge on TV, and carb load." She gave Jennifer an arch look. "But *there* won't always be *there* if you know what I mean."

"You'd turn down the chance to run for DA if you were me?"

"Is your listener broken?" She enunciated loudly. "Go be the DA there. Or not. But you've got the thing everybody wants. You're going to let that go and stay here because you *might* get the chance to *maybe* get elected for a thankless job in a moldy city that floods every time it's even humid outside? Don't do that unless you want the job more than him. If you do, then, hey, you're not in the relationship I thought you were, and more power to you, sister."

Jennifer stared at Alayah. This was *so* not the advice she'd expected from her friend. "You're scaring me."

"Good." Alayah nodded briskly. "Go pack."

"Maybe if I went back up there, I could convince him to come back here with me. Then I could still run for DA."

"Maybe. But now, since you're not dead, and I'm done kicking your ass, I need to get back to work. Whatever you decide, I'll still love you. Hell, I might even come visit you up in Idaho."

Jennifer didn't bother correcting her. They kissed and hugged goodbye. Jennifer shut the door behind Alayah and leaned against it. She stared at the blond hardwoods she'd selected herself, comparing them unfavorably to the old wood floors at the lodge. *I've got working bathrooms here, too.* Her phone chimed in the pocket of her robe. She pulled it out.

Aaron again. *George asked me if I thought you'd help him. Will you come try again with me and give him a hand?*

An energy that had been missing for the last few days surged through her. Alayah was right. Jennifer couldn't just leave Aaron in

Wyoming. They were supposed to be together forever. Some of what he'd said had hurt, but now that she was calmer, she could admit things had been out of balance in her favor for a long time. She'd thought he'd wanted what she did, but she hadn't asked him.

She started to type a reply to his text, then stopped. She'd save it for in-person. The ball of emotion inside her burst like a firework. She raced to her phone and pulled up Quentin's number, then pressed Call.

His face filled the screen, smiling. "Jennifer! Lovely dinner last night. Do you have my yes for me?"

She didn't have the bandwidth for niceties. "How long can you give me to make a decision?"

He frowned. "That's not a yes."

"I have some personal issues to deal with."

He looked offscreen, thinking. Then he trained his steely eyes back on her. "A month. No more. It's a long campaign, and we need to get started. With you, or someone else."

She nodded. "Understood."

"But we need a yes from both you and your husband. No scandals before a campaign, Jennifer."

Being the Harris County DA is conditional on staying married to Aaron? That hardly seemed fair. Now was not the time to dwell on it, though. She wanted to work things out with her husband, so her goal was aligned with Quentin's. "I'll have your answer within a month."

Ending the call without saying goodbye, she straightened her shoulders. Her brain, which had been recycling on all the reasons things couldn't work out, went into problem solving mode. She and Aaron could afford the high rise and the Wyoming place. She didn't make a ton as an ADA, but Aaron's practice minted money, and, since they didn't have kids, they had a lot of disposable income. Wyoming could be a vacation house for them. And she was due time off. She would tell everyone she was taking a sabbatical to write a novel. She might even do it. In the meantime, she could give George some advice and reassurances. A month was plenty of time to get his legal situation straightened out, patch things up with Aaron, and change his mind.

They'd be back in Houston in time for her to call Quentin to tell him yes.

NINE

BIG HORN, Wyoming

"SIMMER DOWN, fellas and let me introduce you to our special guest today." Perry Flint held up a hand to quiet the crowd of teenage boys—plus one girl. They were standing in short sleeve jerseys over their pads while snow fell around them in a dense cloud.

The kids made Aaron feel like a wimp zipped into a winter jacket. Mid-September in Wyoming, and outside was white out conditions. He wouldn't have believed it if he wasn't living it. Tuesday had been sunny and seventy-five. And on Wednesday, this. In Houston with his team of middle-schoolers, it would have been double nineties, temperature and humidity. He'd hated bailing on the boys mid-season, but his buddy and assistant coach Tony was an ex-Miami Dolphin middle linebacker, and he had a kid on the team. He'd been happy to take the helm. They would be fine without him, even though he would miss them. But not the double nineties.

He hit send on a text to Jennifer and slipped his phone in his pocket. *Miss you. About to speak to the Big Horn football team at their practice. Pretty cool.*

"Are you J.J. Watt?" one of the boys shouted at Aaron.

Aaron laughed. "No. I'm Aaron Herrington. But I know J.J. Great player. Great guy. And I went up against plenty of talented defensive ends like him when I played tight end for the Detroit Lions." How he wished he could have stayed in the game and lined up against J.J., though. If he'd had a long, healthy career, he would have gotten the chance. "I'll bring a signed ball and jersey from him next time I come talk to you guys."

A buzz swept through the team. "Cool," several players said.

"Enough about J.J. You guys show Aaron a true Ram welcome." Perry clapped for Aaron, and his team followed suit.

Aaron pointed at Perry. "When your coach asked me to talk to you guys, I looked you up. This team has an amazing record. State champs two out of the last three years."

"Woot, woot, woot," the players shouted.

"With some pretty amazing individual talent."

More woots and whistles sounded at that.

"When I played for the University of Tennessee Volunteers, we had some pretty amazing players, too, and we won the SEC championship. You guys might have even heard of our quarterback. Peyton—"

"Manning," they yelled back at him.

Aaron grinned. "And an All-American tight end named Aaron Herrington." That got a few laughs. "When I was in high school, though, I was a quarterback. That's what the Vols recruited me to play. Man was I pumped. But when I got to Knoxville my freshman year, the coach pulled me aside and ran some film from the previous season, a game I'd played in after I'd signed with them. Let's just say he wasn't praising my throwing mechanics."

"What was he doing then?" the female player asked.

"Making me watch myself jeopardize the game by fighting with a player from the other team. Over and over and over."

Eyes widened, watching him intently.

"He told me they had decided to go with another quarterback, one who could keep his cool."

That earned a few groans.

"I was pretty disappointed to say the least. I told the coach I'd do anything to get on the field. And he said he'd hoped that would be my response, because he wanted to redeploy my good hands and understanding of offense and my, ahem, *aggression* into a different position."

"Tight end?" several kids said over each other.

"Tight end. At first, I wasn't very excited about it. I wanted to run the offense. I wanted my hands on the ball, every play. I wanted to throw touchdowns. That's what I told the coach. And he said something I'll never forget." Aaron paused for dramatic effect, aware of individual snowflakes falling on his head as he waited for the pulse of energy from the players that would tell him it was time to deliver his punchline. When he felt it, he said, "All your objections have one thing in common, son. They're all about you. What you need to decide is what's more important here. You. Or the team. You go home for the weekend, talk to your parents, and think about it. Give me your decision Monday." He hadn't wanted to. Too many recent memories, none of them good. But he'd done it.

A tall, lanky boy said, "Why didn't you ask for a transfer?"

"I thought about it. I probably had options. I'd even been recruited by the University of Wyoming. But after I talked with my folks, I realized I wanted to stay in Knoxville, and that I could make a difference to my team by blocking and running and catching. A difference I wouldn't make sitting on the bench anywhere else."

The lanky kid's voice cracked with puberty. "So, you told him yes."

No one laughed at him. All their attention was on Aaron.

"I told him yes. And I learned my position. I lifted and ate like a mad man to put on forty pounds, and I kept my focus on the team. Most of the time. Some of the time, I was blind with jealousy about

Peyton playing in the position I'd wanted. But he was a nice guy, so I only short sheeted his bed a couple of times."

The players laughed.

"I never regretted my decision, and it taught me something important about life. In order to field a winning team, somebody's got to block. To tackle. To play on the second offense so the starters have someone to practice against. Life isn't about glamor. It's about showing up for your team. Not just in football, either. I'm a veterinarian now, and I have partners. They're my team. I have a wife." A lump formed in his throat. "And she's always been my home team." His eyes burned. "If you focus on your team, they'll focus on you. They'll have your back. Team is a two-way street, and your job is to worry about holding up your end of the rope." He realized he was talking in one mixed cliché after another, but his words hit way too close to home, and it was all he could do to keep going. He cleared his throat and turned to Perry. "Thanks for having me here, Coach."

"Thanks for coming out, Aaron." Perry clapped twice. "Let's give him a big Ram thank you."

The players shouted and pretended to butt heads like their namesake animal.

Perry said, "All right. That's it for today, everyone. Good practice."

With a roar, they took off for the locker rooms. Perry shook Aaron's hand, and, after a few parting words, the men turned to go, in opposite directions. As Aaron walked to the gate leading off the field, he saw a truck pulled up to the curb beside it. A magnet on the door read WYO RIDES. A well-built man in his seventies, with jeans creased from the dry cleaners and a thick flannel shirt Aaron envied, grabbed a snow-covered suitcase out of the truck bed. Safety, back in his day. Or punter.

Aaron stopped on the sidewalk. His car was in the lot, parked facing the opposite direction. He smiled at the man. "You looking for a room at the school?"

"You'll have to ask her." He tipped his cowboy hat to someone in the truck and said, "Thank you," as he accepted cash.

A smaller figure climbed out of the passenger side. A familiar blonde head leaned back in to retrieve something, then turned to Aaron.

His breath caught in his chest.

Jennifer slammed the door of the truck. She locked big blue eyes on him, shivering. She was in a short-sleeved top with shoes that exposed half her feet. No coat. She held her arms out to keep from falling. Her steps were wobbly. "I can't believe it was eighty-five when I left Houston."

He met her halfway, catching her elbow to help her balance. "What are you doing here?" He cleared his throat. "I mean, it's great to see you."

She finally smiled. "I came to block for some guy who wants to play quarterback. He texted that he was spinning tall tales for the next generation, so I figured I'd find him here."

He smiled back even bigger. "You're sure?"

Snowflakes were sticking to her lashes. "I'm going to try, anyway. I'm new to that position. Or skill. Or whatever."

He laughed and gathered her into his arms. "I'm so glad about that. And that you're here. God, I can't believe you're here!" She felt good. Really good. "Come with me to the lodge? I was just heading back. The car's over there." He pointed across the parking lot, where snow was accumulating.

She eased back from him and pointed at her feet. "In these shoes?"

"Not very practical." He scooped her into his arms, and she squealed, a happy sound. "I can solve that problem."

"Ma'am," the driver called. "Should I put the suitcase on the sidewalk?"

"Thanks, Rory. That would be great."

Rory saluted.

Aaron buried his face in Jennifer's hair and breathed in deeply.

Mango and coconuts. He picked the bag up and carried it through the handle on one arm. Then he sped to the car, juking and jiving like he was eluding tacklers, with Jennifer giggling into his chest. The sound was like the handbells his mother used to make him play at Christmas in church. He worked the car door open and deposited his wife inside. When he was behind the wheel, he turned to her again, unable to stop grinning.

She crawled across the console and put her soft hands on either side of his face. "I missed you."

"Me, yeah. I mean me, too." He kissed her, his heart thudding, his brain and tongue capable of nothing but nonsense.

"Take me to the lodge or lose me forever," she said.

The line from *Top Gun* instantly became his favorite of all time. "Gladly."

He steered carefully through the storm with one hand and held tightly to hers with his other. There was so much he wanted to say, but he didn't want to break the spell. He felt hopeful. Giddy. He gripped her hand tighter, and they drove on in electric silence.

When they reached the lodge, he said, "Wait here."

He raced in with her bag, then stomped his boots on the mat inside the back door and took off his winter outerwear. The wind up on the mountain was rattling and creaking in howling forty-mile-per-hour gusts. There was a foot of snow drifted against the house.

The place was freezing. Aaron found a wall thermostat. It had tape on it, but he wasn't going to waste time trying to figure out what George meant by it. He slid the lever slightly to the right. In the kitchen, he wet a rag and washed his hands, careful not to let water run down the drain. The scent of burning dust tickled his nostrils. *Good. The heater works, at least.* Because the toilets still didn't, or anything requiring water to drain. *That camp potty and outdoor shower suddenly don't sound as much fun.* Jeremiah jumped onto the counter and chirped at him.

"Down, varmint."

The skunk waddled to the Keurig and sniffed it. He turned to

Aaron, smacking his lips. Aaron laughed and set him on the floor. "No coffee for you." In the last week, Aaron had discovered it was the animal's favorite treat.

He grabbed an afghan from the back of the couch. He ran back outside and shut off the car. "Ready?" he asked, as he wrapped her up.

She eyed the snow. "Can I think about it?"

"Nope." He lifted her, shut the door with his foot, and sprinted across the yard, up the stairs, and onto the porch.

"I can walk now."

He set her down and opened the door.

She ducked in ahead of him. "I just have to run to the bathroom. I'll be fast." She flashed him a sultry look.

He closed the door behind them. "About that. It's uh, not working."

"What? I thought Black Bear Betty had everything she needed to finish the job."

"She did. But it's a crime scene."

Jennifer frowned. "Oh, come on. They haven't released it yet?"

"No." He hurried back to her and drew her into his arms. "But let's not let that ruin things. Where were we?"

"Something about taking me to the lodge or losing me forever." She tilted her head back and her eyelids closed. Then they popped back open. "Except I have to pee."

A voice behind them drew a groan from Aaron. "Aaron, who's— oh, Jennifer! Welcome back."

Aaron released Jennifer slowly and reluctantly.

"Hey, George. How has my favorite little friend Jeremiah been?" Jennifer asked.

"I just came to bring him back to the cottage with me. I'm fixing dinner for him, Liam, and Katya out there tonight."

"He was in here a minute ago," Aaron said.

There was a knock at the door. A red and blue strobe through the window promised trouble.

"Not them again." George stalked to the door and threw it open.

Two bundled-up deputies stood at the door. Aaron recognized them. The man and the woman who had been at the lodge on the day of the murder. The female deputy held up a piece of paper.

The male deputy held up handcuffs. "George Nichols, we have a warrant for your arrest for the murder of Hadley Prescott. Hold out your wrist please."

Expressionless, George held out a wrist. His shoulders slumped.

Jennifer stiffened and backed away from Aaron. "He's not resisting, deputy. You don't need to cuff him."

He gave her a withering gaze. "Hands behind your back, Mr. Nichols, so I can cuff the other wrist."

George complied.

Aaron pulled Jennifer aside. He whispered, "You've got to help him."

"Aaron, I'm not licensed in Wyoming. And I'm not a criminal defense attorney."

"Details. I know he didn't do it. You don't think he did it either. I know you don't."

"But how can we be sure? Do you know who did?"

"No. But George would *never* stab his dog. And whoever killed Hadley stabbed Liam, too."

Jennifer pursed her lips. Then she turned to the deputies, who were leading George out. "I'm Mr. Nichols's attorney. Why are you arresting him?"

The female deputy turned to face her from the front deck. "Because he had a beef with the victim whose murder occurred in the yard here. Plus, there was blood all over him, and he conveniently can't remember how it got there."

Aaron winced.

Jennifer stood taller. "None of that means he killed him."

"Tell it to the judge. Like I said, we've got a warrant."

Jennifer walked briskly after them, Aaron on her heels. "When will he be making an initial appearance?"

"I dunno. Call the circuit court."

The deputies started George down the stairs.

"I'll do that." Jennifer stepped to the edge of the deck. "George, did you get checked out by a doctor last week, after Hadley died?"

He looked back at her and nodded, his eyes glazed, then turned to focus on the steps.

"Everything will be okay, George," Jennifer called after him.

She stood, arms clasped, as the deputies loaded George into the back seat of the truck. Aaron came to stand beside her. The deputies climbed in front. The male deputy whooped the siren, then drove the truck away.

Jennifer shivered. "You really don't think he did it?"

Aaron put his arms around her. "From what I've learned about him in the last week, he just doesn't have it in him to stab someone in the temple, then stab his dog, and leave them both to die."

"People can surprise you." Jennifer pulled away from him and walked inside, rubbing her arms. "I still have to go to the bathroom. And with George gone, we don't have a place to stay." She gave him a hopeful look. "I can book us a flight to Houston."

He shook his head. "No."

"But what will we do?"

"We have a contract to buy this place. We can stay here."

"Not without working septic. Maybe all of this is a sign that we shouldn't go through with this, Aaron."

"You don't believe in signs. I do, and I don't think this is one. This is a speed bump. Besides, you told George you were his attorney."

"I told the deputies I was his attorney."

"Same difference."

She threw the afghan back over her shoulders. "I'll see what I can do for him. But right now I'm getting us a hotel. We need toilets and a shower at least."

"What about the animals? There's no one here to take care of them." When he saw her brow tighten, he added, "Think about poor Jeremiah."

Her face relaxed. "I could call Hank about his guest cabin, I guess. On our way there."

Aaron pulled her to him. "Thank you. I'll just go load up the animals."

Her cheek was pressed against his chest as she said, "You're welcome. I think."

TEN

STORY, Wyoming

THE PHONE CALL to Hank hitting him up for a place to stay at Piney Bottoms Ranch hadn't been as painful as Jennifer had feared, given that they'd chosen not to stay with him in the first place. He'd said, "Hell, yeah, come on down," and told her the guest cabin would be unlocked for them.

Her older cousin had always been one of her heroes.

Aaron at the wheel, they had driven right up to the cabin, holding hands in George's beater truck, which they'd commandeered since it had been clear that they wouldn't be able to fit all of their luggage and animal charges in the Fusion.

"Nice place," Aaron said.

Jennifer nodded, taking it in. "It's cute."

And it was. Aged, hand hewn logs. Faded red shutters. A bright green, new-ish roof. Spruce trees, a grassy yard, and stones bordering the walk-up front porch. Adirondack chairs on either side of the door. The ranch buildings were beautiful, too. A weathered barn. A larger structure that she guessed was some kind of indoor arena, given that its shape matched a nearby outdoor arena. Paddocks of various sizes. In the distance, the familiar two-story ranch house that she'd stayed in as a young child. A smattering of smaller cabins past it. Like the Big Horn Lodge, Piney Bottoms Ranch had an astounding view of the mountains. But Piney Bottoms also had rolling pastures with herds of horses. Big, beautiful horses in every color imaginable, many with foals nearby, bucking and playing. Jennifer had gone through a horsey period as a tween, just like half the girls in her middle school. It had fizzled out after a few years. Aaron's vet practice was small animals only, so she hadn't had any reason to think about horses since, except when she watched *The Horse Whisperer*, or when the Budweiser Clydesdale Superbowl commercials came out. But the horses here were breathtaking. She knew they were part of the Double S Bucking Stock business, and that Hank raised them with his business partner Gene.

"How about we drop in at the main house to say thanks after we've settled Liam, Katya, and Jeremiah?" Aaron said.

"Works for me." She released Aaron's hand and climbed out of the truck, arms wrapped around herself in her jean jacket. She would have to get something heavier, and soon, before she froze to death.

Aaron stopped for Liam to make yellow snow, and Jennifer lugged two cat carriers—one holding Katya, the other Jeremiah—through the white stuff to the porch. The new carriers were from an emergency stop at the Sheridan Wal-Mart. While they were in town, she'd checked on George at the jail. She hadn't been able to see him but had been assured he was safe. It would have to do for now.

Jennifer heard an engine and stopped on the porch. A magenta Ford Pickup as old as the cabin was throwing up snow plumes as it approached. She squinted and recognized the driver. Maggie.

Not yet. Jennifer needed to get her feet under her and wits about her before she had to handle Maggie.

She set the carriers down. Maggie parked and got out. Despite the cold, the woman wasn't even wearing a coat. She moved toward the cabin in a loose, rangy motion that swiveled her hips and made Jennifer's teeth hurt. She was sexy, no doubt, and tall, and talented, but oh-so-superior. From the moment they'd met, Jennifer had felt sized-up and a few inches short. Literally and otherwise.

Liam finished his business and staggered toward Maggie. Aaron waved at her. *Both of them, eating out of her hand already.*

Aaron said, "Hey, there, Maggie. Thanks for letting us crash here."

"It's Hank's place," Jennifer muttered under her breath.

Apparently, Maggie had hearing like the Bionic Woman. "Technically, it's mine, too. I bought Laura out last year." She leaned over and massaged Liam's ears and neck with both hands. Laura and her husband Mickey Begay lived on *his* family's quarter horse racing ranch in New Mexico.

"Is that so?" If she'd known that, it would have been even harder for Jennifer to make the call to Hank begging for a place to stay.

Maggie stood, leaving Liam hangdog. She walked to the cabin door, scraped the snow off her boots before entering, and flipped on the lights like she owned the place, which, to Jennifer's chagrin, she did.

"I stayed here on my first visit to Wyoming. My only visit, I guess, since I made it permanent the next time I came north. It's a nice little cabin. It doesn't have a fireplace, but it heats up fast." Maggie fiddled with a dial on the wall, then moved aside for Jennifer and the pet carriers. "So, you guys bought the Big Horn Lodge. George's truck, too?"

The magnetic Big Horn Lodge logo on the door was a dead giveaway.

Jennifer put the carriers down and opened them. "We just borrowed the truck."

Katya sprinted out and straight to Maggie. Jeremiah stayed hidden inside his safe space.

Maggie crouched and picked up Katya. The calico scrambled into Maggie's arms like it had been doing it every day of its life, without any bloodshed. "Are you going to practice law in Sheridan?"

Aaron and Liam came through the door, both of them tracking in snow. Aaron had something square clutched in one hand. Hearing Maggie's question, he arched a brow at Jennifer. They'd both carefully avoided any controversial topics so far, like Jennifer's professional plans.

Jennifer busied herself crouching down to check on Jeremiah. "I'm not sure yet."

Liam nosed Jennifer's hand, then hobbled around, exploring the little space. It wasn't much cabin for the number of pounds of mammals who would be occupying it. It was barely big enough for Aaron by himself. Just a single homey room, with a kitchen in one quadrant, a sitting area in another, a bedroom in the third, and a closet and bathroom occupying the fourth. Quilts in red, white, and green hung over the windows and covered the bed. Inspection over, Liam lowered himself with a groan onto an oval rug in the same colors as the quilts. The dog was still stiff from the knife wound. His bandage was hanging on by a thread, which she knew Aaron would fix before bedtime, but otherwise the St. Bernard seemed to be recovering fine.

"First you've got to write a best-selling murder mystery." Aaron set a framed photograph on the bedside table and headed back outside.

The square item—the picture of them in college. Always her husband's first contribution to any place they stayed. She felt a flicker of warmth in her core. *He is pretty darn adorable.*

Katya hopped off Maggie's shoulder and nosed along the base of the kitchen cabinets. The way she was sniffing made Jennifer worry about rodents. She hoped there weren't any mice.

Maggie laughed. "You've got a good start on it, then, with a murder right outside your bedroom window at the lodge." She picked up the photo Aaron had set on the nightstand. "Well, well, it's miniature Barbie and football Ken. You were a Tennessee cheerleader?"

"Rah rah, siss boom bah," Jennifer said, her voice dry. She'd buried her cheerleading past deep. The only people who learned about it were friends close enough to visit their home. It was hard enough to overcome the stereotypes related to her looks without the cheerleader issue. "Although I prefer to think of myself as a Baylor law student."

"Two four six eight, who do people love to hate?" Maggie paused, then threw her arms in the air, still holding the picture. "Lawyers."

"Ha ha."

Maggie leaned toward her. "I did the pompom thing in high school, too. But if you ever tell anyone, I'll have to kill you. It would wreck my image."

"Really—you?"

Rebel Maggie seemed more Joan Jett rocker than Doris Day cheerleader type. Jennifer could understand why she was concerned about people finding out. In entertainment, image seemed to be the most important thing, after talent and luck. And recently, Maggie had started re-recording her old hits and some new songs with indie pop princess Ava Butler. Maggie's star was definitely back on the rise, although she was avoiding the "scene" in favor of hiding out in Wyoming with Hank.

"Really. Until I quit school and ran away to become rich and famous. Or, as it turned out, poor and infamous." She set the picture back down and changed the subject. "Seriously, if y'all need a vehicle, Hank has a great one he can lend you. Or maybe sell to you if you like it. It's Wyoming tough, which you'll need."

"I'm not sure we—"

Aaron kicked the door shut behind him, a suitcase in each hand. "Sounds great. I'll talk to Hank."

"How about at dinner? We have some friends coming over. You may have met the Flints at Hank's shindig?"

"Perry?"

"No, his parents and sister."

No. All Jennifer wanted was a quiet evening reuniting with Aaron.

But before she could signal him, he beamed at Maggie. "That would be great. We don't have any food yet."

Just then, Jeremiah finally poked his head out of the carrier door. After a second, his body followed, and he waddled into the middle of the room.

"Oh my God!" Maggie jumped back with her hand over her face. "What is that?"

Jennifer couldn't help feeling a little gleeful. "It's a Jeremiah Johnson. He's a destunk skunk."

Maggie composed herself. "You'd better not let my dog see him. F***** likes to kill rodents."

Jennifer jerked back like she'd been slapped. *Did Maggie just use the F word?* She wasn't a prude—you couldn't be in her line of work—but she was brought up that there was no call for that kind of language, especially from a lady. She decided to give Maggie another chance. "What did you call your dog?"

Maggie repeated it.

Yep, the F word. "That's . . . that's . . ."

"Her name."

"I was going to say 'offensive.'"

"Trust me, if you knew her, you'd have named her that, too. The dog is trouble."

Jennifer's nose pinched up. "So, call her Trouble."

Maggie shook her head. "It's not the same. Plus, she'd be confused."

Jennifer pressed her lips together. "It's your home, not mine."

"If it makes you feel better, I can call her Fornicator when you're around."

Aaron busted out laughing. "You sound like a little old lady, honey. It's not like you don't hear that, and worse, all the time."

"At *work*." Jennifer shot him a dirty look. Where she grew up, manners weren't old fashioned.

Maggie backed to the door and opened it without turning around. "Drinks in half an hour before dinner."

Aaron said, "See you then."

Jennifer waved, then turned to her husband when Maggie was gone. "*Don't* egg her on."

He grinned. "Who, me?"

His grin was so cute that she forgot about her mild irritation instantly. She looked him over. He was still wearing a Lions jersey under his coat. His blond hair was shaggy and curling up in the back. As he took off his coat, his biceps flexed.

Damn. She'd missed him. Missed all of him. For a hot second, she thought about the three animals in the room with them, then decided they weren't a problem.

She took three quick steps across the room and tugged on the hem of his shirt. When he turned to her and saw the look in her eyes, his grin turned into a full, brilliant smile.

***

JENNIFER AND AARON arrived late to happy hour, holding hands again—her with cold, flushed cheeks and untamable hair. Before they even had time to greet the other guests, Hank brought in an enormous platter covered in aluminum foil. "Dinner's served."

"You two grab a drink then join us at the table," Maggie said. She gestured at an array of bottles and glasses on a tall server.

Aaron put his hand under Jennifer's elbow. "You don't have to tell us twice."

Jennifer's skin tingled where her husband's fingers warmed her through her shirt. She stayed close to him as they perused the selections together. "Drinks" was an assortment of liquors and liqueurs with a choice of water or ice as mixers. Aaron poured himself two fingers of Buffalo Trace bourbon. Jennifer opted for the Koltiska 90 she'd had at Hank's party. She thought she'd liked it, but it had been wicked strong. So strong she barely remembered anything afterwards. Maybe that was best, since the night had ended badly, at least from Aaron's perspective.

As she made her drink, she glanced up. The dining room opened onto a kitchen with an amazing wood burning stove. On the wall by the server, old ranch implements were arranged over shiplap. She'd always loved this room.

She and Aaron turned toward the table. It was long, wide, and farm-house style with benches. The other guests were seated on one side. Hank had claimed a short bench at the head of the table. Maggie stood beside him.

She gestured along the other long bench. "Herringtons, you're on this side with me."

Jennifer nudged Aaron ahead as a buffer between her and Maggie. They took their seats. A yellow lab puppy lunged against a leash tied to the leg of a bench and yapped at them from under the table.

"Hush, Moose," an older man said. Jennifer had a hazy memory of seeing him at Hank's party.

Hank was making introductions. "Jennifer and Aaron, meet Patrick and Susanne Flint and their daughter Trish. Patrick is a retired Buffalo physician. Susanne teaches Zumba at the senior center and plays a mean game of pickleball. Trish runs the National Forest Service office in Sheridan. Flints, meet Aaron and Jennifer Herrington. Aaron's a vet, Jennifer's a lawyer and my cousin, and they've just bought the Big Horn Lodge."

Moose barked louder.

"And, of course, Patrick's birthday puppy, Moose."

Everyone laughed, and then a flurry of greetings passed back and forth across the table. Patrick and Susanne looked to be in their seventies. Patrick had thinning gray hair, light blue eyes, and the tan of an outdoorsman. Susanne's chin length hair was a rich brown with blonde and white highlights. She was cheerful and petite in jeans and a red turtleneck. Trish was in her forties or fifties—it was hard to tell which. She wore her blonde hair in a messy bun, and her blue eyes matched her father's, although she mostly favored her mother.

Hank blessed the food, and everyone started peeling back foil and passing platters. Steaks. Baked potatoes. A big tossed salad of iceberg, tomatoes, and grated carrots. Corn casserole. Ice box rolls. Moose tried to intercept the steak platter by putting his front paws on the bench and leaning in, but Patrick corrected him.

"Sorry." Patrick beamed with the sparkling eyes of a proud parent. "Puppy training."

Trish shook her head. "That dog is going to be spoiled, Dad. You were never as easy on us, or any of your other pets, for that matter."

Her father ignored her.

Jennifer accepted the steak platter and bit her lip. She didn't do meat or simple carbs unless it was bread pudding in an emotional emergency. She passed the steak onward and loaded her plate with salad. She eyed the dressing. Bottled French. She'd just eat her salad dry. It wouldn't be the first time. She declined the potatoes and rolls.

Maggie leaned around Aaron. "Sorry, Jennifer. I know you're vegetarian. This meal was already in progress when I invited you."

"I'm fine, Maggie. Really." She forked in a bite of plain iceberg lettuce to prove it.

Trish smiled at Jennifer. "It's easier to be a vegetarian in Sheridan than in Story or Buffalo. I have a friend who's vegan. I'll get a list of her favorite restaurants for you."

Jennifer liked Trish already. "Thanks."

Trish said, "Aaron, are you working with a vet clinic in the area?"

"Not yet, but I'd love to. I got burned out in Houston. My practice there has become very corporate in some ways, and our clientele's owners are too wealthy and pampered for my taste. I've always dreamed of having a simple, country practice."

Patrick nodded. "Our vet in Buffalo retired and shut down his practice. Joe Crumpton. Great guy. But one of my old buddies in

Sheridan could use some help. He's trying to slow down, too. In fact, I'll bet if I contacted him, he'd have you punched in and working tomorrow, if you'd like that."

"Would I ever. I've been off less than a week and I already miss it."

Patrick pulled out the newest model iPhone. He handed it to Susanne. "Would you mind texting Frank?"

She made a face but did it. "How could you get through medical school but not be able to operate an iPhone?"

"Because I don't have to. I've got you."

She swatted him playfully, which got Moose excited again. Susanne typed and ignored the puppy. After a few seconds, she said, "He's already answered. Can you be there at nine tomorrow, Aaron?"

"Absolutely."

Susanne entered a few keystrokes. "Here's the address." She rattled it off.

Aaron typed it in his phone. "Thank you. This will be great."

Patrick's eyes twinkled. "You know, I practiced a little veterinary medicine in my time."

"Really? Were you a vet before you became a doctor?"

"Nope. But in my day, when the vet was out of town, the doctors took turns covering for him."

"You're kidding?"

"I kid you not. I learned a lot of good medicine practicing on animals."

"Between them and your family, you were never short of guinea pigs." Susanne patted her husband's hand. "We're all grateful he's retired."

"Do you enjoy retirement, Dr. Flint?" Jennifer asked.

"Call me Patrick," he said. "And I guess I like it all right. Gives me more time to hike and explore."

Susanne winked at Jennifer. "He's as happy as if he had good sense." When everyone stopped laughing, she said, "We're thrilled you guys are buying the lodge from George. He's been a friend of ours for a long time. A great electrical contractor."

Trish nodded. "And he took us on some of the best snowmobiling trips."

Patrick groaned. "Every time he called, I had to hide my wallet. Snowmobiling isn't a cheap hobby."

Susanne smiled. "You loved it, you know you did."

"Guilty as charged."

"George has had such hard luck, but he's a good man."

Aaron cleared his throat. "So, I take it you haven't heard about . . ." His voice trailed off and he glanced at Jennifer.

Jennifer shrugged. "It's public information now, anyway."

"What is?" Susanne put a hand to her chest.

Aaron said, "George was arrested this afternoon in the death of Hadley Prescott, the man who was killed at the lodge."

"No!" Patrick rubbed his forehead, leaving a bright red mark

Jennifer said, "We're so sorry to bear bad news about your friend."

Susanne took her husband's hand. "George would never hurt anyone on purpose. Never."

Aaron put an arm around Jennifer's shoulders. "I agree. Jennifer is going to help prove that. She's defending George."

"That's wonderful," Susanne said.

Patrick's voice turned serious. "Thank you, Jennifer."

Jennifer sighed. "Honestly, I don't know that I *can* defend him. About the best I can do is find him a good local attorney. I'm not licensed in Wyoming." She turned to Aaron and explained. "I Googled it on my phone while we were driving. I'd have to take the bar exam, which is only offered in February and July. February won't be soon enough to do him any good." She left unsaid that it was her plan to be back in Houston in a month, long before February. With her husband.

"But he wants you to be his attorney." Aaron stroked his chin. "Hey, maybe you could associate with local counsel."

Jennifer was about to change the subject, when Trish put her hands on the table and leaned toward her.

"That vegan co-worker I mentioned has a kid who just graduated from law school at the University of Wyoming. He's put out a shingle as a solo practitioner. Maybe he'd be willing to work with you."

Aaron smiled. "Yes! He has the license, and Jennifer has the experience. Perfect."

"I'm texting her right now." Trish pulled out her phone. Her fingers flew. "Maybe I can get a meeting set up for Jennifer tomorrow morning while you're working at Frank's clinic, Aaron."

Moose barked with excitement and put his paws on the bench by Jennifer's leg, as if it was the best idea he'd heard in his short life.

Jennifer felt like she was being sucked into a vortex. *Hello, I'm right here.* "Great." But inside, she was thinking, *This is so not happening.*

ELEVEN

SHERIDAN, Wyoming

THE NEXT MORNING at Ark Veterinary Hospital, Aaron found himself in the eye of a hurricane.

"We've got a repeat in exam room two." The vet tech held out a chart as Aaron was exiting room one.

The tech was a heavyset Asian guy with salt in his peppery hair that didn't match the smooth skin on his face. Their introduction had been so quick that Aaron hadn't gotten his name, and, in this small practice, no one wore name tags. He reminded Aaron a little of Dat Nguyen, the former Texas A&M (and Dallas Cowboys) linebacker. Their college careers had overlapped, but they weren't in the same conference. Aaron pushed away his musings and refocused on the tech, who was still speaking.

"The customer is the repeat. The cat is new to us."

"Thanks." Aaron took the chart and leaned against the wall of the narrow hallway, making room for the tech to pass. He glanced down at the chart. The heavy card stock was blank except for information filled in for the day's visit.

The vet tech was shaking his head. "I've never seen it this busy here before. Our lobby is insane. Thank God you're here."

The staff had been overjoyed, if surprised, to see Aaron when he'd arrived. The harried practice manager, Patrice, had barely glanced at his credentials before hustling him in to see his first patient. Between cases, he picked up bits and pieces of the clinic's predicament from Patrice and the tech. Frank—Dr. Carson—had been showing up less and less in the last few weeks. Neither of them was sure why. They just knew they needed help. Aaron was happy to give it to them. It was a nice clinic, although not the kind he was looking for—small animal practice only, and he had his heart set on working with big animals, too.

He'd hated having to leave the bed that morning. Jennifer and Aaron's fight and time apart had made their reunion like a honeymoon, albeit one played out in a tiny cabin with skunk, cat, and dog voyeurs. But work called for them both. She had dropped him off at Ark and left with tentative plans to meet the young lawyer and visit George in jail. Aaron already missed her and had been checking his phone for messages from her, but they'd be together soon enough, and this opportunity to make inroads into the local veterinary community was too good to pass up.

He lowered his voice to a rumble. "What's the story on this repeat customer?"

The vet tech shrugged. "I don't want to bias your exam." He leaned in close and whispered, "Just don't give her any drugs."

"What kind?"

"Any kind."

Aaron knew what that meant. He hated it when humans used animals to feed their own nasty habits and addictions. "Got it."

"And keep in mind she's never paid a bill in full. Or even in half. No extras."

Aaron nodded. He walked down the hall to exam room two and rapped his knuckles on the door.

"What?" A woman's voice rasped.

He opened the door and slipped inside the little room. Noah, an ark, and animals by twos cavorted around the room on a wallpaper border at chair rail height. The edges of an enormous poster of dog breeds from around the world curled around thumbtacks.

"I'm Dr. Herrington." He stuck his hand out to an emaciated woman with sleeve tattoos on both arms and jet-black razor cut hair. A silver hoop earring with a yellow stone accented her right eyebrow and matched an earring in her left ear.

She shrunk from him and clutched a metal cat carrier to her chest. The skinny, scroungy animal looked feral. "Denise."

He withdrew his neglected hand. "Denise, who's this you've brought in to see us today?"

The cat hissed and swiped at Denise through the slats of the carrier.

Denise said, "Um, this is my cat."

The cat doesn't think so. But if going by the adage that pets and owners start to resemble each other, it was possible. "How old?"

"Four?"

He took that as a guesstimate. "Male or female?"

"Girl." This she said with more confidence.

He squatted down and squinted at the animal. It yowled at him. Nine months, maybe. And it definitely wouldn't be identifying with the she pronoun. Unaltered. It looked reasonably healthy, although malnourished. Tape worms, possibly. Almost certainly unvaccinated. "Hmm. And what's wrong with him?"

She paused for too long. "He hurt his leg. He's in a lot of pain."

Aaron noticed her quick gender transition. "What's his name?"

"Uh . . . Fluffy."

An odd name for a cat with so little hair. "Will he let me hold him to examine him?"

"I don't know. My dad just died. I haven't been paying a lot of attention to, um, Fluffy, you know? I think he's upset."

Aaron felt a flicker of sympathy. What if she was telling the truth? He took the carrier from Denise and set it on the examination table. "What's wrong with his leg—did he cut it or puncture it?"

"I don't know. It just hurts him, and he keeps making awful noises all the time."

Aaron donned heavy duty gloves and retrieved a thick blanket from a cabinet against the wall. Then he opened the door to the carrier. The cat hissed. Aaron reached inside, and it growled like a demon. For a moment, he considered giving it a sedative. He'd only just dodged cat scratch fever a few days ago from Katya and still had the wounds to prove it. But he hated drugging animals unless he had to. He knew how to handle an angry cat for a simple physical exam. For anything beyond that, he'd need help, but with the tiny lobby crowded with patients, he could let the staff keep the train moving down the tracks.

Aaron adopted a soothing tone. "It's okay, buddy."

With the blanket over his chest and shoulder, he scruffed the cat by the loose skin on the back of its neck, then moved it quickly into the blanket, careful to avoid its extended claws. The sound "Fluffy" made was otherworldly. If Aaron hadn't been accustomed to it, it would have raised every hair on his head.

"He makes that noise all the time," Denise said. "He's in so much pain."

Aaron used his free hand to wrap the cat like a burrito, without releasing its neck. Once he had the cat secured, he set it on the table. He arranged the blanket for easier access to the animal's legs, then he adjusted his hand into the snake hold, moving his first and middle fingers over the cat's forehead at the same time as he slid his thumb and ring fingers under its jaw. While not foolproof, the snake hold worked on most cats, and kept them fairly docile for an examination. The cat's voice box vibrated under his thumb, but its sounds grew quieter.

Sweat dripped down Aaron's forehead. "There you go, boy. I'll just take a look at you now, then I'll put you back in your nice, safe carrier." *Safer for both of us.* "Which leg?" he asked Denise.

"Um, his front paw. On the right."

Aaron didn't believe for a second she knew where the cat was injured. In fact, he didn't believe the animal was even hurt. But it would be negligent not to check. He probed and inspected each leg along with paws, toes, and joints. Since the cat was reacting well to the snake hold, he examined the rest of its body, too, finding no sensitivity to touch or manipulation. Not anywhere. Other than fleas and ear mites and an obvious worm situation based on what he saw coming from the back end of the animal, there was nothing wrong with him.

"Fluffy hasn't been neutered. Do you want to take care of that today?" Aaron asked.

"Would he get pain meds?"

Aaron bent the truth to see how she'd react. "Not to take home with him. We'd keep him here until he was recovered enough to go home without them."

"No, man. I may, um, still want kittens from him."

Right. "Is he current on his vaccinations?"

"Yes."

"Do we have those records?"

"No."

"If you could have them sent to the office before you bring him in next time, we'd appreciate it."

"Yeah, sure."

"He has some ear mites. I'd like to clean his ears and apply some medication. You'll need to continue with his treatment at home. They're very contagious, if you have other pets, and also very irritating for him."

"I have to put stuff in his ears?"

"Yes."

She shook her head violently. "He's wild."

"Could you get someone to help you?"

Again, the head shake. "Maybe that's what's hurting him, though. Meds might help."

Denise has been around this block before. Even if she wouldn't care for the cat, he could at least give the poor animal some temporary relief. Still using one hand for the snake hold, Aaron applied cleanser to the end of two long, cotton-swabbed sticks. He gently cleaned the ears, then applied medication to two more swabs. He rubbed them inside the cat's ears. It remained as frozen as a block of ice.

Aaron returned the animal to the carrier and zipped the closure. Fluffy immediately began expressing displeasure again. Aaron took off his gloves and set them aside. "Well, I have good news, Denise. Other than itchy ears, some tape worms, and fleas, your cat is healthy and sound. All very treatable. I see nothing to make me believe he's in any kind of pain."

Her eyes darkened and narrowed. "What do you mean?"

"I mean he's fine. He doesn't need pain meds." Aaron wrote down the treatment he'd provided the cat on the bare chart and added in his recommendation for medications.

"Yes, he does." Her voice was a shriek. "And I have money. I can pay for them."

"I'm glad to hear that. He's going to need medication for his ear mites and worms, and I highly recommend a parasite preventative as well."

"Well, I mean, I don't have the money now, but I will. I'm inheriting it. My dad was a financial planner. He was loaded. You might have read about him in the paper. He was murdered. Hadley. Hadley Prescott. He loved this cat. He wouldn't want to see him suffering. Furry *needs* pain pills. Even just a couple."

Now the cat's name was Furry instead of Fluffy. But Hadley Prescott? What were the odds that he'd see the daughter of the man murdered at the lodge on his first morning working in Sheridan? It wasn't a huge town, but at thirty thousand county-wide, it wasn't a ghost town either. And what was that about an inheritance? In Jennifer's line of work, an inheritance was motive. More motive than George had.

Aaron reached the door in one stride and opened it. He exited, then poked his head back in. "Check out whenever you're ready. I'm going to pay for the medications for him myself. Please use them."

Denise didn't raise her sullen glance from the floor.

He shut the door. "You're welcome," he said to no one.

In the hall, he pulled his phone from his pocket and texted his wife. *I've got a suspect for you in Hadley's death. Reasonable doubt for George.* He sent it, then added a second text. *Are you meeting with that young lawyer this morning?*

At the front desk, he opened his wallet and took out his credit card. He handed it to Patrice along with the chart. "I think I'm going to need to run a tab today. The cat in exam room two is on me."

She raised an eyebrow and called out to the vet tech. "Tron, call that pizza place you like. Dr. Herrington's buying us lunch."

TWELVE

SHERIDAN, Wyoming

JENNIFER STUDIED the narrow shotgun house behind a pristine, snow-blanketed yard. Jennifer had always thought it was such a clever description—she could picture the rooms connected with aligned doorways and a gunshot traveling the length of the house through open doors without hitting anything. The thermometer inside George's truck read thirty-one degrees, even with the heater going full blast. She pulled the white puffy down jacket tighter around her. The night before, Maggie had insisted she borrow it, despite Jennifer's protests. Jennifer was pretty happy about that right now. There was hope she and Maggie could become friends. Or at least friendlier.

Jeremiah chittered inside the carrier. When she'd grabbed her purse to go, he'd looked at her so sweetly that she hadn't been able to leave him behind, even though Aaron had called her a sucker. "Do you know which house it is, skunk?"

Jeremiah didn't answer.

After she'd dropped Aaron at Ark Veterinary Hospital and was at Albertson's picking up a few necessities for the guest cabin, Wesley James, III had called. In a deep voice, he'd told her he could just "squeeze her in," if she came immediately. She shook her head. She couldn't believe she was scrambling all over town for a baby lawyer, but what kind of jerk face would her husband and their new friends think she was if she didn't, when George needed her, and Trish Flint had gone out of her way to help set up the meeting?

She checked the street number on her phone again. It matched the house number. If Maps had taken her to the right address, why did it still seem wrong? She was looking for a law firm. Specifically, The Law Offices of Wesley James, III, Esquire. But Maps had taken her to this residential house with no signage, in an older neighborhood. Not only that, but the street number Trish had given her ended in a -B. The house didn't.

No, she decided, *this can't be it.*

But the houses before and after this one couldn't be it either—they had completely different numbers. So did the homes across the street.

Then it dawned on her. There had to be another property on the lot. She backed up, truck transmission whining, until she saw a converted detached garage partially hidden behind the house. She didn't see a number on it, with or without a -B. And there was no sign visible for The Law Offices of Wesley James, III, Esquire.

Apparently, she was going to have to do this the hard way.

She put the truck in park, turned it off, and climbed down, leaning back in to retrieve her little shoulder purse and Jeremiah's carrier. Life would be easier if she was in the Fusion, but she hadn't had time yet to traipse to the lodge half an hour up the mountain.

Her phone chimed, and she pulled it from her bag, checking it quickly. All morning, she'd been getting messages from Alayah asking for details about Wyoming and her reunion with Aaron. She hadn't had time to answer her yet. Or her boss, Vivian, who was peppering her with follow-up questions on cases she was temporarily reassigning to—of all people—her nemesis, Evan. Or Quentin, who was bombarding her with links to candidates announcing their campaigns for various offices and pundits pontificating on how the race for DA was shaping up. Or her mom, who wasn't pleased she'd had to hear her own daughter was relocating to Wyoming from her nephew Hank and the rest of her Sibley relatives. Or her twin brother Justin, who had yet another baby on the way with his amazingly fertile wife. Correction: two babies. After the fourth pregnancy, it seemed the generation-skipping nature of twinness went out the window. He was certainly making up for Jennifer's lack of contribution to the family line.

But the current text wasn't from any of them. It was from her husband. She smiled.

Aaron. It had been a great night. Unlike any they'd had in a long time. Such a good start, although she'd had another nightmare, in the little time she'd slept. With a few weeks like this, she was sure she could convince him to make Wyoming part-time to be with her in Houston while she ran for DA. She was still concerned about the night of Hank's party, though, and what she had said or done. It was like she was the Titanic, and what she knew about her behavior— basically, nothing—was the tip of the iceberg. The truth could sink her if she didn't make up for it. But it was hard to apologize for some-thing she couldn't remember. *Hey, Aaron. Sweetie. Honey. My Love. Remember the night of Hank's dinner? I'm sorry. I was a beast. None of that was real. Please forgive me. I love you.* Would that work? Only if he didn't ask her exactly what she was sorry for. She was going to have to try it soon when she got her courage up.

She read his text. *I've got a suspect for you in Hadley's death. Reasonable doubt for George.*

She thought *More like a suspect for Wesley James, III, Esquire, who is going to be George's attorney after I'm gone.*

Another text pinged in from Aaron. *Are you meeting with that young lawyer this morning?*

Walking and carrying Jeremiah, she voice-texted him a reply, then hit send: *Good news for George. Who's the suspect? How's it going, and what time should I pick you up? Trying to locate the attorney's office now for meet-up.*

Her toe smashed into concrete. "Ouch." She put her phone back in her shoulder bag, then climbed concrete steps to the squeaky boards of the main house's porch.

A small piece of paper with a handwritten message was taped inside the half-light window in the door. LAW OFFICE OUT BACK. *Bingo.*

The snow in the yard didn't look deep, so she cut across it to the driveway. Unfortunately, she'd misjudged, and it swamped her loafer-style shoes. Her thin socks were no barrier, either, and the snow quickly melted and seeped through. She wished she'd taken the boots Maggie had offered with the down jacket. Of course, they wouldn't have matched her outfit. Black palazzo pants and a silvery unstructured silk blouse.

She turned left at the driveway, still trudging through wet snow. The garage—her presumed destination— was tucked behind the house, half exposed to the street. When she reached it, she rested, panting. The altitude and cold, dry air were making her short of breath. That, or too many days without hot yoga.

The break gave her a moment to look around. Double vehicle doors hung across the front of the wooden structure. An exterior set of stairs on the side led up to a landing and a door. She eyed them warily. The snow had been cleared from the treads. *Still.* She made her way over and tested the bottom one. She'd be okay, she decided, thanks to the rubber-soles on her loafers. She switched hands to carry Jeremiah on the same side as her shoulder bag. Keeping a tight grip on the handrail, she started the climb.

When she was halfway up, the door opened.

"Ms. Herrington?"

The young man who appeared made Doogie Howser seem over the hill. Pink-cheeked, carrot-topped, and pencil-thin, he was decked out in a gray three-piece suit, white pinpoint oxford, and yellow bow tie. Teenage acne hadn't yet been replaced with facial hair. He had an awkward nose like a pelican's beak. But when he spoke, she could have sworn he was Barry White, if her eyes had only been closed.

"Hello. Call me Jennifer. And you're Wesley James the Third, I presume?" His face was so serious that she automatically gave him a disarming smile.

"I go by Kid."

She bit the inside of her lip to keep from laughing. "Kid. As in 'Billy the . . . ?'"

"Sort of. It's because my grandpa is Wesley, and my dad is Wesley Junior. So, I was Wesley the—"

"—kid. Gotcha." She reached the landing. It rocked slightly. Reluctantly, she let go of the railing and shook his hand.

"Welcome to my offices. Come on in where it's warm."

"Sure. Thanks for meeting with me, Kid. Did your mom fill you in on the situation?" It was the first time a mother had ever arranged a meeting for her with another lawyer. *Kind of like a play date.* Again, mirth bubbled up. Her lip was going to be cut to ribbons at this rate.

"She said your client is George Nichols, who is facing a murder charge, but you're not licensed in Wyoming and need co-counsel who is, so you can help Mr. Nichols at trial."

Close enough. "Yes."

He held the door open. "And that you're a hotshot ADA from Houston."

"I never said that to her!"

Color flamed in his cheeks. "She didn't tell me that part. I Googled you."

Jennifer laughed and stepped into his office. A slab desk, tall bookshelf, and two gently worn upholstered armchairs took up most of the floor space. A law school diploma in a shiny, unscratched frame hung behind the desk, which was completely clear except for a yellow legal pad, two pens, and a Macbook in a snazzy hardcase with a picture of the solar system on it.

He shut the door and stomped his feet on a mat.

Too late, she realized she'd tracked in snow. "Nice office."

"Thank you. Please, have a seat." He stood to the side, giving her access to the desk like he expected her to take it.

She took an armchair and set Jeremiah at her feet. "What kind of law have you been practicing?"

He grabbed his pad and a pen and dropped into the other armchair, leaning forward. "Um, general. I've done some wills. A few contracts. And I helped my mom in small claims court. I'm on the list to take court-appointed cases now, too."

So, basically a legal virgin. "This should be interesting for you, then, if you're willing to take it on. First up is going to be some kind of hearing. To advise George of his rights and charges and to set bond. For the judge or a grand jury to decide whether there's probable cause to bind him over for trial. Then an arraignment." Or whatever they called the various steps in the process in Sheridan. There was so much she didn't know about procedure in Wyoming generally and Sheridan County in particular.

He crossed and uncrossed his legs, like he couldn't figure out where to put his limbs. "Very. Yes. Thank you."

"It will be your malpractice insurance policy on the line."

He stared at her.

"You do have malpractice insurance, don't you?"

"Uh, yes. Of course."

"Good. Then if you'd like to work together, we need to call the court and find out when George will be appearing before the judge. Then I'll need to talk you through the process. You'll be the one standing up in court while I backseat drive."

Kid's Adam's apple bulged in his throat. "I do. Very much. Thanks. Do we need a contract?"

"If you'd like to write one up for us, that would be great. I'm not sure what George can afford to pay, but whatever it is, you can have it. I'm just helping him as his friend since I have some downtime."

"Great. Okay. Thank you."

She was beginning to get a feel for his communication pattern already. *Agree, Amplify, Appreciate.* "All right. Let's get this rolling." She pulled out her phone and pressed and held the home button. It made a tonal sound.

Jeremiah answered it with something like "chirp, chirp, chirrup."

Kid's eyes widened. He seemed to notice the carrier for the first time. He pointed at it and mouthed *What is that?*

Jennifer ignored him and enunciated into the phone, at the same moment that she realized it was probably time for Jeremiah to take a potty break outside. "Phone number for the Sheridan County Court Clerk, Sheridan, Wyoming."

Siri recited the number to her and offered to call it. Jennifer took her up on it. Kid lifted a flap on the carrier to peek inside through a webbed panel. He dropped the flap and pushed back his chair, looking horrified. The call connected and began to ring. Jennifer left the phone on speaker.

"County Clerk," a woman's voice said.

"Hello. I'm Jennifer Herrington with the law office of Wesley James the third. We are representing Mr. George Nichols, who is currently being held by the county. I believe he's going to be making an initial appearance soon, and I'm calling to see when that might occur so we can be there with him."

"George Nichols. Yes. Just a moment." The line went silent for a few seconds.

Jennifer drummed one finger on the desk and smiled at Kid.

"Is that a skunk?" he whispered.

"His name is Jeremiah," she whispered back.

"This is my *office.*"

"Don't worry. He's destunk. But I think he needs to go to the bathroom."

Kid looked even more horrified.

The woman came back on. "The judge is going to hold his preliminary hearing today."

Jennifer was stunned. Harris County never moved this fast. "Do you have an approximate time?"

"Yes. Judge Peters always does her preliminary hearings in the circuit court before lunch. About eleven. That way if the defendant is bound over, she can send them right over to the district court for arraignment, if Judge Ryan can fit it in there. The county attorney has asked us to expedite this one. Speedy justice and all. The timing is good. The courts have been in a bit of a lull. I guess everyone in the county has been on their best behavior." She giggled.

There was fast, and then there was light speed. Jennifer's mouth went slack. Her phone had adjusted to Mountain Time and read ten-forty-five. "Oh, my. We're on our way. Thank you."

"You betcha."

Kid's knee started jiggling. "What do we do now?"

Jennifer stood. "Take Jeremiah out to pee. Then I'll drive, and I'll tell you everything you need to know on our way."

THIRTEEN

SHERIDAN, Wyoming

AARON LEANED on the clinic's front counter and pulled out his phone. The staff had caught up with the morning rush. Patrice and the vet tech, Tron, were chatting behind the counter. Aaron scrolled through Jennifer's texts, frowning.

Good news for George. Who's the suspect? How's it going, and what time should I pick you up? Trying to locate the attorney's office now for meet-up.

A new one came in while he was reading. *Omw to courthouse. George's preliminary hearing in circuit court @ 11!!*

Damn. He wanted to be there, but he didn't have wheels. Hank had brought by an orange 1968 Jeepster Commando right before Aaron had left with Jennifer for Sheridan that morning, offering to lend it to them. The vehicle was a beast, and he couldn't believe Hank was still using it. It could just as easily have been an attraction in a classic car museum. But Aaron had wanted to ride in with his wife. Now, he wished he'd made a different choice on the Jeepster.

He was going to ask Hank for a mulligan when he got back to Piney Bottoms.

Maybe he could walk? He mapped to the courthouse on his phone. *Yes.* It was only a few blocks away from the clinic.

He straightened. "Patrice, I have to get to the courthouse downtown. I shouldn't be gone too long. I'm on foot, or I'd offer to bring that pizza back."

She tilted her head, studying the recently emptied waiting room for a moment. "Tron, can you give Dr. Herrington a ride?"

"Call me Aaron. And I didn't mean to suggest—"

Tron held up his hand. "We close from eleven to noon for lunch, Dr. Aaron. You can call the pizza in. Then I'll drop you off at the courthouse and pick up the food. If you're ready after that, I'll give you a ride back."

Patrice crossed her arms and nodded, looking satisfied. And hungry.

Aaron said, "Thanks! I literally need to leave right now. I can call for the pizza on the way."

Tron pulled keys from his pocket, tossed them up, and snatched them in midair. "Why are we standing here jawing about it, then?"

Aaron grinned. The two of them headed to the door.

"Make sure you get me Canadian bacon and pineapple," Patrice shouted after them.

Tron pressed speed dial on his phone as they walked to his car. "Use my phone."

"What should I order for you?"

"Large supreme."

"Mind if I have a slice of that?"

"Yes."

Aaron laughed. A man answered through the speakers, "Powder River Pizza." Aaron placed an order for a large supreme and a medium Canadian bacon and pineapple. He'd ask Jennifer to grab lunch after the hearing.

The ride in Tron's modified Subaru Outback to the courthouse was short. The vet tech had rally racer driving skills, which he showed off over icy backstreets and alley ways. Aaron's adrenaline red lined. He could face down a three-hundred-pound lineman, but rollercoasters and race cars had always made him feel disturbingly mortal.

When Tron pulled to a stop at the curb in front of the courthouse —a building completely lacking in character, which was surprising in a town as picturesque as Sheridan—Aaron released the hand holds. His knuckles were white. "That was exciting."

Tron revved his engine. "That was nothing. You should see me when I'm really racing."

"What do you race?"

"Anything with an engine. But mostly this and B mods. Come with me to the track, and I'll give you a ride sometime."

Aaron couldn't imagine much he'd less rather do. "Wow."

"Text me when you're done. I'll come back for you since you got me my own pizza."

Until two minutes ago, Aaron would have taken him up on it. "That's okay. My wife will give me a ride back. I appreciate the offer, though."

"Suit yourself." Tron saluted. "Hey, which court are you going to?"

Aaron re-read Jennifer's text. "Circuit court."

Tron pointed. "It's next door."

"Thanks." Aaron shut the door, and the Subaru fishtailed away. The short walk up the sidewalk took Aaron to a handsome neoclassical building with the words SHERIDAN COUNTY capitalized in the old Roman style, with Vs in place of Us.

"This is more like it," he said aloud, as he opened the door.

He hurried up the steps and into the gold-domed building, where a sign with an up arrow read CIRCUIT COURT. He took the split stairs to the second floor, two steps at a time, passing an old-timey gold radiator on the landing. The radiator didn't seem to be working, judging from the sub-Arctic temperature. When he threw open the double doors under the Great Seal of the State of Wyoming, he saw a judge with a full head of long, curly gray hair at the bench. The room was in silence. She was looking down at something in front of her. Jennifer was behind the defense table with George, her head leaned toward a redheaded man beside her. Aaron wanted to let her know he was there, but he knew better than to interrupt at this stage. He'd connect with her afterward. He searched for a place to sit and found a spot on the last row. He slipped into it, and, to his surprise, found himself next to Patrick Flint.

The two men shook hands. Patrick's fingers were like ice.

"How's Moose?" Aaron asked.

Patrick grinned. "Best dog ever."

Lab puppies were notoriously hyper. Hopefully Moose would calm as he matured. Until then, "best dog ever" did not describe the out-of-control beast Aaron had met the night before. "Did I miss anything?"

The doctor shook his silver head. "The judge just announced George's hearing."

"I didn't know you'd be here."

Patrick gave a single nod. "I called this morning to make sure George was on the schedule."

Aaron perused the gallery. Most of the people were unfamiliar to him, but he was surprised to recognize a few of them. The fragile waitress—Melanie? Melinda? Mindy?— from Hank's dinner at Frackelton's was sitting beside an even more-fragile look-alike woman a few decades her senior. Melinda, he was almost positive. Aaron wondered if the older woman was her mother. Her name came back to him instantly. Gerrianne. His own mother was named Annie, so Gerrianne had stuck with him from his conversation with Perry and Melinda about the wreck that had killed her sister. Further down their row was the drug-seeking cat lady Denise from the vet clinic that morning.

The judge looked up and blinked. "For the state?" Her voice was clipped. "Pootie, are you ready?"

The man who stood at the prosecutor's table had a Julius Caesar bowl cut and baggy suit. "County Attorney Alfred Carputin, Judge Peters."

The judge rolled her eyes. "Alfred Carputin, you've been Pootie to me since you ran around in your training pants playing in the sprinklers in the yard next door. However, if it makes you feel any better, I will endeavor to call you by your given name. Please forgive me in advance if I backslide."

"Thank you, Your Honor."

"Defense?"

The red head jumped to his feet. "Yes, Your Honor."

The judge fixed her gaze back on the county attorney. "So, don't keep us waiting. What are the charges against Mr. Nichols?"

Pootie cleared his throat. "The State of Wyoming will be charging George Nichols with first degree murder."

Jennifer was the first person to gasp aloud, but others followed. She gave her co-counsel a hard shove. The young man jumped to his feet, still leaning down to hear whatever Jennifer was whispering in his ear.

The judge cocked her head. "You have something to say, Counsel?" She frowned. "I haven't seen you before. What's your name again, son?"

"Kid James for the defendant, Your Honor. I mean, Wesley James. Attorney James. James, ma'am."

Kid? A titter rippled across the room. Aaron couldn't stop himself from joining in.

The judge smiled. "Take a deep breath, son."

Kid's back heaved. "First degree murder is a ridiculous charge and without grounds." He paused a little too long, then blurted, "Ma'am."

"Pootie—I mean *Carputin*—how do you respond?"

Pootie's voice was sonorous. "The state will prove beyond a reasonable doubt that the defendant invited the victim, Mr. Hadley Prescott, to the Big Horn Lodge with an express intent to take his life.

That the defendant had the means, a motive, and opportunity, and that he in fact did maliciously and with forethought murder Mr. Prescott, his unarmed guest, by stabbing him with a knife through the temple and into the brain."

Instead of groans, this time the gallery responded with oohs.

"That county attorney—what a boob," Aaron whispered.

Patrick leaned sideways at him without turning his head. "Pootie hasn't been the same since his youngest child died."

"That's too bad. So, he wasn't a boob before then?"

A smile creased the weathered skin at the corner of Patrick's mouth. "Not as a big a boob."

Aaron covered a laugh with a fake cough and a fist to his lips.

Jennifer pulled on Kid's arm. Again, the two had a hurried, one-sided conversation. Kid held a hand up as if asking the judge to wait on him to speak.

The judge crossed her arms. "Attorney James, would you like to introduce your co-counsel? Or does she wish to speak on her own behalf?"

"No, sir. I mean, yes, sir. This is Jennifer Herrington, Your Honor. She's assisting me in Mr. Nichol's defense."

"What is she, a legal secretary? A paralegal? A life coach? A psychic?" The judge nodded to her audience, which responded with an organized roar like a laugh track.

Aaron and Patrick exchanged smiles.

Kid's voice cracked. "Ms. Herrington is an ADA in Harris County."

"I'm sorry, son. I've lived in Wyoming all my life, and I'm not familiar with a county named Harris."

"It's in Texas, ma'am. Houston, Texas."

The judge slid her glasses to the end of her nose and peered over them at Jennifer. "Well, Big City, welcome to the Cowboy State. Let me guess. You're not licensed here."

Kid started to answer. "She's pro hac vice, and I'm—"

The judge held up a hand. "I suspect Big City can speak for herself."

Jennifer stood. Aaron felt his chest expand. He was so proud of his wife. She might be small, but even in the simple act of rising from a chair, Jennifer radiated competence, confidence, and power.

"You are correct, Judge Ryan. I can't test until February, so Mr. Nichols requested that I assist a properly licensed Wyoming attorney in his defense until such time as I pass the Wyoming bar exam."

"How fortunate for Mr. Nichols that he found you, all the way down south."

"My husband and I are under contract to purchase a home here, ma'am."

"Good fortune abounds for us all." Her voice was like dust.

Just then, a high-pitched animal noise shocked the courtroom into silence. It seemed to come from Jennifer. The animal made the noise again. Jennifer swatted Kid, who leaned under their table. Suddenly, Aaron knew exactly what the noise maker was. He groaned softly.

"What, may I ask, is making that noise, Big City?"

Jennifer drew in a deep breath. "It's, um, a service-animal-in-training." She lightened her voice. "I have to take it everywhere, ma'am."

"A service animal. In training."

"Yes, ma'am."

"In that bag under your table that Attorney James is fiddling with."

"Yes, ma'am."

"It's awfully small."

"Yes, it is, ma'am."

"May I ask what kind of dog that small aspires to a career of service, Big City?"

"Um, well, it's not a dog, Your Honor."

She wiped her forehead. "Don't keep us waiting, Big City. Tell us what kind of honorable animal you've brought into my courtroom today on its journey to serve others."

"A skunk, ma'am."

There was a pregnant pause, then frenzied laughter broke out, Patrick loudest of all.

"Did you know?" he whispered to Aaron.

Aaron nodded and closed his eyes. "Poor Jennifer," he whispered.

The judge sounded thoughtful. "A skunk. In my courtroom."

"It's been fixed, ma'am. No more stink."

"Oh, my. That's a great consolation."

The gallery was in hysterics now, with people standing up and trying to see Jeremiah.

The judge banged her gavel. "Order." When the gallery quieted, she added, "Never again, Big City, not even if that skunk's special service is to provide first degree murder defense representation. Understood?"

Jennifer's voice was subdued, and Aaron knew if he could see her face, a starburst of bright pink would highlight each cheek. "Yes, Your Honor."

"Thank you, Big City. You can take your seat."

Jennifer sat.

"Now, where were we? Oh, yes. Attorney James, you may continue."

Kid straightened his shoulders, turned toward the County Attorney, and adjusted a bow tie the size and color of Big Bird. "Stand your ground."

"What about it, son?"

"Mr. Nichols will, uh, prove that Hadley Prescott engaged in a campaign of escalating harassment against him." Jennifer prodded him in the back with a pen. "Including trespassing at his home at all hours of the night and day and leaving threatening and libelous posters on Mr. Nichols' home, and that under the "stand your ground" doctrine, Mr. Nichols had a right to defend himself and his property." He glanced at Jennifer, and she nodded.

"Save it for trial, counselor."

"But the charge of first-degree murder, ma'am?"

"The prosecution can lower the charge if warranted later. For now, I'll allow it. I've seen the felony information, and I think everything is in order to bind this matter over for trial in the district court. Mr. Nichols, sir. It's your turn." She proceeded to explain the charge and his constitutional rights to him. She ended with, "You have the right to the assistance of counsel. If you can't afford a lawyer, the state will appoint one for you. And are you satisfied with your counsel, or do you need the court to appoint a new one?"

George swayed. "Satisfied."

"Despite the skunk episode?" the judge said drily.

"Um, yes. Your Honor."

"You may be seated." The judge took her glasses off and mopped her brow with the sleeve of her robe. Aaron thought the room was frigid, but the woman appeared to be sweating. "In the matter of bond, the court hereby sets it at five hundred thousand dollars, cash only. Will you be posting it today, Mr. Nichols?"

Beside Aaron, fabric rustled. To his surprise, Patrick Flint was standing.

"Yes, he will. I'm paying it," Patrick said.

Every head in the courtroom swiveled to stare at the doctor.

FOURTEEN

SHERIDAN, Wyoming

AS IF THE preliminary hearing hadn't moved fast enough, Jennifer found herself swept along into the basement, across original mosaic tile, past a bronze water fountain, and from the old county building through a connecting hallway into the new one, then up to the district court on the third floor. Apparently, Pootie had already arranged for the district court judge to squeeze George's arraignment in before lunch. The speed was unheard of. She was used to a week or two gap between preliminary hearing and arraignment back in Texas.

"Is this normal?" she turned to whisper to Kid. She was carrying Jeremiah in one hand. The other was on George's elbow. George's face was slack, and he didn't appear to be listening to her. "To have a preliminary hearing this fast, then an arraignment on its heels?"

Kid blinked like an owl. "I don't think so. But I, um, I don't really know."

Whether it was normal or not, it was a few weeks less of uncertainty and worry for George. That wasn't a bad thing, if she could just adjust to the feeling of a speedometer spinning out of control.

A hand grasped her shoulder. "Jennifer."

It was Aaron. Her heart leapt. "You made it. Thanks for being here."

"This is crazy."

"Tell me about it. Are you coming to the arraignment?"

"I wouldn't miss it."

"Good." She held up the carrier. "Can you take custody of our *service animal* and keep it out of sight? And quiet?"

He smiled. "I can do that."

"I'll see you afterwards."

He took the carrier and gave her a salute.

She came to a room with a sign outside that read FOURTH JUDICIAL DISTRICT COURT OF WYOMING, THE HONORABLE JUDGE STU RYAN. She pushed open the doors, revealing dark vertical paneling and green carpet. It was an attractive-if-somber room, but she didn't have time to examine it. A judge was seated on the bench, and Pootie was already behind the prosecution table.

The judge's voice boomed. "Are you defense for Mr. Nichols? Judge Peters briefed me."

Uh oh. Jennifer filed ahead of Kid to the defense table, giving her co-counsel a surreptitious poke in the ribs as she did.

"Yes, Your Honor," Kid said. "Wesley James and Jennifer Herrington for the defense."

A smirk creased the judge's cheeks. "Kid and Big City. And are we to have the company of your *service animal*, Big City?"

Judge Peters had clearly filled him in on *all* the juicy details. Jennifer pondered carefully how to answer the judge truthfully, while omitting the damning fact of Jeremiah's presence. "My husband took the skunk for me, Your Honor."

The judge's sloped shoulders shook, and she realized he was chuckling. "I'm Judge Ryan, like the name says on the door. And I'm meeting my wife for lunch at the Flagstaff Café in half an hour. So, let's begin." He nodded at Pootie. "Go, Carputin."

Pootie recited the charges again. Judge Ryan crossed his arms and listened.

When Pootie went silent, the judge gave George his second explanation of the day regarding the charges and his rights. "Do you understand, Mr. Nichols?"

"Stand up," Jennifer whispered.

George half-stood. "I guess so."

"I need a yes or no, Mr. Nichols."

"Uh, yes."

"Regarding the charge of murder in the first degree, Mr. Nichols, how do you plead? Guilty or not guilty?"

Jennifer patted George on the back.

"Not guilty, Your Honor." His voice sounded dazed and weak. Then he crumpled back in his chair, head on the table.

The gasps in the gallery weren't half as loud as Jennifer's own.

***

AFTER GEORGE RECOVERED from his near-fainting episode, the rest of the proceeding had been anti-climactic. George insisted he was all right—just tired, stressed, and hungry. Jennifer wanted to take him to the emergency room, but Patrick Flint gave him a quick examination right there in the courtroom and declared home and bed his best medicine. Judge Ryan then set a trial date four months out and dismissed them all.

Half an hour later, Kid was driving a white Denali with Jennifer and George as passengers, headed toward the lodge. Given the nonexistent income of a wet-behind-the-ears solo practitioner officing out of the family garage, Jennifer was positive Kid's mom owned it.

He'd jogged home to get it after dismissal—in his suit—so Jennifer stole a few minutes to catch up with Aaron. He'd given Jeremiah back to her, then told her about meeting Hadley's daughter Denise, her likely drug habit, and her strong belief she was about to come into daddy's money. Jennifer was encouraged and looked forward to discussing it with George and Kid, when they got to the lodge.

As they passed through Big Horn, George said, "Thanks again for bringing my little buddy." He was holding the skunk in his lap.

She hadn't brought Jeremiah to court for him, but it didn't hurt for him to think so. "You're welcome, George."

"I thought Judge Peters was going to lose it there for a second!" Kid sounded like he thought that would have been the coolest thing ever.

"Me, too," Jennifer admitted, grinning and shaking her head.

She looked out for the mountain view, but it wasn't there. Low clouds hung so thick it was as if the range didn't exist. Even when they reached the lodge, Jennifer couldn't see past the trees at the base of the mountains. She was glad she'd flown in the day before and not in this bad visibility.

George waved his hand. "Just park anywhere."

Kid aimed for the railroad ties separating the parking area from the yard, choosing one next to the undriveable Suburban. He bumped the Denali tires into the tie, and his ears turned pink. Jennifer pretended not to notice.

Jennifer got out last as she juggled with her bags. A faint sound caught her attention. Human voices speaking in a language she didn't recognize. "George, what is that?"

"What's what?"

"I hear someone talking."

"Neighbors, maybe."

"It's not English."

"Not you, too. Black Bear Betty is always telling me she hears Sioux talk." He rubbed his eyes. "Shelly did a time or two herself."

Jennifer hadn't believed it when Black Bear Betty had told her the same thing. She cocked her head, listening harder. The only sound was the wind. That had to have been what it was in the first place, since there was no way she was hearing ghost voices. Was there?

The three of them plus Jeremiah walked into the lodge. Kid's jaw dropped. He wandered the living room, touching everything like an unsupervised kid in FAO Schwartz.

"Liam," George called.

Jennifer put a hand on his arm. "Aaron and I are staying with my cousin Hank at Piney Bottoms Ranch in Story. We weren't sure how long the county would keep you, so we took the animals with us. We still have Liam and Katya there."

His head tilted. "Why aren't you staying here?"

"The septic situation."

George stroked his chin. He looked overdue for a serious scrubbing. A shave wouldn't hurt him either. "All right."

"How about we sit and talk strategy for a few minutes?"

"Let me just change clothes first." He started walking away down the hall before she answered.

"Take your time. I'll make us something to eat." She went to the kitchen and flipped on a switch. No light came on, but a lamp beside a living room armchair did. She tried it again just to be sure. Same result. She turned it off.

George called, "Use whatever you can find. Sorry, I haven't been to the store this week."

A sign for pizza at the Big Horn Mercantile had been calling to Jennifer every time she'd passed it in Big Horn. Hot, cheesy pizza would have been great in the cold. "Don't worry. I'll find us something."

The back door opened and closed. Jennifer set to work scavenging. Kid made no move or offer to help.

She raised her brows. She wasn't his mommy. "A little assistance, co-counsel?"

Kid threw his arms out. His body took up half the kitchen floor, like a scarecrow in a garden. "Um, I'm not much of a cook."

"Can you operate a Keurig?"

"Yeah."

"Hop to it then. Just don't run the tap into the sink. The septic system is down."

"Okaaaay." Kid scrunched his nose. "Do you think George wants coffee?"

"Make some for—" A scurrying sound drew her eye, and she screamed. A little gray mouse was sprinting across the kitchen floor. "Oh, my God!"

Kid spared it a quick glance. "He needs a cat."

The mouse disappeared under a cabinet, and Jennifer shuddered. "He has one. It's just living with Aaron and me at the moment." Katya might have a horrible attitude, but she was a necessary evil, and Jennifer's appreciation of her increased tenfold.

Fifteen minutes later, George returned. Jennifer had no doubt he'd tippled at his cottage, but he was still upright. She had heated a can of tomato soup, made PB&J sandwiches, loaded a plate with saltines, wiped down the table, and laid out lunch on the burn-scarred top. She'd even had time to hide George's booze in the coat closet. Kid, meanwhile, brewed three cups of coffee which he sloshed onto her clean(er) tabletop. He stared at it in dazed horror until she threw him a dishrag.

Jennifer tried to initiate the strategy conversation while they were eating, but a raised hand from George stopped her. She supposed she could let a man just released from jail eat in peace, even though inside she screamed in frustration. So, the three of them dined in silence, unless you counted the sound the table made rocking back and forth on its uneven legs. When she'd finished, Jennifer put her plate, bowl, and spoon in a plastic bin by the sink.

George grunted. "Throw any food that's left in the compost can."

She wrinkled her nose. "How about the disposal?" *Was that hooked to the septic system?*

"Don't got one."

Aaron and I are buying a house with no disposal. I didn't even know they came that way.

She shook it off. Time to get serious about George's defense, even if he had a few bites to go. "George, we need to talk to you about the night Hadley died. What you say to us is covered by the attorney-client privilege, which means we can't disclose it to anyone. And it's critically important you tell us everything. We won't judge you. If you hold things back, it could make it hard for us to help you. Do you understand?"

He sniffed his coffee, then set it down. "Okay."

Kid was still crunching his way through a bag of saltines and didn't seem inclined to interject.

Does okay mean he agrees or understands? And does it even matter? She decided to keep moving forward. "Now can we talk?"

George sighed. "I guess."

She sat back down, cradling her cup of coffee. "What do you remember about the night before Hadley died?"

Jeremiah jumped onto the table. She scooped him off and into her lap, stroking his long, soft fur.

"Going to bed. Next thing was you waking me up in the morning."

"Nothing about Hadley's visit?"

"Nothing."

"You don't have a memory of using a knife or anything to do with one?"

"None. Besides, everyone in Wyoming knows that to get away with murder you follow the three S's."

Jennifer was afraid to hear what they were. *Thank God for attorney-client privilege.* "Which are?"

At exactly the same time, Kid and George said, "Shoot, Shovel, and Shut up."

Jennifer just stared at them. Jeremiah made excited noises.

Apparently, everyone in Wyoming *did* know how to get away with murder.

George nodded at Kid. "What kind of idiot stabs a fellow he doesn't get along with and leaves him in his backyard?"

"Right?" Kid said.

"Much less his own damn dog."

Jennifer nodded. They were fair points. "When was the last time you talked to Hadley?"

"That afternoon."

"On the phone?"

"No. In person. He showed up here." His nose wrinkled like he smelled something foul. "I found another one of his notes on my door after he left."

"Like the one on his body?"

"Could be."

"What did the one you found say?" Jennifer actually remembered it, but she needed his memories, not her own.

"Killer."

Jennifer said, "Can you remember seeing a note anywhere the night Hadley died?"

"No. But it sounds like someone doesn't like something he did, if they left one on his body like I heard."

"Do you still have the note someone left you earlier that day that said Killer on it?"

"Maybe. I saved a few of them."

"Do they all say Killer?"

"Or something like it."

"Can I have them? They might help us."

He shrugged. "I only have copies now. I gave the originals to the sheriff's office."

"What?"

"I went to file a complaint against Hadley for harassing me. They called it stalking though. I didn't like that."

"What happened with the complaint?"

"I changed my mind and withdrew the charges."

"Okay. I want the copies then." It didn't help their case that the sheriff had proof of how upset Hadley had made George, but it couldn't be helped. She needed to verify something else. "So, you saw Hadley when he was here at the lodge at about the time Aaron and I arrived? Not at another time?"

His forehead folded up like an accordion. "Yeah, I guess that's right."

He'd been a little juiced then, on his way to getting juicier. But that's how she remembered it, too. She and Aaron had gone to Hank's party, then she'd sunk into a deep, inebriated slumber when they got back to the lodge. She couldn't vouch for anything that happened during the night, and Aaron hadn't heard anything either. By the time she'd seen George the next morning, he had woken with unexplained blood all over his clothes. From himself or someone else? *Or both?*

Jennifer said, "What did the doctor say when the county had you examined?"

In her lap, Jeremiah had curled into a ball. He was snoring softly.

"I had a big cut on my noggin." He touched his forehead. "Up under my hair."

His longish Rod Stewart mop. No wonder neither she nor Aaron had seen the injury that morning. "From what?"

"They didn't say."

"They didn't mention a knife?"

"No."

"Did you get stitches?" She nudged the skunk. Jeremiah awoke, stretched, hopped off, and shuffled away.

George lifted the hair on his forehead. Jennifer got up and looked at it. A jagged row of small, tight stitches marched in black across his skull. There had to have been a dozen of them. Not an insignificant injury. But did it account for all the blood on his body? There was no way to know without DNA tests, for both George and Hadley, which she felt sure had already been performed. She'd follow-up on those later, as well as on getting a copy of George's medical records.

She walked into the kitchen and leaned against the lower cabinets. "Had you ever talked to Hadley on the phone or by text or email?"

"A few times on the phone. I told him I had had enough of his shit."

"Had you ever invited him to the lodge?"

He snorted. "My wife's ex-husband? Not on your life."

"Okay. Can I take a look at your phone?"

"I don't have it."

"Did the police take it?

"I'm not sure. It wasn't in the cottage when I got home. I looked for it when I went to change clothes. Do you think they took it when they arrested me?"

"Maybe." To Kid, Jennifer said, "We need to ask Carputin about the phone. We'll call as soon as we're done here."

He nodded and kept eating. He'd polished off the rest of the soup and saltines and was working on the last sandwich.

She raised her brows at him. "If you could keep a list for us, I'd appreciate it."

He dropped the sandwich and scrambled in his briefcase for his legal pad and pen. George moved into the kitchen and started rummaging in a cabinet. It was one of the ones where she'd found a half-full bottle of Wyoming Whiskey.

She continued giving Kid instructions. "Add that we need to get the DNA reports and medical records."

George reached into a cabinet behind her legs.

She moved to the side. "George, had you and Hadley ever had any physical altercations before?"

"You mean fights?"

"Yes. Fights."

"Um, no."

"Did you ever threaten to hurt him? Or kill him?"

"Never." George began pulling open kitchen drawers. With each one, he shut it a little harder, until he was rattling utensils and silverware.

Jennifer paused, thinking. It was surreal to be on the side of the defense for the first time in her nearly twenty-year career. In her experience—in her past *belief*—defendants were guilty and all of them lied. She'd assumed defense attorneys knew this and didn't care. But she cared whether George had done it. She cared whether he was truthful. Actually, she was finding she cared a great deal. The thought of him being convicted made her truly apprehensive and, dare she say, sad. She believed in his innocence and couldn't let it happen. She had to give him a good running start, then find him the best criminal defense attorney around. The Alan Dershowitz of Wyoming. And she had to do it fast. Because if one thing was crystal clear from just this brief foray into criminal defense, it was that it could ruin her heart for prosecutorial work forever.

Her eyes stung. She blinked rapidly, hoping Kid and George didn't see the wetness in her eyes. She cleared her throat and squared her shoulders. "Who do you think would want to hurt Hadley?"

"Besides me? I never would have, but that doesn't mean he didn't have it coming."

She winced. "Yes. Besides you. Although let's try to avoid saying that to the cops or the prosecutor."

"Isn't it a job for the sheriff's office to figure this stuff out?"

Ouch. As a prosecutor, it hurt to admit the truth. "No. They've found you and enough evidence to convince the prosecutor to charge you. Now their job is to prove you did it. They won't be looking at anyone else."

Kid dropped his pen. "But that's awful. They should be hunting for the real killer."

Welcome to the grown-up practice of criminal law. It was depressingly different than in law school textbooks sometimes. "From here on out, that's our job. George, can you think of any other possible suspects for the jury?"

"I don't want to blame someone who's innocent."

"Don't worry. We won't railroad anyone. We'll just investigate. Discreetly. If it seems like someone else could have done it, then and only then will we use that as part of your defense. It's called 'the other guy did it' defense, and it can be pretty effective, since the prosecution has to prove beyond a reasonable doubt that *you* killed Hadley. They can't do that if the jury suspects someone else."

"I thought we had a defense. That 'stand in place' thing."

"Stand your ground. And we do. But that's basically like saying you did do it, but you had a right to. It's a last resort. The best possible outcome is if we prove you *didn't* do it, and one way to do that is to hand over the real killer to the court."

His chest heaved with a sigh, like he was carrying the weight of the world on his shoulders, or at least the weight of the people he was considering throwing under the bus. "Okay. My stepdaughter, Denise. She's . . . troubled. She didn't get along with either of her parents. Or me, for that matter. She wanted money when Shelly died, and I would imagine she's after some now that Hadley's dead, too."

Kid scribbled it down.

That matched what Aaron had told her about the young woman earlier. Jennifer wondered if she really would inherit, and how much. "That's good. Who else?"

He shook his head, his eyes sad and droopy. "I didn't know Hadley except for the things he did to me and what Shelly told me."

"Well, if she was here, who would Shelly think had it in for him?"

"She wouldn't believe Denise would hurt her father. But she did tell me that people who lost money with him sometimes held grudges."

"Anyone in particular?"

"None that I remember."

"That's good. Keep going with what Shelly would have said."

"She seemed to think he had a girlfriend he'd been stringing along."

"Who?"

"She didn't know. It was just things she heard from Hadley after they split up. Plus, she'd suspected him of tomcatting around when they were married."

"Okay. Thank you. Keep thinking about it, and if you come up with something or someone else, we'll talk about it."

"What will happen now?"

"Right this second, Kid and I will call the County Attorney before he goes home for the day."

"Okay." George rubbed the toe of his shoe on the floor like he was putting out a cigarette. "Do you, uh, think they might have taken my whiskey when they had that search warrant?"

Jennifer struggled not to let her face reveal her guilt. "I doubt it. Why?"

"It's missing. All of it I kept in the lodge."

"Huh. Well, sorry about that. Now's a good time to lay off it anyway. You need all your wits about you. But maybe you just ran out."

"I don't think so." He retraced his search pattern through the kitchen.

"One last thing, George. Something I hate having to bring up."

George paused to look at her, trepidation etched across his face. "What?"

"Money. I'm happy to donate my time, but you will have expenses. And I can't practice law in Wyoming without associating with Kid and his firm."

"Okay. Thank you."

"Kid, what are your rates? Or do you want to charge George a flat fee?"

Kid's neck turned splotchy pink. He pulled at his bow tie.

"Doesn't matter what his rates are. I don't have money. Not until I sell the lodge to you guys."

Jennifer made her voice as gentle and understanding as she could, while still being firm and businesslike. "Could you pay Kid after our closing?" *If George doesn't have enough money to pay Kid, how will he ever be able to pay for the type of counsel he's going to need?*

"I don't need money," Kid blurted out. "I'm going to do this pro bono, too. I'll learn a lot. Maybe after this, the court will refer me cases."

Jennifer nodded at Kid. *Good on him. Now, I may even ask his input later on lead counsel for George.* "I think your time is well invested in this case. Do a good job, and you'll be set. And, George, you can just run a tab with me on the expenses. We'll settle up later."

George grunted. "Thank you both."

"You're welcome." Jennifer got out her cell phone. "Kid, I'm going to ask the County Attorney's office for witness statements and George's phone records. Anything else?"

He looked at his notes. "Whether they took his phone?"

"Right. Good."

"George's medical records. DNA reports."

While it hadn't been a test per se, she had wanted to see if he was paying attention. She was beginning to think she could rely on him. "Yes. Either on this call, or soon." She asked Siri for the number then called it.

A harried man answered. "Sheridan County Attorney's office."

"County Attorney Carputin, please."

"May I ask who's calling?"

"Jennifer Herrington and Kid James, counsel for George Nichols."

"Wesley," Kid whispered.

"Wesley James," Jennifer amended.

"Hold please," the man said.

Jennifer put the call on speaker and waited. Music played while she was on hold. A remake of "Don't Stop Believin'," made famous by Journey and nausea-inducing by Muzak.

"Carputin here." He sounded even more self-important than he had in the courtroom.

Jennifer couldn't resist. "Attorney *Pootie*, this is Jennifer Herrington. I don't believe we met in court earlier. I'm working with Wesley James representing George Nichols."

His tone could have lasered through diamonds. "That's County Attorney Alfred *Carputin*. And George Nichols is a scumbag. He doesn't deserve a fancy big city lawyer."

"Excuse me?" George walked over to her with his fists balled. She held up a hand to keep him quiet. Now she wished she hadn't put Carputin on speaker.

Pootie's voice was clipped. "What can I do for you, Ms. Herrington?"

"First, we need your direct number. This case is too important to go through the switchboard."

"Fine." He recited some digits with a three-oh-seven area code, which she jotted down quickly.

"Next, we'd like to get a copy of Mr. Nichols's statement, any phone records gathered, other witness statements, and any medical records or test results."

"Put it in writing, counselor. It's called a formal discovery request. Maybe you don't have those down in Texas."

She breezed past his jab. "You'll have it in your hands soon. I just wanted you to be expecting our request, so you could have everything ready."

"When we get the paper, we'll call you."

"Also, we'd like his phone returned to him, along with a list of anything belonging to him that was seized."

"Fine."

Jennifer smiled the smile she usually reserved for intimidating defense attorneys face to face. So, they did have George's phone. "Kid will be by as soon as we hear from you."

"Wesley," Kid mouthed.

Carputin didn't reply.

"Oh, and we need the crime scene at the lodge released so that

George can have his septic installation completed at his home. It's been nearly a week."

"We'll let you know when we're done with it."

"Great. I just suggest it be soon unless you want to explain to the court why we're filing for reimbursement for George's hotel bill."

Carputin growled, low and rumbly. "We'll release it tomorrow."

"There now. That wasn't so hard, was it?" Jennifer hung up and winked at Kid. "How do you feel about drafting discovery requests together this afternoon?"

He whooped.

George kept searching for his whiskey.

FIFTEEN

STORY, Wyoming

AARON CRUSHED the empty Big Horn Mercantile pizza boxes and stuffed them in a heavy-duty garbage bag. There wasn't much room for trash in the Piney Bottoms guest cabin. He'd dispose of it tomorrow. Tonight, the clutter was worth it. After he'd dropped George's truck at the lodge, he and Jennifer had taken the Fusion for the pizza on the way back to Story. It had felt good to visit the restaurant together in their new hometown, and it made up for missing the pizza he'd bought for the clinic staff. Since Jennifer had needed to return to the lodge with Kid and George, Aaron had ended up lunching with Patrick Flint. He really liked the older doctor. And after a long-term, mostly monogamous relationship with Star Pizza in Houston, he was surprised how much he liked the Merc pizza, too. A small veggie for Jennifer, a large meat lover's for him. They'd eaten it on the cabin's tiny porch at Piney Bottoms, while Liam rolled around in the snow.

Aaron turned on the water to fill the sink for dishwashing.

Jennifer had driven into Story after dinner to buy alcohol. She'd learned that morning that the Sheridan grocery stores couldn't sell any. He'd stayed behind for the easier job—cleaning up after dinner.

The front door rattled with a knock. Aaron opened it with a wet hand. Hank stood on the porch beside a funny looking dog. It looked like a black and white border collie chopped off at the knees.

"Hey, Hank. Come on in."

Hank pointed up. "I saw lights. Where's Jennifer?"

"She ran into Story for supplies."

Hank came inside—the dog didn't—and sat down at the table. "Do you guys have everything you need?"

"If you're still willing to rent me that Jeepster, I'd take it."

"Lend, rent, sell. It's great on snow, ice, and mud, which you'll get a lot of up at the lodge. And it's just gathering dust here. My grandfather would want to see it used. He loved the crazy thing."

Aaron paused. He'd sorely tested his wife by buying the lodge and not returning to Houston. What if she didn't want the Jeepster? But, no matter what, he needed an all-season vehicle in Wyoming. And hadn't he decided he was the quarterback of his own life? Not the Monday morning kind. The quarterback in real time. And this quarterback wanted a vintage snow monster. Besides, he and Jennifer had always chosen their own rides. This time would be no different.

"How much do you want for it?"

Hank grinned.

Five minutes of haggling and discussion later, Hank handed Aaron a handwritten bill of sale in exchange for a check. "You're going to love it. Reminds me of riding a seasoned bull. The old boy's still got it and gives you a hell of a ride."

Or going up against an aging linebacker. Aaron pictured the big, orange vehicle. Tough and not afraid to get dirty. DeMarcus Ware was the epitome of a crusty, all-weather beast. He'd started his career with the Dallas Cowboys, but he'd played a few years with the Broncos as an outside linebacker. The Jeepster had lived its life up in Denver Broncos country, but Aaron had lived in Texas for half of his life. The partnership of Aaron and Jeepster synced up with Ware's career perfectly. Bonus: the Broncos wore orange jerseys, the color of the Jeepster.

That settled it. He was definitely going to call it DeMarcus Ware. "I can't wait."

"The keys are in it, and it's parked in the big garage where we store all the vehicles and do our mechanical work. I'll put the title in the glove box for whenever you're ready to do the transfer."

"Perfect." Aaron heard a car engine outside. He went to the door. "Jennifer's back."

"How is she settling in?"

"Better all the time. Just a sec." Aaron met his wife at the car. The odd little dog followed him, sniffing his ankles. "Can I carry the bags?"

She smiled up at him. "Always."

"Hi, Jenny." Hank was walking down the porch steps toward them. "Just checking on you guys."

"Thanks, cuz. We're good." The dog snuffled her feet. "Oh. And hello . . . dog."

Finished with their scents, the dog trotted back toward the ranch house.

"Maggie's dog. She's a weird one." Hank shook his head.

"With a horrible name," Jennifer agreed.

Hank laughed. "True, although it fits her. One last thing, Aaron. Our vet called today. He's moving to Utah. I asked him what he was going to do with his practice, and he said he's selling."

If the guy was the ranch vet, that meant he had a large animal country practice. It could be just what Aaron was looking for. "Intriguing." He looped plastic grocery bags over his wrist. They cut into his skin. Two six-packs, one bottle of KO90—that surprised him —a wine glass, and three bottles of what looked like pinot noir.

"You want me to introduce you?"

Jennifer cut in. "It's a little premature."

He kept his voice mild, trying to sound amused instead of exasperated. "It's a blind date, Jennifer, not a shotgun wedding." To Hank, he said, "Sure. I'd love an introduction. And to meet with him."

Jennifer shut the door to the Fusion more firmly than necessary.

Hank said, "Will do, Aaron. See you later, guys." Then, after checking that Jennifer wasn't looking at him, he mouthed, "Women," and winked at Aaron.

"Tell Maggie hi," Aaron said.

"Will do."

Jennifer was already at the cabin door. Hank set off for the main house. Aaron chased after his wife.

"Is there something we need to talk about?" he said.

He knew it was a dumb question, and not just because he'd disagreed with her in front of Hank. Jennifer and Aaron hadn't talked about anything substantial since she'd been back, not about the lodge or Wyoming, their jobs, their condo, or their relationship.

When she didn't answer, he tried again. "You seem upset."

"I'm tired." She set to work liberating a wine cork from a bottle of pinot noir. "And I miss the skunk."

Jeremiah had stayed with George. "I'm sorry."

"Jeremiah's not mine. I'll get over it."

"But he will be soon. Hang in there. George is including him with the lodge." He thought that would make her happy, but she didn't respond. Then Aaron caught a glimpse of the price tag on her wine bottle. Fifty dollars for a bottle of wine she was drinking alone. On a work night, at home. He nearly mentioned the price, then thought better of it. "You're not mad about me wanting to meet with that vet, are you?"

"Why would I be?"

It was a trick question—he knew it, he hated it, and he ignored it. "Good. Because it shouldn't surprise you."

"I was hoping we'd be a team—the quarterback and his blocker." She threw her voice to mimic Aaron's. "*I'd* love an introduction,

Hank." She resumed her normal voice. "What's that expression? There's no "I" in team?"

Aaron felt his own ire rising, plus a flicker of foreboding. "Meeting with someone is not a big deal, Jennifer."

"*We'll* see."

He took a deep breath, then released it. "While you were in Story, I bought Hank's Jeepster. You know, the one he brought to show me this morning. I got a great price on it. I've decided to call it DeMarcus Ware."

She slammed the wine opener into the drawer. "Congratulations to you and DeMarcus."

He tried to keep his voice pleasant. But he couldn't pretend he wasn't a little mad. "Why don't you look for a car? No reason to keep sinking money into a rental."

Jennifer frowned. "I want my MINI Cooper. I'd rather wait to be reunited with it." She rinsed her new wine glass with tap water.

Jennifer was obsessed with her MINI Cooper. The little car was gorgeous. But he wondered how long it would stay that way at the lodge. He didn't voice his concerns, though, because it was up to her. "Want me to get it shipped for you?"

She hesitated, then said, "No. I'll take care of it." She tilted the wine bottle over the glass, and the liquid made glug-glug-glug noises.

He braved continuing their taboo topics. "Have you put in your notice with Vivian at work?" Then he popped the top on a can of Saddle Bronc Brown from Blacktooth Brewing and put the other five beers in the refrigerator.

She kept her eyes on the wine glass. "Not until I exhaust my paid time off."

"Okay. Well, what did Quentin say when you talked to him about the DA job?"

"He wasn't happy."

"I'll bet." Aaron's anger started to ebb. He wanted to get back to good with Jennifer. "I'm sorry. I'm sure that was hard."

"Yes, it was." She swirled the wine in her glass, watching the legs flow slowly down the side.

"How about our condo?"

Jennifer drank a sip so big it was more like a chug. "I think we should lease it."

"Okay. Have you posted it anywhere yet?"

"Not yet." She added quickly, "But I've got it."

"I appreciate it. And have I mentioned I'm really, really glad you're here?"

She gave him a tight smile. "I'm glad to be with you."

Her answer sounded hollow, although on the outside it appeared solid. "Are you going to work on George's case tonight?"

"Nothing to work on yet. Kid is drafting our discovery requests tonight."

"Want to watch Thursday Night Football with me? The Buccaneers are playing the Panthers." Jennifer used to love to curl up and sleep on his chest while he watched a game. It might be a good way to smooth things over and reconnect. Not that he had any particular interest in the teams playing. He was a Titans fan, remained loyal to the Lions, and followed the Texans. But he devoured all football, at every level, any chance he got.

"No thanks. I think I'll do some writing."

While he was disappointed, writing was a positive sign. He didn't want to pressure her, but he couldn't keep the hopeful note out of his voice. "Really? I wasn't sure you were going to do any writing. That's great."

"I'd be doing more if I hadn't gotten steamrolled into this thing with George." She buried her nose in her glass.

"You don't want to represent him?"

She sighed. "I'm not in private practice, Aaron. I'm a prosecutor who puts bad guys away. It shouldn't be a surprise this isn't my thing."

"George is in a bad spot."

"I realize that."

Aaron backed off. "I get it. Thank you for helping him."

She carried her wine and laptop bag to the far corner of the couch. He watched as she arranged a workstation, including headphones, which she donned without another word.

Aaron watched her out of the corner of his eye. Pushing her wouldn't do any good. When Jennifer shut him out, he was out until she decided to let him in again. He turned the TV to the game, leaned against a pile of pillows and the wall behind the bed, and worked his way through half the six-pack, sneaking glances at his wife every few minutes as he analyzed and argued with the commentators over players, play calling, and game strategy. At halftime, the game was close, but he just wasn't into it. He turned the TV off and went to check on Jennifer.

She was out cold, curled into a ball with her laptop beside her.

"Jennifer?"

She didn't stir. He took her empty wine glass to the kitchen, rinsed it out, and corked the half empty bottle. He returned to her, sitting on the other side of the laptop. Even the weight of his body on the couch didn't wake her. He touched the keys on her laptop. It awoke from screensaver mode. He was curious to see how far she'd gotten with her writing and excited about her return to it after so many years away. She'd been very good once, and he'd been sure it was her destiny. Maybe it still was. After a moment of hesitation, he typed in her password, TNGURL76.

A Microsoft Word document was open on the screen. The cursor blinked in slowmo on a blank page. He accessed the Window pulldown. No other documents were open. A deep ache took hold of his heart.

Jennifer hadn't written a single word.

SIXTEEN

STORY, Wyoming

JENNIFER WOKE on Friday the thirteenth with her heart racing from a bad dream. *Another one.* She was three-for-three on nights in Wyoming with nightmares and was feeling the sleep deprivation. This time, though, she remembered parts of it, unlike the others. The rapid pops of semi-automatic gunfire. Shrill screaming. Pain in her knee. The scent of earth. Grass on her palms. And a snake that looked ready to strike. Not a live snake though. This was a picture of a snake with some words or letters below it. Like the one on the sticker in the back window of the WYO Rides truck. Had that been what triggered this nightmare? Sweat trickled down her chest. But it had seemed so real. Too real. A memory from one of her cases perhaps? Overidentifying with the victims? Whatever it was, nightly terrors weren't going to make her love Wyoming. Maybe this would be the last of them.

She rolled toward Aaron. The room was bitingly cold, which wasn't a good match for her night sweats. So much for the good heater Maggie had promised. But Aaron's body was crazy warm, and she snuggled into him. She hated that they had gotten sideways the night before. Their conversation about all the things she had no intention of doing in Houston had terrified her. Aaron seemed to have accepted her misleading answers, though, and she hadn't told a single outright lie. She was here to reconcile with him and convince him to return to Houston. That wasn't going to happen if she fought with him. Brutal truth would have gotten her nowhere last night. But she knew she had to give him more space to do the things he wanted. Like get an old Jeepster. She hadn't done a very good job of that. *Old habits die hard.* She was just so scared he was auguring further into Wyoming. But she would do better. She would.

She nipped his shoulder blade. "Aaron? Are you awake?"

He flipped and was crouched over her on all-fours in a blink. He kissed her nose. "Good morning, world's cutest nose."

She laughed. "I need to get moving. I'm meeting Kid at 8:30. Do you need a ride into Sheridan?"

His eyes bored into hers. "No."

That's right. He had his new baby, DeMarcus Ware. *It will be okay.* That had to be her new attitude about everything. *It will all be okay.* He could either bring the monster back to Houston or keep it as their vacation vehicle here. "Are you going back to sub at that clinic today?"

"No."

"Can you say anything else besides no?"

"No."

She screwed up her mouth. "Can we buy the lodge and stay in Wyoming?"

He frowned. "Tricky. But yes."

She sighed and wriggled out from under him, grabbing her iPhone and standing. "It was worth a try."

He tugged at her hand. "Don't you have a little bit of time left?"

She glanced at her phone. It was already 7:30. "Honestly, no. It will take me forty-five minutes to get to Kid's, and I have to at least brush my teeth and hair." She slipped from his grasp.

She took two steps and tripped over something big, warm, and hairy. *Liam.* The dog didn't seem to mind, and its tail started thumping the floor. Her next step was into a puddle. She groaned and hot footed past it.

"Dogs that can't hold their tinkle should be outside. Aaron, there's a mess in aisle one." She slipped into the bathroom.

From the other side of a closed door, she heard him say, "Got it."

Jennifer turned on the shower. She checked her phone while the water heated. Messages had stacked up last night when she'd fallen asleep on the couch. She shot off replies.

To her mother: *Still in Wyoming. We may buy a place here.* That wasn't a lie. They had a contract, but the lodge wasn't theirs yet. So "may" was still the most accurate word. *Hank is doing great and says hello. I love you.*

To her twin: *Miss you, Justin. Now, please be responsible and quit impregnating your wife. Sheesh.*

To Quentin: *Thanks for the updates. I'll be in touch with my final decision by the deadline or before.*

To her boss Vivian: *Any problem with me doing pro bono work while I'm on PTO? I don't want to violate my employment agreement, but I have a friend in trouble in Wyoming and I'd like to try to help him.*

And, finally, to Alayah: *Aaron is good—happiest I've seen him in a long time—but I want him to come home with me more than ever. Been roped into a criminal defense thing. What's up with you? Miss you. Love you.*

She hopped in the shower. A moment later, the door opened.

"Lake Liam has been cleaned up. Dog is outside. Cat is MIA. Coffee is brewing."

"Thanks. How can Katya be missing in a one room cabin?" She felt a sharp pang of missing Jeremiah. A skunk had come into her life and was already gone. How awesome would it have been if George would have let her keep him? But she couldn't, not when they went back to Houston. Or could she? He'd miss being outside, but she could get a leash and take him on long walks. She'd have to look at their condo rules. And the city ordinances.

"Cats are mysterious creatures." She heard his weight settle on the commode. "Pretend I'm not in here."

His presence made her chest feel tight. It wasn't that Jennifer minded sharing the bathroom. It reminded her of their early days, when life was simple, the most important thing was each other, and their apartment bathroom had been even smaller than this one, with the toilet practically in the shower. But she could picture her phone, sitting face up and wide awake on the counter, open to her messages, where she'd just sent a couple of incriminating ones. And she knew that Aaron would think nothing of casually browsing her phone, just like she would with his.. She had to distract him before it happened. She also knew she had to come clean with him, soon, about how she'd left things in Houston—suspended, not terminated—when things were calm and good between them, and they were talking face to face.

Water started splashing into the sink from the faucet.

"So, honey, what are your plans for today?" She used a chirpy voice to get his attention.

He didn't answer her.

Is he reading? Please don't be reading. Please, please, please don't be reading. She raised her voice. "Yo, Aaron, what are you doing today?"

"Sorry. I was brushing my teeth. I haven't completely decided yet." The faucet turned off.

She worked shampoo into her hair. "I think I'm going to drag Kid with me to interview people Hadley worked with and see if we can catch up with his daughter."

"She's a piece of work. I told you about the things she said, but I didn't tell you what she did. She brought a cat into the clinic, not even hers—something feral—and pretended it was hurt, to try to get pain pills for herself."

"What'd you do?" She started rinsing. It was harder, but she could still hear him.

"Paid for the cat's treatment myself and sent her home unhappy."

Jennifer put conditioner in her hair and soaped her body up. The toilet flushed. Water ran in the sink then stopped again. She was almost in the clear. *It will be okay.* "Be sure you close the door behind you and don't let the cold air in."

"Gotcha."

As soon as he was gone, she rinsed her body and hair, then wrapped herself in a towel barely big enough for her. For Aaron it would be like drying off with a dishrag. She jumped out and looked for her phone.

It wasn't on the counter.

Her heart rate shot up. *No, no, no.* She needed to open up to Aaron, but not because she was busted by her texts. She hadn't done anything wrong by delaying her confession. Not really. She just didn't want him mad at her. Or to hurt him.

"Aaron?" The tone of his answer would tell her whether he'd read them or not. She held her breath.

He stuck his head back in. "What?"

"Cold air."

He slipped inside.

"Have you seen my phone?"

He patted his jeans pockets, then nodded. "Habit. I thought it was mine." He handed it to her.

"Oh, good. Thank you."

"Is that it?"

"Yes. That's all."

He gave her a strange look and left.

She finished getting ready, alternatively talking herself into and out of believing everything really was going to be okay.

***

THE INTERSTATE WAS WIDE and empty, the speed limit seventy-five miles per hour. Jennifer set the Fusion's cruise to seventy-eight. Driving to Sheridan would take half an hour at that speed. The roadway was completely free of snow, and the south-facing hills were nearly clear, too. Deer and pronghorn antelope were grazing the open patches. The sky was an eye-popping blue. Giant hills undulated in all directions, leading to the mountains in the west and buttes to the east. Sheridan was due north. She glanced at the thermometer. It was already forty-five degrees. *Heat wave.* Houston was probably in the nineties. She didn't mind the break from the heat —or the far superior views—even if she wasn't looking for a perma-nent relocation.

Aaron had acted completely normal after her phone scare. She'd scribbled a quick gratitude message for him on a napkin on her way out the door, while he was in the shower. *I'm grateful you let me take the first shower. <3 Hot water!* Tonight, she'd bite the bullet and apol-ogize to him for last night. For whatever she'd done after Hank's party, too. Maybe she'd even try to write again. *Try* being the opera-tive word, as her efforts the night before hadn't yielded a single soli-tary word.

It hadn't exactly been a confidence boost. She'd had the best of intentions, but when she put her hands on the keys, her mind had gone blank. So blank that it was all she could do to finish her wine before she fell asleep. Once upon a time she'd been bursting with ideas. Half the fun of watching TV for her was the running critique she'd imagine writing for the screenwriters. Didn't it just figure? Now that she had the time to write a novel, she had writer's block.

She looked into the backseat. Empty. She felt an ache in her chest. Toting Jeremiah around with her yesterday had been fun. He seemed to bond with her, too. She hoped he was happy back with George.

She sighed and pressed Kids' number in her Recents. She'd make good use of her drive time, even if they were due to meet when she got to town.

When Kid answered, she put her phone on handsfree. Skipping the niceties, she got straight to the point. "Did you get the discovery request filed and delivered to the county attorney's office?"

"Good morning. Yes."

"Has Pootie called yet?"

"No."

"Shoot. I wanted whatever info they had on Hadley. Like where he worked, so we could go talk to his co-workers ASAP."

"We don't need to hear from Pootie for that. Hadley owned a money management firm."

Jennifer was incredulous. "How do you know this?"

"My mom was a client of his."

Small towns. She couldn't decide whether she loved them or hated them. She guessed she lacked sufficient data yet to decide. She'd grown up in Nashville, gone to school in Knoxville and Waco, and worked in Houston. The *smallest* of them was many, many times the size of Sheridan.

She said, "Go on—do you have a firm name, phone number, and address?"

"I'll text you. It's safer."

A gust of wind blew the rental car over the rumble strips. Luckily the shoulder was dry and free of roadkill. It was amazing to her that there were so incredibly many deer in Wyoming. By all rights, they should be extinct, as bad as they were at staying out of the way of fast-moving vehicles.

She white knuckled the Fusion back into the lane. "Good idea."

"Anything I can do now?"

"Set an appointment up for first thing this morning at Hadley's office, if you don't mind."

"I already did. For 8:30. I was going to text you to go there instead of my place."

"Wow. You're a mind reader." Kid was definitely growing on her. "Are you joining me?"

"I want to. There's a lot I can learn by watching you."

Most attorneys working pro bono would try to minimize their hours. She liked that Kid was all-in. She hoped whoever she found to represent George would keep Kid on the case, too. "Sounds good."

"Texting you the address now."

"Thanks. See you soon."

At the first red light after she exited the interstate in Sheridan, Jennifer mapped to Prescott Financial Services from the address Kid texted. Five minutes later, she pulled in behind him at a small brick building. There was even less snow on the ground in town than there had been near the interstate, but the bushes lining the front of the office were still frosted.

Jennifer walked to the door and waited for Kid. She'd left the down jacket in the car. How could forty-five feel too warm for a coat? "Good morning."

He beamed. Was it her imagination or had he grown an inch since the day before? At this rate, he'd be shaving by Christmas. "Hi, Mrs. Herrington. Ms. Herrington. Miss Herrington? Crap. Should I just call you ADA Herrington?"

Kid was a breath of fresh air, at a time when she was finding it harder to breathe than usual. "You should be calling me Jennifer. Are you ready?"

"Great. Very. Thanks."

She pushed open a glass door into a small vestibule where she opened another glass door. Inside, an unmanned receptionist desk was centered in a narrow room. The colors were one hundred percent mountain themed. Plush forest green carpeting. Pine chairs in the waiting area. Dark paneling from the floor to the chair rail. A wallpaper border up top with a repeating pattern of bears, moose, and elk.

"Welcome to Prescott Financial Services. May I help you?" The voice came from Jennifer's right. She turned and saw an elfin woman with a white cap of hair watering hanging plants. A big satin bow closed her blouse under her chin. The shirt was tucked into a pair of houndstooth pants. Patent leather toes peeked from beneath the hem.

"Hello. I'm Jennifer Herrington and this is Kid James. I believe someone was expecting us?"

The woman's eyes crinkled shut when she smiled. "Come in. Wesley talked to me. How are you, young man?" She stopped short of bussing his cheeks, but her tone suggested she would have liked to.

"Great, Mrs. Murray. How are you?"

"I'm good, thank you. Let's go in the conference room. I made fresh coffee. It's just Harriett and me now, with Hadley gone. Is it okay if you talk to me first?"

Jennifer couldn't help smiling back. "Perfect, all the way around."

The front doors opened, and someone entered.

Mrs. Murray said, "May I—oh, hello, Mr. O'Leary. I have your payment for you right here." She bustled to the reception desk.

A man joined her. Jennifer glanced at him. He was tiny. Shorter than Hank's partner Gene Sobeleski and far less brawny, although this man didn't seem skeletal. Just lean. She could imagine him as a circus acrobat. Or a cat burglar, able to maneuver in tight spaces. He was dressed casually in pressed khakis and a golf-style shirt sweaty at the pit of its long sleeves, a light jacket over one arm. And he was dark-complected, which was unusual for the area. Black hair, nearly black eyes, and skin like a browned nut.

"Who do I talk to about ending your lease now that Hadley is out of the picture and the firm will be closing?" he said.

Mrs. Murray didn't react. "Closing? That's news to me. I'll get Mr. Prescott's attorney to contact you."

"Do that. No offense to Ms. Harriett," he said, wiping beads of moisture from his upper lip. "But I don't see how this place is even still open. I've got a deal pending to tear the building down and put a Kentucky Fried Chicken in. It's worth big bucks. So, I won't be giving you a single day's grace on the rent. If you pay late, you're out."

That got Jennifer's attention. Both because most leases didn't prevent sale of a property, and because Sheridan had a serious shortage of chicken, which Aaron loved. He would have preferred a Popeye's, but was it wrong of her to root for the KFC?

Mrs. Murray handed him an envelope. Her smile was bright and fake. "Here you go. See you next month."

He nodded, tucked the envelope in the pocket of his shirt, and hurried out.

Mrs. Murray grumbled and shook her head. "Tim O'Leary was a good electrician. He's a lousy landlord. He's been trying to break the lease and raise our rent every month and pressuring Hadley to move out by refusing to fix things. One month he didn't pay the utilities and our electricity got turned off. Hadley had to go pay it himself." She harrumphed. "And Harriett Staples is the best financial advisor in Sheridan County. Now that Hadley's passed, anyway."

Kid looked uncomfortable. Jennifer stayed mum, but she made a mental note to look into O'Leary and get a copy of the weird lease. People had killed for less.

The two attorneys followed Mrs. Murray down a short hall made cloying by the chemical perfume of a floral plug-in air freshener. Jennifer put her fingers under her nose to block it. She noticed a kitchenette and break room on one side of the hall. A large flier was posted on the door. It read COME LEARN HOW TO INVEST IN YOUR FUTURE WITH PRESCOTT FINANCIAL in a casual font, all caps. Jennifer stopped to examine it more closely. There was a stock photo of happy people on a cruise ship. Something about the flier kept her rooted in place.

"Are you coming?" Mrs. Murray asked.

"Yes, of course." The free public seminar was scheduled for the following week. "Are you still holding the seminar?"

"What?"

Jennifer pointed at the flier.

"Oh, yes. That's Harriett's flier. The seminar is all her doing. She's expecting a nice crowd."

Jennifer hurried after Mrs. Murray. They entered a conference room across from the kitchenette. The room departed from the mountain theme but built on the green carpet. Jewel tones. A glossy cherry conference table big enough for eight people with a matching side table. Walls painted plum. Rolling armchairs upholstered in a coordinating shade of green. A fake Ficus tree stood in one corner. Aspirational vacation photographs adorned the walls, as if it were a travel agency. Greece. Paris. A cruise ship in front of a glacier. The Great Wall of China.

Mrs. Murray lined up three coffee cups on the side table and held up a carafe. "Cream or sugar?"

"Yes, please." Jennifer set her bag down by a chair at the end of the table closest to the window.

"Black." Kid took the chair beside Jennifer.

Jennifer helped Mrs. Murray with the coffee, delivering one to Kid along with an arch look. So far, she really liked him, but she had him pegged as the only child of a single mother who doted on him. To his credit, he seemed to get her message. His neck pinked again.

When they were all settled around the table, Jennifer laid a pen beside her yellow pad. Kid had his pad, too. Even if he took notes, she needed something for her hands. It helped her think.

She smiled at Mrs. Murray. "Did Kid tell you we represent George Nichols, Mrs. Murray?"

"Just Bonnie will do."

"Bonnie then."

"Yes, he told me." She frowned. "I'll be honest with you, Ms. . . . ."

"Jennifer."

"Jennifer, then. I love my job here. But Hadley wasn't always the nicest man. I liked his ex-wife Shelly a lot better than I did him. I stayed in touch with her even after their divorce. George made her really happy. And Hadley—well, Hadley never did. She was rightly angry with him for being so ugly to George all the time. It only got worse after she died, from what I heard. So, I don't know if George killed Hadley or not, and nobody deserves to be murdered, but Shelly would have wanted me to help George."

"Thank you, Bonnie. And, if it makes you feel any better, I don't believe George killed Hadley. I hope that by showing he didn't do it, we make law enforcement focus on finding who did."

Jennifer watched herself in her mind's eye as if from a distance, marveling at the words from her mouth. She was defending a man charged of first-degree murder. If someone had asked her only one month ago whether this would have been possible, she would have laughed her head off.

She continued. "Because you're right. No one deserves to be murdered, and whoever did this to Hadley should be held accountable. Our laws exist to protect us all."

That last part was a lot more like her normal self, but she knew she meant every word of it. And that it felt shockingly good. She didn't even recognize herself. She'd probably need therapy after this experience. Like someone who'd made it through a temporary bout of schizophrenia or multiple personality disorder. Not that there was such a thing. But if there was, this was how it would feel.

Bonnie cradled her coffee in both hands. She nodded, then held up a finger. Tears welled in her eyes. After a few seconds, she said, "Sorry. I wasn't expecting that."

"It's okay. We aren't in a rush." Jennifer crossed her ankles out of superstition because she was lying. She was always in a rush when it came to work. "Are you ready to talk or do you need a minute?"

"I'm ready. Let's do this." Bonnie gave a sharp nod.

"It shouldn't take too long." Jennifer caught Kid's eye and nodded at his note pad and pen. He picked up the pen and nodded back. "You mentioned that there was some bad blood between Hadley and George. Did you ever hear George threaten to harm Hadley in any way?"

Bonnie pursed her lips. "No. I don't even think I ever saw them together. All of my information came from Shelly and Hadley."

Kid began writing furiously.

"Did Shelly ever tell you that George had threatened to hurt Hadley?"

"Oh, no."

"Or that he *had* hurt Hadley?"

"Never." Bonnie put her hands flat on the table.

"What did Hadley say about George?"

"Nothing *to* me. And I already told you about the things Shelly repeated from him. But I also overheard him saying things on the phone."

"Like what?" Jennifer asked.

"Like that George deserved to die for . . . for . . . for killing Shelly."

Jennifer patted Bonnie's hand. "Was he talking to George when he said that?"

She nodded. "To George and to other people. He said it a lot."

"Okay. Thank you. What can you tell me about his daughter Denise?"

"Don't bother that poor child." Bonnie stiffened and pulled her hands into her lap. Then her shoulders sagged. "She was always such a cute little girl. I used to sneak her candy from my drawer when she'd come up here. She loved Starburst chews. And now, well, she's just been through enough."

Jennifer was careful not to agree she would leave Denise out of it. "Why do you say that?"

"Her parents splitting up did a number on her. That girl loved her father. I promise you, she would never do anything to hurt him."

Mentally, Jennifer put a big star next to Denise's name.

"She used to babysit me," Kid said.

His voice startled Jennifer. He'd been so quiet she'd forgotten he was there. "Oh? Did you know her?"

"Yeah. A little."

Bonnie gave him a stern look. "Then you know what a nice, sweet girl she's always been."

"Um, yeah." He looked away from Bonnie and doodled on his note pad.

Jennifer had great peripheral vision and saw he'd written HELLION. She added a second mental star to Denise.

"Bonnie, what about other people who might have had conflicts with Hadley? Did anyone else argue with him, threaten him, dislike him, or get mad at him that you remember?"

Bonnie tore her eyes away from Kid. "Hmm. Mainly just Shelly and George. But sometimes clients would be unhappy if their investments didn't do as well as they'd liked."

"Any clients in particular?"

"Lately?"

"Anytime. Someone upset enough that they bad mouthed Hadley or threatened him. Or made you uncomfortable."

"More coffee?" She stood up. Jennifer shook her head. So did Kid. Bonnie picked up the carafe. "William Marton." She filled her cup.

Jennifer wrote down the name. "Tell me about him."

Bonnie sat back down. "This last summer, he threatened to sue Hadley."

"Over what?"

"He said Hadley shouldn't have lost his money. He came in several times and the two of them would scream at each other at the tops of their lungs. Once, I asked Harriett if I should call the cops. She said they would work it out."

"Did they?"

"I guess. He didn't come back."

Jennifer chewed the inside of her lip, thinking. "Anyone else?"

"No. Even when he lost money, he'd make it back. Mostly people put up with him because he was good at his work."

"My mom did," Kid said.

That earned him a smile from Bonnie.

"How long have you worked here, Bonnie?" Jennifer said.

"Twenty-one years in February."

"And Harriett? What is her role?"

"She's a financial advisor, too. She came on with us about ten years ago."

"Is she a partner?"

"I'm not sure. You'll have to ask her."

Jennifer turned to Kid. "Can you think of anything else, Kid?"

Kid looked up from his note taking. He pointed at his chest and mouthed *me?* Jennifer nodded.

He cleared his throat and spoke in his deep, deep voice. "Will Prescott Financial stay in business?"

Bonnie looked at her hands. "Harriett says she doesn't know yet."

Jennifer jotted down notes to herself, her notepad coming in handy after all. *Figure out who inherits firm. Talk to the landlord, Tim O'Leary. Get a copy of the lease.*

"Thank you, Bonnie. For talking to us and for the coffee. Could you send Harriett in now?"

Bonnie stood. She wrung her hands together. "Is George all right? He has a tendency to drink too much, I hear."

"He'll be fine." Jennifer smiled at her.

Bonnie nodded. "That's good." Then she disappeared, leaving the door open.

When she was sure Bonnie was far enough away not to overhear, Jennifer spoke to Kid in a low voice. "What did you think?"

"She's the nicest little old lady in the world."

"Besides that."

"That Denise has always been a train wreck. She used to water down my mom's vodka when she babysat me. Random guys would come and go the whole time." His phone vibrated on the table. He turned it over. "Call coming in from the County Attorney's office."

"Good. Maybe they're ready for you."

"Hello?" Kid said.

"Knock, knock." The throaty voice at the door sounded young and twangy. Midwestern.

Jennifer pointed at Kid, then at the hallway. He nodded and left.

A young woman—late twenties? Early thirties?—with forearm crutches stood inside the doorway. Her almost-black hair hung in a thick curtain to her shoulders. She had eyes so blue that Jennifer would have thought contact lenses if not for her glasses. She still wasn't convinced.

"I heard you want to talk to me. I'm Harriett Staples."

Jennifer smiled at her. "Jennifer Herrington. Please, join me."

Harriett moved swiftly to the chair nearest the door. She rested her crutches against the empty chair beside her.

Jennifer walked Harriett through the same explanation she'd used with Bonnie. "I appreciate you talking to us."

Harriett's smile was stiff. She took off her glasses and cleaned them on the sleeve of her shirt. It was red and sheer with a black undershirt. "I don't have much to say."

"Well, how about you start by telling me what you do here and how long you've worked with Hadley?"

"I'm a certified financial planner. I've worked here for nine years, ever since I moved to Sheridan."

"Where are you from?"

"Des Moines."

"How did you meet Hadley?"

"At a seminar."

Her answers were taut and quick, like volleys from a well-strung tennis racket. Jennifer decided she needed to slow her down. Leaning forward on her elbows, Jennifer said, "I hear he wasn't very popular."

Her nostrils flared. "People are assholes."

"You liked him."

She swallowed. "We had our ups and downs, but I'm still here."

An odd answer, but she was beginning to realize Harriett was an odd woman. "Do you know of anyone who you think would have wanted to hurt him?"

"Besides your client?"

Jennifer half-smiled. "We can talk about him in a moment."

Harriett's eyes flashed. She pushed her sleeves up. "No, let's talk about him now. He was a mean drunk who stole Mr. Prescott's wife and then killed her. I know everyone is entitled to a legal defense, but I don't know how you can do it and live with yourself."

Jennifer had learned long ago to ignore personal attacks from witnesses. Still, Harriett's words stung like a slap across her face. "Did you ever hear my client threaten or see him harm Hadley?"

"I heard Hadley when he was on the phone with George, and from his responses, it sure sounded like George was threatening him."

"In what way?"

Her tone was reptilian. "When Hadley said, 'you couldn't kill me if I was tied up and unconscious.' Is that good enough for you?"

"And you heard George's voice on the other end of the phone?"

Harriett blinked slowly like an owl. "No. But Hadley said it was him."

Jennifer gave her a whole smile. "Back to my earlier question. Did you ever hear or see my client threaten Hadley or try to harm him?"

"No." Harriett's voice was sullen.

"Do you have any first-hand knowledge that George threatened or harmed him?"

"He stabbed Hadley to death."

"Leaving aside Hadley's death for now, do you have any first-hand knowledge that George threatened or harmed Hadley?"

Harriett grabbed her crutches. "I don't have anything more to say."

Jennifer held her hand out, palm down. "Will this firm be remaining open?"

Harriett slid her arms into the crutches. "I wasn't a partner. I suppose if someone buys it from whoever inherits it, it will. But it won't be me. I don't have the money."

"Was the landlord pressuring Hadley to move?"

She snorted. "The man is a weasel. Hadley ignored him."

"Do you know of anyone besides George who you think would have wanted to hurt Hadley?"

"Besides him? No."

"What about his daughter?"

Harriett snorted. "She was usually too high to care about him. But they seemed to get along fine. He was supporting her, for the most part."

"No disagreements between them?"

"I mean, she's a drug addict. Yes, there were disagreements. But no threats or violent fights."

"William—" Jennifer read her notes "—Marton."

"What about him?"

"I heard he was upset with Hadley."

"I guess."

"Bonnie wanted to call the cops on him."

"Bonnie is a drama queen."

"You see it differently?"

"Marton lost money. He flipped his lid. He got over it. Lots of people get upset when the markets don't favor them." Harriett rotated on a crutch and headed for the door. Over her shoulder, she said, "I hope your client rots in prison for what he did. Do you know how hard it will be for me to find a job in finance in this town if this place closes?"

She hurried out before Jennifer could respond.

"Thank you," Jennifer called after her.

Harriett didn't answer.

On her legal pad, Jennifer wrote *Find out what has Harriett Staples so emotional.*

Kid walked back in. "The County has our discovery ready. Did I miss anything?"

Jennifer's antenna were up, but in reality, Harriett hadn't told her much. "That remains to be seen."

SEVENTEEN

SHERIDAN, Wyoming

AARON SMILED at the woman behind the counter at Sheridan Vet Clinic. He opened his mouth to speak, but she beat him to it.

"Do you have an appointment?" Her voice matched her appearance. Bleak. Leathery skin with as many furrows as a tilled field. Hair like steel wool. Watery eyes. Lips stuck in a permanent downturn. A drab cotton shirt washed so many times it had no shape.

"I do. I'm—"

"Pet's name?"

"I'm actually here to see Doc Billy."

"You and everybody else. But we have to get through the paperwork first."

"I don't have a pet with me. I have a meeting with him."

"Why didn't you just say so?"

"I tr . . . you're right. My bad. I'm Aaron Herrington."

She used her middle finger to point him to the chairs in a waiting area crowded with metal-legged chairs. Most of them were taken.

And most of the people in the formed plastic seats had animals in their laps or in front of them on the floor. One chair remained, in between two others occupied by men that rivalled Aaron in size. Their thighs overlapped their own chairs onto the empty one.

Aaron remained standing. He looked behind him, then backed toward a standing set of shelves that displayed pet food, dental chews, deodorizers, pill pockets, and animal toys. His foot splashed in something that was definitely not water. The smell of cat urine was unmistakable. None of the pet owners offered an apology or eye contact. Aaron stepped from the puddle. He glanced outside. A teenage boy was coaxing a steer into an examination pen by twisting the animal's tail to move it along. A woman who looked like she could out arm wrestle Aaron had a sheep slung over her neck and was holding its front legs in one hand and back ones in the other.

In his mind's eye, he pictured his own practice back in Houston. Soothing, piped in classical music. An attendant whose sole responsibility was to anticipate clean-up needs and take care of them before they hit the floor. Air fresheners that misted the scent of lilacs at timed intervals. On sale items that included thunder blankets, dog entertainment consoles, canine cologne, pet jewelry and skincare, and, of course, ecologically conscious and organic desserts.

A wave of revulsion surged through him. He *hated* his clinic. Luckily, his partnership contract included a buyout clause with an escalator, so extricating himself was turning out to be fairly simple. He'd given his partners notice that he was activating the clause a week ago, and the closing on the buyout would be in six weeks. That still seemed like forever to him, when he was paying to have a temp vet cover his spot and waiting on the cash. Cash he could spend to buy a practice here. He rotated his neck. How had he let himself stray so far from his upbringing on a farm and the big plans he'd made in vet school? A large animal practice hadn't been feasible in central Houston, but here he could have the best of both worlds.

He belonged somewhere like this.

He started thinking about what he'd change if it was his. Bigger chairs in the waiting room for starters. Maybe a new receptionist. He'd barely gotten started on his list when a voice interrupted his daydreams.

"Dr. Aaron Herrington?" a man said.

A tall, blond man stood in front of him. He was lanky bordering on beanpole. Maybe a forward for the basketball team, but he would have been crushed on the football field. "Doc Billy?"

The two men shook hands. Aaron felt hostile glares lasering into his back from all the people in the waiting room who'd arrived before him.

"I gotta admit, I Googled you," Doc Billy said. "Detroit Lions, huh?"

The staring from the peanut gallery went from hostile to curious.

Aaron smiled. "Not for long. Too many head injuries."

"I've always told people you'd have to get hit in the head to want to become a vet. And now here you are to prove my story true."

Aaron laughed. "Happy to be of service."

"Follow me. I've only got a minute. Full house today, but I appreciate your interest."

"I understand."

Aaron single filed behind Doc Billy through a doorway, down a narrow hall, and into a cramped office with two Brigham Young University diplomas on the wall—one in Biology and one for a DVM from the Idaho campus. Stacks of papers were everywhere. On shelves. The floor. The desk. Even the chairs in front of the desk. What little space wasn't taken by dead trees was covered with random animal paraphernalia. Aaron saw a horseshoe, a cattle ear tag, a coiled woven loaner leash, and Ivermectin samples.

He loved it.

"Just shove the junk anywhere and have a seat," Doc Billy said.

Aaron put a stack carefully on the floor before he sat. "So, you're selling and moving on, I hear."

"Yeah. Sheridan is a nice town, but my wife had some trouble here, and I lost my shirt with a shyster who invested my money negligently and refused to make it right. I'm suing the firm, but that won't help my cash flow in the short run."

"Sorry to hear that."

"It'll be okay. We want to be close to family, in Utah. My dad has a practice there he wants me to take over." Doc Billy pawed through the mess in front of him and came up with bound papers in a transparent red plastic cover. "Here's a prospectus, of sorts. It gives you all the information on the clinic's performance and customer base. My cell number is in there if you have questions."

The crusty receptionist stuck her head in the door. "We've got a problem. Patrick Flint just brought in his puppy. He took him over to Dr. Carson first. I have the x-rays. Dr. Carson said the dog has a broken hip at the growth plate and needs pins."

"Ouch. Thanks, Loretta. Tell him I'm coming." After she shut the door, Doc Billy said, "My staff is top notch, although Loretta's an acquired taste. I can probably free up a few more minutes after I check on this puppy and a cat that's coming out from under anesthesia, if you want to look through that prospectus while you wait."

"Perfect." Aaron pictured the wriggly yellow lab he'd met only two nights before. The puppy was the apple of Patrick's eye. He felt terrible for the dog and its owner. "Good luck with the puppy. Those are tough surgeries."

"You've done them?"

"A fair number."

Doc Billy nodded, looking thoughtful, and left. Aaron began reading through the prospectus. The financial statements had been issued by a CPA firm in town attesting to their validity. The bottom line was healthy for a small-town practice, although it netted about one quarter of what Aaron was currently drawing annually. That was okay. He was looking to scale back. And if money was lean, he and Jennifer could operate the lodge. Lease the acreage for cattle grazing. Jennifer could practice law in Sheridan. He pulled up the website for the clinic on his phone. As he'd already seen, it was both a large and small animal practice, and, in addition to running the clinic, they did farm and ranch visits.

He imagined what it would be like to have a paid reason to drive around the county-side and get to see all the properties.

Pretty darn awesome.

Jennifer was going to love this. She'd left him a gratitude message that morning. Granted, it was about hot water, not about having a hot husband, but it was progress. He couldn't wait to tell her about the clinic.

A knock sounded on the door.

Doc Billy poked his head back in. "Good. You're still here. Any questions?"

"Thanks. Just a few. Are you the only vet on staff?"

"No. I have a youngster that hired on with me two years ago. She's coming along fine, but it's far too early in her career for her to buy a practice. She's interested in staying under new ownership. I think it would help the clients through the transition, too."

"I imagine so."

The two men chatted about the challenges and opportunities the practice faced. When Aaron explained that he was newly arrived from Texas, Doc Billy related his experience as an outsider moving into the community from Utah, ten years before.

Finally, Doc Billy said, "How about you scrub in on this surgery? I've only done one before, and this puppy is awfully young."

"I'd love to." Aaron said, "And I'd like to make you an offer on the practice, subject to verifying the financial statements. And talking to my wife." He quoted a number five percent lower than the asking price in the prospectus.

Doc Billy stroked his chin. "I'll meet you halfway."

"Would it include the trailers, tractor, mobile van, and truck?"

"Yes. Everything."

"Could we close in seven weeks? The sale of my Houston practice to my partners closes in six."

"Works for me. I can call my attorney after the surgery and have her draw up the papers."

Aaron stood and stuck out his hand. "Sold. Unless my wife vetoes." *Which was a very real possibility. One he'd worry about later.*

Doc Billy laughed and shook Aaron's hand. "Come on, let's go take care of this puppy."

Aaron bounced down the hall behind Doc Billy, his mind already happily churning over how to broach the topic of purchasing the clinic with Jennifer.

EIGHTEEN

SHERIDAN, Wyoming

WHILE KID SWUNG over to the County Attorney's office for his discovery collection errand, Jennifer went back to his office and hunted down an address for Hadley's daughter. There was no phone listing for a Denise Prescott, so she texted Kid, asking if Denise had a different last name.

Little. His reply was almost instantaneous. *And she lives in a trailer park. Or she used to. I'd go with Mom to pick her up sometimes.* He gave her the name. Shangri-La Estates.

Jennifer was feeling crummy that she would have to start her search for George's replacement counsel soon. Kid deserved to see this case through, which she wouldn't be able to guarantee him. If she were in private practice, and if it were in a small town in Wyoming, she'd want him as her associate. He had a great attitude, he was smart, showed initiative, and worked hard, and he'd even taken having Jeremiah along in stride.

Jeremiah. Kid's office felt empty without him. She shot off a quick email to the office at the Houston condo building asking for a copy of the pet policy. If it didn't directly prohibit skunks, it would give her an argument to have him there.

Turning her attention back to the case, she inputted the name of the trailer park into Siri, who spit out directions. It was only a ten-minute drive away. Jennifer decided it would be best to interview Denise without Kid present, since the two knew each other already. She sent Kid another text: *I'm heading to Denise's place. Back soon.* She dashed out to the rental and made her way northwest of town—passing a well-groomed public golf course, which she decided she'd check out, if she ended up with any free time before she hustled Aaron back to Texas—and found the park easily. A sign out front confirmed it: SHANGRI-LA ESTATES. The fake palm trees and pink flamingoes on either side of the entrance matched the name but were incongruous with the silhouette of the stark Bighorn Mountains as a backdrop. She stopped at the trailer marked "office."

The man who came to the door was too large to fit in the frame. She couldn't imagine how the floor was holding up his bulk. She'd seen full sized cars that probably weighed less. Sun glinted off his Mr. Clean bald head. The tips of bird wings showed on either shoulder, stretching across his chest under his tank top. The tattoo had looked like a vat of ink and half a day's work.

"Yes?" He said.

"I'm trying to locate the residence of Denise Little. Siri brought me here."

"Siri doesn't know sic'em."

That one's going in the "someday novel" file. Maybe someday soon. "So, she doesn't live here?"

"Who wants to know?"

"Me. I'm Jennifer Herrington."

The man's attention flicked back to a television blaring from across the room. "Which tells me zippo, princess. Who wants to know?"

Jennifer bristled. "I'm investigating a matter related to her father." Luckily, she couldn't get disbarred in Wyoming since she wasn't licensed here. Besides, it was a true statement—if misleading.

He looked back at her with more interest. "That old dickhead? He's late on rent."

"He's dead."

He grunted. "Might explain why he's late. Police?"

"No. Private." Jennifer fished a twenty out of her shoulder bag. She held it out to him. "I really appreciate your time and trouble, sir."

The twenty disappeared in a ham-sized hand. He barked a laugh. "Drive until you dead end. She's on the right. You can't miss her trailer. Her boyfriend parks his camper out front." He grinned, revealing a missing canine tooth. "Don't tell her I sent you. She can be a little testy."

Jennifer cocked her head. "Big guy like you, scared of a little ole woman?"

"Hell, yes. You've got me shaking in my boots." He shut the door in her face.

Jennifer saluted him with the disrespectful finger, wishing he could see it through the door. Then she fired up the Fusion and cruised down the dirt road. The street appeared to be the only one in the park, and, by her count, there were about twenty sites. Mobile homes in varying states of disrepair lined each side. A few—a very few—looked new. Or less old, anyway. Most had seen better days. Some didn't look like they'd survive a trip to the dump.

She stopped one trailer short of the last site on the right just in case Denise was put off by the thought of a visitor. It gave her time to eyeball Denise's home without being eyeballed in return. Sure enough, there was a camper out front—if a pockmarked pickup with a wooden shed strapped into the bed could be called a camper. The trailer was of the same vein, with cinder block steps that almost made it up to the door of the half-sized unit.

Jennifer got out of the Fusion. With her purse over her shoulder and her notepad in hand, she walked toward Denise's mobile home. Her skin prickled like someone was watching her. She scanned the windows and doors ahead and then the ones on the other homes around her. No eyes were visible. Certainly not from Denise's place, where cardboard covered the windows from the inside. But she did detect an offensive odor. Her eyes started burning, and she realized that what she smelled was ammonia. She'd worked enough murder scenes that smelled like ammonia to know exactly what was going on in the trailer.

Denise's house was a meth lab. *Great.*

She climbed the DIY steps, knocked on the door, then retreated to solid ground ten feet away. There was no answer, no sound.

Jennifer shouted, "Denise Little? Are you in there? This is Jennifer Herrington. I'm here about your dad."

Still, there was no sound from inside. But she heard something around back. *Was Denise making a run for it?*

Jennifer weighed out how desperate she was to talk to Denise versus how much she didn't like the idea of getting beaten up by a crazed meth head. She came out in favor of pretty desperate. Enough to peak around the side of the house, anyway. Which was crazy. When had she started caring this much about George's case? But she did, and she had to check out the noise. In Houston, the cops would have handled this visit for her. But not here. Not as defense counsel. *Something else to appreciate about being a prosecutor.*

The going was rough. If she'd worn hiking boots, or even running shoes, she would have been moving briskly over the hard, hillocky ground. But she'd thought she was straight-up lawyering today, so she had on a pair of cute, zippered ankle boots with three-inch heels. She picked her way through the yard like it was filled with landmines. As she neared the corner of the house, she heard a deep, rumbling noise, like an engine. She half-expected Denise to come flying around on a four-wheeler or dirt bike, until the rumbling erupted into growling.

Loud, menacing growling.

Jennifer checked herself. No water bottle. No bear mace. No cattle prod. *As if.* Nothing to fend a dog off. Just her tiny purse and a pad of paper. Well, she wasn't waiting around to meet the animal and see if it wanted to be friends. She made a beeline for the rental, walking as fast as she could. She hadn't gone two steps before a big ball of muscle and teeth shot around the corner and straight at her. It was mostly white, with short hair and a big neck and head. A pit bull. As a rule, Jennifer didn't fear dogs, and she didn't believe all dogs of certain breeds were vicious. She did know, however, that some breeds had physical characteristics that, combined with training and environment, could make them lethal weapons. Pit bulls fell into that category. She broke into a run. She only had fifteen feet to go, but the driver's door was on the opposite side of the car. The dog had thirty feet and no heels.

The dog had the definite advantage.

She hadn't counted on the impact of adrenaline, though. She ran faster than she'd ever run before, without even stumbling or faltering in the grass and gravel. As she rounded the nose of the car, she steadied herself with a hand on the hood. Just when she thought she was going to make it safely, the dog launched itself through the air and over the car. It sailed past her, inches from her face. Its slobbery lips were pulled back in a snarl, and it snapped the air so close to her that she could have kissed it if she'd just leaned forward a little.

She screamed.

The dog landed, skidding five feet on the gravel before it scrambled to a stop. It wheeled to face her.

The delay of its landing had given her just enough time. Jennifer flipped up the door handle and wrenched the door open. With the door as her fulcrum, she slingshotted into the car. The dog lunged after her. Jennifer slammed the door shut. The dog never slowed down, and its body slammed into the car, yelping, cracking its head.

The collision didn't deter it long. It jumped up in a frenzy. Jennifer stared through the dog fluids smeared on the window. It was an amazing physical specimen, capable of ripping her to shreds. But rather than feeling upset at the dog, she felt sorry for it. Someone had trained it to act this way. It could have made a wonderful companion in the right household. *Could* have. Not now. Now it was a lethal weapon. Aaron had worked with many pits during his stints volunteering in a free spay and neuter program, and the mistreatment of some of the animals had gutted him so much that she was afraid they were going to end up fostering a pack of them in their condo.

This one was scratching the hound out of the metal on the Fusion. *That's going to cost me.* But the damage to the car was done, and she was safe, so, she stayed put for a moment while the dog raged on. She gave the surrounding homes and yards one more close inspection, looking for a strung-out woman in her late thirties making an escape.

Besides neighbors peering through gaps in curtains, she didn't see anyone.

So much for her visit to Denise. She put the Fusion in drive and pressed the accelerator, following the cul-de-sac in a semi-circle until she was pointing back toward the park exit and safety. She'd try again later—with mace and a squirt bottle of water.

Or that's what she thought she'd do, anyway, until a percussive blast buffeted her ears and pushed the car away from Denise's trailer, just a fraction of a second before her rear-view mirror reflected flames shooting twenty feet in the air.

Jennifer clapped her hands over her ears. "Ow!" Then she put them back on the wheel and floored the car until she was out of the blast zone and could turn around to survey the damage.

A blackened crater was all that was left of the small trailer, and the dog was nowhere in sight.

NINETEEN

AARON TURNED up the classic rock on local station Z94. He belted out "More Than a Feeling" in his best falsetto—which wasn't saying much—as he cruised away from Sheridan Vet Clinic toward Piney Bottoms. DeMarcus Ware might not be young anymore, but someone had invested in a decent set of speakers for the old Jeepster. He cranked down the window. Cool air flooded the cab. It felt great. *He* felt great. The surgery on the puppy at Ark Veterinary with Doc Billy had gone perfectly. Jennifer was here with him in this amazing location, and, if all went well, he'd be free of his practice in Houston and own the clinic of his dreams by Thanksgiving.

Life felt like an adventure again. In fact, it was so great that he decided to take Jennifer on a dinner date. He needed to talk to her about his old and new practice opportunities and their bright future—with a good bottle of pinot noir ready to pour in case she had any reservations. He'd heard about a new place that was hot. Aspen?

Spruce? Birch? Birch sounded right. He'd reserve a table and call his wife.

His phone rang as he stopped at a red light. Glancing at the screen, he saw a number with a three-oh-seven area code. He turned the volume down on the radio and pressed accept. Since he didn't have his headphones, he activated speaker and put the phone in his lap.

"Hello?" he said, as he rolled the window back up.

"Aaron? This is Perry Flint."

"Hey. Gotcha on speaker. I'm driving."

"I'll make it quick then. Do you have some time to talk today?"

"I was heading back to Story from Sheridan. I could swing by the school now and be there in ten."

"Make it five at the Big Horny, and we can grab a sandwich."

"The what?"

"The Big Horn Y. It's the gas station between Sheridan and Big Horn. They have a walk-up restaurant and bar. I call it the Big Horny because that's how their name reads on Instagram."

Aaron couldn't keep the laugh out of his voice. "You're on Instagram?" He knew the Big Horn Y, though. He'd gassed up there several times.

"All my players are. It's how I keep tabs on them. And I follow the Big Horny to see what bands are playing on Friday nights in the summer."

Aaron glanced at his watch. It was eleven thirty. "The Big Horny it is, then. See you in five."

He turned left onto Coffeen Avenue and rumbled past Sheridan College. Twenty or so pronghorn antelope were munching in the Antelope Habitat there, a project of the University of Wyoming Research and Extension Center. The early summer fawns were nearly as big as the adults now. The herd was sharing space with a loud flock of Canadian geese and two mating pairs of long-legged sandhill cranes. Aaron smiled. So much wildlife so close to town.

Just as he crossed Little Goose Creek, his phone buzzed and lit up with an incoming text. There was no traffic in either direction, so he held his phone at eye level and glanced at it quickly.

Jennifer: *I've had a situation, but I'm all right.*

A situation? And she was texting? A *situation* necessitated a phone call, especially when he was driving. He punched her number in his Favorites.

She answered on the first ring "I can only talk for a sec."

He heard sirens in the background. *Sirens.* Every muscle in his body tensed, ready to change course if needed. "What's going on?"

"I went to talk to a witness—Denise, the one with the cat that you met yesterday?"

"I remember."

"She didn't answer her door. Then a dog tried to attack me. And her trailer blew up."

He eased off the accelerator and parked on the side of the road in front of a house with a bizarre concrete rhino statue in the yard. It barely registered on him. "Wait, what?"

"Hold on."

A deep male voice was speaking in the background, but the words were indistinguishable.

Jennifer's voice was muffled but audible. "Okay. Let me just hang up with my husband." Then she spoke clearly into the mouthpiece. "I'm all right, Aaron, but I have to go. I need to give the police a statement."

"Shit, Jennifer. Are you sure you're good?"

"I am. Really."

"Call me as soon as you can."

"I will."

The call ended. Aaron kept his foot on the brake and stared at his hands. A trailer had exploded? And a dog had attacked his wife? Where in the world was she? He could check her location on his phone. Give Perry his apologies. Rush to her side. He drummed his thumbs. But she'd said she was good, and she didn't like to be babied. The police were there. She'd called to let him know what was going on. He needed to trust her, even though he was worried about her. He checked the lane behind him, then eased onto the road, still thinking about his capable wife. She was a pro. And she'd given him an earful on multiple occasions about people who showed up at crime scenes without good reason. They made it harder for emergency personnel to do their jobs.

Distracted, Aaron zoomed past the first two entrances to the Y, which forced him to enter on the far side. Then he drove past the gas pumps and executed a wide, looping turn to park at an angle near the door to the convenience store. Before he got out of the car, he sent a quick text to Jennifer. *I'm worried. Call if I can help you.* If she called, he'd drop everything.

He'd never been inside this convenience store before since he always paid for his gas at the pump. He entered through the front vestibule, passing a drink cooler, an ice cream freezer, and a community bulletin board that spilled over onto the walls around it. Fliers were push pinned onto every available inch of space. LAYING HENS FOR SALE. EXPERIENCED ONSITE HORSE CARE. COME LEARN HOW TO INVEST IN YOUR FUTURE WITH PRESCOTT FINANCIAL. And one that was a few weeks out of date: DON KING DAYS SEPT 1-2 WITH POLO, BRONC RIDING, AND STEER ROPING.

Once inside the main building, he scanned it quickly. On the left, the interior looked like a normal C-store. But in a larger area on the right was a fully stocked liquor store.

Only in Wyoming.

A young guy—average height and weight, with a long, curly beard—greeted Aaron from behind the register. *Special teams. Third string safety.*

"Restaurant?" Aaron said.

The man pointed back out the door. "There's a pick-up window down the sidewalk, and if you keep going, there's seating on the patio."

Pick-up window? Patio? How had he missed all of that? He really had been distracted by Jennifer's situation. "Thanks."

Aaron walked out past DeMarcus Ware and kept going. Sure enough, the structure continued into a boxy addition with a covered pick-up window. A concrete slab patio took up about nine hundred square feet of real estate on the far side of the building. The patio was partially fenced in, with plastic chairs and dark brown picnic tables. About half the tables were full.

Aaron stopped at the food window. Perry Flint, wearing a Big Horn Rams windbreaker with blue jeans and sneakers, was standing in a short line. He nodded when he saw Aaron. The two men shook hands.

"I never realized this was more than a gas station and convenience stores." Aaron gestured at the patio, then the window. "A whole restaurant."

"And bar. The Big Horny complex."

"Guess I'm not very observant."

"Well, it's just a concrete slab in a parking lot. Easy to miss. But the food's not half bad. When you teach at Big Horn, it's this, pizza from the Merc, or last night's leftovers. And this place is only open in the warm months, so I try to hit it every day I can until it closes for winter."

Aaron glanced around at a few remaining mounds of snow. "This is still considered a warm month?"

"Oh, trust me. It's definitely warm."

"What's good to eat here?"

"Everything. I usually get the pulled pork sandwich, but Friday is fish-fry day."

Aaron didn't have to look at the menu. While he wouldn't be caught dead eating barbecue outside the south, he never passed up fish and chips. "Fish-fry it is."

After they'd ordered, they grabbed a table. The view wasn't much —the building, the parking lot, the road, and a bluff behind the gas station. But Aaron had to admit, the fifty-degree temperature was pleasant, and, if not warm, it was at least not cold.

"Thanks for meeting me." Perry popped the top on a Snapple Arnold Palmer.

The tea and lemonade combo was too much for Aaron. He positioned his phone face up so he could watch for messages from Jennifer, then stuck a straw in his normal, unsweetened iced tea. He'd be thrown out of Tennessee for drinking it without sugar. "My pleasure. What's up?"

"I've got a problem, and I hope you're the solution."

Aaron grinned. "I don't kneecap guys, if that's what you're after."

Perry shook his head. "Nah, what I need won't get you a stint in the slammer. My assistant coach has to leave town for a few months. Family emergency. And I've got a team making a run for the state championship."

"That's the pits. I hope he's okay." Aaron took a sip of tea.

"Aging parents. You know."

Aaron thought of his own. As the youngest of a big tribe and the only one who'd left Tennessee, he felt bad that he wasn't around to help out more. So far, his parents were healthy and hearty, but time would ultimately have its way. He didn't know what he'd do when they started to decline. "Can you find a substitute?"

"A substitute teacher for his history classes, yes. But not for a coach of the caliber I need. That's where you come in. You mentioned you'd been coaching youth club football in Houston."

Aaron put his tea down, excitement flickering. "Yep. For years now." Until he'd moved here. He still felt a little sad about leaving the kids in Houston mid-season. But they were in good hands with Tony.

"And you said you were sticking around and buying the Big Horn Lodge."

"Also true."

"Could you coach the high school football team with me here, then?" He held up a hand. "I hate to say this, but it would be a volunteer gig. We're a tiny school, and we're still paying my assistant while he's on leave."

Aaron wanted to break out into *More Than a Feeling* again. And dance to it. "I was doing the club coaching gratis, too. I just love being involved with the game and the players." He leaned in. "Keep this between us, but I may buy the Sheridan Vet Clinic from Doc Billy. If so, we'd close on the sale around Thanksgiving." Then Aaron thought about the operation he'd just done on Perry's father's dog. "Oh, man, your dad's puppy. You knew about his injury?"

"Yeah, Dad's been really torn up about Moose's hip."

"I just operated on him with Doc Billy."

Is he going to be all right?"

"The surgery went well. He should be fine."

"That's great news. Thanks."

"But as to the timing and coaching . . . playoffs wrap up before Thanksgiving, right?"

Perry rubbed at his beard, eyes glittering. "Mid-November."

"Then I'd love to do it."

"Hell, yeah. When can you start?"

"When do you need me?"

"Today, if you can. We play Greybull at home tonight."

Aaron thought about his idea to take Jennifer to Birch. Guilt tore at him. He hated doing it, but he could push that back to Saturday. As important as Jennifer's work was to her, surely she'd understand. "Outstanding."

Perry held up a fist, and Aaron bumped it. "Excellent, man. Welcome aboard."

Aaron grinned. "Thanks, Coach."

A cowgirl-looking woman too fresh-faced to be older than her twenties sashayed up in dusty boots and faded jeans. She set the fish and chips baskets in front of them with ketchup and tartar sauce. "Anything else, guys?"

Aaron said, "Thanks, no."

Perry nodded in agreement.

She turned on a bootheel and walked back inside the building, pony-tail swinging.

Perry doused his fish in ketchup. "I didn't know Doc Billy was selling his clinic. Is he leaving Sheridan?"

Aaron made a pool of ketchup for dipping. "Yeah. He said he had some financial setbacks with his investments. He's going back home to Utah to take over his dad's practice."

Perry talked around a mouthful of fried fish, ketchup on the whisps of beard nearest his lips. "Funny about his investments. Pretty sure he had the same financial advisor as me. The guy that was murdered up at George's place. Hadley Prescott."

"Really?" Aaron dipped his fish in a cardboard container of tartar sauce and took a bite. It was good. Not the best he'd ever had, but good enough to bring him back, especially with the name of the place. The Big Horny. Perry was a funny guy.

"Yeah. Used to run into him occasionally at their offices. I didn't lose money with Hadley, though. I was pretty happy with him and Harriett."

Aaron chewed, thinking. He needed to relay this conversation to Jennifer. Dark, black smoke was curling upwards in the distance above the town. He wiped his hands and picked up his phone. He had good signal, but no texts and no missed calls or voice mails from her. *Come on, Jennifer.* He had so much to tell her. So much to ask her. Most of all, what had happened at Denise's trailer, and whether she was really, truly fine.

The column of smoke gnawed at him. But he and Perry had just started eating. He'd call her when they were done with their lunch.

TWENTY

SHERIDAN, Wyoming

JENNIFER'S STOMACH GROWLED, doing a good impression of the pit bull that had come after her earlier. She'd been in such a hurry to leave the trailer park after being stuck there for two hours that she'd driven straight to Kid's place without stopping for food.

She hadn't really been stuck there, though. Things had moved efficiently enough. But she'd decided to hang around to see if the police or fire department learned anything significant. Like whether Denise Little had been in the trailer when it blew. Or confirmation of what had caused the fire. The fire department had finally shooed her off after she gave her statement, and she hadn't gotten answers on either count. She'd have to wait for the information to be made public, like everyone else.

She accelerated up the hill from downtown toward Kid's place. The hilly neighborhood of stately old houses was charming, and someday—before she and Aaron went back to Houston and when she wasn't chasing her tail on this case—she planned to explore it. She parked in the muddy driveway in front of Kid's office. He'd been blowing up her phone, first with messages about the spoils from the County Attorney's Office, then with questions once he realized she was at the site of the explosion everyone was posting about on social media.

Before she went upstairs, though, she was going to call Aaron back. She should have done it while she was still at the crime scene. As she got out her phone, Kid came galloping down the stairs, shaking the entire garage.

She'd have to call Aaron in a minute. She got out of the Fusion.

"Your car!" Kid said, pointing.

Half of the cobalt car was coated in soot. *Talk about black and blue all over.* Only she knew that under the dark were deep scratches from dog claws, too. "Yeah. It was something."

Kid's eyes were bugging out. "So, you were really, really close to the explosion?"

"Too close."

"Was Denise in the trailer when it blew up?"

"No idea yet."

"What have they found?"

"Nothing so far. The fire was too hot. I guess that's what happens when you're cooking meth in the kitchen. They were still trying to cool it down when I left."

"You could have been fried!"

Jennifer pictured herself knocking on the front door, then walking through the yard. An eerie realization struck her. If the dog hadn't attacked, she'd be dead. The poor animal had disappeared after the explosion. It hadn't come back while the emergency vehicles were there, although that wasn't surprising. It was probably terrified and possibly in pain. She'd told the officers about it, and she hoped someone had gone to look for it.

"I got lucky."

Kid started walking back up the stairs, his steps lighter, and the shaking of the garage less dramatic. "I picked up our discovery file."

Jennifer followed. "That's what your messages said."

He opened the door, and she walked through it ahead of him. "They didn't give us George's cell phone."

She dropped her bags and notebook on the desk, then turned back toward him. "What excuse did they give you?"

His neck splotched. "I, uh, didn't realize it until I got back here."

Jennifer crossed her arms and tapped her foot, frustration oozing from her pores. Then she made a concerted effort to relax her posture and stay calm. It wasn't Kid's fault that the County Attorney was a jerk, or that Jennifer was having a bad day. "Okay. But we need to go through the rest of it with a fine-tooth comb. I don't trust Pootie." Her stomach growled again. She pressed it with one palm. "Do you have any food?"

"Not in here. But I can make you a sandwich over at Mom's."

"That would be fantastic. Thanks." Bonus—she would get no small measure of satisfaction out of Kid doing a little service work.

"What do you want?"

"Whatever you've got, except no meat, please."

"Then what do I put in it?"

"Everything but meat." She gave him an encouraging thumbs up. "You can do this, Kid. I'll inventory the boxes while you're gone."

"I've got it. Great. Back in a flash." Kid disappeared and the door slammed behind him.

Jennifer surveyed the desk. Two boxes sat on it, their tops open and ripped tape hanging from the flaps. She got out her notebook. "Let's see what we have here."

Quickly, she did a high-level inventory of the contents of the first box, repeating the process for the second. Then she scanned what she'd written. Witness statements from George, Aaron, Jennifer herself, Black Bear Betty, and Hadley's employees. The sheriff's office's paperwork. Hadley's phone records—home, cell, and office. George's phone records—home and cell. Fingerprint results on the knife and the GUILTY note found on Hadley. Crime scene photos and analysis. With the exception of the cell phone, everything they'd *requested* was there. But not everything she'd *expected*. She'd have thought the county would have tested George and Hadley's DNA and have results in by this time. More than a week had passed since the murder. And where was the medical report for the examination George had been subjected to? She jotted down a separate list of the missing items, underlining the words "missing phone" twice.

She was most concerned about communication between George and Hadley, especially on the day of the murder. She took a seat with the stack of phone records in front of her. There were no recent texts or calls to or from Hadley's personal numbers on George's cell, or, in the case of his landline home phone, calls only. She cross-referenced Prescott Financial and scanned George's records again. She didn't find any outgoing calls to the financial services firm, but she did find an incoming call of a few seconds duration made to George's cell phone, on the evening Hadley died. *Hadley called George.* Then she corrected herself. *Someone called George from Prescott Financial.* She circled it and set the records aside.

She made a "huh" sound in her throat. "Not exactly the call and invite Pootie suggested we'd find."

She couldn't check the content of texts from the phone records. Just because she didn't see recent texts between George's and Hadley's cell phones wasn't dispositive. Hadley could have been using another number Jennifer didn't know about yet. The messages themselves would tell Jennifer whether Pootie's argument at George's arraignment had been wishful thinking or based on reality. Getting the phone back had just jumped up to job number one. She added a third underline to "missing phone."

She did a quick review of Hadley's cell phone, looking for repeat numbers. She jotted down three of them, all in the local area code. One was the office. She checked online and discovered the second belonged to Denise Little. But with the third she came up empty. Interestingly, it was the most frequently called. Who would a man call on his cell phone? *His mother and his girlfriend.* But did Hadley even have a girlfriend or a living mother? She started a third list titled

Follow-up Items and parked the number there. Then she consolidated her notes from the interviews at Prescott Financial into the same list. *Talk to William Marton. Figure out who inherits firm. Interview the landlord, Tim O'Leary. Get a copy of the lease. Find out what has Harriett Staples so emotional.*

She eyed the tall stack of witness statements and other documents. She was more interested in the fingerprint analysis than anything else remaining, and she fished them out of the pile. A quick read yielded no surprises. The knife had no fingerprints. The report described it as a Swiss Army Sentinel. Black plastic handle, four-inch folding blade. She studied the pictures of it. No engraving. No scarring. The very definition of ordinary. She added it to follow-ups: *George/look at knife.* There were no fingerprints on the GUILTY note, either, although the report noted the word was typed in Marker Felt Wide, seventy-two-point font. She retrieved an envelope from her laptop bag containing three notes George had given her. The ones Hadley had left for him. She compared the most recent one, KILLER, to the one found with Hadley. The lettering looked the same to her. Precise, centered capitals that almost looked like handwriting, only too perfect to be real. She paged through the other two: another KILLER and one YOU KILLED HER. They matched as well. In fact, they matched so well that she was certain they were printed in the same font. Was the note one of Hadley's, or had his murderer left it? If it was Hadley's, had he been keeping his prints off the notes in case George sicced the cops on him? She didn't have an answer. Which meant it was unclear whether George's notes would hurt or help his case. She'd keep them to herself for now, but she needed to know whether George had a printer, because the cops certainly would be searching for the same thing. In fact, they probably already had, but she didn't find mention of it anywhere in the file, suggesting they hadn't found one. She wrote *George/printer?*

She riffled through the rest of the papers, looking more closely for anything related to DNA. If she was the County Attorney, she'd have ordered a DNA test on George and Hadley first thing, so that they could search for their DNA on each other. George's DNA would have been simple to obtain during a medical exam, without need to ask his consent. But there was nothing in the file to indicate DNA tests had been performed on the men. She did find the analysis of the crime scene—lots of organic matter and unidentifiable DNA. Nothing helpful. She made another note on her legal pad: *DNA test results for George and Hadley.*

She tapped her lips with her pen. She needed to think like a defense attorney. As an ADA, she usually had a charged defendant by the time she received a case—or at least a strong suspect. Motive mattered to her, since it would be part of what she presented to a jury to prove guilt beyond a reasonable doubt. In other words, she was looking to *bolster* the defendant's motive. As a defense attorney, she wanted to *disprove* what the prosecutor would argue was the defendant's motive, as well as show compelling motives for other potential suspects. *Like a modern-day Matlock. Except I'm a woman and representing George pro bono instead of for big bucks. But other than that, totally Matlock.*

That meant she needed to explore the most common motives and who might have them toward Hadley. Things like love, lust, loathing, or loot. Whether he was or had been involved sexually or romantically with anyone. Whether he'd made anyone angry enough to kill, like a client who blamed Hadley for his big financial loss. She already had the name of one, but there might be others. Who inherited from Hadley, by will, insurance, or business contract? Denise or someone else?

She expanded her list of follow-ups: *Life insurance policy. Will. Client list. Girlfriend?*

Just because Hadley was obsessed with his dead ex-wife didn't mean there were no women in his life. Shelly had told George she thought Hadley was involved with someone. And then there were those unidentified calls on his cell phone records.

Her phone rang. She was so deep in concentration that she almost missed it. A last-second glance at caller ID changed her mind.

Aaron. She'd forgotten to call him back. *Crap.* He wasn't going to be happy, with good reason. She thought for a second about trying to fake still being at the crime scene but decided on the mea culpa approach instead.

She picked up. "Hey, I was, uh, just about to call you."

"Are you all right?" His voice sounded so concerned that she wanted to sink into the cheap carpet. Except that it was cheap carpet. *Yuck.* And God knew how long it had been since it was cleaned—if ever.

"I am, and I'm so sorry. I left the scene and was going to call, but then I got involved with George's case. I should have called you half an hour ago. I feel terrible that I didn't. But I'm good. Just busy. We got the first round of discovery from the County Attorney. Can I tell you all about it over dinner?"

There was a pause. She winced. She knew it—he was mad at her.

Then Aaron said, "You're sure you're fine?"

"One hundred percent." Normally, when she was deep into her work, she would have ended the call there. But because she had a lot of making up to do, she extended it. "How was your day?" But, meanwhile, she eyed the stack of files. It wasn't getting any shorter. Her mind wandered away from Aaron's words for a second, and she had an epiphany. Sometimes taking a break did more good than harm. Pootie had provided witness *statements*, but not a witness *list*. A list would tell them the witnesses Pootie planned to talk to but hadn't interviewed yet. Like friends, neighbors, disgruntled clients, or girl-friends. *Yes.*

"Excellent. I met with Doc Billy at his clinic—where I repaired a broken hip on Patrick Flint's puppy, believe it or not, and did a damn fine job of it, too."

"Wow. That's great."

"And I had lunch with Perry Flint. Lots to talk about when we get home."

"Sounds good. I'll bring takeout and see you there."

"Wait. There is one thing that's time sensitive."

She started flipping through documents, looking for a witness list. She could have missed a one-pager. "What's that?"

Again, there was a funny pause. "I'll be late. Really late."

"Oh? Why?"

"Perry asked me to help him with the team."

Her hands stilled. "The team?"

"The Big Horn High School football team. His assistant coach had to take personal leave. I'm stepping in for the rest of the season, and there's a home game tonight."

The blood drained from her face. Aaron had found a football team to coach. And it was only September. Playoffs wouldn't be until when—November or so?

She swallowed and tried not to sound panicked and upset, which was hard to do, since she was both. "That's such a big commitment."

"Yeah, but it feels right."

"Okay, then. Great." She hoped her words didn't sound as hollow to him as they felt to her.

"Can you come to the game?"

"I have a mountain of discovery to get through. Would you mind if I came to the next one instead?"

"I wish you could be there. But it will give me time to get my feet wet with the team first."

"Thanks for understanding."

"See you late tonight. I love you."

The door opened. Kid was kicking it with one foot and holding a large tray in his hands. The tray was fully loaded. A plate with a sandwich. A bag of Cool Ranch Doritos. A container of Fig Newtons. A can of Coca Cola. An entire bunch of bananas. Jennifer was slightly amused, since he'd been gone an hour, that he really did return with just a sandwich and finger foods. She suspected he'd run to the store for everything on the tray. Kid donkey-kicked the door shut. The windows rattled.

"I love you, too." She hung up the phone. She had to shake off the unsettling news from Aaron about his coaching gig, and she would. Food would help.

She smiled at Kid. "Wow. I can't eat all that. But thanks."

He set the tray on the desk and perched on the edge of a chair, looking young, vulnerable, and slightly proud of himself. "Anything you don't finish will be snacks."

"For days."

"Did you find anything interesting?" He pointed to the documents on the desk.

Jennifer peeled a banana. "Yes and no." She told him about the call from Prescott Financial to George. That there had been no fingerprints on the knife or GUILTY note, and how the note looked so similar to the ones George received that it suggested they were printed using a handwriting font. The lack of DNA results for George and Hadley. The unidentified frequent caller to Hadley. The missing witness list. "I haven't gone through the witness statements yet." She took a big bite of her banana.

Kid frowned. "The local criminal attorneys talk about the county attorney's open file policy."

"What's that mean?"

"Locally, they give you everything they have, not just what's in the state or federal rules. You know, to be fair."

To be fair. What a concept, and one that would eliminate half the acrimony and arguing pre-trial. "And they would have an ongoing duty to supplement, I would assume. If that's the case, we should get it, but sooner is far better than later."

"What do we have to produce for them?"

"Anything we have that isn't attorney-client privileged or work product." She grinned. "In other words, nothing." And, strangely, she didn't even feel guilty about it, even after all the times she'd cursed defense attorneys for their liberal interpretation of the concept.

Kid looked a little uncertain. "What do we do now? Besides finish going through the file."

A banana had never tasted so good. She grabbed her sandwich.

Avocado, onion, tomato, Swiss, and mayo. *Yum.* "We get George's darn phone back so we can read his texts and emails and listen to any voice mail. We get a witness list." She paused to add that to her notes. "His will. His insurance policy. Results from the medical exam the county did on him. And we find out about the DNA tests for George and Hadley. It's standard procedure to do them. But, after we call Pootie, I'm going to want you to go over everything. The stuff I've already reviewed, plus the rest of it. We've got two brains and two sets of eyes, and we need to use them to backstop each other."

"Good. Very. I will."

She bit the inside of her lip to keep from smiling at his reply. He wouldn't understand. "I also want you to get a client list from his firm, past and present. And research a phone number for me. I'm thinking it may be a girlfriend of Hadley's. If so, we need to know who she is and talk to her. Let's get George to look at pictures of the knife in case he recognizes it and find out whether he has a printer."

"I didn't see one at his place."

"Yeah, but there are a lot of rooms. Maybe he uses one as an office. Then I have a few things I thought of when we were at Prescott Financial, like a copy of their lease. Talking to William Marton, the angry client, and Tim O'Leary, the landlord who wants to bring chicken to the masses. And I'd like for you to see if you can figure out what has Harriett Staples so worked up, if you can."

Kid said, "Is *that* all," under his breath as he frantically wrote down her instructions, and not as a question.

"Ready for the call to Pootie?"

"Go ahead."

She took a bite of the sandwich, then put her phone in the center of the desk and pulled up Pootie in her Recents. Kid scooted up a chair while the phone rang.

To her surprise, Pootie picked up. "County Attorney Alfred Carputin speaking."

"Hello, Mr. Carputin. It's Jennifer Herrington and Kid James. You remember us—George Nichols's attorneys."

Pootie sighed. "I left the discovery for you. Didn't you get the message?"

"Oh, we got the message and copies. What we didn't get was George's phone."

Silence.

"Pootie?"

"Alfred *Carputin*. I'm here."

"Where's the phone?"

Silence from Pootie's end again.

"Do Kid and I need to take this to the judge?"

"No. We'll get it to you."

She winked at Kid. "Great. Now, what about the results of George and Hadley's DNA tests?"

"What DNA tests?"

She rolled her eyes and wished Pootie could see her doing it. "The DNA tests you ran on them."

"Uh..."

"Unless you're completely incompetent, it was the first thing you did after you tested for fingerprints on the knife and the note."

"Are you calling me incompetent?" His tone was hostile.

"I'm demanding a copy of the DNA results."

Pootie's voice was stilted. "There was a delay."

"What kind of delay?"

"A mix-up. They're redoing the analysis as a rush job. It should be back any day now."

"What kind of *mix-up*?"

"They sent us the same set of results twice. We're having them redo the work."

Jennifer crossed her eyes. "Great lab you're working with."

"They are. It's the State Crime Lab. We've never had a problem like this before."

"So, we'll get it tomorrow?"

"If I do. Is that all?" He sounded weary now.

"Nope. I need a copy of Hadley's will and his life insurance policy. And an updated witness list."

"We sent the statements."

"I want a list."

"Fine. A list of witnesses. His will. His life insurance. The DNA analysis."

"And his phone."

"And his phone."

"Nice doing business with you, Pootie."

"My. Name. Is. Carputin."

"One last thing, Carputin."

There was an explosion of air in the phone. "What?" His tone was curt.

"When will the crime scene be released? Our client is being forced to live in a home without plumbing."

Kid nodded vigorously.

"There's plumbing in the jail."

"Funny. When?"

"Today. It was released about an hour ago."

"Oh, wow. Thanks for the heads-up." She crossed her eyes at the phone, and Kid put a hand over his mouth, muffling his laugh. She shot off a text to George and Aaron: *Put Black Bear Betty back on the septic tank case. Sheridan County has released the crime scene.*

"Ms. Herrington, are you still there?"

"I was. Not anymore. You have a good day."

The line went dead.

Kid clapped. "You kicked Pootie's ass."

For a split second, Jennifer wondered if it was the right time to ask Kid about defense attorneys in Sheridan. Someone she could refer into the lead counsel position on George's case. But then she dismissed the thought. Not now. She could always ask him tomorrow.

She shrugged, smiling. *All in a day's work.* "Yeah, well, we'll know whether it did any good when we get what we asked for. Now, let's dig back into this file."

TWENTY-ONE

BIG HORN, Wyoming

AARON SLUNG an athletic bag with BIG HORN RAMS emblazoned on it over his shoulder. It was filled with gear, play books, and notes. The Rams had won their home game against Greybull fifty-five to zero, despite putting in their third stringers and playing a short ground ball game the entire second half. Aaron had spent most of the game soaking things in like an oversized sponge, but he'd managed to help. Their offense was one he was familiar with from many seasons past, so he took over running it in the fourth quarter.

Big Horn was a tiny town, but their stadium was brand new and their facilities pristine. He'd sure never played anywhere half as nice in high school. When he remarked on it, Perry told him that, with the state coffers flush from energy money in the last decade, libraries, schools, and athletic facilities had benefitted greatly.

It wasn't just the facilities that were nicer than Aaron's high school days. The crisp fall air was invigorating, unlike the hot, humid Friday nights in Tennessee. The looming mountains that felt close enough to touch weren't bad either, although, to give it its due, Tennessee didn't lack for scenic beauty. It was just beauty of a different kind. And the bright lights, the whistles of the refs, the cracking of helmets and creaking of shoulder pads, the smell of sweat and fear, the butterflies in Aaron's stomach. All of it took him back to his own playing days. He'd missed it more than he realized.

Maybe best of all was the line of parents who'd welcomed him after the game. They were nothing like the ones who'd made coaching a challenge back in the city.

"Make my boy work for it," one had said.

"You let me know if Kenny is gold bricking," another told him.

"Josh enjoys practice. He may never get in a game but being on a team is good for him. His mother and I appreciate the opportunity," said a third.

It had been refreshing. More than that. It had been inspiring and life-affirming. It made him question why he was still a vet. Coaching high school football—now *that* would be a rewarding career. But he loved the animals, too, and he appreciated the income that veterinary medicine afforded. He was pretty darn lucky to have them both. Or, as his mom would have said, blessed.

Aaron waved and called goodnight to the players. He left the main locker room, walked down a hall, and stuck his head in Perry's office. "See you tomorrow, Coach Flint."

Perry looked up from a spiral bound notebook. "Have you got a second?"

"Sure."

He motioned Aaron in. "I was thinking we could divvy up the team. I take defense and special teams, you take the offense."

Aaron leaned against the wall just inside the door. "Sounds like a good plan."

"Daddy!" a little girl's voice screeched from somewhere nearby.

Heavy footsteps pounded down the hall. Two freckle-faced kids barreled in, knocking into Aaron's legs. From their height, they looked to be only a year or two apart in age. One wore pigtails. The other a flat top.

"Sorry about that." A female voice at Aaron's shoulder made him turn his head. A woman was standing behind him. She was Jennifer's height—which was to say *short*—but thicker than his wife, with red hair and freckles, like the children. Shaking her head and smiling, she said, "They love coming to congratulate Daddy after a game."

Perry had a child's shoulders under each arm. "Aaron, this is my wife Bethany."

"Welcome, Aaron. I'd shake, but my hands are full." Bethany had a blanket tucked under one arm and stadium seats clutched in her other hand.

"Nice to meet you, Bethany."

"Perry sure is grateful you're helping him out."

"I'm already loving it."

Perry pulled the kids tight against him. "And these rascals are Willy and Silly."

"No, Daddy," the little girl said, wriggling away. "It's Sally."

"I could have sworn we changed it to Silly."

She started giggling in little snorts through her nose.

"I'll let you guys get on with your celebration. Have a nice night, and I'll see you tomorrow, Perry."

"Thanks again, Aaron. You were wonderful with the players. I can't believe how lucky I am to have you on board. It's going to be a great season."

The kids, prompted by Bethany, called out their goodbyes as Aaron departed.

On the walk to his car, he started humming. By the time he was in the parking lot, he was singing "Standing on Top of the World" under his breath and fighting the urge to play air guitar along with the vocals. *Sammy Hagar, eat your heart out.* Aaron had a football team. He had a new veterinary practice, almost. And his lodge was about to get septic so he could move Jennifer back up to it. Not that Piney Bottoms and the guest cabin weren't nice, but the quarters were tight with Liam and Katya, and there was no substitute for having his own space.

He glanced at the time on his phone screen as he shut DeMarcus Ware's door. He'd be home by ten thirty. That wasn't too bad. But then the phone rang while it was still in his hand. The screen said GEORGE.

Aaron picked up. "What's up, George?"

"I need a ride." His voice was flat.

"Where are you?"

"The hospital."

Aaron turned on the ignition. "I'm on my way. Are you okay?"

"A little banged up. I've been released. My truck's totaled, though."

"You weren't . . ." Aaron couldn't make himself utter the word *drunk*. He pulled the Jeepster out of the parking lot and onto the road toward Sheridan and the hospital.

"I hadn't been drinking. Not to speak of, anyway. Someone ran me off the road."

"Are you serious?"

George sighed. "The police don't believe me either."

"I believe you, George." He at least believed that George was telling his truth. But Aaron couldn't understand why anyone would run him off the road unless it was an accident. He eased off the gas. He didn't want to get stopped for speeding. Again. Just then, he saw a white Ram Sheridan County Deputy truck. *Good thing I was proactive with the accelerator.* "Do you know who did it?"

"No. Came up out of nowhere and rammed me as I crossed a bridge over Little Goose. I almost went over and into the creek." He said it "crick" as everyone local to the region did.

Either George was the world's unluckiest man, or someone had just tried to kill him. Either way, Aaron was worried about him. Really worried. "I'm just glad you're all right. Hang tight, buddy. I'm on my way."

⁂

AN HOUR LATER, Aaron pulled DeMarcus Ware to a stop in front of the Big Horn Lodge for the Jeepster's first visit to its future home. George climbed out into the pitch black without a word, favoring his left leg and holding his left arm to his belly as he lumbered toward the cabin. Cuts from broken glass crisscrossed his forearms. A white bandage on his forehead had him looking like an extra on *Grey's Anatomy*. He was banged up all over and was going to have some humdinger bruises, too. His mood——glum since his arrest—was closing in on depressed.

Aaron hustled after him, putting a hand on his upper back.

George didn't break stride. "I'm all right. Go eat dinner with your wife."

"I'll just walk you in. We both know you're not as okay as you say you are."

"I miss my dog." George lumbered up the steps.

"I'll bring him and Katya back tomorrow. I promise."

"And I don't have any wheels, unless you count the Suburban, which hasn't run in over a year."

Aaron opened the front door. Jeremiah was scurrying in circles right inside. It gave Aaron a pang in his chest. How cute Jennifer was about the animal. The skunk leapt in George's arms before he'd crossed the thresh hold. George grimaced with pain, but he let go of his hurt arm to cradle his little buddy.

Aaron said, "We'll go get you something to drive tomorrow, too. Your insurance will cover a rental. Or you could go ahead and buy something, since your truck is toast."

"Hello, fellas," a gruff voice said.

Both men startled. Aaron peered into the dim living room, but he didn't see anyone. He flipped on the lights. Black Bear Betty was sitting at the kitchen table. At midnight. When George wasn't home.

The woman certainly made herself at home. But if it bothered George, he didn't show it.

"I was waiting for you, George. I was sitting outside, but I couldn't hear myself think. Too many of those voices."

"For the last time, woman, you're crazy or drunk. Maybe both. There are no voices, except Wilma and Butch."

"Who are Wilma and Butch?" Aaron asked.

"Neighbors," Black Bear Betty said. "And it wasn't them. Besides, tonight I saw them, too."

Aaron was really confused now. "Saw them, who?"

"Indians. A woman and a child. Lakota Sioux, I suspect."

George shook his head. Aaron was intrigued. He hadn't heard anything, but Black Bear Betty wasn't crazy. Or drunk. He wouldn't discount anything she said.

She brandished a mug at them. "Anyway, the reason I'm here. Bad news." Aaron almost smiled inappropriately at her accent, as bad came out as bed.

George collapsed into an armchair, Jeremiah still snuggled into his shoulder. He groaned and put his head back and his feet on the ottoman. "More bad news? Because I've been charged with a murder I didn't commit, my truck is totaled, and I just got out of the hospital. All I want is whiskey and a hot bath."

Black Bear Betty winced. "Sorry to hear about the truck and the hospital. But it's the hot bath I need to tell you about."

"Then get to telling me, woman. My patience is a little thin tonight."

Black Bear Betty rose, like a dog with its hackles up. "You don't have to be so snippy with me. I'm trying to help you. But when the work here got delayed by the sheriff, I gave your new septic tank to another customer. I've had another one on order, but the truck that was bringing it here got caught in a crosswind in Casper. Flipped the trailer and crushed the tank. They're expediting me another, and it should be here soon."

"Well, that's just peachy."

"I'm sorry, George."

He closed his eyes for a few seconds. When he opened them, he spoke in a calmer voice. "At least the weather is warming up. I've been using outdoor facilities for weeks now. I guess another couple of days won't kill me."

Aaron held his tongue. He felt bad for George, but this wasn't good news for Aaron either. He'd been counting on coaxing Jennifer back to the lodge. On helping her fall in love with their place. He needed the septic tank worse than George did.

But, in the meantime, George would be fine with Black Bear Betty, or, at least, good enough. It was late, and Aaron had things to talk about with his wife. Important things.

It would have been a great night to bring home daisies.

TWENTY-TWO

STORY, Wyoming

WHEN AARON HAD TEXTED her that the Rams had won but that he was giving George a ride home from the hospital, Jennifer was sitting at the bar in Frackelton's, waiting on a to go order. She should have eaten hours ago, but she'd waited for her husband. She knew she had to pull out all the stops if she was going to tear him away from football, the lodge, and Wyoming.

The evening hadn't been bad, up until that moment. She'd managed to squeeze in hitting a bucket of balls at the public golf course, even though it was chilly out. She'd nearly whiffed more than once, distracted first by the killer view and then by a red fox sprinting across the grass not ten yards away from her. The snow had finished melting on the course, but the tops of the mountains were still capped in the white stuff. When she'd managed to connect with the balls, though, she'd gotten some serious distance. She could get used to golfing in thinner air.

Of course, she'd also put the time to good use on George's case.

George. The reason for Aaron's further delay. The man at the center of the upheaval in her life, too. She sighed. She needed to keep a positive attitude. Whatever she did, she couldn't take her frustration out on Aaron. It wasn't his fault.

She texted Aaron back. *Congrats on the win. Is George okay? What happened?*

Then she ordered a glass of pinot noir. Just one, plus truffle fries to make sure she absorbed the alcohol. She deserved the wine, though. Her plans for a romantic evening had been ruined. The food would be cold and spoiled when Aaron got home. A Delmonico steak was best served fresh, not microwaved to warm it up when he rolled in at—when, midnight, maybe?

Two more hours. *Ugh.*

At least the fries were crisp and hot and the wine velvety smooth. She enjoyed them slowly, killing an hour while scrolling through social media and fending off a parade of hopeful men between the ages of twenty and seventy. She was like a giant blue light in a room crowded with moths. Was it just her, or was there a critical shortage of women in Wyoming?

The heavily tattooed bartender held up a check. "Another round?"

"No. I'm ready to cash out," Jennifer said. She glanced over the bill then slid it back with her credit card. "Thanks."

"Sure."

Beside her, a man she'd rebuffed earlier made conversation with the bartender. "Did you hear about the trailer home that blew up north of town today?"

Jennifer was suddenly all ears.

The bartender swung her head to the man as she pulled a draft beer from the tap. "No. That's terrible."

He nodded. "They found a body in it. Burned to a crisp."

Jennifer's insides clenched. *Denise?*

"Who was it?"

"They say they don't know yet."

The bartender handed Jennifer the charge slip. She took her time adding a tip and signing it, stalling so she could keep listening in. But the lonely man changed the subject to the time the bartender was getting off work, and Jennifer left.

The drive back to Story was uneventful, save for the deer launching themselves across the interstate. What was it that made deer so heedless of vehicle danger? You didn't see that kind of behavior from antelope, cows, horses, or even dogs. Deer all but disproved Darwin's theory of evolution on their own. By the time she turned into Piney Bottoms and parked at the cabin, her hands hurt from her death grip on the steering wheel.

Lugging her purse, her laptop carrier, and the takeout bag, she struggled to the porch with her eyes on her feet, deep in thought. She needed to talk to Alayah. A girlfriend who understood everything Jennifer was up against without the need to explain the history and context. Jennifer hadn't realized until she'd come to Wyoming how much she counted on the short daily chats at work with her best friend.

"Hey, there, ADA Herrington. You're home late." The slow, husky drawl stopped Jennifer short. *Maggie. On the porch. Ugh.*

Jennifer resumed walking, trying to hide the fact that Maggie's presence rattled her. She didn't want Hank's needling girlfriend here. She wanted Aaron, with her, back in their Houston high-rise, celebrating her DA candidacy. Short of that, she wanted Alayah, on the phone, and a serious gab session, followed by a Hailey Dean mystery on the Hallmark channel. And a bottle of wine. A hot bath was out of the question, but it would have been nice, too.

"Hello, Maggie."

Maggie's odd looking and inappropriately named dog snuffled Jennifer's feet.

"Where's Aaron?"

Jennifer unlocked the door. The explanation was just too long. "On his way. What has you hanging out on the porch here?" She swung the door open and walked in, bags banging against her legs and the doorframe. She hefted them all onto the little kitchen table.

Maggie was hot on her heels. "Just being neighborly. Need anything, cousin?"

Jennifer didn't bite her tongue fast enough. "You're not my cousin."

Maggie peeked inside the Frackelton's bag. "Honey, you better get used to Hank and me. We're together. We own this ranch together, we sleep together, and we've made a life, together. You can either be happy about it and stand up with us when we make it official someday, or you can alienate your *cousin* Hank, because we're a package deal."

Jennifer sank into one of the kitchen chairs. After a few shallow breaths that had trouble getting past the lump in her throat, she said, "I'm sorry. That was uncalled for. I know all that. You're right."

Maggie crossed her arms. "Bet that made your tongue sting like you'd swallowed a bull nettle."

Jennifer laughed, but tears leaked out. "It did, kind of."

Maggie took the other chair. "Thank you. Now, besides the thought of me as family, what's up your butt?"

Jennifer eyed the refrigerator. "Want a glass of wine with my answer?"

"I'd prefer KO 90."

Jennifer got out her wine glass and a coffee mug. She emptied the rest of the bottle of pinot noir in her own then broke the seal on the KO 90 and poured two fingers for Maggie.

"Keep going."

Jennifer doubled the amount, then brought it to her "cousin." She took a big sip of red wine—it was too cold, after having spent a night in the fridge—and turned on the oven. She put Aaron's dinner on a cookie sheet, then slid it onto the middle rack. *Pre-heating is for sissies.*

"Well?" Maggie prompted.

Jennifer sat, took another sip, and said, "It was a hectic day."

"Oh, that tells me everything. Glad we had this talk."

Jennifer slit her eyes at Maggie. "You really don't make it easy on anyone, ever, do you?"

"Where's the fun in that?"

"A dog attacked me, a trailer home blew up when I was thirty-feet away and someone burned to a crisp inside, George totaled his truck, and—I saved the best for last—Aaron is the new assistant coach for the Big Horn Rams high school football team. Yay." She shook her hands like they were holding pompoms.

Maggie rotated her coffee mug. "What do you have against your husband being happy?"

Heat flooded Jennifer's cheeks. "What did you just say?"

The door to the cabin opened, and Aaron stuck his head in. "Honey, I'm . . . oh, hey Maggie. Jennifer. It smells good in here." From the bushwhacked expression on his face, he felt the tension in the room.

"I got us dinner from Frackelton's. A Delmonico steak for you. Pasta for me. Yours is warming in the oven."

He grinned, one eyebrow up. "You didn't eat without me."

Maggie stood. "I think I kept her from it. Jennifer, thanks for the chat and the drink." She rinsed the cup out and left it in the sink. "Y'all have a nice night."

"Night, Maggie." Aaron walked to Jennifer and put a hand on her shoulder.

"Night." Jennifer's tone of voice said she hoped it was Maggie's last one on earth.

The door closed, leaving Jennifer and Aaron alone.

He stood next to her, like he was waiting for her to stand up and hug him. She was too steamed to move. In fact, she was afraid she was going to break her wine glass with her bare hands, so she pushed it away.

"What's the matter?" Aaron asked.

She forced a bright tone to her voice. She wasn't going to let Maggie ruin things. "I'm hungry. Are you ready to eat?"

"Sure. I'll get plates." He turned and reached into the cabinets for plates and the drawer for utensils without moving his feet.

Jennifer stood then, safe from a hug that would have betrayed to her husband the bitterness she was fighting inside herself. "I'll microwave my pasta."

They worked in silence for a few minutes, sidling past each other in the small kitchen. Aaron opened a beer. Jennifer kept sipping her wine, and her anger receded.

When they sat with their food at the table, she gave him a smile that was fifty percent genuine. "You said you had a lot to talk to me about tonight."

A guarded expression crossed his face. "It's late. Are you sure you want to get into it tonight?"

"I'm good if you are."

He blew out a lungful of air. "Okay then. I met with Doc Billy this morning. He's the vet that owns Sheridan Vet Clinic."

"That's what you said earlier. I'd figured you would, after Hank told you about him."

"It turns out that he's selling, in part, because he lost a bunch of money in bad investments."

Jennifer's eyebrows shot up so high it stretched her forehead. It felt good and helped with the Maggie headache building behind her eyes. Aaron's words lined up with what she knew and clicked. "And I learned today that Hadley had a seriously disgruntled client named *William* Marton making threats against him."

They smiled at each other, and both said "Doc Billy" at the same time.

Aaron took a bite of his Delmonico. "My God, this is so good." He chewed, then added, "Another potential suspect."

"Which we need, since our first potential suspect may have just burned up in that trailer today. The police found a body they haven't identified yet."

"No!"

"I need to talk to William Marton—Doc Billy—tomorrow. Before he does something crazy like moves out of town. You know him. Want to come with me and introduce us?"

Aaron started coughing. Jennifer was afraid he was choking, and she pounded his back. He held up a hand. "I'm okay."

"You scared me for a second. So, yes or no on going with me to talk to the vet?"

Aaron drank his beer in one long series of gulps. When he'd drained it, he said, "Yeah, sure."

"Great. Now, tell me how George and Jeremiah are doing, then I want to hear about your football team."

While the two of them ate, Aaron filled her in. When they'd finished, he offered to do the dishes.

Jennifer handed him her plate. She bounced her hip against his leg. "Sure, pick a night when it's takeout."

"I'm no dummy." He didn't meet her eyes.

Usually, when she hip bumped him, he did it back to her. She watched him as he prepped the sink for the utensils and cookie sheet. "Aaron, is there something you're not telling me?"

"What makes you say that?"

"I don't know. I've just been getting a weird vibe from you."

"Don't do that. It sounds contagious."

"Ha."

He brandished a sponge. "I've got this. Do you want to write a little more tonight?"

Now it was Jennifer's turn to get cagey. "Uh, yeah, sure."

"Well, get after it. I can't wait to hear what you've come up with."

As she got out her Mac, Jennifer chewed on the inside of her cheek. She claimed her couch corner, then booted up. Every few seconds, she snuck a look at her husband. He was whistling, but it felt false. Like he was an actor on a television sitcom doing a scene—the happy modern husband washing dishes. But she didn't push him on it.

When the startup sequence was complete, she opened Messages on her laptop.

She texted Alayah: *I need out of my cousin's guest cabin. His girlfriend is evil. And it feels like Aaron is holding something back from me. He got a job as assistant coach of a high school football team. And I'm stuck representing the guy he's buying the lodge from. On a murder charge. Did I say I needed out of the cabin? I need out of THE STATE.*

She hesitated a few moments, seeing if Alayah would answer. But it was Friday night. Friday the thirteenth, she realized, as she looked at her calendar icon. No wonder everything had gone so crazy today. When Alayah didn't reply, Jennifer decided to check in with Quentin.

Hope you're good. All is well here. Thanks for your understanding as I work through the only issues delaying my yes to a campaign for District Attorney.

"How's the writing?" Aaron's voice was inches away from her.

She gasped and jumped, spilling her wine on the floor with her foot.

"I've got it," Aaron said.

She slammed the laptop shut. "Sorry. Thanks."

He returned with paper towels and sopped up the wine from the wood floor. "So . . . you didn't answer me. How is the writing?"

Jennifer looked him straight in the eyes and batted hers. "Great. But it's getting kind of late." She motioned toward the bed with her head. "Meet you in the bedroom?"

He stared back at her for long seconds. Her heartbeat quickened. She remembered her phone in his possession that morning after she'd sent texts about her plan to lure him back to Texas. Was he on to her?

But then he smiled and with one clean, effortless motion, he lifted her off the couch, strode to the bed, and tossed her onto it. "You were saying?"

TWENTY-THREE

SHERIDAN, Wyoming

THE NEXT MORNING, Aaron readjusted his sweaty palms on the steering wheel. The stereo was playing the Rolling Stones' "Wild Horses" just loud enough that talking was impossible. On the one hand, that wasn't a bad thing, since he was scared to talk to Jennifer. On the other, it was problematic, because he needed to. He snuck a glance at her. Behind her, the high, rolling Wyoming prairie flashed by outside the passenger window of DeMarcus Ware. Jennifer looked good. Great in fact. And by some measures, their relationship was better than it had been in a long time. Years, maybe. He sure wasn't going to complain about their physical closeness. But if he wasn't evaluating them by the count of notches in the bedpost, they were farther apart than ever.

He couldn't continue hiding things from her. He had made the choice to disrupt their Houston lives. Jennifer had a right to react the way she had, even if he hadn't liked it. He knew that. Yet it was because of how she had reacted initially that he was still holding back. He already should have talked to her about the pending sale of his Houston clinic to his partners. He should have told her he wanted to purchase the Sheridan practice and that he had made a conditional offer to buy it. He should have made the time to sit down with her and *really* ask about *her* plans for Wyoming. Find out how it had gone when she resigned with the DA's office. How the party bigwigs had reacted to her decision not to run for DA. How she felt about leaving her best friend Alayah.

Now, unless he found the courage to open his mouth and speak, DeMarcus Ware's wheels were just spinning toward doom at one thousand rotations per minute. Because at the end of this drive lay the Sheridan Vet Clinic, Doc Billy, and a whole lot of truth.

Talking to his wife was scarier than facing any NFL linebacker had ever been. *Toughen up, Herrington.*

He turned off the stereo. Jennifer shot him a puzzled look. She knew he liked his rock classic and his volume loud when he was driving.

"Jennifer, I have a few things I want to go over with you before we get to Sheridan."

She raised her eyebrows. "You better hurry, then. We're only ten miles out."

He swallowed. "Right. Okay. Well, yesterday with Doc Billy went really well. He's got just the type of practice I've always dreamed of owning. And the price is right, too."

"Aaron, you just bought a lodge. We own a condo, and you have a clinic in Houston."

"Not really."

"Not really, what?"

"I don't really have a clinic in Houston." His breath came out in a rush, and he felt lightheaded.

She turned to face him. Her tone changed to reasonable-with-an-edge, one he called her "cross examination" voice. "Since the clinic is a major asset in our portfolio, that sounds like something we should decide together. Do you or do you not own a veterinary clinic in Houston?"

"On paper. But I have an agreement with my partners for them to buy me out, and we close in a couple of weeks."

He had a sensation of heat. Malevolent heat emanating from the petite woman sitting next to him.

"When exactly were you going to tell me?"

"As soon as we talked, which we've been putting off. Both of us. But it's not a big deal. All I did was activate the clause in our agreement. We'd anticipated this, and it's been practically automatic."

"Well, good for you, Aaron. Only you left one partner out of the automatic part."

Her sarcastic tone started getting under his skin. "That partner had run off to Houston."

"*Her* partner had ditched her in Wyoming for a decrepit lodge."

He took a deep breath, recentering himself. "I didn't ditch you, and you came back. We're good now, aren't we?" He snuck a glance at her.

Her mouth opened and closed like a goldfish. The fire in her eyes went from raging to flickering. "Yes. Of course."

Eyes back on the road, he reached for her hand, and she clasped his. "Good. I'm sorry I didn't mention this sooner. The more time that went by where we didn't talk, the more nervous I got about it. But when Doc Billy congratulates me on buying his clinic, I didn't want you to—"

She jerked her hand away. "Wait! You already bought it?"

Shit. "I made an offer, conditional on talking to you about it first. He accepted. We don't have it in writing yet, and the closing isn't planned until after the Houston closing, assuming you say yes."

"Nice."

"Jennifer, I have to work. I want it to be there."

"You're rushing into things."

"We have to move forward with our life here."

"No, we don't."

"What's that supposed to mean?"

She crossed her arms over her mid-section and stared out the window. "Nothing. It means nothing."

"Are you telling *me* everything?"

Her voice was muffled. "Of course."

His radar pinged wildly. She was hiding something from him. The evidence screamed at him. "How is the writing going?"

She whirled at him and scowled. "Fine."

"Really? Because I saw your screen two nights ago, and you hadn't written a single word."

Her eyes were red and wild, like a cornered animal. "What are you accusing me of, Aaron?"

"I just want to know the truth."

Aaron turned on his blinker. They'd already reached their exit in Sheridan. They'd be at the clinic in three minutes. He lowered the Jeepster's speed and barreled down the ramp.

"My writing sucks. But I don't appreciate you trying to read it without my permission."

"Thank you." He nodded, thinking *there was nothing to read.* "I won't look at it again until you're ready for me to see it."

"Good."

He turned right and caught sight of her face in profile. A single, fat tear was sliding down her cheek. "We don't have to go in the clinic right now, Jennifer. We could get a coffee first. Or reschedule altogether."

She shook her head. Blonde waves stuck to her wet cheek. "I made a commitment to George. I can't let our problems keep me from giving him the defense he deserves."

But what about what I deserve? Aaron didn't have a comeback to cut the bitter taste in his mouth, so he steered into the Sheridan Vet Clinic parking lot and didn't say another word.

TWENTY-FOUR

SHERIDAN, Wyoming

JENNIFER FOUGHT to get her game face on as she entered the clinic. The lack of sleep from another night of bad, vivid dreams didn't help. She was numb to the details around her of the vet practice, even as it registered with her that this place was her husband's future, which made it hers, too. Unless she said no, of course. But what choice did she have in the matter, really? If Aaron wanted to sell his clinic and buy this one, she couldn't stop him. And if she tried, she'd lose him. She was sure of it.

A week ago, she'd been devastated when Aaron hadn't followed her back to Houston. But Alayah had reminded her of what was important. How lucky she was. And she'd returned to Wyoming determined to win her husband back not just to her but to their life. Their *Houston* life. No matter how hard she'd tried to rekindle things, though, Wyoming was winning.

He wanted her, but only if he could have Wyoming, too.

This place—this dump, really, not unlike the lodge—was

winning. It was dingy. Dated. And probably unsanitary. How could he prefer this to his beautiful, immaculate Houston clinic?

Aaron walked up to the woman at the front desk. "Hello, Loretta."

The woman answered in a voice that sounded like a horse hoof against a rasp. "Doc Billy said to send you right back. You know the way."

Hoof against a rasp? Where the hell did that come from? Now that she'd admired a few—admittedly gorgeous—fancy bucking horses cavorting around at Piney Bottoms, she'd lost her Tennessee born-and-bred mind to a western one. *Great.*

"Thanks." Aaron smiled, one eyebrow up.

Loretta's return look was simpery. The Aaron effect. Today, it made Jennifer want to scream. The crusty woman gave Jennifer the once over. Jennifer was too discombobulated to throw back any shade. Besides, it looked like those piercing black eyes could see right through her.

Aaron opened a door to the interior of the clinic and gestured her ahead of him. She escaped Loretta's censure down a tight hallway.

"On the right," Aaron said.

She straightened her shoulders. She was here as George's attorney. She and Aaron could work on their issues later. Now, it was time to shuck off her self-pitying haze. At an open doorway on the right, she stopped, sucked in a breath, then preceded Aaron into the room.

If she'd thought the front of the clinic was a disappointing mess, the stacks of paper teetering on every available flat space took it to another level in the office. She looked up from them. Two diplomas, both from BYU. Which made sense—the vet was moving back to Utah.

A rangy man with curling blond hair stood behind the desk. He was like the scarecrow version of Aaron. "William Marton." He stuck out his hand. "People call me Doc Billy."

"Jennifer Herrington. Nice to meet you."

The three of them traded handshakes.

"Good to see you again, Aaron. You aren't here to tell me your wife didn't approve our deal, are you?"

Doc Billy shuffled a stack of paper off one of the two utilitarian metal chairs crowded in front of his desk and onto the floor. He paused with the second stack, looking unsure where to put it. Jennifer took pity on him and scooched two floor stacks closer together. He nodded at her and put his stack down beside them.

Aaron wiped his hands on his thighs. "Nope. Jennifer and I were just talking about how excited I am. My practice in Houston is nothing but rich, pampered clients and their spoiled small pets. I've dreamed of a country practice since I was a teenage boy."

Jennifer seethed. So much for a chance to give her input. She'd just been rubberstamped. But that wasn't fair. She was a grown-ass woman and could have given her opinion before she and Aaron had come in the clinic. She'd held it back then and she was going to now. Her choice.

"Great. Have a seat. Tell me what I can do for you? More questions?"

Jennifer sat first and waited for the men. Then she said, "I have a few."

"Happy to answer them. But if I'd known, I'd have asked my wife to join us." He winked at Aaron. "Mary's a vet tech, but she has Saturdays off."

"Oh, my questions are definitely for you, not her."

"Fire away, then."

"Did Aaron tell you what I do? Professionally, I mean."

"Things were a bit rushed when we had to operate on the Flint puppy," Aaron interjected. "How is Moose by the way?"

"Resting comfortably. We'll let Patrick take him home to recuperate quietly in a few days."

"Great news. Well, Jennifer's a criminal attorney. Excuse my brag, but she was a real hot shot with the Homicide Division in the DA's office in Houston."

Jennifer cringed at Aaron's use of the word "was." Shame was welling up inside her, though. She hadn't been honest and open with Aaron during their argument in the truck. He'd asked her point blank if she was holding anything back, and she'd lied. She'd been so angry about the things he'd kept from her. But she wasn't any better. How could she tell him? He believed things were good with them in Wyoming. And she believed they could be if they returned to Houston.

"Impressive." Doc Billy sounded sincere, but a little confused.

"Jennifer?" Aaron said.

She'd zoned out, instead of concentrating on her client's business. She *really* had to get it together. "Sorry. Skipped my coffee this morning. Thanks, Aaron. So, here in Sheridan, I took a pro bono case. Criminal defense this time."

"You've changed teams?" Doc Billy smiled at her.

"For the best of reasons. We're buying the Big Horn Lodge from George Nichols, who was charged with Hadley Prescott's murder. George has become a friend, and he asked for my help. I couldn't say no to that."

"I heard about that. Poor George. I don't know him personally, but I knew his wife. She used to bring their animals in here. I don't know who's taking care of them now—if anyone."

"He dotes on them." Aaron held up a hand. "But as for their veterinary needs, I'd guess no one, until I moved into the lodge, but only what George will let me do."

Doc Billy nodded. "You'll find that's not unusual here. Almost everybody, especially the ranchers, doctor up their own animals. And when it comes to stock, most times the big stuff is solved with a bullet."

"Oh, my God," Jennifer said.

"I understand their dilemma. A ranch is a business. Stock aren't pets, they're assets. If the cost of repair and upkeep is greater than their value, then they need to be put out of service."

Jennifer had really never considered this part of ranching before.

Her cousin, Hank. All those amazing horses and enormous, wily cattle. They were assets.

"Don't get me wrong. They care for them better than most people care for their pets. They depend on them. It's not a bad life at all. Not for the people or the animals."

Aaron reached over and squeezed her hand. "The realities of a large animal practice in ranching country are new when you're from the city. I grew up on a farm, so I get it. It's exactly how my pops operated."

Doc Billy held up his palms like he was under arrest. "Anyway, I got us a little off topic when you mentioned George. Sorry. Go on."

Jennifer hated that she was starting to like this guy. She cleared her throat. "Right. So, my job is to clear George of the murder charges."

"He didn't do it?"

"No, actually, I don't believe he did. Aaron and I were there the night Hadley Prescott was murdered."

"Oh, my. Did you see or hear anything?"

"Yes. Hadley's body. And George's shock. It was real."

Aaron added, "And someone stabbed George's dog Liam, too."

"A man doesn't stab his own dog." Doc Billy shook his head. "So, you can give him an alibi?"

"Well, we didn't spend the night in his bedroom, so, no."

He laughed. "Yeah, I guess not. Well, I can't give him one either, I'm afraid."

She smiled at him. "Has the County Attorney's office talked to you about it?"

"An alibi? No."

"About Hadley."

A shadow crossed his face. "Why would they talk to me about him?"

"Because of the bad blood between the two of you."

Long seconds passed as a shadow descended and darkened on

Doc Billy's face. Then he turned to Aaron. He pointed with his middle finger. "You. What did you tell your wife?"

Jennifer shook her head. "He told me nothing." *Almost nothing anyway*. "I heard about your disagreements from Hadley's employees."

"Hadley Prescott lost my life savings in bad investments when he was too busy making eyes at his young associate to manage my money." Doc Billy's eyes narrowed. "Wait—why are you asking me about this?"

Jennifer didn't answer, letting the silence speak for her.

His face turned red. "I'm suing his firm, but I didn't kill him over it."

Again, Jennifer didn't say a word.

"You're here trying to pin a murder on me? When I thought you were coming to buy my clinic?" Doc Billy jumped to his feet and shoved a stack of papers off his desk with both hands. The documents crashed to the floor, except for a few stragglers that wafted lazily down. "Both of you, out of my office."

Jennifer was stuck on two things. His mention of Hadley's goo goo eyes at his associate. Harriett? Or had there been someone else? She'd certainly find out. The second was Doc Billy's shocking temper. Now she understood why his behavior had made such an impression on Bonnie Morrow at Prescott Financial. And what could that temper lead him to do? Could he have killed Hadley? She wasn't sure she'd have believed it until this minute. Now she wished she had his reaction on video to show a jury.

Jennifer said, "I'm just—"

"You're just a shyster. And you." Doc Billy used his unorthodox pointing style on Aaron again. "You set me up. I wouldn't sell to you if you were the last person on earth. The deal is off."

Jennifer glanced at her husband. His face was deathly pale. She hadn't wanted him to buy the clinic, but she sure didn't want to be the cause of his heartbreak either.

TWENTY-FIVE

SHERIDAN, Wyoming

"I'M SORRY." Jennifer chewed her lip and stared at her husband's stony profile.

"It's not your fault." He kept his eyes on the road and hands on the wheel as they drove away from his dream of owning Doc Billy's clinic.

"Still, I'm sorry he bailed on you."

"Thank you." His jaw bulged and flexed.

The phone rang in her lap. She flipped it over. It was Pootie. On a Saturday. "I have to take this."

"Who is it?"

"The County Attorney." She pressed Accept. "Jennifer Herrington speaking."

"This is County Attorney Alfred Carputin."

She wondered if he ever got tired of repeating that mouthful. *Doubtful.* "Wow, I never dreamed I'd hear from you on a weekend."

"You Houston ADAs are nine-to-fivers?"

She laughed. "No."

"So, what would make you think we are here?"

"Touché. So, what has you calling me on a Saturday?" Jennifer surreptitiously watched her husband as he drove. He looked so sad that it made her insides heavy. He veered into the Holiday gas station and up to a pump.

"I have the will and insurance policy for you. But I can give you the Cliff Notes version verbally. The daughter gets everything under both."

"Even the firm?"

"Everything."

"In the Houston DA's office, that's what we call a powerful motive."

"Have you met Denise?"

Aaron started pumping gas.

"I haven't. Is she still alive after the explosion in her trailer?"

"I have no reason to think she isn't. They identified a body they found in there, and it wasn't her. A guy named Yori Baryshnikov. Known meth chef, and Denise's boyfriend."

"But they haven't found her?"

"I don't think so."

Aaron had disappeared. Jennifer looked toward the C-store. Her husband was standing by the front door talking to a woman who was facing away from Jennifer, showing a stellar backside. Jennifer frowned. "She has motive, and she's on the run."

"We already have the murderer."

"We'll see about that. What about the DNA analysis?" Aaron threw his head back, laughing. Jennifer craned for a better look. All she saw was shiny black hair, a tiny waist, and long legs. The woman was tall. Up to Aaron's shoulder anyway. Jennifer fought an urge to honk.

"Don't have it yet."

"Witness list?"

His sigh was long suffering. "We'll put it together this week. But you can pick up the will and insurance if you catch me before lunch. I'm only working a half day and no one else is here."

Aaron was typing something on his phone while he talked to the woman. She scowled. "In Houston we don't work half days when we have cases this big. Anyway, can we get George's phone then, too?"

Crickets. A familiar response from Pootie when it came to this topic.

She jerked her attention away from the Aaron effect. "Pootie, I said, can we pick up George's phone when we come in for the documents today?"

"Carputin," he said, sounding like his teeth were clenched. "And, yes, you can pick up the damn phone." He ended the call without saying goodbye.

Aaron climbed back in the Jeepster. She waited for him to tell her about the woman, but all he did was fire up the ignition. What had he typed in his phone? Hopefully it was a recommendation on where to get the best sushi in Wyoming. She didn't want to have to ask him. She waited. He put the vehicle in drive. She gave in.

"Who were you talking to?"

"When?"

"In front of the Holiday store. The young woman with the long black hair."

"Oh. I'm not sure. She bumped into me and spilled her coffee on my jeans."

"That was a long conversation about spilled coffee."

"Well, you know. She asked what I did and if I was from around here. Neighborly stuff. Being friendly."

Jennifer snorted. "Is that what the kids are calling it?"

He frowned. "I didn't do anything wrong."

"Then what were you typing on your phone?"

"Here." He took it out of his pocket and tossed it to her. "If you don't trust me, take a look. And why don't you show me yours while you're at it."

Jennifer's mouth went dry. The messages to Alayah. To Quentin.

To Vivian. She wasn't ready for him to see them. She had to come clean with him first about where things stood in Houston. "Don't be ridiculous. I just want you to tell me. I don't need to check up on you."

"She gave me the name of a kid on the team. Her nephew."

Was that so hard? "Fine."

"Fine."

Suddenly, Jennifer realized that Aaron was driving back toward Story. She tried to inject a lighter tone. "Um, after talking to the County Attorney, I have good news and bad. Which do you want first?"

His tone was flat. "Start with the good."

"Denise Little inherits everything from her dad, under the will and life insurance."

He nodded. As an ADA's spouse, she knew he would recognize confirmation of motive when he heard it. "What's the bad?"

"I need you to drop me off at Kid's office."

His expression could have melted paint. "It's Saturday."

"It's first-degree murder."

Aaron spun the steering wheel and DeMarcus Ware made a nimble U-turn.

The words, "I'm sorry," seemed to get stuck in Jennifer's throat, but she reached over and put her hand on his thigh.

TWENTY-SIX

BIG HORN, Wyoming

SINCE HE WAS at loose ends while Jennifer was working with Kid, Aaron decided to swing by the lodge. He could make a surprise welfare check on George, give him the ride into town he'd promised, and maybe even find him a vehicle. That would kill a few hours, until Jennifer was ready for pick up.

He drove on autopilot for the first fifteen minutes out of Sheridan, through Big Horn and toward the lodge, still stinging from the loss of the clinic and his argument with Jennifer. Then, as he was navigating a dog leg turn to the right, an enormous bird swooped low over the road ahead. He slammed on the brakes, although the raptor had already soared skyward. Pulling over, he rolled down the window and stuck his head out. He tented a hand over his eyes. The bird descended and gripped the branch of a cottonwood along a creek bed. With its summer leaves shed, the tree offered up a spectacular view of a mature bald eagle.

Aaron sucked in a breath. The bird turned and stared right at him. Its gaze—glare, really—was so intense, that Aaron shuddered. "Hey, brother."

The eagle looked away. It cocked its head, then took flight. At first, it struggled, its wings seeming insufficient to heft its body into the air. But with a mighty surge, the bird gained speed and altitude until it became a part of the sky. When it was only a speck above him, it stopped, hanging in place, then dove like a missile. Aaron's breath caught in his throat. The bird rocketed toward the earth and, at the last possible second, it pulled up and extended its talons into the tall, brown grass. Its flight pattern resumed, almost horizontal to the ground at first. Something was grasped in its claws. Rabbit? Prairie dog? Aaron was too far away to be sure.

Rising slowly, the bird flew a straight course toward a stand of pines nearer the mountains. Aaron lost sight of it, but he kept searching for a full minute, in case it came back. The majesty, sheer power, and daring of the bird held him in thrall. *To have the freedom to be like him,* he thought. To live life on the edge, as if there was no tomorrow. Hunt or die. Decide and provide.

He put DeMarcus Ware in gear, mulling over the encounter for the rest of the drive to the lodge. He didn't *not* believe in signs. Could this be one? His gut told him it was too significant not to be . . . something. If so, he wondered what he was to take from it. A laugh bubbled up from his core. *Of course.* The message was simple. Live. *Live.* He felt surer than ever of the decision to move to Big Horn.

He parked beside the dead Suburban in front of the lodge. As he got out of the Jeepster, a scowling, backpack-laden young man stumbled around the corner. Aaron recognized him from the first day he and Jennifer were in Wyoming. They'd seen him in the barn.

Then George came running, still wearing the bandage on his forehead. "Get. I'm not telling you again, Will. Next time I call the sheriff."

"You think they're gonna help you, old man? Besides, I came looking for my knife. I lost it last time I was out here."

"You could have said so. What did it look like?"

"Black. Four-inch blade. A little Swiss flag on the handle. My granddad gave it to me."

"Haven't seen it."

Aaron frowned. He'd seen one like that recently. An awful image flashed into his mind. Hadley. The handle protruding from his temple. Had that been a black Swiss Army knife?

Will scoffed. "Right. I'll bet you stole it and used it to off the guy here. You're a killer, man."

George shook his head. "I've never taken anything of yours. But if you think I'm a killer, then you should think twice next time about squatting here."

"Camping, not squatting."

George gave him a shove, and Will stumbled forward.

Will pivoted and launched himself into George's face. The back-packer's voice was a snarl, his face contorted and nearly purple. He shoved a palm in George's chest, knocking him backwards. "Don't *ever* put your hands on me again. Understand?" He pushed George again, and the older man fell to his rear.

It was the second violent display of temper Aaron had witnessed that day. What was it with these people—drugs? Mental illness? Whatever it was, it wasn't okay to hurt George. Not okay at all.

"Hey!" Aaron yelled. He ran toward the two men.

Will faced him, fists up. His eyes popped when he caught sight of Aaron. Aaron knew he looked like a charging bull to most people, even when he wasn't wearing cleats and shoulder pads. Will's fists opened by his shoulders. *Hands up.* "Dude, relax. We're good."

Aaron grabbed Will by his shirt front and hauled him up, then shoved him against the lodge. "That's not what I saw, *dude*. I saw a trespasser attacking a property owner."

Will shook his head, feet scrambling without finding the ground. "He assaulted me, man."

Aaron shook his head. Maybe under the technical laws that made any unwanted touching an assault, but that wasn't enough for Aaron to support Will's version. There was the law, and then there was reality. And in real life, this shit was not happening on Aaron's watch.

He ground Will's shoulders against the rough logs. "You okay, George?"

George was struggling to his feet, his face contorted with pain. The day after a car wreck—or a football game—was always the worst. Aaron let go of Will. His feet crashed back to the ground, and he crumpled to his knees.

Aaron rushed over and gave George a hand up, careful not to pull too hard.

George brushed off his jeans and elbows. "I'm fine. If I hadn't been in that wreck yesterday, he wouldn't have gotten the better of me."

An engine, tires on the dirt road, and a loud clanking jerked Aaron's attention away from the two men for a moment. It was a truck. Behind it was a trailer, and on the trailer was a giant, light blue plastic tank. A septic tank. And in the driver's seat was a beaming Black Bear Betty. Aaron waved, and she returned the gesture as she parked.

He wheeled on Will. "Why are you still here?"

"What are you, George's enforcer?" The expression on Will's face was malevolent.

Aaron considered it for a moment, then gave him a maniacal grin, the kind he'd perfected over four years in the SEC. "Yes. And I'm buying the place, so be warned. Next time, if George catches you, he calls the sheriff. But I won't. Your family will think you're lost in the woods, and they'll never find your body."

"You're nuts, man." Will stomped past Black Bear Betty's rig and up the road. He turned when he was thirty feet away and shouted, "You'll get what's coming to you. Both of you."

George snorted. "Can you believe I hired that kid when Shelly and I were first out here? We had more business then. He lived in the cottage. I had to let him go when . . . after Shelly died. He can't get it through his thick skull that nothing is like it was before." George's eyes looked red and filmy. Sad, not angry.

Aaron clapped George on the shoulder he hoped was the uninjured one. "Ignore the punk. You've got a septic tank. B-cubed has come through.

George squinted at him. "Who?"

"B-cubed. Black Bear Betty."

George still stared at him.

"You know. Black Bear Betty. B-B-B. Three Bs. B-cubed."

George shook his head. "I don't think you should call her that."

Black Bear Betty strode toward them, rocking back and forth from the hitch in her gait. "Time to fix you up, George."

"Robbing Peter to pay Paul again?" George said.

She stretched her suspender straps. "I'm a master of prioritization."

George brushed dead grass, dirt, and small rocks off his shirt. "You've wasted your time."

"How's that?"

"Tractor's not running."

"I'd bring my own tractor out, but it's broke, too. I'm waiting on a part. You know that old dinosaur is down more often than not. What's the matter with yours?"

"Wouldn't start. Battery, I suspect. I'd run to town to get one, but I don't have a vehicle."

Aaron smiled. "That's why I'm here. Let me give you a ride, and we'll get you that battery after we go look for some wheels in town."

George made a harrumphing sound.

B-cubed nodded. "I'll come out tomorrow and do the install."

"And charge me Sunday emergency visit rates? No thanks."

"Have I ever done that to you?"

George turned and gazed up into the mountains like he hadn't heard her.

"I've never," Black Bear Betty said to Aaron. Then to George she said, "Fine. Monday."

George kept his eyes on higher elevations. "We can go to town. But I want to fetch Katya and Liam while I'm out. Things here don't seem right without them."

Aaron said, "Sounds like a plan."

"I'll get my wallet." George stomped up the front steps of the house.

Black Bear Betty raised her eyebrows at Aaron. "He's difficult, our George."

Aaron couldn't disagree. "I've got a question for you."

"Can't promise I have an answer, but I'll try."

"What would you think if I were to call you B-cubed?"

Her expression remained neutral. "Is this an initials thing? Because if I'm not mistaken yours are A.H. What's that stand for? Ass Hole?"

Aaron bit the inside of his lip. She was quick. And the way she said it—Ess Hole—was downright funny. "Black Bear Betty it is, then."

"Now, I've got to go dump this tank off my trailer."

"You need help?"

She gave him a withering look. Without another word, she hobbled back to her truck and pulled the trailer around to the back of the lodge.

Aaron checked his phone to see if he'd heard from Jennifer. No word. But he did have a new text. *Hi, Coach Aaron. My nephew said your awesome. I agree. He gave me your digits. I hope you dont mind. ~ Etta from Holiday.*

He pulled at the collar of his shirt. Etta from Holiday? The only person he'd talked to at Holiday, besides Jennifer, of course, was the woman whose nephew Trey played on the Rams. It had to be her. But why was she texting him? He stared daggers at the phone, wishing the text would disappear. The woman was putting him in a bad position. Jennifer would be pissed if she saw this. She had been suspicious of the woman. Etta. And it seemed a little flirty. He started to delete it without answering, not that it would do any good. She had his number. She could just contact him again. It had happened before. People acted weird when they mistook him for a celebrity. Then he stopped. What if he was misreading the text? Would it be rude not to answer? It might put Trey in the middle and make him uncomfortable. Aaron lifted his thumb in mid swipe.

The front door to the lodge slammed. At the same time, another vehicle started making its way up the long drive from Red Grade Road to the cabin, a plume of dust billowing in its wake. George came to stand beside Aaron. They watched together.

"The lodge is the place to be today. Who's this?" Aaron said.

Aaron felt rather than saw George shrug.

The white, circa 2000 Chevy Impala with oversized mirrors—obviously a former patrol car—lumbered toward them. It lurched to a stop three feet away from them, but neither George nor Aaron moved a muscle.

A dark-skinned man with an infectious grin bounced out. He was plump. Roly poly was the word that came to Aaron's mind, really, with a belly that lapped over the waistband of a pair of skinny chinos.

"Yo, is this the Big Horn Lodge?" he said.

"No vacancy. Sorry." George's expression was wary.

The man advanced anyway. "You the owner?"

"I am."

"George Nichols?"

George's voice moved to the testy range. It hadn't had far to go to. "Yes. Why?"

Too late, Aaron spied the papers the man produced from behind his leg. *Oh, no.*

The man slapped them into the hand George automatically held out for them. "You've been served, my man."

George stared at him, a look of incomprehension on his face.

The man saluted him with two fingers to the temple and walked back to the Impala, his shoulders juking as he sang *Bust A Move*. Then the Impala bounced away on loose shocks, juking like its driver.

Aaron said, "May I see?"

George didn't respond. Aaron slipped the papers from his unresisting hands. He read the style on the first page, then the content on the first few pages.

George was being sued by Gerrianne Williams in civil court for the wrongful death of her daughter, Mary Stiles.

Can anything else go wrong for this poor guy?

TWENTY-SEVEN

SHERIDAN, Wyoming

JENNIFER PUSHED WISPS of hair off her face and back into a headband. The relaxed dress and make-up, hairdo-optional Wyoming code was rubbing off on her, and on a Monday morning no less. In her jeans, up-do, and oversized plaid shirt with rolled sleeves she'd taken from Aaron's suitcase, she barely recognized herself in the mirror of the little bathroom at Kid's office. She looked more like a poster for Rosie the Riveter than the high-powered ADA of the last fifteen years. And younger. More rested, with no thanks to Saturday.

Ugh, Saturday. The fight with Aaron. The drama with Doc Billy. The unsettling interaction between the woman and Aaron at the gas station. Pootie failing to produce George's phone, again, despite dumping a mound of additional documents on her and Kid. Why wasn't she surprised Pootie had reneged? Because of him, she'd spent the rest of Saturday drafting an emergency motion for the judge, asking for the return of George's phone. She couldn't wait to ream Pootie a new one in court.

Rest had come on Sunday when she'd taken the day off. At first, she'd hoped to reconnect with Aaron, but he was outside with Hank, being a ranch hand. *The unplumbed depths of Aaron Herrington, as revealed in Wyoming.* The cabin was sad and quiet since George had picked up Liam and Katya in his new-to-him pickup. She'd known she'd miss Jeremiah, but she'd been surprised how large the absence of the dog and cat loomed. So, at loose ends, she'd sat down to write. When that failed miserably, she'd taken a long, slow walk, stopping to pet horse noses over fences. Then, feeling western, she'd finished the day streaming *Longmire* episodes. She figured she'd deserved the mental downtime.

Somehow, over thirty-six hours, she and Aaron had barely spoken to each other, much less discussed anything important. He'd been acting weird, too, fiddling with his phone to keep from having to look at her. It was her fault. She was the one with things she needed to tell him. That she wanted to tell him. She'd just chickened out. She was so blue about it all that she hadn't wanted to talk to anyone, and she'd ignored calls and messages from Alayah and her family and gone to sleep early. Luckily, the nightmares had been less disruptive, although they were still repetitive. Screams. Grass. Gunshots. A coiled snake. A pile of rocks. Some letters. An acronym, maybe? A-T-O-M? Darned if she could figure out what it was all about. If she could, maybe she'd be able to make it stop.

Which brought her to the harsh reality of Monday and the dismal confines of Kid's office bathroom. The little space had an RV-sized plastic shower stall and a plastic sink basin set in the top of a single cabinet. A knee-knocker toilet sat too close to the sink and at eye-level with a mirror propped behind the faucet. Aaron wouldn't have been able to fit one thigh in the tiny room. Not that he would have wanted to. She wouldn't even be in here if she had the choice. The floor was squishy and uneven. The walls were stained and bare. The light was a bare bulb with a pull string. The fixtures were rusted, in the sink and in the shower. And there was a smell. Like a wet dog locked in a closet.

She splashed cold water on her face and neck. The high temp yesterday had been an amazing sixty-eight. Her shirt would have been perfect for yesterday. But today it was already seventy-five out. She'd adjusted to the cooler weather faster than she could have imagined, and now her body was resistant to the warming trend. And Kid didn't have an air conditioner. Or a hand towel.

She shook her hands dry and returned to the office. Kid had arranged the originals of the discovery documents into piles on the desk. He was digging redrope pocket folders from a plastic shopping bag and creating files.

She said, "Did you get a chance to read the motion?"

He nodded, not pausing his organizing. "Yes. Amazing. Thanks."

"Anything you think I missed or should change?"

His eyes bugged. "You want my input?"

"I didn't send it to you for your entertainment. We're co-counsel. Two brains, two sets of eyes, remember?"

His chest seemed to enlarge a shirt size. "Well, you heard Denise Little is okay, right?"

She cocked a hip. "Uh, no. I'm not plugged into the Sheridan grapevine, Kid. Next time, use that touch screen communication device you carry in your pocket and let me know when you learn important stuff like that."

He gave her a sheepish grin.

"What's the story?"

"I just heard this morning. My mom had coffee with Bonnie. You know, from Prescott Financial?"

"I remember her."

"Bonnie said Denise has been staying with her ever since her trailer blew up."

Gotcha, Denise. "That means we can interview her."

"I think the county already did. Bonnie said Pootie came to see Denise on Sunday."

Jennifer growled.

Kid put down his latest redrope. "I was thinking we should ask for Denise's statement and the DNA analysis in the motion, too."

"I like your thinking."

Arguably, Pootie wasn't technically in violation of any rules yet, but he was ignoring repeated requests and lying about the phone, which was getting him toward a violation in a hurry. They had plenty for the judge to show him the defendant's faith in the system was being tested. He might deny the motion, and it might cost her some points with him, but annoying Pootie and putting the judge on notice that the county attorney was a problem was more than worth it. Jennifer couldn't afford any delays. Every day they lost was another opportunity for Aaron to embed himself further into the greater Sheridan community.

She mused aloud. "So, if we went to trial tomorrow, we'd have the *stand your ground* defense. 'He did it, but he had the right to stand his ground, Your Honor.' We've got two possible suspects—Billy Marton and Denise Little—who the police haven't taken seriously. Honestly, though, neither thing is enough. We need that DNA." She smiled at Kid. "Want to add your ideas into the motion real quick?"

Kid's eyes sparkled. He opened his laptop, sat down behind it, and started typing with the impossible speed of a serious gamer. While he worked, Jennifer revisited their to do list for the case. Kid was working on the phone, DNA, and—bonus—a statement from Denise. Pootie had promised them the witness list later in the week. She and Kid had the will and insurance policy and knew that Denise inherited the firm and everything else. Hopefully they'd be able to discuss those things soon. They still needed to talk to Tim O'Leary, the landlord at Prescott Financial. And to get their hands on that lease.

"Kid?"

"Huh?" He didn't look away from his screen.

"Do we have a copy of the Prescott Financial lease yet?"

"I'm supposed to pick it up today."

Thinking about Prescott Financial brought Hadley's supposed fling back to her mind. "What about that phone number Hadley was calling? Any luck?"

"No. I think it's a prepaid. You know, a burner?"

"Hmm. I have a lead on a girlfriend."

Now she had his attention. His fingers stopped, and his eyes lifted up to hers a second later. "Who?"

"Doc Billy said Hadley was sweet on a young associate at the office."

"Whoa. There are no young associates there."

She drilled him with her eyes. Harriett was ten years younger than Jennifer. But from the perspective of an early-twenty-something, anyone out of college was one foot in the grave. "Um, Harriett?"

"She's not young. Maybe they had somebody else that quit. Or an intern."

She wasn't as sure as Kid. She'd ask Denise about her father's love life when they talked to her. But there was another way Jennifer could try to find out about the girlfriend, and she couldn't believe she hadn't already thought of it. She fished Hadley's phone records from one of Kid's neat stacks and dialed the number. It went straight to a recorded voice mail that didn't give a name. Jennifer hung up on it. No sense in showing her hand.

She returned to O'Leary, looking his number up online and making a note of it.

"Done," Kid said, punching a fist in the air. "Printing."

"Sign it, and let's get moving," Jennifer said.

Kid looked crestfallen. "That's it?"

"What—did you want a cookie?"

His frown bordered on a pout.

Her lips twitched. "Would you like me to read it and tell you it's wonderful?"

He smiled and handed it to her.

· · ·

***

JENNIFER MARCHED into Pootie's office with Kid scrambling to keep up with her. It was in a quaint two-story house with white trim, a deep porch, and a wide balcony, catty-corner across the street from the county buildings. The county attorney's quarters were twice the size of hers in Houston and decorated with real wood furniture and Western prints. Her fishbowl was crowded with an L-shaped metal desk and matching cabinets, handed down from multiple predecessors, and complete with the dents they'd left behind. No prints on the walls. A lonely, framed picture of her and Aaron at a Habitat for Humanity charity event on her desk.

Pootie peered over tortoise shell glasses at them. An expanse of white forehead suggested a weekend shortening of his hair. "How does your client feel about getting sued?"

"What?" Kid said.

Aaron had texted her the news about the wrongful death complaint, but she hadn't had a chance to bring Kid up to speed on it yet. "I'll fill you in later." Coolly, she said to Pootie, "George is having a much worse time than he deserves."

Pootie's face was feral. "On that we will have to disagree."

"On that, and much more, I suspect. Speaking of which, it's time for you to cough up his phone."

"Sorry. I tried. It's still in evidence." He sounded decidedly glib.

"The county has had ample time to get any data off it they want to."

Pootie didn't respond.

She'd save it for the judge instead of wasting her energy on a futile debate. "I heard you visited Denise Little."

He nodded.

She gave him a moment, but he didn't elaborate. "We're on our way to file this with the court. Here's a courtesy copy, *Pootie*." She dropped the motion on his desk.

He frowned at it. Jennifer watched him for a moment, then looked down, too. The motion had landed beside a copy of *The Sheridan Press*, the town's daily print newspaper. She'd seen it for sale all over town and had been wanting to pick one up and check it out. Actual *print* papers. So last decade. But curiosity wasn't what drew her attention to the paper now. It was the front page, above-the-fold picture of her husband.

Pootie flicked his hand at the motion. "What is this?"

Jennifer ignored him. She snatched up the paper and read *NFL Alum Joins Rams Coaching Staff*. If she'd worried Aaron would get even more entrenched in the community, she didn't have to wonder anymore. The article practically promised a statute of him at the Big Horn city limits. It included gushing quotes from Coach Flint, parents, players, and boosters. The article continued on an inner page. She flipped with dread, speed reading. She couldn't believe the depth they went into about his college and pro career, even explaining that his move to tight end had come about when he and Peyton Manning had gone head-to-head for quarterback at Tennessee.

Kid read over her shoulder. "Holy moly, Jennifer. Is that your husband?"

Pootie stood, joining in the reading party.

Through clenched teeth, Jennifer said, "Yes."

"He's famous."

She sighed. "Not famous. Well-known long ago. But he was a really, really good tight end." She swallowed hard. Maggie's words popped back into her head, tormenting her. *What do you have against your husband being happy?* She needed to spit out the sour grapes she was sucking and support him, like he deserved. This was wonderful for Aaron. She smiled and tried to match it with her tone of voice. "And he's a great coach. Those kids are lucky."

"He was going to be a big star. I remember him. Definitely famous." Pootie's mouth moved as he continued reading. Then he said, "Is he friends with Peyton Manning?"

"We both are. The Mannings are lovely people."

Pootie and Kid stared at her, two matching human fly traps.

Jennifer refolded the newspaper and put it back on Pootie's desk. "Would you like to read the motion before we take it to the judge?"

Pootie waved her off with his fingers. "Do your worst, counselor. Stu doesn't like big city games."

Jennifer smiled. She'd been hoping he'd say that. "Stu?"

"Judge Ryan."

He was trying to hometown her. *Newsflash, buddy. That's not going to work.* "All righty then. See you in court."

"Wait—I do have one piece of news for you."

Jennifer and Kid exchanged a glance.

"Yes?"

"We got the DNA analysis back, but it was still messed up."

"Of course, it was."

"I'm serious. George and Hadley's results came back identical, which is impossible. We'd like to do a fresh sample on George and send that in."

Over my dead body. Her hands started to shake. Sweat beaded on her brow. Her last victory in Houston replayed in her mind. The murder defendant had tried to create reasonable doubt with the identical DNA results of his identical twin brother. She'd convinced Harris County to pay for the special Eurofins test that could distinguish between them, only to have the court reject it. There was no way Sheridan County would pay big bucks for a test that wasn't generally accepted yet.

With indistinguishable DNA, Pootie couldn't prove George was at the crime scene or in contact with Hadley. It was her trump card to reasonable doubt in George's case. Maybe even to a dismissal in the absence of other evidence.

But that wasn't what was making her hands tremble and bringing on a sudden sweat. *No.* It was the inescapable fact that if their DNA was identical and the lab *hadn't* made an error, George and Hadley—

sworn worst enemies who'd married the same woman—were identical twins.

TWENTY-EIGHT

BIG HORN, Wyoming

JENNIFER'S MIND was racing as fast as her heartbeat as she skidded to a stop at the Big Horn Lodge. Even the ticket a friendly Deputy Travis had given her in the thirty-mile per hour zone in Big Horn hadn't slowed the churn inside her.

She threw the door to the rental car open, glad she was wearing jeans and casual cruiser shoes. Breaking into a run, she took the porch steps two at a time.

"Wait," Kid called.

She didn't wait. Nor did she knock. She barreled into the living room. "George? Are you in here?"

She paused, listening for a response. She heard loud mechanical noises from behind the lodge. Tractor-like noises. And a chittering.

"Jeremiah!" she called.

The fluffy little animal stretched and rolled on the sofa like a cat waking from a nap. She picked him up and held him to her face, crooning baby nonsense.

Kid caught up with her. "It's the little stink pot."

"Shh. Don't listen to him," Jennifer said into Jeremiah's fur.

"You should get one of your own."

His words pole axed her heart. She didn't want one of her own. She wanted Jeremiah. But an ugly truth hit her. He belonged to George, in Wyoming, no matter what George had said about pets coming with the purchase of the lodge. She could research her condo building's rules and talk to the property manager all she wanted to, but it wouldn't matter. She knew this skunk would never be coming to Texas. Feeling like she was amputating a limb, she forced herself to set Jeremiah back on the couch.

"What's the matter?" Kid sounded confused.

How can he know, at his tender age, the pain of true love? "We've got to find George." She raised her voice. "George? Are you in here?"

When there was again no response, she trotted toward the back porch with Kid right behind her. Once on the deck, she followed the noise of the tractor to the septic pit. A huge blue plastic tank was perched in the tractor bucket over the hole. George was gesticulating wildly to Black Bear Betty, Liam standing beside him swaying in the wind. George's gestures might mean Black Bear Betty should move the tank slightly to her left. It was hard to be sure, because he abruptly started making the same motions in the opposite direction before she had adjusted the tractor.

The whole scene was bizarre. The last time Jennifer had seen that hole, it had contained Hadley's dead body and an injured Liam. She leaned on her knees, suddenly lightheaded from altitude, exertion, and sheer excitement.

Kid shouted to be heard. "Do you really think George and Hadley are twins?"

She shot him a look. Sometimes he was such a, well, *kid*. "We don't have any new information since we left Pootie's office. All we can do is ask George about it. And it's entirely possible the sample just got contaminated or switched out or something."

"But if they really are twins . . ."

He was only echoing her own thoughts and emotions. She needed to rein both of them in. "These chicks aren't hatched yet. No use counting them."

Black Bear Betty seemed to notice them for the first time. She lowered the bucket and eased the tank into the hole. After she raised the bucket, she turned off the tractor and waved to them. George barely glanced their way.

"Hi, you guys!" Jennifer's enthusiasm was spilling out, no matter what advice she dispensed to Kid.

"Hi, yourself," Black Bear Betty called. "Do you need me?"

"Nope. Just George."

She saluted. "I'll stay up here and return a few calls then."

"Sounds good," Jennifer said. "George, do you have a minute to talk about your case?"

Liam trotted up and shoved a nose in Kid's crotch. Kid fended him off. The geriatric dog walked away and collapsed in a heap by the porch steps.

George looked like he'd swallowed a porcupine. "Which one? The one the state's bringing against me, or the one Mary Stiles' family is?"

She took a deep breath. "The state. That's the one we represent you on."

"What am I supposed to do about the other one?"

"You don't have a civil attorney yet?"

"You're my attorney."

Kid was looking at his feet.

The difference in civil and criminal was lost on George. On most people. Jennifer said, "Well, Kid is really your attorney, since I'm not licensed in Wyoming. Kid, do you think you could help George with his other matter? It's a wrongful death complaint." She wished they'd talked about it on the way up from Sheridan, but all either of them could think about was identical DNA.

Kid's eyes rose slowly. To say he looked unsure of himself was an epic understatement.

"Or maybe you could get started and then find co-counsel?" Not waiting for Kid's response, she turned to George. "Do you have property insurance—like a homeowner's policy on the lodge?"

He scowled. "The lawsuit isn't about the lodge."

"Homeowner's policies usually cover wrongful death. It doesn't have to occur on the premises."

"That doesn't make a lick of sense."

"It doesn't have to. The bottom line, though, is that your insurance company will pay for your attorney, if you've got a policy and it doesn't have a specific exclusion for wrongful death."

The scowl loosened. "I've got one."

"Could you find a copy?"

"If not, my agent can."

"Good. You need to let the insurance company know about the lawsuit ASAP. Your agent can help you get that contact information. You also need to tell them you want Kid as your attorney."

He rubbed the three-day stubble on his chin, enough for an audition for a *Miami Vice* reunion episode. "Okay."

She smiled at Kid. "The policy would mean you'd get paid."

Kid still seemed like he was in pain. "But I—could you work on it with me?"

"I've never defended a civil case. Just file an answer by the deadline and find someone to refer the work to if you're uncomfortable after that."

He exhaled a rattling breath. "I, um, I can do that."

Jennifer's mouth opened to raise the issue of finding substitute counsel for herself on the murder charge, but something stilled her tongue. A flicker. An energy. An *interest*. Comprehension dawned on her. Unwelcome comprehension. She wanted this stupid case. Curmudgeonly George had grown on her, but it was more than that. The potential twin angle fascinated her, between her own twin-ship and the case she'd prosecuted in Houston with "the other twin did it" defense angle. But it didn't matter what she *wanted*. She had to get back to Houston for the DA campaign. She had to. She'd been thinking about it before she fell asleep the night before, with her husband a million emotional miles away beside her on the bed. Their relationship was in a dip, but all marriages had ups and downs. They belonged together. They'd make it through this. And now, with his clinic purchase off the table and his coaching commitment in Big Horn only running through football season, she could lure him back to Houston. She'd go ahead and move back at the end of the month Quentin had given her for her decision. She and Aaron would do the distance thing for a few months. Then Aaron would come home.

And just because she cared about George's case didn't mean she had to sign on to it for the long haul. She'd be here a few more weeks. Why couldn't she just give it her absolute best a little longer, without the interference of replacement counsel? Then she'd hand off a rock-solid case she was proud of to a local hot shot in a couple of weeks.

I don't have to give the case up. I won't give it up. Not yet. A slow smile broke over her face. The decision felt good, like unbuttoning tight jeans or taking her hair out of a ponytail holder at the end of the day.

The two men were staring at her like they were waiting for something, so she cleared her throat. "Now that we've settled that issue, George, we need to talk to you about Hadley." She motioned him toward the porch, then thought better of it. Talk by the septic hole where a grisly murder had occurred or by the actively used camp potty? She split the difference and moved into the open yard between them.

George grunted and followed her. Black Bear Betty restarted the tractor.

When George and Kid were both an arm's length away, Jennifer said, "Bear with me, George. I'm going to ask some odd questions, but I have good reasons."

That got an eyebrow raise out of him.

Jennifer took a deep breath. This was going to sound crazy to George, so she might as well just spit it out. "Is there any chance you're related to Hadley?"

George's words exploded from his mouth. "Not no, but hell no!"

Black Bear Betty lifted a scoop of dirt.

"Tell me about your parents and where you were born."

His eyes narrowed to a squint. "What's this about?"

"Humor me." She gave him a toothy smile and put some eye sparkle into it.

He softened. "Lorene and Carlton Nichols. They were good people. I was born and raised right here in Sheridan."

"Were you adopted?"

His arms crossed over his chest in a gesture more protective than assertive. "No. What is this crazy talk?"

Her eyes were drawn again to the tractor. The bucket of dirt was still hovering in the air. Black Bear Betty was on the ground, looking at one of the arms to the bucket. She wasn't smiling.

"Are you one hundred percent sure?"

His eyes cut to the tractor and Black Bear Betty. "They kept it a pretty good secret if I was."

"Would you mind if I talked to them and asked them myself?"

"They're beyond answering."

"What do you mean?"

"They're both deceased."

An acute disappointment welled inside her. Her best source of information, forever unavailable to her. "I'm sorry. Anyone else I could ask?"

He pursed his lips, rubbing the upper one. "My mother's little sister—my aunt—lives in Billings."

"I need to talk to her. Today."

Black Bear Betty kicked the tractor and hollered something unprintable that Maggie's dog would have answered to.

"Today?"

"If possible."

"Okay. I'll call her."

"How about your birth certificate? What does it say?"

"I dunno. I've got a copy in my safety deposit box. I assume it says what I told you."

Jennifer pulled a photo of the murder weapon from her bag. "New topic. Do you have a knife like this one, or have you ever seen one like it before?"

George leaned close to the picture. "Don't have one. Seen a lot like it. And Will says he lost one like it here."

"Will?"

"The kid who thinks he should be allowed to live in a tent on my land."

Jennifer nodded. She remembered him. "Did he have a beef with Hadley?"

"None that I knew of."

"Next question. Do you have a printer here?"

"A printer?"

"A printer. The thing you connect to a computer so you can print what you type onto paper."

He shook his head. "I keep my records on paper. If I need to print something, I can do it at The UPS Store. People these days don't even remember how to write anything by hand. All this emailing and texting. They aren't even teaching kids cursive in school anymore in some places. It's a national tragedy." *I wouldn't go that far, but the man has a point.* Then his eyes widened. "Denise. Melinda. I didn't know you were coming."

Denise? Melinda? She hadn't heard a car, but, then again, the tractor was loud enough to cover an air raid siren. Jennifer whirled. Denise was standing right behind her. The young woman looked even worse than the last time she'd seen her. Which made sense. She'd lost a father, a drug-cooking partner, and a home since then. A stiff wind would carry her away, along with the woman beside her, a red head with a pissed-off expression on her face. By process of elimination, Melinda. She looked familiar, but Jennifer couldn't place her.

Denise spoke, and her voice had the tonal quality of a thrumming high-tension wire. "I need money, George."

"Get a job."

Denise launched herself at him. Her lips were curled back over bad teeth. Her face was drawn like a weasel's. Her bloodshot eyes bulged. "Yori's dead. You've taken everything from me, you bastard. You owe me."

Melinda cocked her head, smiling.

Kid moved faster and with more confidence than Jennifer would have given him credit for, getting in between Denise and George.

"Move it, pipsqueak."

"Denise, it's me. Kid. Kid James. Calm down."

She locked her eyes on George without sparing Kid a glance.

George didn't flinch. "Who's Yori?"

"My boyfriend. And I loved him." Her voice broke on a sob.

"I'm sorry about that. But I don't know anything about him, Denise."

"Ask her. Your lawyer." Denise pointed at Jennifer.

Denise was out of control. Probably high. Potentially homicidal. Jennifer dialed her voice to soothing as she scanned both women for weapons. When she didn't see any, she raised her hands. "I didn't know him either, Ms. Little. I'm very sorry for your loss."

Denise spit a gob of saliva at Jennifer. "You'll get what's coming to you."

The loogie fell short of Jennifer's feet.

Denise redirected her rage at George. "You killed my mother. You took everything she should have left to me."

"You know that's not true. You're a spoiled brat who should have been nicer to Shelly when she was alive. Your mother didn't owe you anything, and I don't either."

Way to poke the bear, George.

Denise lunged at him again, shrieking, rabid. Kid caught her by the upper arms. Her fists flailed, pounding his shoulders. She landed a vicious kick on his shin, but he didn't let go. Melinda watched, amused and motionless.

Denise snarled at George over Kid's shoulder. "This place was half my mother's. Why should you get it and not me?"

Even though Jennifer had seen no signs of weapons, fists, feet, teeth, and nails could do a lot of damage. She decided the best way she could help Kid and George was by distracting Denise. She stepped into her field of vision. "Was your father adopted?"

Denise refocused on Jennifer. "I saw you in court. But I don't know you, Lawyer Lady. And that's a personal question that I don't have to answer."

"My husband took care of your cat. You don't know me, but you know him."

"I don't have a cat." Then she laughed. More a cackle, really. "Oh, yeah. The cat."

"So is your father adopted?"

"Um, yeah, I think he was. What's it to you?"

Kid kept his hands on her arms, but his grip relaxed.

Yes! "Can you get me a copy of his birth certificate?"

"I don't have it. But why would I give one to you anyway?"

Instead of answering, Jennifer fired a lightning round question at her. "Where were you the night he died?"

"What did you say your name was?"

"I'm Jennifer Herrington. My husband is the vet."

Denise thought about it for a second. It didn't make sense to her, clearly, but she was just high enough that she gave up and gave in. "Home. In bed."

Kid released her.

"Was anyone with you?"

Melinda took a step closer. "Don't answer that. It's bullshit, Denise. I mean, come on. She's the attorney for the man who killed my sister. You can't trust her."

"What?" Jennifer said. "Who?"

Melinda sneered at her. "Sarah Stiles is my sister."

Suddenly Jennifer understood Melinda's presence and behavior.

The sense that she'd met the redhead before grew stronger. Then it hit her. Melinda worked as a server at the restaurant where Hank's dinner had been.

Denise's venom returned. She bristled at Jennifer, and, although her words had the empty sound of the chemically altered, they were defiant. "Listen, lady, I'm not answering any more of your—"

Jennifer pressed. "Can you get me a copy of his birth certificate? I really need it. Maybe from his attorney?"

Denise and Melinda shared a look. *I'm losing her.*

"Why are you hassling me, Lawyer Lady?"

Jennifer stepped between the women, blocking Denise's eye contact with her friend. "Because you're his heir. Anything that was his is yours. And you seem like you'd like to make some cash."

A shrewd look came into Denise's lizard eyes. "How much?"

Jennifer slowly and deliberately pulled her wallet out of her shoulder bag and extracted a one-hundred-dollar bill.

"One now, one when you give it to me. I can come get it after lunch. Are you still staying at Bonnie Morrow's?"

Denise's mouth opened and closed like a fish gasping to breathe. "How did you know . . . Okay."

"You can borrow my phone to call the attorney and then pick it up on your way back to Bonnie's." Jennifer put the phone in Denise's hands.

Denise swallowed. "What do you think, Lindy?"

Melinda licked her lips. "It seems all right."

Kid and George were staring at Jennifer, speechless. She winked without smiling. Steely confidence had always been one of her best weapons. And she hated it, but junkies' objections almost always evaporated when cash for their next hit was on the table. Maybe the women would use the money for lunch. But probably not.

Denise dialed and put the phone to her ear. She cleared her throat. "Uh, yeah, can I speak to Alistair McClain. This is Denise Little about my dad, Hadley Prescott." She was silent for a few seconds. "Yeah, hi. I need to come get a copy of my dad's birth certificate. Do you have one?" Then, "Can I come today?" A pause. "I'm fine. Good. Thank you."

She handed the phone back to Jennifer and left her open palm extended. "One hundred dollars."

Jennifer withheld the bill. "One more thing. Did your dad have a girlfriend?"

The answer came out as a whine. "He was in love with my mother until the day he died."

"That's what I hear. But who did he date?"

"He was with women sometimes."

"Did any of them get attached?"

"What do you mean?"

"Did any of them have trouble accepting that they wouldn't replace your mother?"

"I don't know. Maybe."

"Like who?"

"Another hundred."

"Twenty."

Denise growled low in her throat. "Etta."

"Etta what?"

Denise stuck out her hand. Jennifer put the hundred in it, then another twenty.

Denise crumpled the bills and stuffed them down her bra. "Don't know her last name. Good luck, sucker."

She and Melinda walked away, their heads together, whispering.

Just when Jennifer thought things between her and Denise had been improving. Clearly they'd never be BFFs. But she'd gotten what she wanted and protected George. Manis, pedis, and mimosas weren't her thing anyway.

The noise of the tractor was suddenly absent.

Black Bear Betty walked up to George, Kid, and Jennifer. "I've got some bad news about your tractor, George."

George stood stock still. Jennifer was beginning to wonder if he had a medical issue, but he snorted and stalked off toward the cottage.

"George?" she called.

"I've had all the bad news I can handle for today." He shut the cottage door so hard the glass panes in it shattered and glass rained onto his porch.

TWENTY-NINE

STORY, Wyoming

AARON WIPED sweat from his brow, scratching hay across his forehead. He sneezed from the tickle of dust in his nose. Stacking bales was itchy work, but the barn and the hay smelled sweet, like summer and horses. He'd loved barns ever since his childhood. The one on his family's farm had been an old wooden structure like the Piney Bottoms barn. Dirt floors. Dark, cool corners in the steamy days of summer. Warm shafts of sunlight shooting through drafty cracks in the depths of winter. Barn cats on patrol. The odor of manure, oddly pleasant. And, today, in this barn, dry heat. It was hard to believe he'd been bundled up against snow, cold, and wind only a few days before. Now here he was, stacking bales of hay in the oven-like confines of a loft.

And it felt *good*. Honest labor. Close contact with the land. Tending to livestock. Paying his keep with Hank and Maggie. Getting in some much-needed strength work, something he missed without a gym. Distracting himself from disappointment—losing the clinic and the tension in his marriage. That morning, he'd helped a mare through a difficult birth and been there for the first wobbly steps of a perfect stud colt. He'd spent most of the day before vaccinating bucking horses. The wily, muscly creatures were surprisingly docile with him, and Hank had explained the process of training them to buck. Bucking in the arena was an athletic performance, not a measure of meanness.

On the subject of athletics, last night he'd studied the Rams' play book. He'd realized Friday night that they were running an offense he knew. But after seeing the skills of the players, he had ideas about how to use their unique talents to complement each other. He couldn't wait to get to practice that afternoon.

He stacked the last bale, eyed it, and scooted it back and to the left. Alignment was critical. One bale out of line could magnify over many rows and throw a barn's storage capacity out of whack. One thing out of line in a marriage could do the same thing. He hated that he and Jennifer had gotten sideways about the clinics. He felt even worse that he'd let everything stick in his craw the last few days.

The distance between them was his fault. He was just so damn frustrated. He wanted her to love it here. There was so much that was promising, so much for both of them to build their lives around. The community was welcoming, and people were friendly. The scenic beauty was unmatched, with possibilities for endless outdoor activities. He had the team and the lodge. Eventually he'd find the perfect veterinary practice, too. Jennifer had thrown herself into representing George. She could have a great Northern Wyoming law practice if she wanted. And, in time, when things settled, maybe words would come, and she could write here.

He climbed down from the loft to throw more bales up from the trailer. His phone buzzed with a text. When he reached the bottom, he pulled it from his pocket.

Gene Soboleski was stacking hay on the ground floor. "No personal calls on the job. The boss has fired people for less."

"You mean he *pays* other people to do this work? Man, I'm

getting screwed." Aaron logged in to his phone with his thumbprint. There were two texts. One from a three-oh-seven number. The other from Jennifer.

Hank came around the side of the trailer, grinning. "I offered you all the hay you could eat. We've got bona fide rodeo super stars around here who don't get a better deal than that."

Aaron read the three-oh-seven message first. It was another one from Etta. *Just checking to see if you got my text. How about lunch this week? You deserve a warm welcome to WYO, and I'm the one to give it to you.* Definitely flirty. He was going to have to deal with her, sooner or later. And later sounded good to him.

He moved on to Jennifer's text. *BBB putting in septic tank. Kid & I came out to talk to G. Breakthru on case!* She was trying to reconnect. A warmth spread through him. He wanted that, too.

He typed back to her. *All good news.* He hesitated, thumb motionless, then added *Date tonight after practice?* and hit send.

Hank clapped Aaron on the shoulder. "Hey, buddy. Seriously, it's great having you and Jenny here. I never thought she'd come back, after everything that happened. Her parents felt like it would be best to keep her away."

Aaron frowned. "What do you mean?"

"She hasn't told you about it?"

Told him about what? "I have no clue what you're talking about."

"Well, it's all ancient history anyway. No big deal. But it's her story to tell, so I'll leave it to her. Sorry if my bringing this up was awkward. I just wanted you to know I'm glad she's back and you're with her."

Awkward was one way to describe it. Excluded was another. Aaron would have to figure out how to get Jennifer to talk about her past in Wyoming, although why she hadn't in their twenty years together was a mystery. A troubling mystery. If she did, it might clue him in on her objection to the place. He'd have to approach the subject carefully, though. It wasn't like he hadn't kept his own secrets. Maybe he'd own up to his own, too. Tonight after their date would be good. He glanced down at his phone. The time read eleven-thirty. He hadn't realized it was that late. Before practice, he still needed to talk to George about scheduling a closing. Something told him that would go best in person. No time to toss more bales today.

He said, "I'm going to run back to the cabin and grab a bite then head to my other unpaid gig."

Hank clapped him on the back with a work-glove-clad hand. "Thanks for the muscle."

"Thanks for giving us a roof over our heads."

Hank took off his gloves and stuffed them in his back pocket. "You're family. Anytime. Maggie isn't big on girlfriends, but she's met her match for feistiness in our Jenny. If they don't kill each other, I think they might become friends."

Aaron laughed. "Maybe. They were having a drink at the cabin when I got back last night."

"That's promising."

"Listen, the septic situation at the lodge should be fixed today. I imagine we'll be moving back up there in the next few days. After we close on the place, we'll have you guys up for dinner."

"Sounds good."

Aaron stopped in the supply room to put up his borrowed gloves and—tight—bull-rider sized chaps on his way out. Outside, a vehicle door slammed, and he heard footsteps entering the barn.

Gene's voice called a greeting. "Yo, Doc Billy, man, how's it hanging?"

Flesh slapped against flesh.

The vet's familiar voice answered. "A little to the left, but I can't complain."

Aaron didn't want to make things uncomfortable for everyone, so he leaned against the shelves in the supply room. He'd hide out until Doc Billy left.

Hank said, "What's up? We weren't expecting you. We'd better not get a bill for this. I know how you shysters operate."

Doc Billy laughed. "Just swinging by to bid farewell to my favorite clients and thank you for your business."

"You make it sound like you're dying."

"Nah. But Mary and I are leaving for Utah tomorrow."

"I thought you weren't moving until November. What about your clinic?"

"I'm going to bring in a temp vet to help out. Things have gotten . . . well, let's just say it's time for us to go."

"Sorry to hear it," Gene said. "Did you sell your practice?"

"I'll have to worry about that later."

"I was really hoping you'd sell the practice to that guy I sent you," Hank said.

Doc Billy snorted. "Not that it reflects on you, Hank, but he was a jerk. He brought his wife in. She's some kind of investigator, and she all but accused me of murder."

Aaron's forehead folded up like it had been squeezed in a vise. A jerk? He'd offered the man top dollar for his practice. He hadn't lied to him about Jennifer. All he'd done was introduce them.

"Murder? Who'd you off, buddy?"

"That a-hole who lost all my money. Or so she's telling people. I don't need her badmouthing me."

Aaron winced. Jennifer wasn't telling people William Marton had murdered Hadley Prescott. The person doing the badmouthing was Doc Billy. He'd liked the man when they first met, but nobody was going to get away with disrespecting Jennifer. He was a heartbeat away from surprising Doc Billy with the opportunity for a heart to heart when Hank jumped to their defense.

"Sorry to hear that. But I gotta tell you, Aaron and Jennifer are all right. Both of them. They're staying here in our guest cabin. She's actually my favorite cousin. And Aaron really wants to buy a local practice. I think it would be a perfect match."

An awkward silence followed. When Doc Billy spoke, his voice was stiff and cold. "I'd appreciate it if you didn't tell them we've spoken."

"Sure, Billy. Whatever you say. I hope you and Mary are nothing but happy and successful back in Utah."

"Stay cool," Gene said.

"Always," Doc Billy answered.

Footsteps receded. A vehicle door slammed. Then an engine started, and tires crunched gravel.

Hank said, "Aaron, you can come out now."

Aaron walked back in the barn, throwing air punches. It leeched off some of the adrenaline that had surged at Doc Billy. "Sorry. I kind of got stuck in a corner there."

Hank nodded. "Looks like you came out swinging."

Gene laughed. "What the hell did you guys say to scare Doc Billy out of town?"

THIRTY

SHERIDAN, Wyoming

AFTER A QUICK LUNCH in the car—sandwiches and salads called in for pick-up from Java Moon, Jennifer's treat—Jennifer and Kid swung by the county courthouse and filed their emergency motion. They'd skipped the filing earlier in their rush to talk to George about the DNA. Back in the Fusion, Jennifer eased out of her parallel parking spot and onto Main, heading north. She missed her MINI Cooper, parked in her reserved spot inside the condo building's garage back in Houston. She couldn't wait to drive it again. For a fleeting moment, she wondered if she should get it shipped. But, by the time it got here, she'd be heading south. And from the looks of the Wyoming-plated SUVs and trucks parked along the street, the MINI wouldn't exactly fit in here.

"Where are we headed now?" Kid asked.

"To pick up the birth certificate from Denise. Do you have an address for Bonnie Morrow?"

Kid barked a laugh.

Jennifer frowned. "What?"

"She lives two houses down from my mom and me."

"Denise has literally been hiding out next door for the last few days?"

"It appears so."

Jennifer knew the way, and she did a U-turn in the middle of the busy street, earning her a few honks, but none of the middle finger salutes she would have gotten in Houston.

"That's not legal here," Kid said.

"Or most anywhere," she agreed. "But I'm in a hurry. This birth certificate could tie Hadley to George."

"Do you think the Nichols were Hadley's parents? Like they had twins and gave one of the babies away?"

Jennifer braked for a red light. "I don't know what to think. I just know Denise said Hadley was adopted, and that's left the door open to twin-ship. The birth certificate could be our first documented clue."

Kid nodded. "Makes sense."

Jennifer paused, then continued. "I know a lot about this type of defense. I *am* a twin. Fraternal, not identical. And I had a case against a guy who murdered some school kids. He almost escaped conviction by blaming things on his twin brother. Lyle, he was the defendant. Jake was the twin."

"How did you convict Lyle?"

"I got lucky and found an exculpatory witness for Jake. Not that he was happy about it either. Jake *wanted* to be Lyle's get-out-of-jail-free card. And there was no risk to Jake, other than people think he might be the kind of person to shoot up a school playground. If one of them couldn't be convicted because of the DNA, neither of them could." Jennifer pulled into the driveway at Kid's garage office. "I assume we'll walk from here?"

He pointed the way they'd been headed, further up the hill. "Yeah. It's just up there."

Jennifer jumped out, leaving her keys, purse, and laptop in the car.

"Aren't you bringing your stuff?"

"I'm too excited to waste the time hauling them to the office. We'll get them on the way back. Sheridan's a safe place, right?"

"Well, yeah, but that's a nice laptop. And you strike me as someone with really high credit card limits."

He was right, but no one would guess that by looking at the modest Fusion. "Come on." She trotted past a white Tahoe parked in front of the James house.

"Jennifer?" a woman's voice called.

It wasn't Maggie's voice. *What other woman do I know in Sheridan?* Jennifer wheeled. A blonde in forest-green pants and a khaki shirt with some kind of emblem on the pocket was waving to her from Kid's front porch. She was tall, fit, and familiar.

The woman put a hand to her breastbone. "Trish Flint. We met at the Sibley's. I see you and Wesley have connected?"

Jennifer waved back. "Hi! Thank you so much. We have connected. In fact, we're late to a meeting."

"Hi, Ms. Flint," Kid said.

"Hey, there, Wesley." Trish motioned them on. "Good to see you both. Come by the National Forest Service offices someday, and I'll give you a tour and a coffee, Jennifer."

"I will." Jennifer meant it. She liked Trish. The woman was older than her, but Jennifer had a feeling the age difference wouldn't stop them from becoming friends.

She hurried up the street ahead of Kid, skipping the house next door, and stopping at the walkway leading to a well-preserved mid-century Craftsman-style home. "This one?"

He nodded. "Speaking of high credit card limits, it must be really cool being married to an NFL star. Did he get a huge signing bonus and a bunch of endorsements deals?"

She barreled up the walk, not waiting for him. "He's a vet, Kid."

"Still."

A tiny flame of jealousy ignited inside her. Kid had thought Jennifer was the cool one when he'd learned she was an ADA and headed up the Homicide Division in Harris County. Most people got goofy about Aaron's past. Football was a national obsession. Kid would get over it soon enough, and she'd be his hero again. Just thinking it made her feel ridiculous. Childish. But still. "It was fun while it lasted. But he's always put his jeans on one leg at a time just like you and me."

She reached the front door and pressed the doorbell.

Kid caught up with her. "You walk really fast for someone who's so . . . who isn't very tall."

She gave him an arch look as Bonnie Morrow opened the door a crack. For a moment, the woman stared at Jennifer, like she was trying to place her, but when she saw Kid's face, she smiled and threw the door wide open.

"Wesley James, twice in one week. How did I get this lucky? Come on in for some homemade cookies. I just baked them last night."

Kid bounced up the steps and through the door. "I remember when you used to make cookies and bring them outside for us kids." He paused. "But why aren't you at work?"

Jennifer followed Kid in, shutting the door behind her. The house smelled strongly of cinnamon and vanilla. Two of her favorite scents.

"Just popped in to make myself a bite to eat."

"You don't happen to have that lease with you, do you?"

"I do, actually."

"It would save me a trip to your offices later."

"Is that why you came by, dear?"

"No."

"Then, if you thought I'd be at work, why are you here?"

That was Jennifer's cue. "Hi, Ms. Murray. I'm Jennifer Herrington. We met at your offices."

She cocked her head. "I remember you."

"We're hoping to talk to Denise."

"Denise?"

"Yes. Denise Little."

Bonnie bit her lip. Her eyes shifted toward the hallway at the end of her foyer. "Oh, dear."

"What's wrong?"

Bonnie whispered, "I promised I wouldn't tell anyone she was here."

"Oh, she told us herself. And she's expecting us." Jennifer smiled encouragingly at Bonnie.

The doorbell rang.

Bonnie frowned. "More company? I wasn't expecting anyone. And I have to get back to work."

"If you'd let Denise know we're here, we won't keep you."

"Just let me get the door first." Bonnie scurried back and opened it a few inches.

A hand reached around and pulled it the rest of the way open. The Volkswagen-sized man on the front porch was someone Jennifer had met before, and recently—the manager at the trailer park where Denise's trailer had exploded and burned to the ground with her boyfriend and business partner in it. The man looked past Bonnie. "You." He pointed at Jennifer. "What are you doing here?"

She pointed back. "You. What are *you* doing here?"

"None of your damn beeswax."

"Likewise."

Bonnie's voice quavered. "This is my home. Please state your name and your business, sir."

"Never mind." He backed away, then wheeled and jogged down the street, his big arms and shoulders making him more gorilla than gazelle.

Bonnie gazed after him, looking worried. "Oh, my. What do you think that was all about?"

"I think he was here to see Denise, too."

Bonnie closed the door, shaking her head. "So troubling. And you said Denise is expecting you?"

"Yes. Please tell her Jennifer Herrington is here."

"I suppose you can come with me to her room."

Kid grinned at Bonnie. "Can I steal a cookie first?"

"Of course. And the lease is on the kitchen table." She looked pleased. "Grab a cookie for your friend, too."

Jennifer held up a hand. "Oh, I don't—"

Kid shook his head, throwing Jennifer a significant look.

She changed her answer. "And one for me, too, please, Kid."

Kid ducked into the kitchen and returned with two cookies in one hand and the lease in the other. He stuffed a cookie in his mouth. "Oatmeal craisin chocolate chip. Ms. Murray's specialty."

Bonnie led the way down the hall. "Don't talk with your mouth full, Wesley."

He winked at Jennifer.

Bonnie stopped at a door on the rear side of the house's main story. "I did this addition years ago. It's so nice for guests, although it gets a little cold in the winter." She knocked softly on the door. "Denise, your guests are here. Jennifer and Wesley."

"Kid," Kid said.

Bonnie smiled but didn't repeat his nickname for Denise. There was no answer from inside the room. "Denise?" Bonnie knocked again. Her face puckered. "That's odd. She said she'd be home at lunch. I *did* wonder about that when she didn't come out to eat, but I assumed she was napping. She's had such a terrible time, losing her mother and then her father so close together. Her boyfriend and her home, too." Bonnie opened the door. "Denise?" Then she put her fingers against her lips. "Oh, goodness."

Jennifer stepped quickly into the room. A pink floral comforter had been pulled up over pillows, although the bed wasn't made to Jennifer's mother's exacting standards of hospital corners and artfully arranged throw pillows. The closet door was open, exposing a row of empty hangers on the clothes rod. In the little en suite bathroom, a towel lay crumpled on the floor. Steam covered the mirror. The door to the back yard was ajar.

Jennifer asked, even though she already knew the answer. "What's the matter, Bonnie?"

"Her suitcase . . . her belongings . . . her car . . . everything is gone."

THIRTY-ONE

BILLINGS, Montana

SIRI TOLD Jennifer the drive to Billings would take an hour and forty-five minutes, but she shaved fifteen minutes off that estimate, with Kid white-knuckle gripping the armrest the entire way. The two of them had left straight from Bonnie's, right after George had called to give them an address for his Aunt Angela. His aunt lived in a nursing home that required family authorization for visitors. George promised he had them on the list, and Jennifer had laid rubber on Main Street getting out of town. She wasn't about to miss out on this lead. If George was a twin, then the case against him was all but over. The sooner she could present that evidence to Pootie, the sooner this monkey would be off George's back . . . and hers. Plus, there was the thrill of the chase for evidence. She couldn't deny it. She'd always thought the adrenaline came from the pursuit of justice, but it turned out that wasn't true. It was just the same for her on the defense side.

She eased up on the accelerator as they entered Billings.

Kid exhaled a shaky breath. "Were you a Formula 1 driver in a past life or something?"

She wished. All she had was a long history of speeding tickets dating back to joyriding in the classic Mustang her dad still kept under a tarp in his garage. "Ha. Did you put Angela's address in Maps?"

"Yes. Sorry. I had the sound turned off. We're ten minutes away."

"Good."

"Hey, if I look car sick, it's because I just finished reading that lease. It was a strange one."

"Give me the punchline."

"It specifically prevents the owner from entering a contract for sale during the term of the lease. There's an annual sixty-day period for notice of non-renewal by either party. Otherwise, Prescott can only be kicked out for cause. Like non-payment, illegal activity conducted from the premises, or destruction of property."

"Wow. How Draconian. And completely opposite of how the relation of landlord to tenant usually goes. So, O'Leary can't sell the place while Prescott Financial is there, and he can't get rid of them except for cause, until their lease is up. Hence, no KFC for Northern Wyoming anytime soon."

"That's how I read it." He glanced at his phone. "Take the next exit, then go right at the light."

Jennifer put on her blinker. "We need to call O'Leary on our way back to Sheridan."

"I don't think it's safe to make calls at the speed you drive."

Jennifer rolled her eyes at him. "Chillax, Grandma."

Non-plussed, Kid continued to call out the directions, and Jennifer obeyed the speed limit the rest of the way. Maps took them right to the Mountain Sunshine Adult Living Center, a long one-story building. They approached driving downhill with a birds-eye view of the facility. Jennifer counted eight wings branching from a central hub, like tentacles from the body of an octopus. She parked in a marked visitor's spot and the two of them hustled in. At the front door, the peculiar odor endemic to nursing homes hit them full force. To Jennifer, it smelled like boiled socks and overcooked carrots with a hint of soiled diaper.

Jennifer presented their driver's licenses to a woman behind a desk in the reception area. Large, framed prints of western vistas and cattle drives hung behind wooden framed chairs with arms, seats, and backs upholstered in browns and golds. There was just enough room left between the furniture and welcome desk to wheel a chair through the space.

The receptionist was a sweet-voiced woman with carefully coiffed orange hair. She was dressed as if for afternoon tea in New York City at the Ritz. Pumps, hose, pearls, a tweed suit dress, and a dainty gold watch darkened by the patina of age.

When Jennifer asked for Angela Arens, she beamed at her and Kid. "Angela is such a sweetie. She'll be delighted to have visitors. She and my mother are suite mates."

"That's great. Thank you," Jennifer said.

The woman stood. "I'll escort you to her room." She set off down the terrazzo floors of one of the hospital-like corridors, talking over her shoulder. "When George told us you were on your way, Angela asked to be taken back to her room to get ready."

Something about that made Jennifer's chest tighten. "I counted eight wings. What determines how patients are assigned to each wing?"

"Each of the wings is self-contained, with some common central spaces. Two of the wings are full skilled nursing care areas. Two are for residents who are physically capable but suffering from memory challenges. We keep the memory wings secured so that our guests don't wander out and lose their way back. The other four wings are assisted living of varying degrees, and residents are assigned living quarters there as they become available."

"What level of care is Angela receiving?"

"Oh, she's in one of our assisted living wings."

Jennifer had prosecuted a case a few years before that had nearly broken her heart. A nursing home health aide had been charged with the murder of several residents of Houston-area nursing homes. His M.O. was to medicate then rape the women after they were incapacitated. Inevitably, one had woken and recognized him, and he'd smothered her to death. Initially, he seemed to have gotten away with it. He then moved from facility to facility without a single negative reference, assaulting women at every location. When the police had finally caught him, he'd admitted to the woman's murder, but then he'd shocked them all by confessing to four more murders of women whose deaths had been classified until then as natural causes. His attorney had tried to retract his confession, calling it coerced, and the case had gone to trial. The jury had convicted the man after only two hours of deliberation. He was on death row now and probably would be most of his life while he worked his way through the appeals system. He was one of the reasons it terrified Jennifer to contemplate the aging of her own parents. At some point, each would probably need care. She knew there were many wonderful people that worked in the industry. Far more good ones than bad. But after the case she'd had? Trust would be an issue for Jennifer, for sure.

As they walked, sounds from the rooms drew her eyes. She tried not to stare. Singing. Maniacal laughter. Wailing. Snoring. And barking. Not from a dog, but from a tiny woman leaning forward from her wheelchair in the doorway to a room.

"Woof." She locked serious eyes with Jennifer.

"Don't mind Thelma," the receptionist said. "She doesn't bite."

Kid laughed. Jennifer looked back at Thelma. The old woman winked at her.

"Here we are," the receptionist said. She knocked on the frame of the open door and stuck her head in. "Angela, your visitors are here."

The woman that tottered to her feet reached for a glossy wooden cane with a tarnished silver ball handle. Even stooped and leaning heavily on the cane, Angela's height was startling. She was easily a head taller than Jennifer. Steel gray hair in tight curls. A pinched mouth with fine puckered lines radiating outward. Birdlike dark eyes. Pale skin with slightly pinked cheeks. *Austere.*

"Good afternoon," Angela said. Her clear, bright voice was as surprising as her height.

"Buzz the front desk if you need anything, hon," the receptionist said.

Angela shooed her with long fingers.

"Hello, Ms. Arens. I'm Jennifer Herrington. This is Kid James. George Nichols sent us." Jennifer moved within an arm's length of her, in case she wanted to shake, but Angela didn't offer her hand.

Kid bowed. "Good afternoon, Ms. Arens."

"Have a seat. And call me Angela." Angela leaned more weight on her cane, aiming her posterior for a walker that doubled as a chair.

Jennifer held her breath until the older woman was safely seated. Angela set her cane against the wall. Jennifer sat in an armchair by the bed. Kid took a folding chair that seemed to have been set up for their visit.

Angela tented her hands on her thighs, fingertips barely touching. Her knees poked sharply up from polyester slacks. "My sweet George. I never had children of my own. He visits me once a week, you know."

Jennifer hid her surprise. George doted on his aunt, clearly. She wondered how many times George had made the drive to Billings under the influence. It was a scary thought. She prayed he hadn't found where she'd hidden all his booze but didn't hold out much hope. "He's your nephew?"

"He's my sister's son, God rest her soul. Here's a picture of her." The picture she handed Jennifer was laying on top of a stack of framed photos on a bedside table within easy reach of the walker. "That's Lorene with George."

The young woman in the picture had jet black hair and almond-shaped dark eyes. Early thirties, maybe? She was holding the hand of a tow-headed toddler.

"Your sister is lovely." Jennifer passed the picture to Kid.

"People say we favored each other. She passed ten years ago."

"You must miss her."

Angela nodded. "George is the only family I have left. Here's Lorene and Carlton's wedding picture."

Jennifer accepted another framed photo. The bride and groom in the picture were achingly young. Carlton was wearing a military uniform of some sort, and Lorene was in a simple white tea-length dress with a round skirt. Carlton was less dark then his wife, but his distinctive jutting chin, dimples, heavy-set eyes, and thick, wavy hair still looked nothing like their son. "Carlton served?"

"The Korean war. Made it through without a scratch then died of influenza in his fifties. Lorene was never the same after."

"Not much family resemblance between George and his parents." Jennifer handed the wedding picture to Kid. He raised his eyebrows and nodded.

Angela started humming softly as she flipped through the rest of the stack of pictures. "Sentimental Journey," it sounded like.

Jennifer lowered her voice to just above a whisper. "Angela, is it possible George was adopted?"

Angela's sharp eyes cut to Jennifer's. Her words were like a pecking beak. "Why would you say something like that?"

Jennifer collected the pictures from Kid. She let her eyes linger on the one of Lorene and young George. "Did George tell you why he sent us to see you?"

"No."

"We're his attorneys. He's been charged with murder. We don't believe he did it. I'm very sorry if this is the first you're hearing of it."

Angela sucked in a breath. Her meager color drained from her face, leaving it gray instead of white. Jennifer had shocked the old woman, and she felt bad about it. Really bad. Kid stood, nervous, and hovered near them. Jennifer took Angela's hand, patted it, and kept holding it.

"Who?" Angela finally croaked. "Who are they saying he killed?"

"A man named Hadley Scott. Did you know George's wife, Shelly?"

"Yes."

"Shelly used to be married to Hadley."

Angela nodded listlessly. "Yes. And he started causing trouble for George after Shelly passed."

"Yes."

"How did he die?"

"Someone stabbed him, out at George's place."

"Oh, my. That's bad."

"It is. And there are no witnesses. No fingerprints. The case is mostly what's called 'circumstantial' at this point."

She nodded. "I watch *Law & Order*."

"Good. So, this next part may make sense, too. As part of the case against George, DNA tests were done. On George and on Hadley. The DNA came back identical for them."

Angela frowned, head tilted. "Is that even possible?"

"It is if they're identical twins."

Her eyes turned damp and filmy.

Jennifer smiled at her, trying to encourage without pushing too hard. "Now, there's a chance of lab error, but there's also a chance the information is right. If it's right, that's very, very good for George's case."

"Why?"

"Because if his DNA and Hadley's DNA are the same, then it would be as if George was never there. It will be next-to-impossible for the prosecution to ever prove George was at the scene of the crime."

"Was he?"

"I don't think he was. But it's not about what I believe. It's about whether the prosecution can prove beyond a reasonable doubt he killed Hadley. With identical DNA, no fingerprints or other direct evidence, and no witnesses, they can't."

"The bad blood between Hadley and George, and the fact that he

died at George's place. That shows motive. And opportunity." Her
voice was growing threadier.

"Right. But we know something the prosecution doesn't know
yet."

"What's that?"

"Hadley was adopted. At this point, we don't know who his birth
parents were. We're going to get a copy of his birth certificate." *If we
ever track Denise down again.* "But if it was a closed adoption, that
won't get us anywhere. That's why we wanted to talk to you. To see if
Lorene had twins and had to give one up."

Angela's gray curls bounced as she shook her head no.

"I thought so. Because of the pictures. And that's why I had to ask
if there's a chance George was adopted."

The woman's shoulders sagged.

"Angela, we're not interested in pulling skeletons out of closets. If
George is adopted, well, then, there's a reason it's been kept a secret
all these years. A good one, I'm sure. But things are different now.
We're trying to keep George from going to prison for the rest of his
life."

A tap on the door was followed quickly by the footsteps of
someone in soft-soled shoes. Then a voice, shrill. "Angela, are you all
right?"

A short, round woman in pink scrubs bustled in. A nurse or
health aide. She grabbed Angela's wrist and, with her eyes on her
watch, she mouthed numbers, counting the beats of the older
woman's pulse. Angela's eyes drifted to the floor. Tears welled in
their corners.

When the medical worker looked up, her eyes were stern. "I'm
going to have to ask you leave now. Angela needs to lie down."

"Angela?" Jennifer stood. Panic gripped her. They were so close.
"Is it possible?"

Angela didn't seem to hear her.

"Enough. Go." The medical worker helped Angela up and
walked her to the bed, where she sat Angela down.

"Come on, Jennifer." Kid tugged at Jennifer's sleeve.

Jennifer followed him to the door, then turned, hoping Angela would give her a sign.

But the old woman was already lying corpse-like on her back, eyes closed, hands folded over her stomach.

THIRTY-TWO

BIG HORN, Wyoming

AARON WALKED to the lodge's back yard, his mind on where he was going to build a gym after he and Jennifer closed on the place. She'd want somewhere to do yoga, too. He could even put a driving range and putting green in for her. Thinking about the projects kept his mind off what Hank had told him earlier about Jennifer's secret past in Wyoming. Or mostly did. Then he saw George, who was leaning from a ladder in front of the tractor, next to the partially buried septic tank. Patrick Flint was standing at the base of the ladder. Liam bounded toward Aaron on stiff legs. Aaron roughed up the big dog's ears.

"Looks like a septic setback," Aaron said by way of greeting.

Liam nosed him for more petting.

George brandished a wrench. "Temporary hydraulic delay."

Patrick Flint laughed. "Careful, George. You're starting to sound like an optimist."

Aaron shook hands with Patrick. "He'd never be accused of that. How's Moose?"

"Good. We pick him up tomorrow. Thank you for saving his hip."

"My pleasure."

"I have an idea. Do you mind if I take a shot, George?" Patrick said.

George nodded. "You already fixed the window in the cottage door. But be my guest." He climbed down. "Good timing. A word, Aaron?" He gestured toward the house.

"What's up?" Aaron said.

"Let's talk inside. I need a drink."

Aaron hoped George was talking about hydration. He followed George into the lodge kitchen. George went straight to a cabinet for a plastic tumbler, which he filled from the tap, carefully turning it off before the cup was full.

Aaron selected a chair at the kitchen table. It creaked under his weight. "What's up?"

George walked to the refrigerator, turned on his heel, paced back to the living room, turned on his heel, returned to the refrigerator, turned on his heel, and kept repeating the pattern. After a few more laps, he gulped his water down. "Listen. I'm too old to get hired as a snowmobile guide. I don't know what I was thinking when I agreed to sell this place. I need a roof over my head and a way to earn a living." He refilled his water, then started pacing again, this time muttering something Aaron couldn't understand, even if he'd been listening, which he wasn't. His mind was fixed on what George had said.

Aaron's lungs deflated. He was losing everything. First the vet practice, now the lodge. When he got to football practice, would Perry send him packing? Worse, would Jennifer leave again? He swallowed. His mouth was dry, and he wished he had a glass of water, too. He scrambled for the right play. It was fourth and long on the forty with one-minute left in the game. The defense was making a heck of a stand. Sticking with the same strategy wasn't going to work. It was time for some razzle dazzle. Something akin to an outside pass to J.J. Watt in the slot. The fact that the big man didn't play offense is what made the gambit so brilliant. That, and his great hands.

Aaron didn't have J.J., but he did have an idea. He drummed his fingers on the table. "We have a contract you know."

George's steps froze, but his lips kept moving.

"I'm not going to force you to sell to me."

The explosion of George's exhale was percussive. "Good."

"But I really want you to."

George's rhythmic footsteps resumed.

"What if you stayed on with us here as the property manager?" *If you're not in prison. And despite the fact that you're a pretty awful caretaker.* "With a salary. And a place to live."

George's brows drew together in a deep V, but he stopped pacing. "I thought you and Jennifer were planning to run the lodge?"

"Being a vet is a full-time job. And Jennifer, well, she's busy all the time. I think she's going to have a thriving law practice here after representing you. We'd live at the lodge, so we'd consume one bedroom and bath, but that would still leave—" He started to count bedrooms and realized he didn't even know how many there were. That he'd never even had a full tour of the giant cabin. He congratulated himself on being such a savvy home buyer. *Not.*

"Six suites."

"There you go. Six suites to rent."

George scratched his chin whiskers. "It would make me feel closer to Shelly if I stayed on. But where would I live?"

"How about the cottage you're in now?"

"You said you wanted that as an office for Jennifer to write in."

Jennifer. Would this conversation with George fall in the category of things he should have talked to her about first? Especially in light of the mystery Hank had alluded to. But all he was doing was salvaging their purchase. "It's not a deal killer if you keep it." He pictured his wife and her love for Jeremiah. "But the skunk has to stay at the lodge."

George nodded, then his eyes took on a glow. "There's the other cabin. I've been wanting to fix it up for years."

"What cabin?" Aaron frowned. Not only had he not known how many rooms the lodge had, the existence of yet *another* cabin on the property took him by surprise.

George chinned toward the mountains. "Want to see it?"

Suddenly, Aaron liked the way the play was developing. He jumped to his feet and bounced on his toes. "Let's do it."

"Can we take your Jeepster?"

"DeMarcus Ware."

"What's he got to do with it?"

"That's what I call him."

"Who?"

Aaron grinned. "Never mind. Let's go."

Ten minutes of rough two-track road later, the men alit from DeMarcus Ware. A small cabin with grayed logs and torn window screens was tucked back into the trees. The forest gave way to a sheer hundred-foot cliff practically in the cabin's backyard.

George rocked back on his heels, arms crossed. "It doesn't look like much, but it's in decent shape. It was a summer cabin. The original structure on the property, actually. There's a creek a few hundred yards away, but it's across the property line to the neighbors. I'd have to haul in water, but the previous owner already ran power out here."

"What about plumbing?"

"Chemical toilet. But that's a small price to pay for this setting."

Aaron couldn't argue with that. "Why aren't you already out here?"

"Somebody has to live onsite with guests in the lodge. If you and Jennifer were there in case of emergencies, I could be here and commute in on my four-wheeler or—" he grinned, "—a snowmobile."

"And Jennifer could still have her office." *Writing retreat.* Aaron stuck out a hand. "Shake on it?"

George bit his lip, but the corners of his mouth were still curving up. He grabbed Aaron's bigger hand and shook.

Touchdown. "Now, how about we go see about scheduling a closing?"

"I know the folks where Shelly and I closed when we bought it."

"Perfect."

The two men drove back to the lodge, talking through what needed to be done around the place. Aaron was thinking about marketing to potential guests. George had his heart set on making improvements. The work list for both of them was long, but they were each happy about it.

Patrick waved them down as they arrived. George lowered his window.

Patrick leaned in. "I think I fixed it. The hydraulics on the tractor bucket."

George and Aaron got out and stood back while Patrick demonstrated the operational bucket.

George clapped Patrick on the back. "Thanks, Flint. You missed your calling."

Patrick laughed. "The human body. The hydraulics on a tractor. There are some similarities."

"I owe you one."

"Nah. I had nothing better to do today. But I'd best get back to Buffalo before Susanne reports me missing. Mind if I clean myself up before I get back on the road?"

"Don't forget not to run water down the drain. Otherwise, my lodge is your lodge. For now. Until it's Aaron's soon."

Patrick smiled and headed into the cabin.

"Ready?" Aaron said.

"I am," George said.

The two men jumped back into the Jeepster.

Aaron shifted into first. "Let's go make this official."

THIRTY-THREE

BIG HORN, Wyoming

"HOW QUICKLY CAN you be in my courtroom?" Judge Ryan's voice boomed over the handsfree speaker in the rental when Jennifer picked up the call from the county.

Kid put his face in his hands.

They were already nearly back to Sheridan. She'd just left a voice mail for Tim O'Leary asking if they could get together. Jennifer smiled sweetly at her law partner as she answered the judge. "Fifteen minutes, sir."

"Good. I can fit a hearing on your motion in at the end of my day. Don't be late." He ended the call.

Never in the history of ever had a judge called a hearing on the same day she'd filed a motion. *Jennifer, I have a feeling you're not in Kansas anymore.* She floored the gas pedal. The Fusion responded with all the zip of a drunk turtle. Maybe she would drop by the rental company and upgrade tomorrow to something with more power.

Kid gasped. "We won't make it on time if we're dead."

"We'll make it."

"Are you going to tell the judge about Angela and your twin theory?"

"Not unless I want to sound like a lunatic. I have zero evidence."

"Angela all but confirmed George was adopted."

"That and a head of lettuce would make a nice salad, but I'm afraid we're going hungry tonight."

"You're giving up on it?" Kid sounded aghast.

"I didn't say that. It's just not ready for prime time."

He nodded, seeming mollified. She appreciated his passion. It mirrored her own. In a crazy way, she felt more invested in keeping George *out* of prison than she'd ever felt about putting someone *in* it. It was about justice with a capital J. Not big picture. Not theoretical. Personal. Justice for George. One man's life, a man who without her could fall victim to the system.

One innocent man.

A thrill ran through her. A convertible-with-the-top-down type of thrill. But she chastised herself before she could relish the feeling. This was not the way a woman about to run for District Attorney of one of the largest counties in the United States should be thinking. But instead of acting guilty, her inner self stood her ground, her hair still blowing joyously in the wind. This experience was essential to becoming the best DA she could be. She needed to understand both sides of the system firsthand. She was already writing it into her campaign speeches.

Kid's stressed voice interrupted her thoughts. "Jennifer, slow down. You're going to miss the exit!"

She slammed on the brakes. The rental fishtailed. She eased off in time to veer onto the ramp. "You were saying?"

"You owe me a year of my life back."

She turned onto Fifth. "You're getting an expedited legal education in a first-degree murder case. Consider it my payment in full."

"Isn't it the devil you pay with your life?"

She threw back her head and laughed. "I think you pay him with your soul. That's safe with me."

In front of them, a truck slammed on its brakes, barely stopping in time for a red light. Jennifer ground the Fusion to a halt inches behind its back bumper. A bumper sticker with a coiled snake and the words Don't Tread on Me looked so close she could have almost touched it over the short front end of her rental car. It was so much like her recurring nightmare that it raised the hair on her arms, yet something about it was different.

"Whoa," Kid said.

"Too late, we're already stopped." Kid laughed. "Hey, that Don't Tread On Me thing on the back of that truck—is that the only version of that around?"

"The Gadsden Flag?"

"It has a name?"

"Yeah. They're a big deal in Wyoming. It's practically the state motto."

"But does it always look exactly like that one?"

He pursed his lips. "Yellow flag, rattlesnake coiled in the grass ready to strike, and the words. Yeah, pretty much always the same. Why?"

Jennifer compared it to the snake in her dream. No yellow background. And the snake wasn't in grass. It seemed like she always pictured it in rocks. And that there were no words. Only letters. A-T-O-M or something like that, accompanied by screams and gunfire. But she wasn't going to fess up to Kid about her nightmares. "I thought I'd seen a different one. That's all."

The truck in front of them started moving. Jennifer gave the Fusion some gas and dropped the unsettling subject.

Five minutes later, the two of them were running up the stairs to the courtroom.

Jennifer checked time on her phone. "We're not going to make it." She could barely get the words out between her panting gasps.

Kid was in better shape than she was, and he spoke without

effort. "It will be okay. The judge likes you, Big City, as long as you don't bring Jeremiah into his courtroom again."

She opened the door as she slowed from a jog to a walk. Everyone in the courtroom turned to look. More than a couple did a raised brow double-take. She stopped and smoothed her hair. Glancing down, she realized she was dressed more like a lumberjack than a lawyer. It couldn't be helped now. She straightened her shoulders, lifted her chin, and marched forward. Kid slunk in using her as his human shield.

She took a seat in the front row of the gallery on the defense side, where she'd be able to get to the defense table quickly when the judge called their motion.

Judge Ryan cocked his head and took off his glasses. He wiped them with his robe, taking his time on the job. When he was done, he drilled Jennifer with his eyes. "I said, 'Big City and Kid for George Nichols, where are you?'"

Jennifer leapt to her feet. The defense table was empty. Only then did she notice Pootie peering down his nose from the prosecution table. "Sorry, sir. Right here."

She double-timed to the table, waited for Kid to take the seat nearest the aisle, then slid into the one beside him.

"Kid? Are you ready to argue your motion?" The judge sounded amused.

Kid got to his feet, nearly knocking over his chair. "Sir?"

"Let's go, son. I haven't got all day. Explain to me why I should rule for the defense on this one."

"Your Honor," Pootie whined.

The judge held his hand up in the stop motion.

Kid's throat croaked and swallowed. His Adam's apple looked like a bullfrog fighting its way out of plastic bag. "Um, can Big City, I mean, can Ms. Herrington do that?"

"Is she licensed in the great state of Wyoming?" the judge asked. "Sir?"

"It's not a trick question, Kid. Is she or isn't she?"

"No, she's not."

"Then no she may not!" the judge bellowed. But his eyes were sparkling.

"A minute to confer with my co-counsel?"

"You had plenty of time for that before you got here. So much so that you were late for my hearing. Get on with it, Counselor."

Pootie smirked. Jennifer squirmed. She'd thought Kid would be prepared for this after they'd worked on the motion together.

"Just talk him through it, Kid," she whispered.

The judge gave her a withering glance but let it go.

Kid cleared his throat, looked around for a glass of water that wasn't there, and then pressed on his Adam's apple and tried clearing his throat again. "May it please the court." His voice cracked. He closed his eyes. Cleared his throat one more time. Took a deep breath. When he opened his eyes, something had changed—a certain calmness had settled over his features. Jennifer breathed easier.

"Your Honor, the prosecutor has had Mr. Nichols' private and business cell phone in his possession for over a week now, adequate time to retrieve all the data off of it. In the meantime, Mr. Nichols has been without a phone of any kind, which has hurt his business and harmed him personally. We, his counsel, have been unable to review his phone data or even a transcript of it. While, technically, discovery is still ongoing, it is our contention that the prosecution is withholding the phone from Mr. Nichols because it didn't provide the evidence they were seeking, namely, something to support their contention that Mr. Nichols' invited the decedent to his home on the night the decedent died. Without that invitation, not only will they be unable to support a first-degree charge of murder, but our stand your ground defense will succeed." He took a breath.

Jennifer was speechless. Kid was like a Chia pet. Just add water, and watch it grow. He sounded like a *real* attorney, not a baby lawyer right out of law school. He was, well, he was *fabulous*.

"Judge, this is ridiculous," Pootie complained.

"Are you done, Mr. James?" Judge Ryan asked, a new respect in his voice.

"Nearly, but not quite, Your Honor. The prosecution has also twice submitted Mr. Nichols' DNA for analysis but failed to provide us with a copy of the report, because they're not happy with the results."

"That's a gross—" Pootie interjected.

Johnson's voice boomed. "Quiet."

"Between their failure to provide the DNA analysis, their refusal to return the phone and our belief the data on it will confirm the lack of invitation and, at a minimum, overcharging—this should never have been a *first-degree* murder charge, if Mr. Nichols should have been charged with anything at all—as well as our strong stand your ground defense, *and* the multiple suspects the prosecution has refused to investigate, we move for a dismissal of all charges against Mr. Nichols."

Jennifer closed her eyes and sucked in a quick breath. And he'd been doing so well.

The judge's tone was now sardonic. "Oh, really, a dismissal, that's what you're here for today? And I thought you wanted a phone. Well, I could just make that easy for you and deny your motion to dismiss, if you'd like."

"Uh . . ."

Jennifer stabbed Kid in the leg with her pen. She would have liked him to argue some of the other items in the motion, but now was not the time. The judge wanted to compel production on the phone. *Let him and live to fight another day.*

"Ow."

"What's that?" the judge asked.

"I meant to say that the defense is merely requesting that you grant our motion to compel production without further delay of Mr. Nichols' phone, sir."

"I should hope so. And Pootie, what says the prosecution?"

Jennifer poked Kid in the leg again. He turned to her. She

pointed at the seat in his chair. He dropped into it.

"CARPUTIN. It's not as easy as the kid makes it sound." Jennifer gritted her teeth at Pootie's deliberate disrespect of his opposing counsel. She made a mental note to take the arrogant prosecutor down a notch next chance she got.

"Enlighten us."

"The phone is in evidence with the sheriff's department."

A heavy silence followed. Then, his voice dripping sarcasm, the judge said, "And?"

"And we're a small county, sir. We don't have unlimited personnel to make emergency copies of the data on phones, and our employee who would normally perform this function has been on paid time off. A family vacation to Hawaii. Nonrefundable tickets."

The judge rolled his eyes. "Has the data been copied from Mr. Nichols' phone or not?"

"I, um, I believe it may have been."

"There's probably an answer in there somewhere, I just can't figure out what it was."

"Yes, Your Honor. The data has been copied."

"Is there any impediment to retrieving the phone from evidence now, say, by five p.m. today?"

Jennifer glanced down at her own phone. It was four-forty-five. She suppressed a smile.

"As I mentioned, it's in evidence."

"Then get it!" Judge Ryan thundered.

Pootie literally jumped three inches off the ground. "Yes, sir. I just wanted the court to understand that the time that has passed up until now has been for legitimate reasons."

"Put the phone in Mr. Wesley's hands by nine a.m. at his offices tomorrow."

"Deliver it to him?"

"Did I stutter?"

"No, Your Honor."

"Ask me even one more question, and I'll require you do the delivery *personally*."

"Yes, Your Honor."

The judge stared at Pootie. "Sit, Counselor."

Pootie sat.

The judge bestowed a huge smile on Kid. "Motion granted. Court dismissed."

The flush of victory on Kid's face was a beautiful thing to see.

THIRTY-FOUR

STORY, Wyoming

BACK AT PINEY BOTTOMS, Jennifer found a depressingly empty cabin. No cute, cuddly skunk. No incontinent St. Bernard. No aloof calico cat. And no Aaron. She was dying to tell him about the huge strides she and Kid had made in George's case. She hadn't heard from him all afternoon, not since his text before lunch about a date tonight. *One I didn't answer until after the hearing.*

She'd sent the message two hours before, as she'd walked out of the courtroom. *Sorry I couldn't communicate. Drove to Billings & back. Court hearing. Yes, to a date, whenever you get home. Which will be when? And where are you?*

She was starting to get worried about him. He could have hit a deer. Run off the road into a ditch. Been detained by a pretty young woman at a Holiday gas station. *I know better. I do. Irrational jealousy won't help anything.* She just hoped she hadn't messed things up by taking so long to answer him. She wanted the date. She'd just been consumed by the case. He knew how she got, though. Maybe he was still at practice. She checked the time on her phone. It was nearly seven. Time for players and coaches to be home having dinner with their families. She checked her messages again.

None from him.

There were, however, quite a few others. She'd been wondering why she hadn't heard back from her family, Alayah, and Quentin. Apparently, they'd texted, but her phone had chosen not to receive anything today while she was motoring back and forth to Montana. Until now.

She uncorked a new bottle of wine and took a seat on the porch glider. It would be good to catch up with everyone in her life, and it would distract her from worrying about Aaron. First, though, she savored a sip of pinot noir and closed her eyes. The wine was smooth, and the weather was glorious. *Indian summer.* Then she felt guilty about even thinking the phrase. Did it have a hidden meaning that fell into the insensitive category? She Googled it and was relieved. No secret offensive meanings.

Her phone chimed with a voice mail. *Odd.* The screen said the message had come in two minutes ago, but her phone had never rung. She played it.

"This is Tim O'Leary returning your call. I know who you are, Ms. Herrington, and I won't talk to George Nichols' lawyer without a court order. I owned a contracting business with him for thirty years or more, and he swindled me. SWINDLED me. Tell him if he pays me what he owes me, I might change my mind. As for Prescott Financial, they pay their rent on time. End of story."

The message ended. She stared at the phone, her mouth in a capital O. The Prescott Financial landlord was George's former business partner? Everyone in this town was related in some way to everyone else. Six degrees of separation. Or less. Where was Kevin Bacon when she needed him? She'd have to deal with O'Leary tomorrow.

She started scanning her text messages.

Alayah: *I can't keep up with you. You're representing a*

murderer? How is that? And don't you think it's time you talked to Aaron? Try honesty. It's supposed to be the cornerstone of great relationships. Not that I'd know personally. And speaking of which, I met someone. He's a Texas Ranger. I know, I know. Not my type. But he is H-O-T.

Jennifer laughed aloud. She was the one who couldn't keep up with Alayah. She sent a short reply: *Tell me about the Texas Ranger!*

From her mother: *Why are you avoiding us?*

She wasn't avoiding them, she—oh, who was she kidding? She totally was. Because her mother would see right through her, asking questions she didn't want to answer. She'd wait until later to respond to that one.

From Justin: *Here are Cherilyn and Jennifer, both 5 lbs even. When are Aunt Jennifer & Uncle Aaron coming to see them?* The text included a picture of two indistinguishable, pink-swaddled, angry-faced infants.

Jennifer's heart swelled. They'd named one of their daughters after her! She answered as fast as she could thumb type. *OMG, they're adorbs. Be there soon, I hope. Love you all. Yay baby Cherilyn and Jennifer!* The text wasn't enough. She tried to Facetime him but got voicemail. "This is your twin. Stop it with the cute babies. They're hurting my ovaries. Seriously, though, congratulations! I'll talk to you and hopefully see you all soon. Love you."

She jumped on Amazon and sent two impractical, frilly newborn dresses with matching booties and hairbows.

From Quentin: *Thanks for checking in. You're still our top choice, but, as you can imagine, we are working on our back-up candidate list now.*

The words sent terror through her heart. This might be her only shot at becoming the Harris County DA. But how could she complain? She'd do the same thing in his shoes. She answered quickly. *Sorry for the delay in my response. Connectivity is in the dark ages here. Don't give up on me. Things are going great. I'll be back with my answer soon.*

From her boss Vivian: *Be careful this pro bono work doesn't take you permanently to the other side.*

How close Vivian's words were to the truth. Representing George was rewarding. But, if Jennifer decided to move over to the defense side of the docket someday, her value in the private practice sector would be much, much higher after a successful DA stint. She decided Vivian's message didn't require an answer.

From Kid: *Check your email. I want to make sure I did the answer right in the Sarah Stiles wrongful death case. And read the complaint. You won't believe who her father is.*

Kid's wrongful death answer could wait until later. Like *tomorrow*. Kid's enthusiasm and conscientiousness was commendable, but it couldn't dictate her choices. She'd already given all of herself to the George and Kid cause today. She knew from experience that she needed bounce back time, or she'd be worthless the rest of the week.

Just as she was getting up to go inside to scrounge for food, Maggie and Hank strolled up hand in hand. Jennifer bristled. She'd thought she was over her last encounter with Maggie, the one about Aaron's happiness. Clearly, her emotional reaction said she wasn't. But it wasn't Hank's fault, and she couldn't take it out on him.

Maggie spoke first. "Hank is making me walk with him. I think I'm breaking a sweat."

Jennifer gave a stilted laugh.

Hank defended himself with a hand over his heart. "She needs to show more concern about my health."

"You're in great shape," Jennifer said.

Maggie put her arms around Hank and gazed into his eyes. "Hank's body and cardio are great. But his brain doctor wants him to add meditation or yoga into his schedule. Since he refuses to do that, a peaceful walk will have to do as a substitute."

"Brain doctor?" Jennifer looked at her cousin.

Maggie released Hank, her eyebrows raised at him.

Hank's answer took a few extra seconds to work its way out. "Too many knocks to the noggin during my bull riding days."

"You know that's why Aaron had to quit football?"

"I didn't know football players rode bulls."

Maggie socked him in the arm.

Hank grinned. "Does he still have problems?"

"Some. Not bad. But he'd probably love to talk to you about it if you're willing."

"Sure."

Something about his tone said the chances of such a conversation were slim. *Men.*

"Where is Aaron?" Maggie looped her arm through Hank's.

"He was supposed to be here after football practice, but I haven't heard from him yet."

Hank chuckled. "I think I messed up today. Told him something you've kept secret. Sorry about that."

Did Hank know that she hadn't quit her job, hadn't dropped out of consideration to run for DA, hadn't sublet their apartment, and planned to lure Aaron back to Texas? But how? It had to have been Maggie that told him. Maggie might not know any of it for certain, but she'd made that comment about Jennifer having something against Aaron being happy.

"What are you talking about?" She tried to keep her voice steady.

"You know. The reason your family quit bringing you to Wyoming."

Jennifer drew a blank. "I don't. What happened?"

"Seriously? The shooting at my school that day you came to the playground to get me." He pulled his shirt away from his right shoulder, exposing a puckered scar. "At first they didn't know which one of us had been shot because I bled all over you. But my body stopped the bullet."

Jennifer sank into one of the kitchen table chairs. "I . . . I . . ." She was going to continue to protest that she didn't know what he was talking about, but the noise in her head was too loud. The screaming. The rapid gunshots.

Hank crouched in front of her. "You really don't remember, do you?"

Open-mouthed, she shook her head.

"God, I'm sorry. I had no idea. You were all right. And I'm fine. It was a scary time. You were only four years old."

"I can't believe I don't remember this." She swallowed, her mouth suddenly dry. "Did anyone . . .?"

He nodded. His eyes were grave. "Two kids died."

"And the shooter?"

"He got away."

"Got away?"

"No one knows who did it. He was never caught."

Jennifer pressed her fingers against her temple. "Wow. I thought I didn't remember, but I've been having these dreams ever since we got to Wyoming. Screaming, shooting. I must have been remembering it on some level."

"Well, I'm sorry to bring it all up again."

"That's okay. I'm a grown-up now. I can handle it. Do handle things like this. My gosh, I just prosecuted a school shooter case."

"Still. And I didn't tell Aaron the whole story, but he knows something traumatic happened to you. You may have to deal with that."

She nodded. Her phone rang. Caller id said it was Aaron. "Speak of the devil."

"We'll let you get it," Hank said.

Maggie waved. "Tell him hey for me. Hank, walk on."

The two left, and Jennifer drew a deep, centering breath, then she answered her phone. "Aaron, where are you?"

The man who answered sounded like her husband, except for the sloshy, slurred way he spoke. "Jennifurrrrrr. I looooove youuuuuu."

"Aaron, have you been drinking?" He liked his craft beer, but not usually to excess.

"Celebrations are in order."

"What's going on? I thought you were at practice?"

"I was. But *before* practice, George agreed to work for us and live in the forest cabin."

"What?"

"Great, right? Then we met with the title company. Our closing is in two weeks."

Drunk. Giving job offers to George. Scheduling their closing. Aaron had been a busy boy. "Wow."

"George asked me to come back after practice for a celebratory drink. Come join us."

So much for their date. She wanted to tell him about her nightmares and Hank's revelation, but obviously, tonight was not the night. And the invite to join them was too little, too late. "You're drinking with George? George doesn't need to be drinking."

"I'm with him. It's all good."

That was obviously a matter upon which they'd have to disagree. As George's attorney, she felt strongly he needed to stay sober while he was facing first degree murder charges. "You're still at the lodge?"

"Yes. I wish you would come." Suddenly, he burst out laughing. A second voice joined in. Or maybe two more voices.

"I don't think so. But thanks. I think."

"I can't drive home. Because of the ce-le-bra-ting. But more good news. B-cubed is going to finish the septic tank tomorrow. We can move back in."

In the background, Jennifer heard, "That's not my name, dammit."

From the distinct pronunciation—demmit—she knew who it was. "Black Bear Betty is there, too?"

"The woman can put them away. Impressive."

"Sounds like it."

"If you wanna come get me I can sleep in the same bed as you." He sounded sweet and cuddly.

She wasn't swayed. "Aaron. Babe. The lodge is forty-five minutes away. And we'd have to go back again tomorrow to pick up your . . . DeMarcus Ware. Two round trips of one and a half hours each."

"You're already at Piney Bottoms?"

"It's seven-thirty."

"Ooooh. I thought you were at the office. Must have lost track of time. I'll just spend the night here then. S'okay. But will you miss me?"

"Less right now than half an hour ago."

"Don't be like that."

What do you have against your husband being happy? Maggie's words ricocheted in her brain again. She shuddered and bit back a snarky reply. She willed her voice to sound sincere. "It's fine."

"Really?"

"Really."

"But you're all by yourself. The animals are here with us."

"I'll write."

"You say that now, but you've said it before when you didn't."

She gritted her teeth. He wasn't wrong. "Tell George I have news for him tomorrow." Under her breath, she added, "If you can remember." Then in a louder voice. "And Aaron?"

"Yes."

"No more booze tonight."

"Can't promise that. B-cubed just broke out some Jager. I love you. Good night."

"I love you, too." She hung up the phone, her words seeming to echo in the empty house. Or maybe it was just in the empty space inside *her*.

Full dark had fallen. She carried her empty wine glass inside to the sink. As she made a cheese, tomato, and mayo sandwich with dill pickle slices, she asked herself if she really wanted to write. If she even could write with the thoughts swirling in her head after Hank's visit. She could find a mystery on TV. An old school *Murder, She Wrote* marathon might be just the distraction she needed. Or she could Google the incident that had left Hank injured and her with a case of selective amnesia. But by the time she had put away the food, poured another glass of wine—up to the rim—and had her dishes rinsing in the drainer, she'd shocked herself with a decision: she was giving her writing another try. Save Google for another day. Reading about being shot at sounded too scary alone by herself in the dark.

Instead of curling up on the couch, she carried a bag of dark chocolate chips and her laptop to the dinette table. If she really wanted to write a book, she needed to quit treating writing time like a glorified nap. Back when she'd thrown her heart and soul into writing in college, she hadn't curled up like a kitten. She'd sat at the desk in her little apartment near the campus. She'd been striving for the top grades in her classes, and she treated writing like the serious business it was. Like the *work* it was. As her writing evolved into legal briefs and motions, she kept the discipline. She pictured her blonde self in front of laptop screens at desks in a succession of offices. Had she thought creative writing was going to come to her automatically, like she'd paid her dues and it was the reward? That the muse would dance through her fingers on satin toe shoes?

There was a reason people talked about suffering for art. Art was work. Plain and simple. She'd never been afraid of work before.

She considered her wine and dark chocolate chips. That didn't mean she couldn't quench thirst and abate hunger. Hadn't Ernest Hemingway said to write drunk and edit sober? Not that she should channel him too literally—he was an alcoholic who had taken his own life. But he wrote like a beast, and she knew to filter the bad from the good when taking advice.

Staring at a blank screen waiting for an idea and perfect first sentence wasn't getting her anywhere. She wiggled her fingers. Time to try something different. She pulled up the emails she had sent herself over the last week and re-read them. Snippets of dialog. Story ideas. Descriptions of vivid Wyoming landscape and Zeus-like weather.

Out of nowhere, flickering fear stole her breath. Her hands trembled over the keys. Then she shook her head. What was wrong with her? Just the thought of creative writing terrified her. It was more than writer's block. It was writer's panic. But what was she scared of?

Her mind was as blank on that issue as it was on what to write. She popped another chocolate chip and chased it with wine. *Once more unto the breach, dear Jennifer.*

That gave her an idea. She typed, "Once upon a time" then hit the return key ten times and typed "and they lived happily ever after."

A giggle burbled out of her. *It's just the middle part that needs work.* Work. The part she was good at. She started typing.

Once upon a time there was an attorney named Jennifer who got stuck defending a drunken innkeeper against a murder charge in Godforsaken Wyoming after her too-cute-for-his-own-good husband practically kidnapped her and made her live there.

She lifted her hands from the keys and reread what she wrote. It was silly. It was awful. It wasn't even really a true version of events. *Is this cheating?* But Microsoft Word told her she'd typed thirty-nine words. *I didn't get skunked tonight.* Jeremiah waddled through her brain, as if he was congratulating her on her progress. Her giggle turned into full-fledged laughter, and she started typing again, furiously this time. Before too long, she realized her giddy energy had morphed into organized thought and that she was documenting George's case. Nonfiction? True crime? It wasn't what she'd planned. She wanted to write a novel, and she didn't have permission to write this story.

Change the names.

She could do that. She did a find-and-replace on a few key players. *If Aaron were here, he'd be proud of me.* He'd tell her that it was a start. That it still counted as creative writing. It didn't matter that it wasn't from her own imagination.

"Keep going," she said aloud, just like he would have. Then she added some coaching to herself, something she remembered from one of her creative writing classes. "You can worry about rewriting it later. For now, let it flow and write what you know."

And, so, she did. Into the wee hours. After twenty pages, her fingers were swollen and her eyelids heavy. She laid her head on the table. *Just a quick nap.* She fell into a satisfying sleep, until she heard a woman's voice.

"Yuhica. Okokipe."

She opened her eyes. The words were in a foreign language. She couldn't understand them.

The woman repeated, "Yuhica!" with an urgency that sent chills down her spine.

She had to be dreaming. There was no one in the room. She closed her eyes again to shake the bad feeling. Clear as day, she saw a shirtless man in camo pants with an AR-15 like the one she knew well from her recent case. He was spraying bullets toward her. She heard screaming and a young boy's voice say, "Jenny, get down," and felt a heavy weight on her back. Then everything went black.

Shattering glass ripped Jennifer from bad dream state and into nightmare reality.

She screamed, but there was no one to hear her. Aaron, Liam, even Jeremiah and Katya. At George's. Hank, Maggie, and Hank's partner Gene— a hundred yards away or more. All too far.

She was alone, except for whoever or whatever just broke the window.

She jumped to her feet. Broken glass blanketed the floor nearest the bed. Worse, there was more glass and a rock—a big one—in the middle of the bed. This wasn't a confused bird or a hailstorm. The window had definitely been broken by a human. Which meant there was a person outside the cabin. She dropped into a crouch. Whoever it was might decide to follow up with more rocks. Or worse. She needed to call for help. *Aaron.* But he was too far away. *Hank and Maggie.* Closer. Her phone was on the dinette table, so she started moving back toward it.

Outside, tires spun on gravel. She heard the sound of an engine receding, heading toward the ranch gate, she thought. At first, she was relieved—whoever it was had left. Then she started shaking. Someone had just tried to brain her in bed with a rock. Someone who had driven onto the ranch in the middle of the night. But who? A burglar who was going to break in through the window until she screamed? Maybe. A serial killer traveling through on the interstate? Less likely. Someone targeting her or Aaron? That seemed ridiculous.

She scrambled up and grabbed her phone. Two-thirty a.m. She scrolled through her contacts for the Sibley's home number and pressed it. While it rang, she walked back to the bed, glass crunching under her shoes. She hefted the rock. It was really big. Three or four pounds maybe? With a rock that size, whoever threw it either used a rocket launcher or had been *really* close to the cabin. She turned it over on the bed and her heart caught in her throat. There were words written on it in black marker.

TEXAS, GO HOME

"Hello?" Hank's voice. "Jenny?"

She sank to the bed, barely registering she'd just planted her tush in broken glass. A messenger. With a threat. Was this a sign that she was getting close to a killer? Her mind raced back through the people she'd made angry. Denise and her friends. Doc Billy. Tim O'Leary.

Outside, a blinding light flashed. Thunder boomed. The quiet of moments before gave way to a mighty deluge of water pelting the roof.

THIRTY-FIVE

BIG HORN, Wyoming

AARON'S first waking thought was that his mouth had been superglued shut, but only after someone had filled it with Sahara dust. He pried his jaws apart and his lips opened. *So dry.*

"Oh, jeez, close that thing until you brush your teeth." The voice was like a chisel to his brain, each word a heavy-handed mallet strike.

He opened eyes only slightly less dry than his mouth. The world's cutest nose was inches from his face. Above it were cerulean blue eyes and a halo of gold. An angel. He blinked. Hair. A head of blonde hair. "Jennifer?"

"Your breath could knock out a wart hog at twenty paces," she said.

He grunted.

"Do you realize it's nearly noon?"

"Huh?"

"You haven't been answering your phone."

He shielded his eyes. It was so bright in the bedroom. And

Jennifer's voice was so loud. He patted around on the bed beside him until he found his phone under the pillow. He pressed the home button, but nothing happened. "Dead." His charger was plugged into the wall, he just hadn't managed to connect the phone. He did it now.

"I've been calling you since two-thirty last night."

He managed a smile. "I tried to get home, but the dude at WYO Rides refused to come out here. Missed me?"

"Someone snuck onto the ranch and threw a rock through the bedroom window with the words 'TEXAS GO HOME' on it. I've gotten a few threats and made a few people mad before, but nothing like this."

"Threats?"

She looked away from him. "Normal stuff with a murder case. Anyway, I thought you'd want to know."

"A rock?" Aaron sat up in bed. His stomach lurched but he ignored it and reached for her.

She shied away from him, her mouth tight as she spoke. "I called you after I called Hank and Maggie, and while the deputies were on the way. And I called you every half hour until they were gone. Then I started calling this morning at six. My guess is a total of twelve or thirteen calls. That doesn't count text messages."

"Oh, my God. Are you okay?" He ignored her hostility and wrapped her up in his arms. She felt tiny there, like a baby bird. Soft. Delicate. Heart beating rapidly against him.

Her voice was muffled in his chest. "Tired. Angry. Worried. But otherwise, fine."

He stroked her hair and pressed his lips into it. She was breathing so fast. "I'm sorry. I should have been there."

"Yes."

After long moments, her breathing started to slow down. He leaned back and tilted her chin up so he could look into her eyes. "I feel terrible. And if something had happened to you, oh my God. I can't even think about it."

"It wasn't your fault. I know that." A tear slipped out of one of her eyes.

He groaned. "Oh, Jenny." The name just came out. *Wishful thinking? That the woman before him was the one he'd fallen in love with?* But she was. Whoever she'd become, his girl was still in there. And he'd let her down.

She brushed the tear away and straightened her spine. "The deputies didn't find any evidence. No fingerprints. Gravel roads, so no useful tire tracks."

"Shit. They have no idea who it was?"

"None."

"I wonder if you rattled the wrong cage working on George's case?"

"Or if you did."

"Me?"

"That crazy vet hates you."

Something else rattled in his brain. Had he made someone besides Doc Billy mad? The squatter here at the lodge. Will. Or maybe a parent or player. *Warmer.* Someone related to the team. He concentrated for a few seconds, but he drew a blank. "I don't know."

"My point is we have absolutely no idea who did this, or which of us it was directed at. All we know is someone wants to scare one of us. Or both of us."

"It's working." He shook his head. "We've got to get you out of there."

"I've had all night to think about this. I was alone in that cabin with nothing but a flimsy push lock on the door. The curtains were open. If they'd meant to hurt me, they could have."

Aaron grimaced.

She held up a hand. "I'm not going to let a cowardly bully chase me away. Or you. When we leave, it will be on our terms."

"Well, the timing is good, because I hear the tractor. The septic should be finished up within the hour."

Aaron's phone dinged, and Jennifer picked it up. She typed in his code and scrolled through his messages. Her jaw dropped. She kept reading. Got to her feet. Turned on him.

And then he figured out what had been niggling his brain. *Etta.* The aunt of his player, Trey. She'd kept texting him last night. Then she'd called. He'd picked up, thinking it was Jennifer. He'd been so drunk. What had he even said? He knew he'd tried to let her down gently. It hadn't gone well. He'd finally hung up on her. She'd called again, but he let it go to voice mail.

"Jennifer . . . "

Jennifer had pushed speakerphone on his voicemail.

The voice that intruded in their bedroom was aiming for sultry. "Aaron, it's Etta. No matter what, I'm here for you if you need to talk. Or not talk. Any time. Day or night." The message ended.

His wife reared back and chunked his phone at him. He threw his arms up to shield his face, and it bounced off one of them.

Her voice was scary quiet. "The woman from the gas station."

"I haven't encouraged her. I was going to tell you."

Suddenly, his phone rang. *Don't let it be Etta. Please, please, no.*

Jennifer snatched up his phone. She frowned. "This number. It looks familiar."

"Is it her again? Jennifer, I swear, I've been ignoring her. And when that didn't work, I tried to tell her to leave me alone. This woman is a head case who doesn't take no for an answer."

"Obviously." She shook her head. "And it's her. But that's not why it's familiar. What's her name again?"

"Etta."

Jennifer dropped the phone on the bed. "Crap, Aaron. You've gone and gotten yourself mixed up with Hadley's ex-girlfriend. And I'm almost positive that's the number I've seen all over his cell records."

Aaron closed his eyes. He was doubly in trouble, and he hadn't done anything wrong.

The phone chimed its voicemail notification like Etta was in the room with them.

Jennifer put one hand on a hip. "If she calls again, I'm picking up. I've got to talk to her."

Aaron stood, wearing nothing but his boxer briefs. "Jennifer, she's crazy. This isn't me. You know me. It's her." He tried to encircle her with his arms, but she ducked away. "Come on. Don't let this person drive a wedge between us. I love you. I'm glad you're here. Everything is going to be good. The lodge is about to have plumbing again, and we can move back in here whenever you're ready."

She walked to the doorway and turned to watch him. "That will work until I wrap up George's case."

"Hopefully the threat will end then, and we'll get this woman to leave me alone. We'll be safe out here." He smiled at her. "I'd like to see someone try to get past me to you."

"You're missing my point. I'll come to the lodge for now, but when this case is over, I'm going back to Houston. I'm not happy you hadn't told me about this, this *Etta,* but, notwithstanding that, I would very much like for you to come with me."

He would have been upset if a guy had been chasing after Jennifer and he found out by reading her phone, but this was overreacting. "The lodge . . . the closing . . . my coaching . . ."

"I understand if you want to finish up the season. And the lodge will make a nice vacation home for us. You said yourself last night that George will live onsite and run it. It doesn't need us. Our lives are back in Houston." She folded her arms over her middle. "Cancel the sale of your practice and come home with me."

Outside the window, Black Bear Betty motored by. She glanced in the window and quickly averted her gaze. Aaron was dazed. This was so out of left field from Jennifer.

He scrubbed his head with a palm, trying to wake up his hungover brain. "What about your job? Didn't you already quit?"

Jennifer broke eye contact. She suddenly seemed to find the pattern of the quilt exceptionally interesting.

That was a no. His blood began to simmer. "Our apartment."

"Is still ours."

"And the DA campaign?"

She took a deep breath. "I haven't given them an answer yet. I need to. They're waiting on me for a few more weeks."

He was so angry his vision blurred. This wasn't about Etta. It was about Jennifer. He wanted to punch something. To ram a tackling dummy at full speed. To beat his head against a brick wall. When his rage simmered down enough for him to speak, he spoke in a dangerous whisper. "What happened to you blocking for me for a change?"

"I have been. And I promise I'll do better from now on. I've learned my lesson. But don't other players get to have input on a team? This is *not* our future. It's wild here. Crude. Lawless." She put her hands on her hips. "Tell me I'm wrong."

She was beautiful. She was smart, passionate, and loving. But his gut and every cell in his body screamed that she was wrong. If he told her that now, he was afraid he'd lose her, though. And what about what Hank had told him? That Jennifer's objection to Wyoming might have more to do with the past than the present?

He bit his tongue and stared at her while his brain spun in an off-kilter wobble like a muffed pass.

THIRTY-SIX

BIG HORN, Wyoming

JENNIFER DROPPED her head to the steering wheel. She'd escaped to the Fusion with the intention of leaving after things had gone badly with Aaron, but now that she was in the car, the force that had been driving her away had fizzled. What had gotten into her? She'd planned to take the better part of a month to lure Aaron back to Houston. One rock through a bedroom window and a crazy woman texting her husband, and she'd bailed on the plan after a week. She'd left her dazed husband staring out the bedroom window, watching Black Bear Betty tamp earth around the installed septic tank like a gravedigger putting the finishing touches on a burial mound. And she hadn't said word one about Hank's revelations about her past trauma. Aaron needed to know about it.

Her phone rang. She answered quickly, ready to make things better. "Aaron?"

"No, it's Kid. I have George's phone. I messaged you. Where are you?"

She shook her head to clear the sadness. "I've been a little preoc-cupied." She told him about the rock through the window. She left out the problems with her husband.

"That's hard core. Are you okay?"

"More or less."

"It's a threat about George, isn't it?"

Her shoulders rose and fell. "I don't know. Maybe. But tell me about the phone. George's texts and email and voice mail. Does the prosecution have their smoking gun?"

His voice was incredulous. "Jennifer, they've got nothing. No messages to Hadley. No voice mail from that call that was made from Prescott Financial. Not from Hadley or anyone. How could they be moving forward with a first-degree murder case against George with such flimsy evidence?"

Jennifer knew how. Pootie had been working a bluff. To his credit, his IT guy had been on a trip to Hawaii, so he'd probably only found out he couldn't put his money where his mouth was a day or two ago. She thought back on a few of her own cases where they'd filed charges in haste and repented at leisure, trying desperately to make good on the promise of evidence that didn't materialize. Had she dropped charges against those defendants? The thought made her feel trapped and uncomfortable. No. She'd sweetened plea deals to buy the quiet departure of the defense attorneys and their clients. Most of the time she'd refused to let herself entertain the thought that the defendant actually wasn't guilty. Kid hadn't been through this before. He hadn't seen the ugly underbelly of the criminal justice system. She'd lived it, and believed she was in the right.

She wasn't so sure about that anymore.

"You've done great, Kid. Take the day off this case. I'll work on a motion to dismiss and send it over when I'm ready for you to add your thoughts to it."

"But what about O'Leary? And Hadley's girlfriend? And the twin issue?"

"Not our job, if we can get the case dismissed." She could feel his energy drop through the phone connection. *Join the club, Kid.* What should have felt great—impending victory—was incredibly unsatisfying.

"If you're sure."

"I am. Thanks for the good news."

Just as she pressed End Call, she heard his voice again. "About my wrongful death answer, did—"

But it was too late. *Oh, well. If it's important he'll call back.* She shook her head. She wasn't ready to write the motion. Yes, she wanted to clear George as quickly as possible. Yes, she wanted to get back to Houston. But she hadn't been entirely truthful with Kid. She was missing a piece of evidence key to *her*: an explanation for the DNA. And the rock and note had made her more aware than ever that *someone* killed Hadley right outside the window where she and Aaron had been sleeping less than two weeks before. If George didn't do it, she needed to know who did. It wasn't Kid's job, but she was going to make it hers. Because if she didn't, they might be back with something more permanent for her and Aaron than a rock and note next time.

Movement outside the Fusion caught her attention. Before she registered what it was, something whapped the window by her head. She screamed, then realized it was two hairy paws. Liam. She put her hand over her chest. Then George appeared behind his dog. Good. It was time to have another talk with her client. To update him on the evidence, and lack thereof.

She opened the door, pushing Liam back gently. When she was out of the car, she smiled at George. "Out for a stroll?" She couldn't help but notice that he didn't look nearly as hung over as her husband. But then George had a lot more practice recovering from hard nights than Aaron did.

"It's good to have him back."

"I miss him. I miss Jeremiah more, and I wish Liam peed outside, but I missed him, too. Especially last night. I had an unwelcome visitor." One more time, she recounted the rock-through-the-window story.

George gaped at her. "Because you're defending me?"

"I don't know. Kid and I got aggressive on the case yesterday, and it might have spurred someone to action. Can we talk about that for a minute?"

He motioned to a swing on the porch. "It's nice out. We can watch Liam from there."

They sat on opposite sides. Jennifer's toes barely touched the ground, but George pushed off to start the swing rocking. Neither of them said anything for a minute. Liam stayed in the grass of the front yard, rolling like he'd found something dead.

Jennifer broke the silence. "Where's my skunk friend?"

"Napping in the cottage." George gave another push. "Did you visit my aunt?"

"Angela was lovely." Jennifer sighed. "She also wouldn't confirm you were adopted. In fact, she got so agitated talking about it that a nurse made us leave."

"What do you mean she wouldn't confirm it?"

"I mean she wouldn't give us an answer. Which is an answer, George. But it's not evidence."

He nodded. "That's a lot for me to take in."

"You understand that it's impossible for you and Hadley to have identical DNA unless you're identical twins? Either the test is wrong or, well, it is what it is."

He rubbed his eyes. "Yes, as much as I hate the thought."

"Denise wasn't there when we went to pick up Hadley's birth certificate. It looked like she'd moved out in a hurry. So that's a dead end, for now."

"I have my suspicions about her, I'm sad to say."

"Me, too. And she's not the only one. There are a number of other strong suspects for the county to look at. Hadley had an on-and-off secret girlfriend." *Who's after my husband now.* "Unhappy clients. A landlord desperate to evict him." She held up a finger.

"Speaking of which, what's the name of your former business partner?"

"Tim."

Well, O'Leary hadn't lied about his partnership with George. "He's the Prescott Financial landlord. I haven't talked to him, but he left a pretty angry voice mail for me last night. He's not your biggest fan. Or mine either."

"Tim thinks everyone owes him something. He's harmless though."

"I hope so." Jennifer heard noises in the lodge. *Aaron.* Her dejection threatened to swamp her, but she held it off. George deserved her best right now. She took a cleansing breath. "I think the biggest news is that we finally got your phone back."

"When can I have it?"

"Kid has it. I'll get him to bring it out to you."

"How soon?"

"Let me ask him." She shot Kid a text. "But remember how Pootie said you invited Hadley out to the lodge that night?"

"Which is a lie."

Kid's reply came in. *I'll drop it with him in thirty minutes.*

"You'll have it back in half an hour or so."

"Good."

"Anyway, your phone all but proves you right and Pootie wrong. With that and the complete lack of any direct evidence, I'm drafting a motion to dismiss the charges."

His eyes lit up. "This will be over?"

"If the judge agrees with us. And I don't want you to get your hopes up too much. It's hard to get a dismissal."

He jumped to his feet. "But it's possible."

"Yes, it is."

He exhaled like he'd been holding his breath. "I needed to hear that."

She stood, too. "Good. Well, I'll update you when I know more. But George?"

George whistled up Liam. The old dog had fallen asleep in the grass. "Yes?"

"I know you and Aaron had a fun night last night, but unless and until we get these charges dropped, I need you to stay sober. Can you do that, please?"

He gave her a crisp nod. "I can." He disappeared with his dog into the lodge.

She had her doubts. But it didn't hurt to ask.

Jennifer walked around the side of the lodge, looking for her husband. She was glad she hadn't left. She needed to talk to him. She wanted to fix things. A powerful gust of wind nearly blew her over backwards. She steadied herself on the log wall. Above the mountains, dark clouds were gathering. By the time a system was visible, it was almost upon the lodge. This one looked like quite a storm.

Her phone rang. Caller ID announced Quentin. She took a deep breath. She might as well answer it, even though she didn't have anything new to tell him yet. Soon, though.

She pressed Accept. "Hello, Quentin."

"Hi, Jennifer. What's that loud noise? It sounds like a train."

She needed a quieter place. "Sorry. Just a second. Between the wind and the tractor, it's a little loud here."

"Wind and tractor? Where are you?"

She couldn't take this call in the lodge where Aaron might hear. The barn would be good. She jogged toward it, one hand covering her mouth and the mouthpiece. "Still in Wyoming, sir. The weather here, especially the wind, is pretty wild. And a tractor is installing a septic tank at the lodge where we're staying."

His voice was dry. "I don't want to touch that one."

"Best not to." She slid open one side of the barn door and hunkered behind the other. "Is that better?"

"Much."

She closed herself in. Low light trickled through dirty windows. The wind howled and rattled the panes. She shivered. The temperature had fallen ten or more degrees in the last few minutes, by the feel of it. "Did you get my latest text?"

"I did. I have to say, our selection committee is shocked that you're really taking a month to make a decision."

"It's only been a week." Dust danced in the light beams and tickled her nose. Her eyes had adjusted, and she was able to make out the hulking form of the tractor carcass and its odd log splitter attachment.

"That's a year in politics. We're offering you the launching pad for a political career that could be beyond your wildest expectations. Being the Harris County DA can lead to great things. Who knows? Senator, Governor, President. The sky is the limit for you. And yet you're on the fence."

Politics? She hadn't thought beyond DA. Quentin seemed to be suggesting the party had expectations for her. Wind buffeted the walls and rattled the tin roof above her. Instead of feeling flattered and excited, she felt like she was being herded into a cage.

"I have to get my husband's buy-in on that, Quentin." Which she didn't have, after she'd ambushed him this morning. She'd been so rattled by the messages on his phone and the threatening visit last night. But the attack could have happened anywhere. She'd received threats as an ADA in Houston, too. Never accompanied by a rock through a window, but serious enough that she'd been assigned protection detail more than once. And as DA—she was bound to find this a more frequent occurrence. That was something else to think about. "We just need one more conversation.".

"If you don't have it yet, what makes you think you're going to get it? We have it on good authority that our second-choice candidate doesn't have personal issues standing in the way."

Personal issues? Up until now, she had deferred to Quentin. Shown respect for his position. But Aaron was more than a personal issue. As she was wrestling with these heavy thoughts, the light in the barn suddenly disappeared. She gasped.

"Jennifer?"

She wrapped her arms around herself. It was darker *and* colder. "Sorry. There's a storm blowing in, and, well, never mind. I'm here."

"Are you? I'm beginning to wonder if this isn't about your husband at all. If it's about you and what you want."

His words made her skin prickle. What if it was about her and not Aaron? How dare he even suggest that! But she didn't dwell on his words long. Instead, her mind substituted other names into another situation. What if the murder had been about *George* and not *Hadley*? What if Hadley wasn't murdered because of being Hadley, but because someone thought he was George? Hadley had been at George's place in the middle of the night, with Liam, and he looked like George. For goodness sake's, they were possibly identical twins.

The murderer could have killed Hadley by accident, might *still* be after George. Which could mean they'd been looking in all the wrong places for the killer.

THIRTY-SEVEN

BIG HORN, Wyoming

JENNIFER HURRIED to the barn door. She needed off the call with Quentin. She had to talk to George again, right that second. "I understand what you're saying. I'll call you tomorrow with an answer."

"That's what I needed to hear. And—"

"I have to go now. Sorry." She ended the call.

She dragged open the barn door, shut it behind her, and sprinted toward the lodge. With the wind at her back, she fairly flew, hair levitating, and hands, nose, and ears nipped by the cold air.

She flung open the door from the back porch to the lodge. "George? George, where are you?"

Black Bear Betty peered around the corner.

Jennifer squeaked and clapped a hand over her mouth. "You surprised me. I was looking for George."

"Me, too. The plumbing is fixed. I need to get out of here before the storm. I'm going to put up the tractor and get gone. Can you tell him for me?"

"Of course."

Black Bear Betty clomped past her and re-opened the door. A gust blew in and knocked a picture off the wall in the hallway. Glass shattered, flashing Jennifer back to the night before. The back door shut, and the abrupt pressure change left a vacuum behind it. Jennifer put her hands to ears for a moment, then headed toward the kitchen, skirting the broken glass on the floor.

"George?" If Black Bear Betty hadn't found him in the lodge, Jennifer wasn't going to either. Maybe George was in the cottage. She'd check there next, after she cleaned up the glass and found a jacket. The temperature had fallen inside, too. She wrapped her arms around herself and stepped into the living room.

Liam was staring balefully at a puddle on the floor. It figured that George was gone just when his dog made a mess. Katya yowled from the rolltop desk.

"Aaron?" she called.

Her husband didn't answer either.

"I guess I'm on clean-up duty." She fetched supplies.

After she'd dealt with the broken frame and Liam's mess, she stopped at the thermostat. She could hear the heater running, but a piece of tape covered the numbers. She scooted the temperature lever to the right, hoping for the best. A fire would be good. She glanced at the fireplace. The log basket was empty.

The front door banged open. Aaron stomped in, laughing.

"Talk to you later, Perry." Aaron's face shuttered when his eyes met Jennifer's. He put his phone in his pocket. "I saw your car out front. I didn't know you were planning on sticking around."

"I, uh, I need to talk to George."

Aaron's flat expression turned hard. "To George."

"And you."

"George is in the cottage. I'm going up to the office."

"Office?"

"The upstairs office. I guess it used to be Shelly's. Perry's emailing me some plays to look over." But he didn't make a move to leave.

The back door opened. More weather gusted in, then the door shut. Jennifer heard George singing, "You are my sunshine." He walked in, Jeremiah cuddled against his chest in a towel.

"I've been looking for you," she said.

George lifted a shoulder. "I was giving Jeremiah a bath."

George bathed his pet skunk and sang to it. He had to be the sweetest defendant in the history of first-degree murder defendants. Sweet *and* innocent. How many sweet and innocent defendants had she inadvertently put away in her career? Her eyes burned. She didn't want to know the answer.

"There's been a development."

"In the last half hour?" George looked dubious. "It's lunch time. Can you talk to me while we eat?"

"Yes to both."

Jennifer followed George to the kitchen, with Liam and Aaron behind her. Outside the window, snow started to fall. A few flakes, then more. Harder, faster. It gave a strange white glow to the landscape. And made her think about staying warm.

She said, "I tried to set the thermostat."

"Gotta dress for the weather." He shot a pointed look at her fall shirt sans jacket. "And don't touch the thermostat. I have it set at the right place. It got installed backwards, so the numbers don't mean anything. That's why I put the tape over them."

Not helpful, but not surprising. "I was going to light a fire. You're out of firewood."

He shrugged. "I can cut more with my splitter." He got out a gallon of milk and a family size box of Honey Nut Cheerios.

Maybe. But, until he did it, it was still an empty fireplace not giving off any heat. "Maybe I'll have to borrow a jacket until I can get mine from Piney Bottoms." Jennifer moved past Aaron, who was standing like a hunk of granite by the table. She stuck a mug under the spout of the Keurig, inserted a pod, and pressed start.

"Sure. But you have to be prepared for anything, any time up here. Survival can depend on it. Easy enough to keep an extra jacket in a car."

It was good advice, based on how fast the weather turned bad. Thinking about the cold brought Black Bear Betty and her departure back to mind. "Black Bear Betty finished the septic tank and put up the tractor. She said the plumbing works again now."

George grunted. He carried the milk and cereal to the table.

A knock sounded at the front door, then it opened. Kid stuck his head in. "Hi, everyone. George, I've got your phone."

Jennifer and Aaron greeted Kid as he brushed snow off his jacket.

George met him halfway across the living room and took the phone.

Kid eyeballed George's retreating back. "You're welcome."

George lifted the phone in the air in response.

"Thank you, Kid. Do you want to stay for cereal and coffee?" Jennifer asked.

"No. My mom needs her car back."

"Drive safe then."

He was gone as quickly as he had come.

Jennifer got out spoons and bowls and took them to the table, almost tripping over Jeremiah, who had rolled onto his back in the middle of the floor. By the time she returned with her coffee, the men were seated and pouring cereal.

She warmed her hands around the mug. "You know how we talked earlier about whether it's possible you and Hadley could be twins, and how that could be key to your defense?"

"Been hard to think about anything else."

"I feel stupid for not thinking of this earlier, but your physical similarities and Hadley's death occurring here raise another possibility."

Aaron's head jerked up. His spoon clanked the table. "Mistaken identity."

Jennifer pointed at him. "Bingo." She poured her own cereal.

George frowned. "I don't follow."

Aaron grinned, seeming to forget how upset he was at Jennifer. "What if someone meant to kill you instead of Hadley?"

George's eyebrows crept toward his hairline. "I could understand wanting to kill Hadley. The man was impossible. But me? I'm the most likeable guy I know."

Jennifer added milk to her bowl. "We've been focusing on you *not* committing this murder, and to a lesser extent, who else had the motive, means, and opportunity to kill *Hadley*. The smarter question might be who had the motive, means, and opportunity to kill *you?*"

George pulled at his baby beard. "Well, I'll be. That thought never even crossed my mind."

Jennifer nodded. "Think about it. Who has it in for you George?" She shoveled in a bite of her cereal. She was hungrier than she'd realized, and it was good. Cold, crisp, and sweet. She would have preferred hot soup, but this would do.

"Hadley, but he's dead. Denise wants the lodge."

Jennifer swallowed her bite. "She's my top suspect, because she had motive to kill Hadley, too, if it turns out it was about him after all."

"Maybe it's about both of them instead of one or the other," Aaron mused.

"Boy, that would complicate things even further. But it's possible. Anyone else, George?" Jennifer asked.

"Will has threatened me a time or two."

"That hiker?"

"He says he has squatter's rights to the place. Like it's his or something. And the knife that killed Hadley might be his."

Jennifer remembered George mentioning that before. It took on new significance now. "Who else?" she prompted.

"It could be Sarah Stiles' family. You know. The mother filed the wrongful death suit against me."

Jennifer nodded. "But filing a lawsuit says they want you suffering, not dead." Still, the sister, Melinda, had shown up with Denise to harangue George, and it wasn't her who had filed the lawsuit. Maybe Melinda wanted George dead and was working with Denise to make it happen. "What about Tim O'Leary? He seemed pretty angry at you."

"Yes, there's him. And he thinks he is going to inherit money from me in my will."

"What gave him that idea?"

"I told him that to get him off my back."

"Great." Jennifer shook her head. "Okay. He goes on the list. What about Doc Billy? He seemed like he had a good motive to kill Hadley."

"Doc Billy takes care of my animals."

"Any bad blood between you?"

George ducked his head.

Jennifer had expected a negative answer. "What?"

"Billy is Shelly's little brother."

"Wait," Jennifer said. She and Aaron stared at each other. He looked as confused as she felt. She cut her eyes back to George, lunch cereal forgotten. "Doc Billy and Hadley used to be *brothers-in-law*?" The connections almost defied belief, the whole six degrees of separation thing notwithstanding. This town wasn't *that* small.

"Yes. Billy moved here originally because Shelly talked him into it. He and Hadley stayed tight after the divorce, too. Used to rile Shelly up good that Billy picked Hadley over her. I'm not sure that's accurate, but the fact remains that things between Billy and Hadley only ended because of money. And then they ended really badly."

"Did Billy blame you for Shelly's death, too?"

"He never said it directly. But he was never as friendly to me after she died. I was even thinking about changing vets. I only take the critters in once a year, and the last visit was pretty uncomfortable."

"All right. Last one. What about Etta?"

"Who?"

"Etta. Hadley's secret girlfriend." Jennifer couldn't help giving Aaron a slightly dirty look when she said it.

"Didn't know her."

"Well, that's one less complication anyway." Jennifer pressed her fingers to her temples. "Wow. My head is spinning."

"Did any of that help?"

"I don't know yet. I'm more confused than ever. I have a lot to think about and look into. But I'm going forward with the motion to dismiss as we discussed and leaving this mistaken identity thing out of it until we have an idea who did it. Right now, I'm more concerned about keeping you safe than anything else. Whoever killed Hadley may have sent me a warning to back off, and, if they meant to kill you in the first place, they might try again."

"I wonder if me getting run off the road has anything to do with all this?"

"Crap. I'd completely forgotten about that. It could have been the second attempt on your life. Has law enforcement made any progress on it?"

George frowned. "If they have, they're keeping it a secret from me."

A heavy, tense silence fell over them. Liam whined. Jennifer didn't like this. Not one bit.

Aaron pushed his bowl back. "Why don't I stay here again tonight?"

"I wouldn't say no," George said.

Part of Jennifer smarted. Aaron hadn't said "we." Had he forgotten about the rock through their window the night before? Of course, Aaron's presence at the lodge might not matter anyway. He'd been there the night Hadley was killed and Liam and George were hurt. Which reminded her—she really needed the paperwork from the medical exam the county did on George.

Aaron stood. "Let's go get your bag, Jennifer.

Jennifer wasn't sure if the lightness in her chest was because she wouldn't be alone, she'd be getting away from Maggie, or her husband wanted her with him.

Whichever it was, she couldn't help the smile that lifted the corners of her lips.

THIRTY-EIGHT

BIG HORN, Wyoming

"WAS Maggie nice to you last night?" Aaron said. He helped himself to another slice of meat lover's pizza. He and Jennifer had stopped for takeout on their way back to the lodge from Piney Bottoms since the Merc was the only place open and on the way. By then, DeMarcus Ware was earning his keep, cruising through six inches of snow on the unplowed roads.

George's phone was beside him on the table, inches from his hand, like he couldn't bear to be parted from it now that he had it back. He took a fourth piece. Aaron regretted agreeing to split a pizza with him. The smaller man could put it away.

"She's never nice to me." Jennifer was sipping Koltiska 90 and iced tea. Hard liquor was not her go-to. But it was her turn to cut loose tonight if she wanted it to be. She pointed at some printer pages Aaron had placed on the table a couple of inches from his plate, safely away from pizza grease. "Your plays?"

He nodded. "I promised I'd mark them up and send them back to

Perry before practice tomorrow." He wasn't letting her distract him from the subject of Maggie, so he doubled back on it. "I thought you and Maggie were becoming friends."

"As if."

"But you said she came over."

"Just a drop by with Hank."

He really wished she'd make a Sheridan friend. At least she had Jeremiah. The skunk was curled up in her lap asleep. "Okay. I thought they spent the evening with you. So, what did you do last night—catch up on the Aurora Tea Party mysteries?"

She gave him a withering look. "Aurora Teagarden. And no. I didn't."

Something in her voice got his full attention. "What did you do, then?"

She lifted her glass to him. "I wrote."

He kept his tone guarded. "All right."

"I'm serious. I wrote twenty pages."

This felt momentous. A breakthrough for her that might lead to a breakthrough for them. He kept it calm. "What did you write?"

She took a gulp of her drink and shrugged. "Crime stuff. About the case."

"Are you going to keep going?"

"Maybe."

God, he hoped so. "What do you think inspired you?"

Jennifer bit her lip, looking down. When her eyes met his, there were tears in them. "Something Hank told me. About when we were kids."

Aaron froze. He wanted to reach out to her, but he didn't want to interrupt her flow if she was going to open up. "Go on."

"I don't know how I'd forgotten it or repressed it or whatever, but when I was four, we were visiting Hank's family. I went to his school and met him on the playground. A man opened fire on us. Two kids were killed. Hank was shot. But he—" Jennifer's voice broke, "—he saved me."

"Oh, honey." Aaron was horrified. He never dreamed the event in her past was this traumatic. "I'm so sorry."

"He's still out there."

"Who?"

"The killer. He was never caught."

"You're kidding?"

George spoke. "I remember that case and young Hank being injured. Parents were scared about it for years."

"My parents never brought me back to Wyoming."

Aaron took her hand. "And now I've brought you here. Right after your Texas case, too. I'm sorry."

Jennifer nodded, her eyes wet. For a split second, Aaron considered telling her about his past. *Not with George here.* He could ask her to step into the bedroom with him. Then George spoke, and the moment passed.

George pointed out the window with his pizza slice. "Snow's stopped. See the stars?" His words came out slurred. Aaron had a bad feeling he'd found the booze Jennifer had hidden away again.

Aaron craned his head. Brilliant lights were twinkling against a velvet blue background. "It's beautiful."

He walked to the window for a better look. Jennifer set Jeremiah on the floor and joined Aaron, her steps just a little unsteady. Had she eaten any pizza with her liquid dinner? He glanced at her plate. Her veggie pizza slice had only one small bite out of it. He held his hand out to her. Her eyes met his, and, after only a second's hesitation, she slipped under his arm and snuggled into him. Her warmth spread to his core in seconds. He wanted their fight to be over. He wasn't happy with the choices she'd made, but they couldn't fix anything without speaking to each other. And he couldn't comfort her unless she let him back in. This was a good start.

"I'm going to turn in. See you in the morning." George's tone was flat. Aaron would have expected him to be on top of the world. What was wrong with him?

"Goodnight," Aaron said.

"N'night," Jennifer called.

George stumbled down the hallway, leaving Aaron and Jennifer alone, still intertwined. Aaron held perfectly still, afraid to break the spell. She was so small and yet so strong. Fear and longing ripped through him. If she really moved back to Houston to run for DA, he'd do everything he could to make a long-distance relationship work. But if she was leaving soon, he wanted to make every moment count. No more time wasted on fighting. No more holding back.

He whispered in her ear. "Come to bed with me."

She turned toward him, her face turned up. "We still have things to talk about."

"How about we talk tomorrow?" He kissed her temple, his lips lingering. "And tonight we *don't* talk?"

Her eyelashes fanned his cheek. "I just have one question first. An important one."

"What is it?"

"That night after Hank's party. You said I did something or said something bad to you. I'm so sorry, but I don't remember it, Aaron. I need to know what it was."

He guided her back by her shoulders. Such big blue eyes. The look in them was sad and a little embarrassed. He couldn't believe she didn't remember. But she needed to know. He bit the inside of his lip, nodding. This was going to hurt. "You said you never wanted to have kids with me."

She jerked back like he'd slapped her. "What brought that up?"

"We didn't have the appropriate contraceptive devices. You took antibiotics last month and were afraid the pill might not be working. I said maybe it was fate, and you pushed me off of you."

"Oh, God."

"You said you weren't taking any chances."

"And then . . ."

"Then nothing. After you told me you never wanted to have kids with me, you rolled over and went to sleep."

She clutched his arms. "Aaron, I was drunk. I know it sounded terrible, but, honestly, I didn't mean it that way."

"What other way is there to mean it?"

Her fingers dug into him. "I just, I was being overly dramatic and . . . and . . ."

He wished he could believe her. "And truthful, under the influence of alcohol. You don't want to have kids. Ever. Or at least never with me. I've been coming to grips with it."

She walked to the table and downed the rest of her drink, swaying. She steadied herself on her chair. Her eyes were closed, and her lips were moving.

"What are you saying?"

When she opened her eyes, they were wet with tears. "That I'm an idiot. Aaron, if I ever have kids, I want them to be with you. I haven't wanted to yet because I'm afraid I'll lose everything I've been working for. Plus, there's a part of me that feels guilty about bringing a child into such a dangerous world, and to a mother who will still be working. But that doesn't mean I won't ever want to."

"We're forty, Jennifer. Can you even still have a baby?"

"Women my age have babies all the time!"

"But you don't know you'll be able to. A lot of those women go through fertility treatments. There's no guarantee."

"We could adopt."

"Even if we did, we'd be the oldest parents in our kids' classes, parenting from fifteen hundred miles apart. I think our door is about to close, Jennifer."

Her voice was anguished. "Aaron, you're the man I want."

"But you want to be the Harris County DA, too, and you don't think being a mother is compatible with that. You know what's funny, though? I think it would make you more electable, not less. And better at your job."

"People will say kids would distract me."

"Male candidates have children."

She looked down.

Aaron softened his voice. "I understand that you're going back to Houston. That you're going to run for office. *I love you anyway.*"

Her amazing eyes came back up and locked on his. "I love you, too."

He sighed. "Now you know what you said." He guided her gently back into his arms. "Please. Let's save the rest of it for tomorrow. Be with me tonight, Jennifer. Just be with me. Just *be.*"

She tilted her head back and stood on her tiptoes. He leaned over, and she laid a soft kiss on his cheek. "I can do that."

He took her hand and led her to their bedroom.

THIRTY-NINE

BIG HORN, Wyoming

THE CLOUDS DRIFTED in front of the sliver of a moon, blocking Jennifer's view of the snowscape behind the house. Deck boards creaked, and the cold against her bare feet shocked her fully awake. *What am I doing outside in the middle of the night, barefoot and without a robe, much less a coat?* She wasn't sleepwalking, per se. Something had woken her from a deep, warm slumber, and she'd responded on autopilot, like a reluctant protagonist from a Mary Higgins Clark novel.

She wrapped her arms around herself and shivered. In the distance, muffled by the wind, she heard sounds that didn't belong. Maybe that was what had lured her from bed. *Is it a voice?* The only people onsite were Jennifer, Aaron, and George, and she'd left Aaron snoring in bed, worn out by the emotion of the evening. There was a desperation to their union now that she'd announced she was leaving soon. So, who was it? Unless George was yelling at himself—not an impossibility, if he were drinking again—then either her ears were playing tricks on her, or the sound was coming from somewhere else.

Only there was no one else around.

The wind swept the sounds to her again. Definitely voices. Male, maybe more than one. Agitated. Angry.

"... your fault ..."

"... can't ... sorry ..."

Light shining from a window of George's cottage caught her eye. She grabbed the porch railing and peered more closely at the little house, wondering if that's where the sound was coming from. She heard them again. Definitely coming from another direction. But she paused. Something seemed off about the cottage, and she squinted. *What is it?* Then it clicked for her. His front door was ajar. *In the middle of the night when it's thirty-degrees outside?* If he was passed out near the door, he might die of exposure before morning. She had to do something about it.

For a split second, she thought about waking Aaron. Sexy, probably still smiling-in-his-sleep, strong Aaron. But as she turned back toward the lodge, she saw a pair of men's muck boots by the doormat. It would only take her a minute to check on George. She'd left her phone in the bedroom, but, if she needed Aaron's help, she could call him from George's phone. She slipped her feet into the too-big boots and clomped off the deck. Goose flesh pimpled her arms and legs. Her Texas fall sleepwear of silky pants and a baby doll tee wasn't cutting it in Wyoming, certainly not outdoors in this onslaught of early cold and snow. In her sleepy state—made worse by nightmares and insomnia that had plagued her since their arrival—the dry air had tricked her into thinking she didn't need a coat, but she wished she had one now. She broke into a trot, and her heels rode up in the boots. She caught a toe on a hidden rock and tripped, crashing onto her hands and knees.

"Ow!" The snow had an icy bite to it. Did the vodka still have a hold in her? She didn't think so—her last drink had been hours ago.

She climbed to her feet, brushed off her hands, and ran faster, lifting her knees as high as she could while still moving forward. Her quads and butt felt the weight of the boots almost immediately.

At George's front door, she poked her head inside. The light she'd seen was from the kitchen. "George?" she called. She knocked for good measure. Her eyes swept the floor. She was relieved not to see him crumpled around a bottle. "George?" Best to do a quick bed check.

She walked in and made her way to the only bedroom and stopped at the open door. The drapes were drawn, and it was dark inside.

"George?"

The silence mocked her.

"George?"

This time, there was a noise, but not from his room. It was from somewhere outside again. The same man sounds, elevated. Her pulse quickened. Dread rooted her to the ground, but she forced herself to enter the room. The bed was empty. She hurried through. *No George, anywhere.*

Moonlight returned and shone through the window. Jennifer saw an old woman outside it. The woman's hair was black shot through with streaks of white and pulled back from her face. Jennifer clutched the collar of her pajama tee.

Faintly, Jennifer heard the woman's voice through the glass. "Wecahcala."

"What?" She didn't recognize the language, but it seemed familiar to her somehow. Had she heard someone speak it recently? Then it hit her. The night the rock was thrown through her window. She'd heard a woman speaking a language that sounded similar. "Where is he?"

The woman pointed east.

Jennifer wasn't sure what she meant. The shop? The stable? The barn? "Where?"

The woman disappeared.

Gooseflesh rose on Jennifer's arms. Who was that woman? And should she call Aaron? But she didn't see a phone on the TV tray that was serving as a bedside table. She ran into the kitchen. No phone on the wall, the counter, or the table. In the living room—nothing, save an empty bottle of Wyoming Whiskey on the coffee table. She put her hand on the wooden surface and felt a few dribbles of liquid. Darn it. He'd found the liquor she'd hidden from him. Or bought more in town.

No phone anywhere.

The voices grew louder outside. One of them rose to a roar. Or was it really a voice? It could be a mountain lion. Or a bear. She went out onto the porch and lifted her hair from her ear. The roar came from the barn, where a faint light glimmered. Only it wasn't a roar. It wasn't even a voice. She recognized the noise.

It was the log splitter in the barn.

Panic ripped through her. *George is out there after drinking so much whiskey that he left his door open in the middle of the night?* She'd urged him to replenish the low logs in the cabin earlier in the day, and now she regretted it.

Jennifer would have preferred to have her big husband with her, but she didn't have time to go after him. She took off at a sprint for the barn, slipping and tripping but somehow managing to stay upright. It was only twenty yards away, but at seven thousand feet in altitude, her chest heaved, and frigid air seared her lungs like she was sucking on a blow torch. A few feet from the hanging barn doors, she tried to slow down. She lost traction and caught herself on one side of the doors.

A person barreled out and past her, knocking her aside. Medium-to-tall height, a ball cap covering the hair and pulled low over the face, layers of bulky clothing hiding body type. Except for the shoulder, where the clothing was ripped away, exposing skin. Not just skin. Skin and a dark patch. The brief glimpse slammed into her brain like a battering ram. A tattoo of a snake coiled in rocks with D-T-O-M below it.

She'd seen it before. It was a recurring image in her nightmares. For a fraction of a second, she was frozen in place, speechless. The tattoo was real, although it read DTOM and not ATOM as she'd thought. Did that mean the man in her nightmares was real, too—a memory instead of a phantom? That it might be George, who she'd let into her inner circle? It was too horrible to contemplate. Because that man pulled out an AR-15 and opened fire on a schoolyard. On her and other children. And he'd never been caught. But having a tattoo she dreamed about didn't mean that George was the only person who had it.

She pushed the thoughts away. The ripped clothing. The log splitter. Those weren't good things. She had to stay in the present for now.

"George?" she cried.

The person didn't stop. Didn't answer her. *George. It has to be.*

Inside the barn, the roar hadn't stopped either. *Why did George leave the log splitter on? Was the exposed shoulder a sign he'd been injured?* He'd moved like he was okay. Okay enough, anyway. She'd just go turn the machine off, then she'd follow him back to his cottage and make sure he was all right. She stepped into the barn. A single caged bulb hung from the ceiling, illuminating the interior in meager light that was mostly shadows. Jennifer frowned, inhaling the scents of sawdust and motor oil. It was spooky, but warmer. She rubbed her prickly arms and strode past the orange tractor to the little tractor carcass that housed the engine powering George's splitter contraption. As she drew closer, hair rose on her neck like hackles. Something felt *wrong*. Instead of turning off the key, she kept going, intuition drawing her toward the splitter on the back of the tractor.

When she reached the rear corner, she looked around it toward the evil-looking cone. What she saw, she wouldn't be able to wash from her memory with a gallon of bleach and a stiff bristle brush.

Bloody boots. Red-splashed legs. A torso drenched in blood. A note on its chest. I AM A MURDERER. Beside it, a photo.

And an arm, ripped and thrown two feet away from the rest of the body.

She had to do something. Render aid, somehow. Go for help. Anything but nothing.

"Help," a weak male voice called, barely more than a rasp. "Help me." It was coming from the bloody body behind the tractor.

The person was alive.

She ran to the man. When she squatted beside him, she saw George's face. Her heart nearly shattered. What else would this poor man have to go through? *He's not the bad man in my dreams.* For a moment, her eyes left his face and focused on the note and picture. I AM A MURDERER, that looked like the notes on George's door. Like the note on Hadley's body. The photo, a woman and two men picnicking beside snowmobiles. One of the men was George, eating sausage and cheese with a knife. She squinted. A black Swiss Army knife. The woman had her head on his shoulder. Shelly? And the other man, younger, was someone she'd met. Will. The squatter. But her mind stayed fixed on the knife in George's hand.

George, with a knife like the murder weapon.

The note, from a printer. A *printer.* George had said he didn't have a printer, but Aaron had printed out the plays earlier. Upstairs. At the lodge. Could George have printed this note? *Oh, my God.* Could George have printed *all* the notes?

What had George done?!? Was this the suicide attempt of a guilty man? Had she been blinded by her own bias—her relationship with George and his animals, her own experience as a twin and with a twin case? Had the person with the tattoo running from the barn been going for help?

No. Good Samaritans didn't hide their faces. They stopped. They asked for help. They didn't run off. *They didn't have her nightmare tattoo.*

George couldn't have done this to himself. And a killer had just gotten away. Again.

"George, what were you doing with the log splitter in the middle of the night?" She heard the distress in her voice verging on hysteria. She had to calm down for his sake. She searched for something to staunch the bleeding. George's jacket was on the ground beside the splitter. She crawled over to it and back to him, pressing it into the wound.

His words were barely audible over the loud tractor engine. She leaned in close to hear him.

"You said . . . low on wood. Wanted to do something . . . nice. Know you don't . . . like it here much."

"Oh, George." Tears welled in her eyes. She should never have doubted him. "You didn't have to do that. The lodge is growing on me." It was. He was.

She spied a log stump and rolled it over to him, positioning it tightly against where his arm had been, and his coat now was. "Lean into that for me. Don't roll away." He shifted slightly, groaning. "Good. I know it hurts, but please don't move. I'm going for help now, George. Hang in there." She squeezed the hand he had left, staring into his eyes as she did, and away from the bloody stump where his other arm had been.

She backed away two steps, still looking at George and trying to decide if she was doing the right thing.

Behind her, she heard a grating noise as the barn doors slid further open. *Aaron!* She felt a dizzying relief—help was here. Then she heard the distinctive action of a shell chambering into a shot gun.

Aaron didn't have a shotgun in Wyoming.

Acting on pure instinct, she dove to the side, scraping her hands, knees, and chin on the packed dirt floor.

BOOM.

Someone had shot at her. Shot at her! And she was still exposed. She scrambled on her hands and her knees. The boots didn't make it easy.

She felt certain to the marrow of her bones that whoever this was had killed Hadley. The picture on George's torso flashed back into her mind. Will. The angry former employee who blamed George for Shelly's death. He had a knife like the murder weapon. Was it him shooting at her?

A connection that had eluded her before became blindingly, suddenly clear in her mind. Harriett had used the same font on her seminar fliers as the one on the notes. Did Harriett bear a grudge against Hadley?

Will . . . Harriett . . . who was out there? But neither of them was old enough to have shot up a school playground thirty-five years ago. Her brain spun in a crazy loop, rocking and off kilter.

The shooter worked the action.

BOOM.

This time the shotgun pellets displaced air around her. Splinters of wood peppered her legs. She was nearly to the wall, but what then? As she crawled, she bumped her head on something hard and metal. *The wood stove.* She threw herself behind its bulk as the action on the gun made its lethal noise again.

BOOM.

PING PING PING PING PING.

The pellets slammed into the stove but missed her. Jennifer wasn't a hunter. But she'd gone with Aaron when he duck hunted, and she'd fired a shotgun many times. She knew most shotguns didn't hold more than three shells unless they'd been modified.

She had a few precious seconds—maybe—to figure out what to do. Because she had to do something. She saw the shooter walking across the barn, looking to get a bead on her. She looked around frantically. What she wanted most was to make a break for the doors. To get out of the barn. But the exit was fifteen feet away, and the shooter was between her and the doors. If she stood up and ran, she made herself an unmissable pointblank target. For now, she needed to keep the stove between herself and the hunter. And she needed a weapon in case she got a chance to use it. She surveyed her options. Tools, a chunk of wood, rocks. Then she saw something promising leaning against a work bench only a few feet away.

The long-handled log splitter. It was shaped like a club—a club with a hefty steel head. Unfortunately, it probably weighed twenty pounds. Too much for her to handle well. But what choice did she have? The footsteps were coming closer, and she moved carefully around the stove in her unwieldy boots, trying not to make a sound. She couldn't quite reach the splitter, not without exposing her head to a kill shot. She lowered herself to the ground and pushed forward on her belly. As she reached the splitter, she looked back and saw work boots under the opposite side of the stove. She grabbed the wooden handle and pulled it toward her. The head drug and caught in the dirt floor. She wasn't going to be able to get it to her unless she stood.

The footsteps were closer, moving around the stove. She pressed her cheek into the dirt. She had no choice. She had to take a swing. Maybe she'd land a stomach or kneecap blow or one that would knock the gun from the shooter's hands.

She pushed off with her hands, bursting from a plank to her feet and grabbing the handle on her way up. Without hesitating, she swung the splitter head back and around. Even using all her strength and her beautiful golfer's form, she couldn't get the height she needed. The splitter hurtled through the air in a low arc, connecting with one of the shooter's ankles.

THUD.

"Argh!" the shooter screamed, in a voice that was neither clearly male nor female.

The impact jolted Jennifer's arms and shoulders so hard that she dropped the splitter. The shooter crumpled to the ground, shrieking. She risked a glance and saw the same low-slung ball cap she'd seen earlier. The bundled-up form was clutching an ankle with one hand but still holding the shotgun in the other.

Now. She had to make a run for it. There was no time to waste. She exploded toward the doors. On her second step, she caught the toe of her enormous boots on the head of the splitter. Her body launched forward and crashed into something that collapsed under her weight with a clatter and cloud of dust. Her hands searched for something to push off of, and she immediately recognized familiar shapes. Long, slender shafts. Cold, hard wedges. Bulky club heads.

She'd knocked over the old golf bag she'd seen on her first visit to the barn.

Behind her, the voice said, "Gotcha now, you nosey big city bitch."

Definitely male. Not Harriett. But was it Will? She'd heard the voice before, but she couldn't be sure.

The dreaded sound of the shotgun spurred her into action. She closed her fingers around the slim handle of a club. It didn't matter which one. Any would do. There was no time to stand or get in her stance. To take a backswing. To think about her form. All she had time to do was use it in the most literal sense of its name. As a club. She rolled toward the shooter, raised the club as high as she could, and smashed it down on him.

CRACK.

Whatever she'd hit, it was solid. The shooter moaned. She clubbed him again.

CRACK.

Had she hit bone? Revulsion roiled through her. She'd never intentionally harmed another human being before. She didn't want to kill him. But if she didn't incapacitate him, he was going to kill her.

In the low light, she saw the man's hand. It was open and no longer grasping the gun. With the club poised high in one hand to strike again if necessary, she levered herself to her feet and kicked the gun away. The man had fallen to his side with his face turned from her. She tossed the bloody club across the barn, then picked up the gun.

She ran back to George. She set the shotgun down beside him, then checked his wound. The bleeding was heavy. Too heavy. She leaned close to him when she saw his lips moving.

He croaked out a few words. "Did Pootie get away?"

"Pootie?"

"Sarah's father. Pushed me . . . left me to die . . . only got my arm."

"Sarah Stiles—the one who died in your wreck?" And the one whose mother Gerrianne had filed a wrongful death lawsuit against George for it.

He nodded, and his eyes fluttered closed. He was unconscious. Jennifer knew she had to do more to stop the bleeding, and she ran back to the battered, bloody, and unconscious body of the shooter.

Pootie. *Sarah's father.* Jennifer kicked herself for not listening to Kid when he had tried to tell her who Sarah's father was. Pootie had pursued the case against George for Hadley's death to the point of framing him, despite the lack of evidence. Like someone who was on a mission to punish. No matter how grief-stricken he was at the loss of his daughter, nothing justified trying to kill George. And Pootie had succeeded with Hadley, believing him to be George. It was the only explanation that fit.

She pulled Pootie's jacket off. His shirt shifted, exposing the hateful tattoo again. *The age fits.* Had Pootie opened fire on a school playground, killing two children, and wounding God knew how many more? Was he the central figure in her nightmares? She couldn't be sure, but it was possible. And suddenly she wanted that child killer caught and brought to justice for the long-ago crime, wanted it with an intensity and ferocity that came out as a snarl. *If it is you, Pootie, I'm taking you down. For Hadley, for George, and for the kids. For Hank. For me.*

She took the coat back to George, heaving him up and tying the sleeves around his shoulder and chest as tightly as she could. Then she lowered him and pushed him back against the log. It was all she could do, except call 911 and fetch her husband, who, with his veterinary experience, could take care of George until an ambulance made it out here.

"Jennifer!" Aaron's voice from the doorway was the most wonderful sound she'd ever heard.

"In here."

The tractor engine suddenly shut off.

"I heard shots." His voice was stressed. "Where are you?"

"I'm fine, I promise. Bring your vet kit. Hurry, and call an ambulance on the way. George lost his arm in the splitter, and he's bleeding and unconscious." After a split second's hesitation, she grudgingly added, "Alfred Carputin has taken a few blows to the head and needs medical attention, too. And handcuffs."

FORTY

SHERIDAN, Wyoming

"IN THE MATTER of the State of Wyoming versus George Nichols, Mr. Wesley, are you and Big City ready?" Judge Ryan's voice was jovial.

Kid straightened his red bow tie for the capacity crowd. It was a big day for him, and he needed to look the part. Jennifer just wished he hadn't felt the need to smell the part and had gone lighter on his cologne. The people in the back row could probably smell him, too. But she understood his enthusiasm. They were here for Justice with a capital J.

Kid's deep voice filled the courtroom. "We are, Your Honor."

Jennifer beamed like a proud parent.

"And for the county—I don't believe we've met, have we?"

Opposing counsel today was two decades younger than Pootie and several shades darker. Apparently, according to Patrick Flint— who'd whispered it to her on her way in—the interim county attorney was the first Black attorney he could remember practicing in

Sheridan County on either side of the docket, brought in from Cheyenne due to the relative inexperience of the attorneys on the Sheridan staff. "Ollie Singletary as Prosecuting Attorney for Sheridan County, Your Honor. The county is ready."

"Mr. Singletary. Got it. Welcome to Sheridan. How's it treating you?"

"Thank you, Your Honor. I'll miss Cheyenne, but I like it here so far."

The judge nodded. "All right, then. Mr. James, introduce your motion, please."

Jennifer itched to get to her feet and present the evidence she'd worked so hard with Kid to gather, and, ultimately, almost paid for with her life. Over the last few days, she'd spent every waking hour either at the hospital with George or in the office with Kid. George would survive. Without his left arm, but he was already sanguine about that, sharing tasteless jokes with Patrick and Aaron about one-armed men. Kid had done the heavy lifting on drafting the motion to dismiss while Jennifer had gathered the last few pieces of evidence to support it. And when she'd stolen away to meet with the sheriff and one of the attorneys from the county about the thirty-five-year-old crime. There was no proof that Pootie had done it, but they were investigating, and Jennifer was hopeful, although her nightmares hadn't stopped.

The biggest piece of evidence for their dismissal motion was the DNA results from the second round of submissions. They again showed George and Hadley as having identical DNA. How the two men could have turned out so differently was a marvel. And yet they'd married the same woman. Earlier that day, Bonnie Morrow had even showed up at Kid's office with Denise in tow. Denise had handed over a copy of Hadley's original birth certificate. The names of the parents had been blacked out, but it did give his birthdate and named Sheridan as the location. While it was still a mystery who George and Hadley's birth parents were and might remain one, Jennifer had a notarized statement from George's Aunt Angela confirming that the Nichols adopted George in Sheridan. That was more than enough for the motion.

What's more, they finally had the medical report from the county's examination of George. "Injury consistent with a fall and contact with a hard, smooth surface," it read. Some of George's memories from the night were returning, which was also consistent with his injury. He had a vague recollection of falling in the bathroom.

There had still been the matter of George being run off the road, as well as the rock through her bedroom window. The police, under pressure from her, had matched paint from George's truck to a scrape on Pootie's SUV, enough to link Pootie to the incident, especially given his lack of alibi. The Johnson County sheriff's department hadn't been able to tie him to the rock through her window, but no one seriously doubted it had been him. If nothing else, there was the TEXAS, GO HOME note in the Marker Felt Bold font, but, like the other notes Pootie had planted, it had no fingerprints. She would have to live with that. As she'd have to live with her unsettling encounters with the women—apparitions?—who'd spoken to her in the strange language, warning her about the rock and about Pootie's attack on George. Remembering the face outside George's cottage window, Jennifer had come to believe the women were Lakota Sioux, whether they were real, or she'd imagined them. Maybe she would never know which.

She turned to the gallery. Aaron was directly behind her. He nodded, and she nodded back. She could count on one hand the motion arguments he'd come to court to watch. George had a hold on them both, it seemed. Aaron had spent even more time at the hospital than she had. Of course, he was holding down the fort at the lodge and with the animals. And coaching, too. She'd never seen him this content and fulfilled before. She couldn't think about what that meant for her. For them. Not now, in court. It made her eyes burn.

She returned her attention to her co-counsel. Kid stepped away from the defense table and cleared his throat. He was auditioning for future defense counsel roles, and he'd rehearsed his monologue ad nauseam for her. She could almost recite it, and it took effort to keep her lips from moving.

"If it pleases the court, I'm here to present a Motion to Dismiss All Charges, With Prejudice, on behalf of George Nichols, my client. Mr. Nichols was charged with the first-degree murder of Hadley Prescott on flimsy evidence that completely fell apart during discovery. It is undisputed that Mr. Prescott died at a lodge owned by Mr. Nichols. DNA results have proved that Mr. Nichols and the decedent are identical twins. In the absence of any fingerprints or other direct evidence, it is impossible to determine if Mr. Nichols was present at the scene of the crime or whether Mr. Nichols and Mr. Prescott had any physical contact on that evening. The prosecution has argued that Mr. Prescott was at Mr. Nichols' home due to an express invitation, yet there is no record of any such invitation being extended by Mr. Nichols. The only real evidence the prosecution is able to present was that Mr. Prescott had a great deal of animus toward Mr. Nichols, relating to Mr. Nichols' deceased wife. Despite Mr. Prescott's ongoing harassment of Mr. Nichols, the prosecution cannot prove the same animus extended from Mr. Nichols *toward* Mr. Prescott. Lastly, Mr. Prescott was found stabbed with a commonly available knife, the same knife used to stab Mr. Nichols' beloved dog, Liam. There is no evidence to suggest Mr. Nichols stabbed anyone, and it is ludicrous to believe he would have stabbed his own dog."

And if we had to, we would have gone further and proved the knife belonged to Squatter Will.

"As if all of this shoddy evidence were not conclusive enough, on the night of Tuesday September 17, 2019, the former County Attorney, Alfred "Pootie" Carputin pushed Mr. Nichols into a log splitter at Mr. Nichols' home and left him there bleeding profusely, with his arm completely ripped from his body. Special Counsel to the Defense, Jennifer Herrington, found Mr. Nichols and saved his life with the help of her husband, Aaron Herrington, but not until after she had to defend her own life from Mr. Carputin, who fired at her multiple times at close range with a shotgun."

If Jennifer had been a murderer like Pootie, she wouldn't have come back to the scene of his attack on George. But Pootie had been loopy when he'd regained consciousness, and he'd admitted that he had been afraid Jennifer had recognized him. He'd been convinced he'd killed George and that Jennifer was the only witness. He stopped just short of admitting he intended to kill her, but that much was obvious by his actions.

"Because Mr. Nichols lived, thank the Lord, he was able to give an affidavit from his hospital bed. He said that in the course of attacking him, Mr. Carputin confessed to having killed Mr. Prescott, believing him to be Mr. Nichols, because he wanted to punish Mr. Nichols for the death of Sarah Stiles, Mr. Carputin's daughter, in an automobile accident. Mr. Nichols was also involved in that accident and was exonerated by law enforcement, with the cause of the accident determined to be Ms. Stiles running a red light. Mr. Carputin even admitted to Mr. Nichols that he stabbed Liam, the dog, when it defended Mr. Prescott. Mr. Carputin killed Mr. Prescott and stabbed Liam the dog. He attempted to kill Mr. Nichols and Ms. Herrington. He also attempted to punish and frame Mr. Nichols for Mr. Prescott's death by pursuing this trumped-up first-degree murder charge, going so far as using notes designed to be nearly identical to those Mr. Prescott had been leaving for Mr. Nichols and that Mr. Carputin knew about because Mr. Nichols presented those notes to Mr. Carputin earlier when taking the matter to the sheriff's office."

Jennifer had followed a hunch and discovered that Pootie had checked out the file from the stalking complaint George had filed—and withdrawn—against Hadley, which is where he had found Hadley's notes and been able to emulate them.

And Pootie didn't oppose his ex-wife Gerrianne's wrongful death lawsuit against George, either. The death of Sarah Stiles was a tragedy that had been compounded many times over by the actions of her parents.

All of what Kid said was true, and Pootie was undoubtedly guilty, but for a moment, Jennifer's mind returned to George's bloody body the morning after the murder and her initial doubts. She was thankful that for her first and possibly only foray into criminal defense, she'd had the chance to represent a truly innocent defendant. She'd had her moment of doubt on the night Pootie had attacked George, when she'd seen the picture of George with the Swiss Army knife and had thought George had lied about the printer. George wasn't even guilty of a falsehood though. Aaron had found the printer in Shelly's office closet, packed away in a box that, somehow, fortuitously, the sheriff's office crime scene investigators hadn't found when they'd exercised their search warrant.

"For all these reasons, and any others I forgot to mention, I ask the court to grant Mr. Nichols' a dismissal with prejudice." Kid inclined his head as if in a slight bow toward the judge.

There was a smattering of applause from the gallery behind the defense. Jennifer turned toward the prosecution side of the gallery. The first person that caught her eye was Tim O'Leary. She'd never ended up interviewing him. The man wasn't a murderer, but George should still watch his back around him. Denise was sitting in the row in front of Tim. Hadley had wisely made his daughter's inheritance subject to her successfully completing rehab first. Two rows behind Denise, Melinda was sitting with an older woman. Gerrianne Williams, Jennifer felt sure. She wondered if they knew yet that the county was investigating Pootie in the old school shooting. It wasn't lost on Jennifer that Denise wasn't beside the friend whose father had murdered her own. Were Melinda and Gerrianne there in support of Pootie? In opposition to George? In the end, it didn't matter. George would not be unjustly punished. And Pootie would not get away with murder.

Judge Ryan nodded and turned to Ollie Singletary. "Mr. Singletary, what say you?"

Ollie stood, bowed, and said, "We support the motion." Then he returned to his seat.

The judge winked at Kid. "Would you like Pootie disbarred, too?"

Kid stuttered. "I, uh, I, um, I don't think that's a decision for me to make."

"True. But would you *like* it?"

"Very much so."

Laughter rolled from the gallery.

The judge smiled at Jennifer. "Anything to add, Big City?"

She stood and inclined her head. "Just my thanks for permitting me to work with Kid in your courtroom. He's a fine lawyer, and I think he'll do the system proud." She returned to her seat.

"I agree." He straightened his robe on his sloping shoulders. "All right. Normally I have to deliberate a bit on motions of this import. But not this time. I just wish Mr. Nichols was out of the hospital so I could have the prosecution beg his forgiveness in my presence. I'm going to swing by after we adjourn and give him my personal apology, and if the county attorney's office is worth a lick, they'll have someone do the same." He nodded emphatically, sending his glasses down the bridge of his nose. "Motion granted." He banged his gavel. "Court dismissed so the judge can get to the hospital."

And with that, he stood, robes swirling like dark smoke, and disappeared from the courtroom.

Kid shook Jennifer's hand.

She pulled him into a big hug. "You did great, Kid. I'm happy to be a reference for you any time you need one."

"Your help with the motion for summary judgment in the wrongful death case was great. I just got a text. Gerrianne Williams has dropped the suit."

"Congratulations!"

"I hope we can try a case together again some time."

"I'll be heading back to Houston soon." An unexpected melancholy fell over her. She would have enjoyed practicing law with Kid. Letting him learn from her years of experience, feeling a mission bigger than herself, and drawing enthusiasm from his energy. She wondered how he'd feel about working as an ADA in Houston? She could get him an interview. Nothing beat it for sharpening courtroom skills.

She was about to ask him. Really, she was. Maybe she was, anyway. But then they were interrupted.

"Congratulations to you." Maggie's voice was, for once, welcome, cutting off a difficult topic.

Jennifer turned to face her frenemy and almost cousin-in-law. "Thanks. I wish George still had his arm, but at least he has his freedom."

Aaron put an arm around Jennifer's shoulders. "I'm so proud of you. And now you have an ending to the book you're working on."

"Book?" Maggie asked. "You wrote your book?"

When Jennifer didn't respond, Aaron said, "She's still working on it, but she's got a good start. She's fictionalizing the story of George's case." He squeezed her. "Don't forget to make the veterinarian husband a Super Bowl MVP quarterback."

Jennifer decided to talk to her husband about telling people about her writing, later. As in, *not* telling them.

Maggie said, "You need to talk to my friend Michele about her agent. I'm going to text her right now."

Jennifer had met Michele Lopez Hanson, a former Houston attorney turned successful true crime author, and she liked her. But she hated asking for help from anyone. "I don't even have a draft finished yet. You're way ahead of me."

Maggie held up her phone. "Too late. I type fast."

Somehow Maggie had gotten under Jennifer's skin, even doing something nice. The woman had a talent.

"Good news," Maggie said to Aaron. "Hank told me he talked Doc Billy into giving you another chance to buy the clinic."

"You're kidding!" Aaron pumped a "yes" with his fist.

That wasn't what Jennifer wanted to hear. She hesitated, then said, "That's . . . *great*." Because, what else could she say, especially in front of an audience. She'd thought with the case over, the sale fallen apart, and all the violence and trauma past and present that she'd be able to convince him to return to Texas after football season.

Not if he bought a clinic, though.

She gritted her teeth.

"Hi, Aaron," a woman's voice said.

Jennifer turned and saw Harriett from Prescott Financial. Only this time she wasn't using crutches.

"Uh, hi, Etta." Aaron's voice sounded panicked, and he shot a look at Jennifer.

Jennifer saw nothing but red. But her mind wasn't on the relationship between Aaron and Etta. She believed him that there wasn't one. It wasn't the first time a woman had thrown herself at Aaron, and it probably wouldn't be the last. No, Jennifer's focus was on the name Aaron had used. *Etta.* Harriett was Etta. And Etta used to date Hadley, who had dumped her. No wonder she seemed to bear her deceased boss a fair amount of ill will. "I thought your name was Harriett."

She answered without looking at Jennifer, her eyes only for Aaron. "Etta, Harriett. Same thing."

"And where are your crutches?"

"I had knee surgery six weeks ago. I'm off them." Harriett finally really saw Jennifer. Her pleasant expression soured. "Oh, it's you."

"Yes. Me. Aaron's wife."

Harriett's mouth made an O.

"I've read your texts and listened to your messages to him, *Etta.*" Jennifer smiled. "Find your own man."

Aaron put a big hand on Jennifer's shoulder.

"Oh, and I know you lied to me. About Hadley. That wasn't helpful. But, if you still cared about him, then I'm doubly sorry for your loss."

Without a reply, Etta, or Harriett, or whatever she called herself glowered and scurried into the milling crowd.

Just then, Jennifer's phone rang. It was Quentin. She frowned at

Aaron. "I'm sorry. I have to take this. I'm three days late calling Quentin back."

"Okay." Aaron's searching gaze sought answers she didn't think he'd want to hear. That she'd seen George's case through. That she was going to make their marriage a long-distance relationship. That she felt terrible about the things she'd said to him that drunken night after Hank's party. But that she was a damn good lawyer, and she deserved a shot at being the Harris County DA.

Walking through the stragglers in the gallery aisle, she answered the call. "Hi, Quentin. It's been a crazy few days." She opened the courtroom doors and exited to the hallway. "I was physically assaulted, as was my defendant in a pro bono first-degree murder case I'm working. I just got out of the hearing on our successful motion to dismiss, and—"

Quentin broke in. "We've announced that Evan Spitz will be our candidate for DA, Jennifer. The press release went out an hour ago, and the news is all over the wire service and social media. We think he'll make an outstanding DA, and we wish you the very best in your Wyoming endeavors."

Jennifer stopped short. Someone bumped into her from behind. She didn't care. She couldn't believe what she'd just heard. "What?!"

"Jennifer, you said you'd call on Wednesday. If you can't keep your commitments to us, then we don't see any reason to keep ours to you."

"But you'd given me a month."

"When you fell out of touch, we had to move forward."

Tears smarted Jennifer's eyes. Quentin had picked her nemesis instead of her to run for DA. She tuned him out as he droned on and on about Evan's qualifications and their excitement about him, and how he hoped Jennifer would rally behind their choice. She hung up on him mid-sentence. If it came to it, later she would tell him she'd lost their connection. She didn't think it would, though.

Her dream was dead. She was nothing to Quentin and the party now but another voter.

She slumped onto a bench in the hallway. How could this happen, when she had been in the middle of doing what she believed was the right thing? And now all she had left back in Houston besides Alayah was a job she was losing her passion for and a condo without Aaron in it.

The bench creaked. Aaron sat down beside her. The eyes that peered into hers were earnest and concerned. "What's the matter?"

Jennifer struggled to get the words out without losing her cool in public. "Evan Spitz is the candidate for DA."

Aaron frowned. "Wait—I thought you guys were politically aligned. Now you'll be running against him?"

Jennifer's laugh sounded like a cat coughing up a hairball. "No. He's *the* candidate. I'm not. They gave him the spot they offered me."

"I don't get it."

"I took too long to get back to them, and they moved forward without me." She wiped her eyes. Her attempts at decorum were failing.

"I'm sorry." His voice was soft. He moved closer, covered her hand with his, and rubbed it with his thumb. "I really am."

She nodded, not trusting herself to speak without major waterworks.

"I can't help but believe it's for the best, though."

She jerked her hand away from his. "The best? Says who?"

"Hear me out." His knee knocked against hers. "I'm just thinking it might be a way of setting you free so you can be you again and we can be us."

"I *am* me. And I'm not free. I'm an Assistant District Attorney in the Homicide Division for Harris County, Texas."

"I know. But do you want to be? This could be a way out." He repeated, "Maybe it's for the best."

"The best for you, you mean? Because I lost everything, Aaron. Everything."

A coldness seeped over Aaron's face. He moved his knee away from hers and stood. He stared at her like he was trying to solve for X

in a complex equation and something wouldn't compute. And then—
he just stopped. She saw it in his eyes the second he gave up. "Well, I
guess that's that then." He turned and walked away, his footsteps
slow, heavy, and portentous, like the bass drum in the soundtrack of
the end of her life as she knew it. The tenor changed, and his feet
began descending the stairs.

For a moment she didn't understand what was going on. Then
her words replayed in her head. They sounded awful. Like she was
saying he wasn't important enough to count as something. She hadn't
meant that. She'd been feeling petulant, betrayed by Quentin and the
party, resentful of Evan Spitz, and pushed into a Wyoming life that
more and more she was realizing she just might want and yet
somehow felt resentful about.

"Aaron," she called.

But it was too late. He had completely disappeared into the stair-
well. Every cell of her body wanted to run after him and beg him to
understand, but how could she? She barely understood herself.

People streamed by. Suddenly, the sting of being "fired" from the
possibility of campaigning for DA evaporated. The pain of Quentin's
"betrayal" just went away. What part of her had wanted that
campaign? Her ego? Because the only thing that felt wounded right
now was pride, and that was rapidly being replaced by something
else.

By . . . relief.

Oh, my God. Did I not want to be DA? Maybe. Probably. Okay,
yes. She didn't want to do the job of the Harris County DA. She'd
wanted to be picked to run and to be elected. But not to spend the
next four years in the job. *Then what the heck do I want?*

She closed her eyes.

At first, nothing came to her. Her thoughts receded and the
sounds and smells of the hallway came into focus. Someone walking
by chewing mint gum. The scent of lavender drier sheets, cloying. A
ripping sound as a heel caught on the carpet.

Then she saw Aaron's face. Aaron pacing a sideline. Aaron

hammering a loose door frame. Aaron listening through a stethoscope to the heartbeat of a horse.

Judge Ryan and Kid in court.

George at the lodge. Liam, Katya, and Jeremiah. Especially Jeremiah. Jeremiah two or three more times.

Then, in quick succession, the faces of her parents, her brother and his family, Hank, and even Maggie. Herds of horses at Piney Bottoms.

The mountains. The golf course with the view of them.

Kids on a playground. Whose they were, she wasn't sure, but they looked happy.

And then Alayah, with a suitcase, getting off a plane at the airport in Sheridan.

But what she didn't see was her Houston office, the condo, or campaign posters with her name on them.

She wanted to stay here. She didn't care who ran for DA in Harris Country.

She grabbed her bags and sprinted down the stairs after Aaron.

FORTY-ONE

BIG HORN, Wyoming

THE CLOSING TRANSACTIONS on the lodge, the sale of Aaron's Houston clinic, and the purchase of Doc Billy's Sheridan practice all ended up being on one chaotic and wonderful day. Chaotic and wonderful were also good descriptions for the surprise party Maggie threw for Jennifer and Aaron at the lodge afterwards. Everyone was there. All of the Flints, Patrick's puppy Moose—who was healing nicely—Kid, the Piney Bottoms crew, George, Black Bear Betty, Judge Ryan, and even Deputy Travis, who by then had given Jennifer her second speeding ticket and was on a first name basis with both Herringtons. Maggie fed everyone hot wings and chips and guacamole and, of course, served TKOs—iced tea and Koltiska Original—by the pitcher.

"You're taking the Wyoming bar exam, aren't you, Big City?" Judge Ryan had asked Jennifer as she stood beside Aaron. "It's a shame you aren't already licensed. You would have made a great County Attorney."

Jennifer had promised him she was taking the bar the next time it was offered. "But Ollie will do a fine job."

The judge had agreed.

All in all, it was a good time, although Aaron and Jennifer were only going through the motions. Things between them had been strained since the day she'd told him he was nothing to her. She'd apologized. Begged for his forgiveness. Explained what she'd really meant. Told him she wanted to be in Wyoming. Re-upped her commitment to him. But he was having trouble believing her. Believing *in* her. Could he trust her with his whole heart? That hadn't gone well for him lately, and he'd lost the energy to force it.

The next few weeks flew by in a blur. Aaron spent weekdays practicing vet medicine in his new clinic—with bigger, more comfortable chairs in the lobby—and weekends working on the lodge with pets underfoot, while George and Black Bear Betty prepped the mountain cabin for winter. By night, Aaron coached, and the Rams team won and won and won.

Mostly, he did it alone, however. After he'd had trouble believing in her, a polite distance had grown between Jennifer and him. He didn't know how to bridge the gap anymore, and the longer it stayed in place, the worse it became.

For weeks, Jennifer holed up in the cottage. Occasionally she'd pop out to hit a bag of orange golf balls into the snow-covered pasture with the old clubs from the barn, then she'd disappear again. Sometimes he'd find her in the living room of the lodge with a yoga video pulled up on Youtube, deep in her flow. But mostly, she was a hermit. She said she was studying for the bar exam and writing. He never asked to see her words, and he wouldn't have been surprised, honestly, if she'd been playing Solitaire, watching cheesy mysteries, and reading. She was in limbo. Kid had begged her to come to work with him, as cases were flooding in. She helped him some but mostly she stayed tucked away in her nest.

On the Houston front, she'd resigned from her Houston ADA job. She put the condo on the market, and someone snapped it up immediately. She hadn't gone back to Houston to pack or clean or even for the closing. She'd just turned it all over to a moving service.

Giving up control wasn't like her.

Sometimes it seemed like she was trying. She came to his games. Shot the stink eye at Etta occasionally. Congratulated him when Big Horn asked if he'd be willing to keep coaching the following year—and be paid for it. Snapped pictures when he gave every kid on the team a ball signed by J.J. Watt. Cheered when they won the state championship. After the season, she'd invited their families to Thanksgiving. Hers accepted. His promised to come next year.

But it felt hollow.

Her days in the cottage started getting longer, until they became all-nighters. He'd sit by the window in their bedroom, staring at the light on in the cottage. It would blend into the outside light at dawn, which is when she'd turn it off, creep over to the lodge, and crawl into bed beside him, unaware he was awake and waiting for her. Then he'd get up and leave for the clinic while she was still asleep.

It didn't help that the county had decided not to pursue charges against Pootie for the school shooting, siting a lack of evidence. The announcement had set her back. Way back.

A week before her family was due to arrive, Aaron found a surprise in the bathroom when he got up to shower for work. A lipstick message was written on the mirror, taking up the entire space.

I am thankful for mean cats, old dogs, and skunks that don't stink.

Hope flickered inside him, but he held himself in check, afraid to scare her away. He smiled and left it up.

The next day he found another.

I am thankful for quirky lodges and snowy days.

This time, he erased hers and printed one of his own. It was harder to do than it looked.

I'm thankful for my wife who calls plays better than Peyton and blocks better than Jason Witten.

Still, he didn't say anything to her aloud. Things between them seemed about the same when they were together, like they were both afraid of making the first move back toward each other.

Then, the evening before her family was due to arrive, he found a message after she'd retreated to the cottage for the night.

I am thankful for YOU.

No frills, no embellishments, and yet this was the one that finally broke him. He bolted out the back door and over to the cottage. He eased the front door open and tiptoed in. He wanted to watch her in her element. He wanted to tell her he was thankful for her and to hold her and never let her go.

He found her in the bedroom she'd converted to an office, Jeremiah curled up in a cat bed at her feet. The skunk yawned, stretched, and went back to sleep. In daylight, the room had a spectacular mountain view. Now, a big yellow moon peeked back in at him. Jennifer's head was down on her desk, cheek pressing against scarred wood, drool pooled by her mouth. Her topknot was a mess. The collar of her Baylor Law sweatshirt hung askew, exposing her delicate collarbone. The screen on her laptop was awake, open to an email.

He read over her shoulder.

Joe: I appreciate you agreeing to review my book at the recommendation of Michele Lopez Hanson. Here's the finished manuscript of my Wyoming murder mystery, BIG HORN. I look forward to hearing from you.

A *finished* book? Over her shoulder, he clicked to open the attachment. As he did, he saw a local obstetrics and gynecology practice brochure beside her elbow on the desk. It was open to a page on their reproductive services. He resisted the urge to touch her, although it was strong.

Then he started to read the words on the screen.

BIG HORN
   A Wyoming Mystery
   By Jenn Herrington

. . .

JENN? He'd never seen her use the name Jenn before. Jenny, when they were younger. Jennifer as a professional. Was this the woman his wife was becoming, this Jenn? His heartbeat accelerated and he scrolled down a page.

DEDICATED TO MY HUSBAND, who knows me better than I know myself.

HIS EYES FELT HOT. He scrolled another page.

PROLOGUE
Big Horn, Wyoming

THE CLOUDS DRIFTED in front of the sliver of a moon, blocking Jenn Herrington's view of the snowscape behind the house. Deck boards creaked, and the cold against her bare feet shocked her fully awake. *What am I doing outside in the middle of the night, barefoot and without a robe, much less a coat?* She wasn't sleepwalking, per se. Something had woken her from a deep, warm slumber, and she'd responded on autopilot, like a reluctant protagonist from a Mary Higgins Clark novel.

AARON DIDN'T NEED to read any further to know she'd done it. She'd really, really done it.

He smiled and closed the laptop. Then he lifted her in his arms. She barely stirred as he carried her to the couch and nestled her into the pillows. He touched a finger to his lips, then pressed them to hers and put a blanket over his Jenn.

Everything he had to say to her could wait. They had all the time in the world.

***

There's more Wyoming mystery, thriller, and suspense from Pamela Fagan Hutchins!

Patrick Flint—Murder, mystery, and medicine in 1970s Wyoming adventures. Start with Switchback: https://www.amazon.com/Switchback-Patrick-Pamela-Fagan-Hutchins-ebook/dp/B07ZJW27S4.

Maggie Killian—Irreverence abounds as rebel Maggie tries to outrun her past and Wyoming bull rider Hank Sibley in three murder mysteries. Start with Live Wire: https://www.amazon.com/gp/product/B07L5RYGHZ.

(For a complete list of PFH mystery/thriller/suspense—in Wyoming and elsewhere!—flip forward to "Books by the Author.")

And to be first to know when the next ***Jenn Herrington Wyoming Mystery/Legal Thriller*** (and other PFH books) comes out PLUS snag a free PFH ebook starter library, join her mailing list at https://www.subscribepage.com/PFHSuperstars.

***

For Joe. Thanks for pitching "myself" to me.
And for Eric, my secret weapon.

ACKNOWLEDGMENTS

Agent Joe Durepos pitched me a story. "A Houston attorney and her husband—he could be an executive in the oil industry, or you could make it something more interesting, like a veterinarian—move to Wyoming and run a mountain B&B, where they have a menagerie of pets and she solves and writes mysteries."

I said, "Joe, that's Eric and me."

He laughed.

I said, "Joe, that's narcissistic."

He said, "It's the type of escape other people dream of. Can you write it?"

Well, duh, of course I could. It's my life, after all. Only, after I sat down to write it, it strayed some from the original blueprint. In a good way, I hope.

The murder idea came from the actual log splitter in our actual "Snowheresville" (aka Big Horn Hideaway Lodge) barn. I may or may not have based characters on real people I know ;-) And the setting is a little bit Snowheresville and a little bit make believe.

Thanks for the idea, Joe. I was able to age up the Patrick Flint characters and draw them into the story and pull across What Doesn't Kill You characters as well. There are already five more books planned for this series, if it turns out people like them and want me to keep going.

And yet there is more thanks to give . . .

Thanks to my dad for advice on all things medical. Love and hugs to my favorite kissin' cousin (who is not really my cousin), Dr. Kristine "Rockey" Millikin for helping Aaron sound like a real vet. Thanks to Stu Healy and Ryan Healy for keeping me from screwing up Wyoming law. If I did, that's on me, not you guys.

Thanks to my husband, Eric, for brainstorming with and encouraging me and beta reading BIG HORN with me despite your busy work, travel, and workout schedule. And for taking a chance on Wyoming and me.

Thanks to our five offspring. I love you guys more than anything, and each time I write a parent/child (birth, adopted, foster, or step), I channel you. I am so touched by how supportive you have been with Poppy, Gigi, Eric, and me.

Big Horn editing credits go to Karen Goodwin. You rock. A big thank you as well to my proofreading and advance review team.

The biggest thanks, though, goes to my readers. It never ceases to amaze me that you read my novels, that your support has resulted in this mid-life career change that gives me so much joy. From the bottom of my heart, I offer you my gratitude.

BOOKS BY THE AUTHOR

Fiction from SkipJack Publishing

THE *PATRICK FLINT* SERIES OF WYOMING MYSTERIES:

Switchback (Patrick Flint #1)

Snake Oil (Patrick Flint #2)

Sawbones (Patrick Flint #3)

Scapegoat (Patrick Flint #4)

Snaggle Tooth (Patrick Flint #5)

Stag Party (Patrick Flint #6)

Sitting Duck (Patrick Flint #7)

Spark (Patrick Flint 1.5): Exclusive to subscribers

THE *JENN HERRINGTON* WYOMING MYSTERIES:

BIG HORN (Jenn Herrington #1)

THE *WHAT DOESN'T KILL YOU* SUPER SERIES:

Wasted in Waco (WDKY Ensemble Prequel Novella): Exclusive to Subscribers

The Essential Guide to the What Doesn't Kill You Series

Katie Connell Caribbean Mysteries:

Saving Grace (Katie Connell #1)

Leaving Annalise (Katie Connell #2)

Finding Harmony (Katie Connell #3)

Seeking Felicity (Katie Connell #4)

Emily Bernal Texas-to-New Mexico Mysteries:

Heaven to Betsy (Emily Bernal #1)

Earth to Emily (Emily Bernal #2)

Hell to Pay (Emily Bernal #3)

Michele Lopez Hanson Texas Mysteries:

Going for Kona (Michele Lopez Hanson #1)

Fighting for Anna (Michele Lopez Hanson #2)

Searching for Dime Box (Michele Lopez Hanson #3)

Maggie Killian Texas-to-Wyoming Mysteries:

Buckle Bunny (Maggie Killian Prequel Novella)

Shock Jock (Maggie Killian Prequel Short Story)

Live Wire (Maggie Killian #1)

Sick Puppy (Maggie Killian #2)

Dead Pile (Maggie Killian #3)

The Ava Butler Caribbean Mysteries Trilogy: A Sexy Spin-off From *What Doesn't Kill You*

Bombshell (Ava Butler #1)

Stunner (Ava Butler #2)

Knockout (Ava Butler #3)

Juvenile Fiction from SkipJack Publishing

Poppy Needs a Puppy (Poppy & Petey #1)

Nonfiction from SkipJack Publishing

The Clark Kent Chronicles

Hot Flashes and Half Ironmans

How to Screw Up Your Kids

How to Screw Up Your Marriage

Puppalicious and Beyond

What Kind of Loser Indie Publishes,

and How Can I Be One, Too?

Audio, e-book, large print, hardcover, and paperback versions of most titles available.

ABOUT THE AUTHOR

Pamela Fagan Hutchins is a *USA Today* best selling author. She writes award-winning romantic mystery/thriller/suspense from way up in the frozen north of Snowheresville, Wyoming, where she lives in an off-the-grid cabin on the face of the Bighorn Mountains. She is passionate about hiking/snow shoeing/cross country skiing with her hunky husband and pack of rescue dogs (and occasional rescue cat) and riding their gigantic horses.

If you'd like Pamela to speak to your book club, women's club, class, or writers group by streaming video or in person, shoot her an email. She's very likely to say yes.

You can connect with Pamela via her website
(http://pamelafaganhutchins.com)
or email (pamela@pamelafaganhutchins.com).

PRAISE FOR PAMELA FAGAN HUTCHINS

2018 USA Today Best Seller
2017 Silver Falchion Award, Best Mystery
2016 USA Best Book Award, Cross-Genre Fiction
2015 USA Best Book Award, Cross-Genre Fiction
2014 Amazon Breakthrough Novel Award Quarter-finalist,
Romance

The Patrick Flint Mysteries

"Best book I've read in a long time!" — Kiersten Marquet, author of
Reluctant Promises
"*Switchback* transports the reader deep into the mountains of
Wyoming for a thriller that has it all--wild animals, criminals, and one
family willing to do whatever is necessary to protect its own. Pamela
Fagan Hutchins writes with the authority of a woman who knows
this world. She weaves the story with both nail-biting suspense and a
healthy dose of humor. You won't want to miss *Switchback*." -
- Danielle Girard, *Wall Street Journal*-bestselling author of
White Out.
"*Switchback* by Pamela Fagan Hutchins has as many twists and turns
as a high-country trail. Every parent's nightmare is the loss or injury
of a child, and this powerful novel taps into that primal fear." -- Reavis
Z. Wortham, two time winner of The Spur and author of *Hawke's
Prey*
"*Switchback* starts at a gallop and had me holding on with both hands
until the riveting finish. This book is highly atmospheric and nearly
crackling with suspense. Highly recommend!" -- Libby Kirsch, Emmy
awardwinning reporter and author of the *Janet Black Mystery Series*

"A Bob Ross painting with Alfred Hitchcock hidden among the trees."
"Edge-of-your seat nail biter."
"Unexpected twists!"
"Wow! Wow! Highly entertaining!"
"A very exciting book (um... actually a nail-biter), soooo beautifully descriptive, with an underlying story of human connection and family. It's full of action. I was so scared and so mad and so relieved... sometimes all at once!"
"Well drawn characters, great scenery, and a kept-me-on-the-edge-of-my-seat story!"
"Absolutely unputdownable wonder of a story."
"Must read!"
"Gripping story. Looking for book two!"
"Intense!"
"Amazing and well-written read."
"Read it in one fell swoop. I could not put it down."

What Doesn't Kill You: Katie Connell Romantic Mysteries

"An exciting tale . . . twisting investigative and legal subplots . . . a character seeking redemption . . . an exhilarating mystery with a touch of voodoo." — *Midwest Book Review Bookwatch*
"A lively romantic mystery." — *Kirkus Reviews*
"A riveting drama . . . exciting read, highly recommended." — *Small Press Bookwatch*
"Katie is the first character I have absolutely fallen in love with since Stephanie Plum!" — *Stephanie Swindell, Bookstore Owner*
"Engaging storyline . . . taut suspense." — *MBR Bookwatch*

What Doesn't Kill You: Emily Bernal Romantic Mysteries

"Fair warning: clear your calendar before you pick it up because you won't be able to put it down." — *Ken Oder, author of* Old Wounds to the Heart

"Full of heart, humor, vivid characters, and suspense. Hutchins has done it again!" — *Gay Yellen, author of* The Body Business

"Hutchins is a master of tension." — *R.L. Nolen, author of* Deadly Thyme

"Intriguing mystery . . . captivating romance." — *Patricia Flaherty Pagan, author of* Trail Ways Pilgrims

"Everything about it shines: the plot, the characters and the writing. Readers are in for a real treat with this story." — *Marcy McKay, author of* Pennies from Burger Heaven

What Doesn't Kill You: Michele Lopez Hanson Romantic Mysteries

"Immediately hooked." — *Terry Sykes-Bradshaw, author of* Sibling Revelry

"Spellbinding." — *Jo Bryan, Dry Creek Book Club*

"Fast-paced mystery." — *Deb Krenzer, Book Reviewer*

"Can't put it down." — *Cathy Bader, Reader*

What Doesn't Kill You: Ava Butler Romantic Mysteries

"Just when I think I couldn't love another Pamela Fagan Hutchins novel more, along comes Ava." — *Marcy McKay, author of* Stars Among the Dead

"Ava personifies bombshell in every sense of word. — *Tara Scheyer, Grammy-nominated musician, Long-Distance Sisters Book Club*

"Entertaining, complex, and thought-provoking." — *Ginger Copeland, power reader*

What Doesn't Kill You: Maggie Killian Romantic Mysteries

"Maggie's gonna break your heart—one way or another." *Tara Scheyer, Grammy-nominated musician, Long-Distance Sisters Book Club*

"Pamela Fagan Hutchins nails that Wyoming scenery and captures the atmosphere of the people there." — *Ken Oder, author of* Old Wounds to the Heart

"I thought I had it all figured out a time or two, but she kept me wondering right to the end." — *Ginger Copeland, power reader*

BOOKS FROM SKIPJACK PUBLISHING

FICTION:
Marcy McKay

Pennies from Burger Heaven, by Marcy McKay

Stars Among the Dead, by Marcy McKay

The Moon Rises at Dawn, by Marcy McKay

Bones and Lies Between Us, by Marcy McKay

When Life Feels Like a House Fire, by Marcy McKay

R.L. Nolen

Deadly Thyme, by R. L. Nolen

The Dry, by Rebecca Nolen

Ken Oder

The Closing, by Ken Oder

Old Wounds to the Heart, by Ken Oder

The Judas Murders, by Ken Oder

The Princess of Sugar Valley, by Ken Oder

Gay Yellen

The Body Business, by Gay Yellen

The Body Next Door, by Gay Yellen

Pamela Fagan Hutchins

THE PATRICK FLINT SERIES OF WYOMING MYSTERIES:

Switchback (Patrick Flint #1), by Pamela Fagan Hutchins

Snake Oil (Patrick Flint #2), by Pamela Fagan Hutchins

Sawbones (Patrick Flint #3), by Pamela Fagan Hutchins

Scapegoat (Patrick Flint #4), by Pamela Fagan Hutchins

Snaggle Tooth (Patrick Flint #5), by Pamela Fagan Hutchins

Stag Party (Patrick Flint #6), by Pamela Fagan Hutchins

Spark (Patrick Flint 1.5): Exclusive to subscribers, by Pamela Fagan Hutchins

THE *WHAT DOESN'T KILL YOU* SUPER SERIES:

Act One (WDKY Ensemble Prequel Novella): Exclusive to Subscribers, by Pamela Fagan Hutchins

The Essential Guide to the What Doesn't Kill You Series, by Pamela Fagan Hutchins

Katie Connell Caribbean Mysteries:

Saving Grace (Katie #1), by Pamela Fagan Hutchins

Leaving Annalise (Katie #2), by Pamela Fagan Hutchins

Finding Harmony (Katie #3), by Pamela Fagan Hutchins

Seeking Felicity (Katie #4), by Pamela Fagan Hutchins

Emily Bernal Texas-to-New Mexico Mysteries:

Heaven to Betsy (Emily #1), by Pamela Fagan Hutchins

Earth to Emily (Emily #2), by Pamela Fagan Hutchins

Hell to Pay (Emily #3), by Pamela Fagan Hutchins

Michele Lopez Hanson Texas Mysteries:

Going for Kona (Michele #1), by Pamela Fagan Hutchins

Fighting for Anna (Michele #2), by Pamela Fagan Hutchins

Searching for Dime Box (Michele #3), by Pamela Fagan Hutchins

Maggie Killian Texas-to-Wyoming Mysteries:

Buckle Bunny (Maggie Prequel Novella), by Pamela Fagan Hutchins

Shock Jock (Maggie Prequel Short Story), by Pamela Fagan Hutchins

Live Wire (Maggie #1), by Pamela Fagan Hutchins

Sick Puppy (Maggie #2), by Pamela Fagan Hutchins

Dead Pile (Maggie #3), by Pamela Fagan Hutchins

The Ava Butler Caribbean Mysteries Trilogy: A Sexy Spin-off From *What Doesn't Kill You*

Bombshell (Ava #1), by Pamela Fagan Hutchins

Stunner (Ava #2), by Pamela Fagan Hutchins

Knockout (Ava #3), by Pamela Fagan Hutchins

Poppy Needs a Puppy (Poppy & Petey #1), by Pamela Fagan Hutchins, illustrated by Laylie Frazier

MULTI-AUTHOR:

Murder, They Wrote: Four SkipJack Mysteries, by Ken Oder, R.L. Nolen, Marcy McKay, and Gay Yellen

Tides of Possibility, edited by K.J. Russell

Tides of Impossibility, edited by K.J. Russell and C. Stuart Hardwick

NONFICTION:
Helen Colin

My Dream of Freedom: From Holocaust to My Beloved America, by Helen Colin

Pamela Fagan Hutchins

CPSIA information can be obtained
at www.ICGtesting.com
Printed in the USA
LVHW080306190722
723847LV00004B/61

9 781956 729177